# WOMEN
## on
## the ROCKS

Author photo: Jonathan Williamson

**Kristin Williamson** is the author of *The Last Bastion*, a political history of World War Two; *Princess Kate*, a novel for young adults; the bestselling novels *Tanglewood* and *The Jacaranda Years*; a biography of anti-apartheid activists, the Watson Brothers, *Brothers to Us*; and an autobiographical novel, *Treading on Dreams*. She has also written for film and television. She has an academic background in history, education and theatre, and spent many years as a teacher and journalist.

Kristin Williamson and her playwright husband David live on Queensland's Sunshine Coast. They have five grown-up children.

**Other books by Kristin Williamson**

The Last Bastion
Princess Kate
Tanglewood
The Jacaranda Years
Brothers to Us
Treading on Dreams

# WOMEN on the ROCKS

## A Tale of Two Convicts

# KRISTIN WILLIAMSON

UQP

First published 2003 by University of Queensland Press
Box 6042, St Lucia, Queensland 4067 Australia
This edition published 2004

www.uqp.uq.edu.au

Typeset by University of Queensland Press
Printed in Australia by McPherson's Printing Group

Distributed in the USA and Canada by
International Specialized Book Services, Inc.,
5824 N.E. Hassalo Street, Portland, Oregon 97213–3640

"Map of The Town of Sydney 1836" courtesy of the
Mitchell Library, State Library of New South Wales.


**Cataloguing in Publication Data**
*National Library of Australia*

Williamson, Kristin, 1940–  .
   Women on the rocks: a tale of two convicts.

   I. Title.

A823.3

ISBN 0 7022 3483 4

*For my husband,*
*who has been tolerant of my obsession*
*with our feisty female forbears,*
*and remains loving*

# The Rocks, Sydney, 1836

DARLING HA[RBOUR]

Soldiers House
Military House
Bathing House
Point

Market Wharf

Sussex Street

Police Magistrate

Windmill

St Philips Church

Watch Hse

Scotch Church

Military Barracks

Barrack Square

Treasury

Clarence Street

York Street

West Street

George Street

Charlotte Place

Post Office

Theatre

Pitt Street

Pitt Street

Oconnel Street

Castlereagh Street

Pitt Street

Hunter Street

Post Office

School Hse

Elizabeth Street

Court House

St James Church

Phillip Street

Government House

[Y]ORK

Bettington Wharf

Millers Point.

OUR

1¼

Stone Quarries

Fort Phillip

Military Hospital

Fort Street

Street

Street

George Street

Kings Wharf

Dock Yard

Custom House

Watch House

Campbells Wharf

Aspinal & Browne's Wharf

Pitmans Wharf

Lambs Wharf

Walkers Wharf

Dawes Battery

Dawes Point

3

3½

4

3½

6½

5

3¼

5

2

2

4¼

6½

SYDNEY COVE

5½

5¼

7

8

6

4

Proposed Public Wharf

2½

3

3½

*N.B. The Soundings are in Fathoms.*

# I
# Rural England
# 1819

# CHAPTER ONE

## My Independent Life Begins
## Sevenoaks, Kent, April, 1819

Spring has come early this year. Crocuses and daffodils are blooming in the garden all around our cottage. I am awake early because today is my birthday and I have come to a decision. I unlatch the casement, lean out of the attic window and sniff the cool air. I can hear church bells in the village below. Today is the last day of my childhood: I am fourteen, old enough to leave all this behind me.

Soon I will put on my cloak and bonnet, walk down the muddy road to the village and up the other side of the hill to Elmtree House and knock on the brass door knob at the servants' entrance. The housekeeper, Mrs Frayne, who is round and red-cheeked, will let me in with a smile and take me into the kitchen which smells of newly baked bread and apples. Perhaps she will offer me a mug of cider after my long walk. And then I will tell her the good news …

'Mary! Stop him hurting me! My arm. Awgh, my arm!'

I pull my head back inside quickly. 'Charley, let her go!'

My young brother is twisting my sister's arm up behind her back and she is squirming to get free. My other sister is hitting him over the head with her pillow. They are still in their nightdresses as it is Sunday and there is no school. The beds we share are all rumpled where the children have been jumping on them, fighting with pillows. Feathers are floating like moonbeams in a shaft of pale light from the open window. I should be cross with them because it is I who will have to mend the pillows and remake the beds but I cannot be cross today because of my secret. Church will not begin until eleven and by then I'll be back from Elmtree House and no one will be any the wiser.

Charley loosens his grip and Sarah springs away from him, hurling herself back into bed with Meg. The twins giggle and snuggle down under the covers. Charley looks at me as if we are the only wise ones. I do not blame him for teasing Sarah. She is a fretful, whining child because she is often ill and must get what she wants and he is the only boy in a family of four women, which must be tiresome for him.

'While Mother's still asleep, let's collect the eggs and make pancakes to surprise her,' I say to Charley.

I wrap myself in an old shawl, take his hand and we creep downstairs, trying not to let them creak. Pancakes are a treat, only served on Sundays or birthdays. The hens have laid only three eggs but there is plenty of lard, milk and flour and we can use the last of the honey to sweeten them. We set about our business quietly, Charley giving me little sidelong smiles for he is pleased to be my assistant. He is growing tall suddenly and his breeches are too short although they've been let down three times in six months.

When I am at Elmtree House I shall be able to use the money I earn for new breeches for him, boots for the twins, a warm cloak for Mother and thatch for the cottage roof. There are so many things we need. I know Mother will be disappointed that I am not taking the dressmaking apprenticeship she has tried so hard to arrange for me, but there is almost no money in a three-year apprenticeship and I do not think we can manage for so long without it.

When the pancakes are ready I dash outside to pick one perfect daffodil to lay beside Mother's platter. She likes beautiful things. I pour fresh goat's milk into her favourite china teacup with faded violets on the rim, and tell Charley to take the Sunday breakfast in to her. The rest of the pancakes can be kept in the pan by the stove until the twins get up. I tell him I am going for a walk to 'welcome the Spring' before church and he looks at me again as if he knows I have a better plan, but nods and smiles to himself and says nothing. He is a smart boy for ten — I wish he could stay at school at least another year.

I have not been to school but Mother has taught me to read and write as well as sew buttonholes and mend stockings. I have no training for the position I wish to apply for at Elmtree House but Mrs Frayne knew my father before he was taken from us and she has told me that once I reach the age of fourteen, if I want to earn

wages, I have only to come to the servants' entrance
and knock. I have been waiting almost a year for this
day.

When I knock it is not Mrs Frayne who opens the
door and I draw back in fright. It is a thin woman with
a nose like a beak, small pink eyes and a mouth that
seems to have just tasted vinegar. Her voice is a low rasp
so that I have to learn forward to catch what she is saying: 'No hawkers here. Away with you!'

I shake my head. I look down at the bunch of crocuses I have brought for Mrs Frayne. 'I am not selling
flowers.'

'Then what do you want?' she snaps.

'If you please, Ma'am, I have come to call on Mrs
Frayne.'

'She hasn't been housekeeper here for six months.
Why do you want her? Are you a relative?'

'No, Ma'am. She said that if I were ever in need of a
position as housemaid, I might call on her. I am fourteen years old today, which Mrs Frayne told me was the
right age to begin my training.'

The thin woman stares at me as if I were a nasty
insect. I think she is going to slam the door in my face.
I thrust the flowers at her. 'For you, Ma'am.'

She bursts into a cackle which is perhaps a laugh. I
am not sure. My knees are trembling and my hands as
well. The crocuses shake their heads. She takes them
from me.

'Come in and let me take a look at you,' she croaks
and pushes me inside. We do not go to the warm
kitchen. She sits me down on a hard chair in the hallway which is dark and smells of furniture polish. She

lifts my chin to the light, pushes back my bonnet and stares hard into my face. Then she takes my hands in hers and turns them over, rubbing them and poking them. I am afraid they are not rough enough, for apart from milking our goat, collecting the hens' eggs, weeding the garden and doing the washing, I do no manual labour at all. She says nothing. I wonder if she is about to look at my teeth. I suppose when you are about to employ someone you want a good return for your wages.

I am relieved when she moves away from me. 'Mrs Frayne retired. I am Mrs Burton. I am housekeeper at Elmtree House now.' She narrows her eyes and squints at me as if she would like to squeeze secrets out of me. Then she snaps suddenly, 'As you have no training your wages will be board and one pound a month.' She pauses to see my reaction. I nod enthusiastically. A pound a month is a fortune to me. 'If you are unsatisfactory or give less than a month's notice when you wish to leave you will get no reference and will never be able to find another position.'

'Thank you, Mrs Burton.' I am beaming with pleasure. 'And which will be my day off, please?'

The Housekeeper stares. 'Day off?' She spits the two words out as if they are poison. 'Day off? So you wish to go gallivanting in the village, eyeing off farmers' boys, do you?'

'Oh no, Ma'am! I only wish to see my family, who live not two miles from here. Once a week on Sundays, if you would be so kind, Ma'am.'

The vinegar look returns to her face. 'And what

makes you think that a servant without training deserves a whole day off every week, girl?'

'My father, before he was taken, worked as a blacksmith and employed two men who were always allowed to go home on Sundays. People like to be with their families on the Sabbath. All kinds of people, whether they are servants or not. Do you not think it so, Mrs Burton?' I am babbling but I only want to explain my meaning so that I do not offend her.

'Your family habits do not interest me, girl,' she snaps. 'You astound me. Do you think that a grand house such as this can be closed up like a blacksmith's shop just because it is Sunday? Who do you think will make the beds, iron the clothes, empty the slops and clean the Master's boots?'

I am silent. I think to myself, perhaps the Master could wear different boots on Sunday … but of course that is a foolish thought. 'I understand, Ma'am.'

'I am glad that you do. You will start tomorrow morning at eight. Do not bring too many belongings. The room you will be sharing is small.'

I hesitate but my curiosity gets the better of me. 'Who will I be sharing with, Mrs Burton?'

'Maria Wilkinson. She has been a servant in the house for six months. She is sixteen.' Again the lips contort as if she has tasted vinegar. 'What is your name, girl?'

'Mary Jones, Ma'am.'

'If your work is satisfactory, Mary Jones, you will be allowed a day off once a month but it may not always be a Sunday. Do not be late tomorrow.'

I walk quickly down the gravel path between the

avenue of elms. As soon as I get outside the tall iron gates I begin to skip. I am about to earn my own money. My life of independence has begun.

'Oh Mary, you have broken my heart!' My mother is pale and her hair lies in damp tendrils on the pillow. I had expected a few tears but not this wailing. I knew she would be hurt that I had chosen to work as a servant for wages when she had planned a different life for me, but I never guessed she would be distraught.

'I have worked so hard to make a good connection with a respectable dressmaker who has at last agreed to take you on as her apprentice, and now you have thrown it all away!'

'Thrown what away? Receiving a few pence for going almost blind sewing buttonholes night after night as you do, Mother?' I speak more harshly than I should but the sight of her, all blotchy and pathetic, makes me angry.

'Foolish girl! After three years of buttonholes and seams, you would have become a dressmaker yourself, making clothes for fine ladies who would pay a small fortune and regard you as a friend, or at least as indispensable.'

'Three years! Too long for us to be scrimping and saving while the debts mount up until we're all starving or out on the road!'

The younger children have crept down the stairs to listen. They hang back in silence. They know the seriousness of our situation.

'The landlord expects us to keep the cottage in good order and if we don't fix the roof he will throw us out.

You know that, Mother. Why do you pretend it isn't so? Why do you think I place every pot and pan we own beneath the leaks each night? To stop us drowning in our beds! The damp does nothing to help Sarah's chest and no doctor will come here unless he sees money first.'

Mother turns her head away and begins sobbing again. I sit down on the bed and gently stroke her hand. 'Mother, you work late into every night sewing shirts, dresses, shifts and bonnets for the village people but often they don't even pay you.'

'They are poor too.' She turns her head back to look at me as if I am a stranger. 'Have you no heart?' This stings me and I do not answer. 'At least we have food to eat,' she says.

'We grow a few onions and potatoes. If the hens do not lay and the goat goes dry we will starve. When I am boarding at Elmtree House there will be one less mouth to feed and I shall earn a pound a month to help the family!'

'And we will not have you at home to lift our spirits. Oh Mary, what has happened to our little family since your poor father was taken from us? I never thought the day would come when a daughter of mine would become a common servant. My father will turn in his grave.'

'Don't cry, Mother. Here, eat this.' I give her the last pancake although it is cold. 'You need not get up to go to church today. Stay here and sleep. I will take the little ones.'

She buries her head in the pillow. She will have a good wail while we are gone.

Her father was a clergyman who left her nothing more than the violet-rimmed china tea service, a mahogany sideboard and an oak table with six balloon-backed chairs. We have already sold the furniture and part of the tea service. Only four teacups remain. Mother wants to leave one to each of her children when she dies, she tell us. Poor Mother. She is so fond of fine things. When she married my father, the blacksmith, her father, the clergyman, barely spoke to her again. I only met my grandfather once. I thought him gruff and bad-mannered. He asked whether I was literate and as I was only five I said I did not know. He then scowled at my mother, passed me a large black Bible and told her, 'If you cannot afford to send her to school, at least teach her to read and write at home.' My mother promised she would do so. She kept her promise. We are the only children in the village who are literate. Charley and Meg have each had a year at the village school and hope to continue for another but Sarah is too ill. Poor families do not often send their children to school.

Winter is back this morning and there is a thin layer of ice on the puddles as I hurry up the hill to Elmtree House with my bundle. I have brought only a few clothes, some small keepsakes, my Bible and a book of poetry. I am feeling excited and cannot wait to meet the girl I am to share a room with — Maria Wilkinson. I have no friends my own age in the village as Mother does not like me to mix with what she calls 'common' girls.

As I pass around the side of the house to the back I

notice there is a fine kitchen garden with fruit trees, vegetables and strawberry beds. In the fields beyond I can see cows grazing and some sheep but no goat. Goats like ours live on scraps, but these sleek cows and fat sheep seem hardly to bother cropping the grass, there is such an abundance of it. I wonder about the family that lives in this grand house. I have heard in the village that the Master, Mr Robinson Doake, is a gentleman farmer, with a bailiff to run his estate and collect the rents from his tenant cottages. He has a wife and two grown-up daughters — they are on a visit to Bath at present. I wonder if they have a library with many books.

I have just met Maria Wilkinson and she is rather wicked! We are to share an attic under the roof at the top of the house. We have a bed each, a luxury I have not enjoyed before, and a washstand and dish for ourselves and one candle, although we must not burn it for long, so my Bible and poetry reading must be brief each evening.

Maria is full of mischief. I had been afraid she might be stern as she is two years older than me and properly trained, but she is kind and so pretty that it is hard not to stare at her. She has dark hair, green eyes, red lips and a perfect complexion, almost as pale as a lady's. As she shows me how to perform my tasks she makes such fun of everything that I find myself weak with laughter. She is clever mimic and has the gentry down perfectly. The Master swaggers when he walks and twirls his riding crop, the Mistress leans forwards and fusses with her shawl, twisting it in her fingers, and blinking her eyelids as fast as candle flicker. As for the Misses Doake, according to Maria, they have certain habits which are rather crude. I cannot wait to see what these might be. Maria herself is quite shockingly bold in her speech, using coarse language I would not expect to hear from such a dainty, innocent looking girl. Perhaps she overhears men in the ale house as she hurries past on an errand. It is only when her betters are not watching that she imitates their speech, their walks and manners. When they are near she is careful to lower her eyes and act respectfully.

She tells me that my clothes are a disgrace. I look like a gypsy, she says, and as soon as I am paid I must have a new frock. In the meantime she has lent me one of hers. When we went to the village to do errands for the mistress she showed me the whorehouse. It looked like an ordinary cottage to me, but Maria swears there are two women there who do nothing but lie on their backs all day wearing fine silk and having a servant bring them meals in bed and prepare baths of rosewater and milk while they wait for gentlemen callers.

Maria herself appears very popular in the village, I notice. She is cheerful to the shopkeepers, and of course Mrs Robinson Doake always pays her bills on time. It is a pleasure to go into a shop and not feel shy about accounts that are overdue. (I hoped to catch sight of one of my sisters or Charley on an errand for my mother but sadly I did not.) Maria has her admirers in the village. The young man at the brewery where we delivered the order for cider seems quite smitten by her, but Maria called him 'a dolt' and said she could do much better than him in the marriage stakes. Why should she waste her time on a 'blithering idiot yokel'?

When we were delivering the order for the house at the grocery shop the shopkeeper asked Maria to read it out to him so that he could check that the goods were on his shelves, and she blushed and handed the list to me. Realising that she could not read, I took it from her quickly to save her feelings. On the way home she said, 'It is better to live by your wits than have learning, Mary. Never forget it.'

I feel sorry she has not had the chances I have had and perhaps when we know each other better I shall offer to teach her reading and writing. I sense she is very proud. She has no love for her parents who live far away up north near Leeds. She told me she never visits them, that they are 'low scum'.

I wondered if she would like to visit my family. I feel sure they would like her. She would make the childen laugh and Mother would be pleased to see that I had made such a clever friend. But when I suggested it she said we would never both be given the same day off and anyway she had too many friends of her own to visit. I felt a little hurt. Maria is allowed a day off once a fort-night because she has been so satisfactory. I hope I shall be allowed the same when I have been here for six months.

I am feeling torn in two today because Mother has sent a note to say that the dressmaker who offered me the apprenticeship has reconsidered and agreed to take me on in six months' time. This is generous of her. I daresay Mother had to plead or offer her some special service and I know it would be ungrateful of me to refuse. But I am enjoying my new life. I am learning how to be a good servant and the work is not hard. I want to earn as much as I can to help the family. It may be heartless to say so but I like living away from the family in a place of my own, even though I miss them sadly and pray for them every night. And I enjoy Maria's company, in spite of the thoughtless things she says sometimes. I do not always do what she advises. I have decided to risk looking like 'a gypsy' as I do not want to waste any of my wages on a new frock. Mrs Burton has provided me with a cap and two aprons so my 'rags' are mostly covered up. I wear Maria's frock for special occasions like going to the village on errands.

Sometimes Maria says daft things. When we were in the village yesterday she overheard another servant say respectfully, 'That is Lady Jane Harrington's carriage.' We looked up and there was a fine lady inside a black carriage drawn by a pair of dappled greys.

'I will be a Lady Jane one day,' said Maria, at which I laughed. She gave me such a scornful look. She was entirely in earnest.

Maria has taught me not to be afraid of Mrs Burton. 'She is an old maid who was once a beauty but was left at the altar and has dried up like a kipper ever since.'

I say that I cannot imagine her ever young, let alone a beauty and ask why her voice is so raspy.

'She was so upset at being jilted that she screamed and screamed until they locked her in a madhouse. There she stayed for seven years, still screaming and now there is nothing left of her voice but a croak.'

I wonder how Maria came to know this sad story, but she only says that it is common knowledge in the village. 'She carried white crocuses as her wedding bouquet and has never been able to stand the sight of them since,' Maria adds.

'But I gave her a bunch of crocuses the day I first came here!' I say in alarm.

'What did she do?'

'She … laughed.'

'And afterwards?'

'I don't know. She took them.'

'Took them? Did you ever see them again?'

'No. I thought she might have put them in her room.'

'Never! She would have chopped them into pieces and burnt them. It's a wonder she didn't strike you.'

'How could I know?'

'You couldn't. That is probably why she let you have the job. You would be the only one at Elmtree House who didn't know her story.'

'Poor Mrs Burton. I shall pretend I still do not know it.'

'Yes, that would be best,' Maria agrees. 'And when she speaks sharply to you don't hang your head, just look her straight in the eye, think of her screaming all those years and give her a look of pity.'

Later I hear Maria and Agnes, the parlour maid, laughing fit to burst in the washhouse and when I ask what the joke is they both stop at once and Maria pretends she was only coughing.

Maria is so fond of pranks. When the weather is threatening we have to rush to the drying lines and bring in the washing before the rain comes down. We climb to the attic above our room, where there are indoor drying lines and hang the half-dry sheets and clothing there. Then Maria will grab a corset and a pair of Mrs Robinson Doake's stockings and parade about with her chest thrust out like a pouting pigeon, saying: 'Oh dear, dear me, where have the gels put my stays? Oh, I am wearing them! How very short-sighted I am becoming. Gels! Bring my chamber pot. I am busting!'

Then I put on a pair of the Master's trousers and a nightcap and strut about twirling an imaginary moustache, but I cannot do imitations like Maria because I have not the talent — and besides, I am laughing too much.

It is only girlish high spirits but I would not like my mother to see me like this.

I have had another letter from home to say that my little sister Sarah has been taken ill again with her chest and cannot leave her bed. The doctor has come once but there is no money for another visit or for medicine, and although my mother is doing her best with hot compresses and herbs, Sarah is growing weaker. I think I must go to Mrs Burton, ask for an advance on my wages and for leave to go home for half a day. Now that I know how she has suffered I feel sure she will understand how I feel. It is only a week until my wages are due and my day off.

Mrs Burton has refused. When I gave her the look of pity Maria advised, she seemed to become more angry and said I had a cheek. She told me I could not have next Sunday off, but Monday instead, which means I cannot go to church with the family as I had promised. I have written to Mother and the little ones to tell them

I will be there as early as possible on Monday morning, just as soon as I have cleaned the bedrooms.

I have made a friend of Michael, the gardener. He is a melancholic Irishman with a thin face and a coarse coat that has even more patches than my frocks. But he is kindly. He told me how much he missed his family in County Cork. When I told him I was to visit my family next Monday he said he would hide some beets, new potatoes, turnips and carrots in a bag he will place in a hedge just outside the gates for me to take home. I have been keeping aside the bacon and beef from my own dinner each day so that the family can have a fine soup.

What a homecoming! It warmed my heart. There were hugs and kisses from everyone and Meg had picked a mass of flowers from the garden to make the cottage look brighter, the fire crackled and there were pancakes such as I haven't eaten for a month. Everyone talked at once, asking questions about life at Elmtree House and I had to tell the same stories over and over. Even Sarah brightened up enough to come downstairs and listen, wrapped in a quilt in a chair by the fire, although she still coughed. Mother was happy too and did not cry once. The fresh vegetables and meat caused cries of pleasure from all.

'Do even the servants eat meat every day?' Charley asked in disbelief.

'Yes. Though this week I have not.' They all laughed, knowing why.

'You have filled out, Mary. The meat agrees with you,' said Mother. Then I proudly handed her the shining gold sovereign. The children all wanted to touch it and turn it over in their hands. Mother did weep a little then. She said that now there would be medicine for Sarah and the roof could be fixed.

I told them stories of Maria's pranks and the children all wanted to meet her, although Mother was anxious that she might be a bad influence on me and cause me to upset Mr Robinson Doake and his family. I said that on the contrary she gave me advice on how to please the Housekeeper and the Master and Mistress were very pleased with me. Then we made the soup, ate as much as we needed and there was still enough left for three more dinners.

After we had eaten Mother recited the whole of the first part of 'The Rime of the Ancyent Marinere' by Samuel Coleridge Taylor to us. She is quite dramatic and performs actions to go with the lines, beating her breast like the Wedding Guest and clutching her throat in horror when the Ancyent Marinere discovers that around his neck there is no longer a cross but an albatross. Mother knows the whole poem by heart. But she left off after '*The Albatross fell off, and sank/Like lead into the sea*' because the fire was burning low in the grate, the sun was sinking and it was time for me to leave.

She said she would recite the rest when I came to visit next month. The little ones cried that they had expected me to stay the night and wanted stories like the ones I used to tell them, but I said severely: 'And who would iron the shirts and empty the slops and clean the Master's boots if I was not there to do it, eh?' They stared at me seriously until I laughed and said that was what the Housekeeper would say.

Then, just as I was leaving, I turned to Mother and promised that I would accept the apprenticeship with the dressmaker in five months time, and thanked her for going to so much trouble to get it for me. I feared that she might cry but she only squeezed my hand tightly and nodded with pursed lips, as if she did not want to let her emotion out.

They went on waving and calling after me until they were just specks in the distance. I was happy to have been at home today, yet pleased to be going back to Elmtree House. As I walked briskly up the hill and into the evening breeze I thanked God for my fortunate life.

# CHAPTER TWO

**Maria Calls Me 'Green Mary' but Says I Do Relieve Her Boredom**
**Elmtree House, Sevenoaks, Kent, May, 1819**

'Lord, I never thought I would still be in this dreary house six months after getting here. Same chores every day, same faces in the village, same deadly dull evenings.' Maria and I were scrubbing the flagstones in the courtyard, getting our hands chapped and red. 'One day I shall escape this wretched life and live in London, where I shall ride in a carriage in a fur-trimmed cloak and go to the theatre and the opera. Just see if I don't!' Maria jumped up from her kneeling position and swirled herself around gracefully. 'Ah, foolish dreams,' she sighed.

'But they lift your spirits, don't they Maria?' I said cheerfully.

She shook her head. 'Sometimes I wonder why I bothered to leave home. Was it worse than here? Yes, it was, now I remember. My mam with her fifth husband. Not wed mind. Never wed except once to my da, the most hopeless of the lot of them. You'd think she'd of learned by now, wouldn't you? Not her! And those squalling brats by the half dozen running around bare-arsed with snotty noses. Agh, but it sickened me. If I'd stayed I'd have taken to the gin just like her.'

I nodded sympathetically.

'Our house was a slum. Two rooms for the lot of us. Never enough to eat. She'd make soup and gruel, soup and gruel and I was supposed to earn my keep collecting coal to sell while my fifth da, the lazy sod, sat at home by the fire burning it up. Mind you, I wasn't as badly off as my little brothers. They was expected to thieve for a living and was often caught and beaten for you can't hang a child. Not as young as eight and six. Imagine three babies under six all sleeping in one bed. The stench! At least here everything is scrubbed and smells of lavender and there's plenty to eat.'

'You say you always wanted to live in the country and now you are,' I told her brightly. Her life sounded so miserable I could hardly bear to listen.

'Yes, I am, so who's complaining eh? But I won't be here for long. I have my 'one great asset' as Mrs Figgs at the haberdashery in the village calls it — 'Your looks, my dear.' She told me I should guard them well and be choosy about a husband. What does she know? I'm never going to marry anyone from around here. Leastways not a villager.'

'But surely there are some in the village quite handsome and eligible, Maria?'

She threw back her head and laughed. 'Not handsome and eligible enough for me, Mary! But listen, I have my wits about me although I have no learning. I watch the gentry and know how to behave with them. More important, I can imitate them well enough to become one! Just see if I don't.'

We picked up our pails and walked to the pump. Maria balanced hers as a lady would carry a parasol above her head, which made me laugh.

Last night as we lay in our beds Maria paid me what I first thought must be a compliment. 'I must say the boredom around here has eased a bit since your arrival, Mary.'

'Why thank you, Maria.'

'But you're so green it makes me want to shake you.' She giggled. 'Such big eyes you make, as if you've never been outside the front gate of your cottage. You're innocent and raw as a skun rabbit. You could be pretty if you tried. Some as I know would kill to have eyes like yours, pale blue as forget-me-nots, and hair as yellow as ripe wheat. But how can you stand to wear such clothes? Has no one ever taught her how to dress?'

I blushed in the darkness and said that although my clothes were not new, they were well mended. This made Maria fairly burst with laughter.

In the house Maria has to teach me everything. 'At least you learn fast. You ain't stupid,' she told me. 'But the notions you have are quite daft. Fancy wanting to ask the Master and Mistress if you can borrow books from their library.'

However, later I overheard her proudly telling Agnes, the parlour maid: 'She was learned to read and write by her mother who's the daughter of a preacher no less.' Then she laughed as she added: 'So you can see how unworldly poor Mary is, and how much work I have to do to "educate" her.'

Today is a special one at Elmtree House. As we splashed our faces and hands in cold water this morning before it was light, Maria sighed. 'Lordy, lord. Guess who's coming home. Miss Dolores and Miss Lydia. Yawn, yawn. I can scarcely wait. So you and I, Mary, must be up at dawn cleaning their bedchambers, polishing their fancy looking-glasses to make everything perfect for the spoilt young darlings.'

'I expect they will have lots of new frocks and bonnets,' I said excitedly. 'They say Bath is just as fashionable as London. People in high society go there to enjoy themselves and take the waters for their health — and go shopping.'

'The young ladies were in the care of their old aunt,' Maria said. 'She was to be their chaperone, the old dragon! She stayed here once. I can't imagine her enjoying anything.'

A few hours later I heard the carriage on the gravel and involuntarily clutched my heart. 'Oh, Maria, how lucky Miss Dolores and Miss Lydia are! They will have danced at the famous Assembly Rooms, attended plays at the theatre and concerts in Sydney Gardens …'

Maria snorted. 'And never escaped the eye of their dragon Aunt for a single moment! All I can say is, if Miss Dolores has taken the waters you speak of, I hope they may have cured her insides. But how do you know about all those things? Have you been to Bath?'

'Only in my imagination. I have read about it.'

My reply seemed to put Maria into a bad humour. I

tried to gentle her. 'The young ladies may have brought you a present.'

Maria gave another rude snort. 'They think of nought but themselves as you will see directly.'

'I hope I may have the chance to see some of their fine clothes,' I said shyly. 'Perhaps I shall even be asked to help them unpack.'

The carriage had stopped at the front of the house and Agnes, who thinks she's above us, shooed us away to the kitchen. Maria stuck out her tongue at her.

Cook was preparing a special repast of baked pheasant with red currant jelly. 'At least Cook will keep us a bowl of scraps,' Maria said.

'Cook is so kind to us,' I remarked. 'How delicious it smells! I have never eaten pheasant.'

'Hark at you, happy as a lark in a hawthorn tree!' teased Maria. 'Sometimes I could throttle you for your sweetness.' I am sure she did not mean it.

Now we heard high-pitched voices and laughter in the hall. Cook was flustered and told us to run quickly and mop the flagstones in the yard. I think she wanted us out of the way. We took the wooden bucket and began to mop. Through the casement window of the dining room we could see the family assembled around the table. I peered at the scene, wanting my first glimpse of the young ladies.

'Which do you prefer, Miss Dolores or Miss Lydia?' I asked Maria.

'Neither. Miss Dolores is the older, about twenty-three, so she's already an old maid. She is full of airs and graces, always dropping her handkerchief in the path of some young gentlemen, hoping he will pick it up, but none ever do.'

'So she is not pretty?'

'Ugly as a hedgehog and bad-tempered, too.'

'How sad. And Miss Lydia? I believe she is not yet twenty. Is she a beauty?'

'Fat as a suet pudding and freckled as a thrush's egg. Eyes so small and close together she could be a piglet. She snorts like a pig when she laughs.'

'Oh, stop it, Maria! You are making fun of me for wanting to believe the best of the young ladies.'

'Believe whatever you like. You'll see the grisly truth soon enough,' she retorted, wringing out her mop and flouncing off.

# CHAPTER THREE

**The Young Ladies Despise Me**
**Elmtree House, June, 1819**

I am disappointed. It has been a whole day and I have not caught more than a glimpse of the young ladies. They must have been so tired after their journey and all that fine food and wine at luncheon that they have been sleeping soundly all afternoon.

When the bell jangles in the kitchen I am down on my hands and knees polishing the floor and I almost jump out of my skin.

'Well, what are you waiting for? It's Miss Dolores' bell,' says Maria. 'Straighten your cap and go!'

'But, but …'

The bell jangles even more urgently. 'Run!' shouts Mrs Burton who has suddenly appeared from the hall.

I knock timidly and a cultured voice calls 'Enter.' Miss Dolores is a pale, thin young lady with mousy hair that floats loosely on her pillow as she lies on her bed reading a book. She has a pointed nose and is wearing spectacles. My heart lifts. She may not be pretty but she certainly appears studious. She does not look up at me. Now I can see that she is reading a volume of poetry. If she enjoys reading verse as I do, surely she cannot be too bad-tempered.

'And who are you?' she asks without much interest.

I curtsy politely. 'Mary Jones, Miss. I am the new girl, training to be a housemaid.'

'Training to be? Where is Maria?'

'She is in the kitchen, Miss.'

'Then send her to me directly. I do not wish to be attended by a half-trained servant.'

'I beg your pardon, Miss, but I am almost completely trained and Mrs Burton is pleased with my progress. It was she who sent me to wait on you.' By now I have managed to make out the title of the book. 'Oh! I see that you are reading *Lyrical Ballads*. I have a copy of that very volume.'

There is silence. Miss Dolores's eyes flash like flint behind her spectacles. She stares at me with contempt. I fear I have upset her. 'Is there nothing I can do for you, Miss Dolores?'

'Yes. Get out and send Maria! Did you not hear me, you insolent hussy?'

I am shocked by her rudeness but I manage to curtsy and take my leave quietly.

But before I close the door I hear the unmistakable sound of the young lady breaking wind very loudly.

I return to the kitchen looking crestfallen. Maria seems to realise at once what has happened for she jumps up from the bench where she is polishing silver. 'Here, you do this. I'll attend to the cranky old witch. Did she ask for me?'

'Yes. I think I have upset her, Maria.'

'Not as much as I will!' And she pulls a sour face that is so like that of Miss Dolores that I have to laugh.

I have not been at the silver for five minutes when another bell jangles.

'Leave that! Off you go,' scolds Cook.

'Miss Lydia?' I stammer.

'Who else, pray?'

I am trembling as I knock on her door. 'Come in!' she calls in a singsong voice.

Her room is not neat like her sister's. There are two large open trunks and littered all over the floor are half-unpacked dresses, shoes, parasols, hats, lace collars, shawls and ribbons, all tossed about.

'Look at this mess!' she laughs gaily. 'I told Agnes to unpack but then I felt sleepy so I told her to leave it and now I'm awake she is busy elsewhere. I have tried to attend to it myself but as you see ...' She laughs again.

I like her much better than her sister. It is true that she is freckled like an egg and too plump and that her eyes are rather small and have such pale lashes that they do remind one of a pig, but at least she seems good-tempered.

I smile and say pleasantly, 'I should be pleased to help you, Miss Lydia.'

'You are the new housemaid, are you not?'

I curtsy and tell her humbly that I am. I do not volunteer my name until she asks for it.

'Well then, what are you called? Don't be bashful.'

'Mary Jones, Miss.'

'What!' She breaks into a peal of laughter. 'Mary Jones! There must be thousands of you. What cruel parents to give you such a common name.'

I blush with anger, which she takes for shame.

'Never mind. You cannot be blamed for your parents' foolishness.'

'If you please Miss, my father's mother was called Mary and my mother's mother as well. I was named for both grandmothers for which I feel proud.'

'Feel proud, do you? Well, well. That is an uncommon quality in a servant.' She stares at me and I feel she is sneering. 'Perhaps you are too fine a lady to unpack my new clothes from Bath.'

'Oh no, Miss. I should be pleased to do so and shall be most careful of your new clothes.'

'A pity, for I have changed my mind. I shall wait for Agnes to return. Better still, you may go and fetch her. At once. I do not trust proud servants, Mary Jones. Be off with you!'

That night in bed I face the wall and try not to let Maria hear my sobs. But my shoulders are heaving and she hears the bed creak. She comes over and sits beside me, stroking my hair. She begins to sing to the tune of 'Mary Had a Little Lamb': 'Little Mary, pray don't cry, pray don't cry, pray don't cry. Gentle Mary, pray don't cry, those two will burn in Hell!'

I begin to giggle in spite of my misery — 'They're a pair of she-devils who'll be loved by nobody, not if they live to be a hundred,' Maria tells me. 'Compared to them you're a blessed angel, so don't waste your tears on them.'

I sit up and throw both arms around Maria's neck and sob loudly with relief. 'How could I be so foolish as to offend them both on their first day at home? Oh, Maria, I don't know how it happened! What was it I said to upset them both?'

'You ain't a cringing liar to their faces as all servants are supposed to be. That's all.'

'So I should not have remarked upon the book Miss Dolores was reading?'

'Never. She wants to believe she's the only one in the world who reads poetry — and you have the cheek to say that you, a humble servant, not only read it, but own the same book! Ooh, I'd love to have seen her face when you said that!'

'And I should not have told Miss Lydia that I was proud of my name even though it is common?'

'Never! A servant ain't expected to have pride. We're there to empty their shite! Don't you know anything, Mary Jones?'

I smile and blink away the tears. 'You know so much about the world, Maria. What would I do without you?'

'You'd be crushed by those ugly crones and grovel at their feet and they would love it.'

'I do not intend to be crushed, but I cannot behave too humbly because I feel it would be dishonest. I do so wish to be a good servant. It is a problem, is it not?'

'No it ain't! You must play-act as I do. Lower your eyes and say little in front of the crones, flash your eyes and smile in front of the Master. Giggle at his bad jokes … but watch out for his wandering hands. He hasn't tried anything yet because you're new, but he will. And never go out to the privy at night. He'll be waiting. He thinks you're his property and there's nought you can do once he catches you. It's the way things are.'

My eyes are wide with wonder. 'But if I can never go out to the privy at night, what should I do?'

'Piss in your nightgown! It is nobler.' I stare so hard that Maria fairly bursts with laughter. 'Use the chamber pot, you booby.'

# CHAPTER FOUR

## Maria Makes Fun of My Family and Finds Herself a Gentleman
### Elmtree House, July, 1819

'So why did you visit them if they was so dull?'

'I knew I shouldn't have agreed to go but Mary insisted because she's so in love with her family that she thinks everyone else will be.' Maria was helping Agnes to polish the dining room table when I passed by and heard this comment. I stopped in shock and lingered out of sight in the hallway to hear what else might be said.

'I couldn't get out of it. You'll remember, Agnes, on Monday the Robinson Doakes took their bored daughters off to town for a spending spree, and we was given the same day off.'

'So you had no excuse not to visit the family. Was they very horrible?'

'Compared to my family they was saints and angels and bustled round trying to make me welcome with little bowls of this and that, which made the visit even more embarrassing. Who wants to eat up their watery stew when here at Elmtree House we have chicken broth and roasted meats with rich brown gravy? To see Mary gulping that wretched turnip stew and yelping "Oh Mother, you have made it taste delicious!" would make you laugh for the shame of it. On the way home she kept saying she was sorry for having uttered "such a falsehood" (she won't call it a lie) but her poor mother had saved the best portions for us and she felt obliged to seem grateful. Well, I wasn't grateful. The stuff made me want to puke all over the floor. The mother saw how I felt and quickly took the bowl away. Then she gave me such a look of sorrow. Well, bad luck for her.'

'So what was the entertainment you mentioned after the soup?'

Maria sighed. 'After the meal we had to sit still for about an hour while her dear mother recited a poem about a madman who lost his wits at sea all because he shot some bird — albatross, it was called. An unlikely tale if ever I've heard one. I hoped one of the little ones would get bored and protest, but no! They sat with their eyes glued on their mother and even joined in the bits they knew. "*Alone, alone, all, all alone, Alone on a wide, wide sea!*" they chanted, just like some dirge at a funeral. The moral of the story seemed to be that those as pray to God and love birds will do all right and the rest will go mad. So there's not much hope for me.'

'There certainly ain't!' Agnes giggled. 'Anyway, Mary worships you. Thinks flowers grow out of your backside, I don't know why.'

'My posterior, you mean? That is a fine word is it not, Agnes? *Posterior.* I am practising using less crude words, you may have noticed. I watch my grammar too and seldom say "ain't" unless I'm too tired to care.'

'And all this is preparation for becoming a lady, is it?' Agnes asked sarcastically.

'Who knows, that might be nearer than you think,' Maria replied with dignity.

'Well, just before you leave off being a servant, could your ladyship take the silver into the kitchen and polish it like I showed you?'

'Be damned if I will. That's your job. You're the bleedin' parlour maid!'

I hurried away as they kept arguing, stumbling because my eyes were blinded by tears. I felt utterly betrayed, not by what Maria had said about me, for I know she finds me odd, but the cruel way she had ridiculed my family, particularly my mother. I resolved not to speak to her ever again.

When Maria found me crying she hugged me close and said she was worse than a whore and deserved my friendship not one jot. Then she took her most treasured tortoiseshell comb from its box under the floorboards and gave it to me, saying 'Forgive me, Mary, and I'll be loyal to you till I'm dead and buried.' When I still said not a word she went on: 'You know I'm nought but a cheap showoff who'll say anything to get a laugh. In truth I quite liked your mother's story of that albatross, but made a joke of it to show Agnes how much cleverer than all of you I was. Well, as you know, that's far from true.'

Maria looked so truly sorry that I forgave her at once, and even offered to teach her reading and writing. I think that if she was literate she would feel better about herself and wouldn't need to be cruel.

Maria had quite an adventure today. She was sent to deliver quail eggs to a gracious mansion known as Mersham Le Hatch, three miles from here. It is the home of Sir Edward Knatchbull and his family. Our mistress sent the eggs to Lady Knatchbull, who wanted them for a special dinner to welcome home one of her sons. Maria said the house is so grand it makes this one look like a gardener's cottage.

There are three grown-up sons of the household as well as numerous younger children. The first son has the title 'Baron', so it is said in the village, the second is in the Church and the third is in the Navy. At the time of Maria's visit the naval son had just returned from the East Indies and the dinner was for him.

As she passed along the path to the kitchen she said she saw a well-built gentlemen, not young or tall, but handsome enough, walking towards her across the lawn. He did not speak to her but smiled and lifted the cloth from her basket to peer inside. 'Ah, the quails have delivered their young,' he said knowingly.

She curtsied and said prettily: 'No, Sir, the eggs are to be eaten, not hatched.'

He seemed to find this most amusing and laughed heartily. He then asked Maria her name and when she told him he introduced himself formally and shook her hand. 'I am Captain John Knatchbull of His Majesty's Navy. I am to remain on shore in the bosom of my family and friends for some time.' Then he looked at her keenly and said, 'It may be that after a short while I shall find their company dull.'

At this point Maria paused and gave me a mysterious look.

'What did he mean?' I asked.

'Oh Mary, you are so innocent!' she cried. 'He was meaning that he might find my company more entertaining than that of his family.'

'Ah,' I said, still not quite understanding.

'The gentleman asked if I would tell him more about myself and I replied, "I should be pleased to, sir, at some time in the future." I said this demurely, with my eyes lowered as if I was not quite sure of the correctness of my offer but did not wish to offend him.

' "Then let us arrange to meet in the village," he says. 'Shall we say tomorrow afternoon at five, at the Hare and Hounds?" At this I drew back in alarm. "A public house, sir? My father, who is a clergyman, would disapprove." He frowned slightly then and drew back as if he'd had a fright. "I do beg your pardon," he said. He was silent and I thought to myself, *Fool! Now you've gone and lost him*. But then he said 'What about tea? At a teashop?'

'Oh yes, tea would be lovely.' I said in a most genteel manner.

'Tuesday would suit me.'

'Capital! Would you like to choose a teashop? I have to say I'm not much of an expert on such places,' he replied.

'Miss Morris at the Millstream serves the finest cucumber sandwiches and her strawberry jam is delicious.'

'He laughed again. Why? Was it my accent, such a contrast to my servant's clothes? He seemed to enjoy my company however, and said enthusiastically, 'We'll meet at the Millstream on Tuesday at four.' Then we shooks hands again and he bade me goodbye. I hope he didn't think I was too forward suggesting the day to meet but Tuesday is my day off, the only one for a fortnight so I had no choice, did I?'

# CHAPTER FIVE

## Maria Falls Into Something More Interesting
## Than a Ditch
## Elmtree House, July, 1819

I am concerned about Maria. It is dark and she hasn't
returned from the village. Today was her day off and
she has been in a strange mood preparing for the meeting with Captain Knatchbull this afternoon. To my
dismay she 'borrowed' a ribbon from Miss Lydia to tie
under her bodice and a pair of fine kid gloves from
Miss Dolores. Of course neither of them knows about
this. I shudder to think what might happen if either
young lady discovers her possessions are missing. I
begged her to take care but she only laughed and said I
was too timid.

Sometimes I am cut by what Maria says because I
am afraid it is true. Compared to her I must seem very
timid indeed. But I cannot afford to displease anyone
in the household and risk losing my position here. The
pound a month I give to Mother is all they have to live
on now that Mother's eyes are so bad she can no longer

sew. Sarah's medicine costs a great deal and although she has seen the doctor twice her cough does not improve. The doctor has told Mother that the cottage is too damp but what can be done about that? The landlord would rather throw them out than spend money on mending the roof. On my day off Charley and I climb up and do the best we can to mend the thatch, but it is beyond us to make it completely water-proof. It needs replacing. So Sarah must suffer.

I must say it was heartening to see my little sister laugh, that day we visited, at Maria's imitations of the Master, Mistress and the two young ladies. Sarah almost never smiles now but Maria was so funny that we were all laughing. Except Mother. It is a pity Mother did not warm to Maria. Yet I think I under-stand why Maria frightens her: I believe Mother fears that if I don't always do as she wants she may turn against me and harm me in some way. That is never likely to happen! For all her faults Maria is the best friend I have in all the world. Since her apology to me she has been quite devoted.

She is a brilliant mimic, so accurate and precise that she should be on the stage. It is like a tonic to watch her performing exaggerated versions of our Master and Mistress's voices, walks and manners. She even broke wind the way Miss Dolores does. I thought Charley and Meg would have fits. They were laughing so much the tears were rolling down their faces. Once you see Maria's version of those people to whom you must be subservient you can never respect them again. She has just perfected an imitation of Mrs Burton and yester-day she crept up behind Cook and croaked in exactly the right low voice. 'Cook, where are the eels I ordered for the Master's broth!' Cook jumped so suddenly she dropped her ladle. Of course when she saw it was Maria she threw the ladle at her full of hot broth and Maria was scalded down one side of her arm and moaned so pitifully that Cook had to treat it with a herb poultice and give Maria an hour off to recover.

Oh, where is Maria? It is almost time for supper. She knows she must be back at Elmtree House by sunset. If the Mistress asks for her I don't know what I shall say. Dare I help Agnes serve their supper instead of Maria? Then they will certainly demand to know where she is — Oh, I am so relieved! I hear her at the back door, taking off her cloak and hood. It is windy and just beginning to rain. I rush out to greet her. 'Maria, I've been so anxious —'

I stop in my tracks and stare. She looks as if she has been dragged through a hedge backwards. Her clothes are torn and her hair is like a bird's nest.

'Don't stare like a booby, Mary. Here, help me off with these wet things.'

The ribbon she borrowed is limp and bedraggled and she is wearing just one glove. She waggles her bare hand at me and whispers, 'Yes, I lost it. How careless of me!'

'Did you fall in a ditch, Maria? Are you hurt?'

She covers her mouth with the gloved hand and laughs. 'No, I fell in something much more interesting than a ditch, but ask me no questions. I cannot tell a falsehood.' And bursts into such peals of laughter that I drag her into the scullery for fear that Cook or Mrs Burton will hear the commotion.

'Well then, you have had a nice day off, I take it,' I say in a peevish voice. I have had to do her evening chores as well as my own to prevent anyone discovering her absence and I have been worried sick about her.

She smiles a mysterious little smile and says sweetly, 'Yes, thank you, Mary. I have had a very nice day off. And I mean to have many more.' And with that she flounces off to change her clothes just in time to serve supper and leaves me almost dying of curiosity.

# CHAPTER SIX

## Maria Snares a Gentleman and He Makes Her a Promise
### Elmtree House, August, 1819

That night in bed, even before she had blown out the candle I made Maria tell me what had happened that day. But first I had to swear on my Bible that I would not tell a soul.

'Well, my meeting with Captain Knatchbull was a "delightful event" as I would say if I was a lady,' she began. 'We met at the Millstream. I pinched my cheeks to make them rosy so that when he arrived just a few minutes late, he was enraptured with me. "My dear Maria, you are even more ravishing than you looked last time we met," he said. I shook my head and blushed modestly. He seemed in fine spirits — Oh, Mary, he is such a man of the world — he has sailed around a good part of it. I asked if he found our little village a dull place after so much travel. He laughed and said not any more, since he'd had the pleasure of meeting me. Then he asked if my father the clergyman preached here, to which I replied that his parish was in Surrey, at which news he seemed somewhat relieved. He asked if I enjoyed my work at Elmtree House and I said it was only temporary for my father and mother wished me to return home to Surrey and take a more genteel position as a governess to a young lady and gentleman who lived nearby.'

'Oh Maria, you are truly wicked!' I laughed. 'Did he believe you?'

She nodded and continued, 'He said I would be the prettiest governess he'd ever laid eyes on and then he told an amusing story of the pranks he and his brothers got up to when they were at school and how their father took them to the head master, who whipped them on their bare posteriors just for going to the woods and collecting nuts.

' "A cruel punishment for such a small crime, sir," said I.

' "Oh no, Maria, we were rascals and did many bad deeds. Another time we were allowed into the town from school and procured a vast quantity of rotten eggs. One of these odoriferous combustibles I threw at our second master, who wore spectacles, and hit him in his glass eye. Ah ha ha ha!" ' Maria gave a perfect imitation of his laugh.

' "Oh, how wicked!" I exclaimed, with a pretty toss of my head. I thought to myself, I must use that phrase "odoriferous combustible" to baffle Cook. I wager not even you, clever Mary, know such a fancy name for a rotten egg.'

I pretended that indeed I did not know.

'He told me his schooldays were happy,' Maria went

on, 'although "mischievous", and hoped the children I taught would have better manners. I then asked about his brothers and he looked sour when he mentioned the oldest, Edward, and said he was trying to cheat him of property his father had left him in his will.

'Then he asked, "Would you honour me by coming for a drive in my carriage, Maria?" I said I would be pleased to do so and as we left the private room the girl who had waited upon us curtsied to him and then to me. I felt such excitement, for at last I had been taken for a lady!

'Captain Knatchbull seemed amused by this too, for as he handed me into the carriage he said, "Up you go, Lady Maria." The carriage had cushions and leather upholstery and as the driver flicked the whip across the flanks of a pair of smart bay horses, I thought to myself, I do not mind where we go, for I could enjoy this ride for ever and ever. But soon he told the driver to stop at the edge of a wood and said we would take a walk and that he should come back for us in an hour.

'It was late afternoon and a glorious golden light was filtering through the trees as we walked along the pathway. The Captain took my arm to help me on the uneven surface of twigs. I must say it was comforting to feel him so close. I have never walked arm-in-arm with a gentleman before. Soon we came to a pleasant glade and he asked if I was tired and would like to rest.

' "I do not see a bench," ' said I, as innocent as a nun.

' "I shall have to make you one, my dear." So saying he sprang forward and dragged a log into a sheltered place away from the path, whipped out his silk handkerchief to cover it and then, with a flourish, bade me sit down as if it were a throne and I a princess. I laughed. He is really quite amusing, more like a boy than a man, although he must be more than thirty. As I sat there he gazed at me and said, "What a pretty picture. If it were painted by Gainsborough it would be called 'Innocence in the Forest'." I wondered if he was trying to seek me out, to see if I would deny being innocent. I decided to look uncomprehending and a little hurt.

' "Ah, my dear Maria, I see that you are not pleased by my fantasy. I meant it as a compliment, believe me." He took my hand in his and keeping his eyes on mine he kissed it very gently. As I did not pull it away he kissed my finger-tips. "You are sweetness itself, Maria," he said with deep feeling. Then, very tenderly he kissed my lips. I responded to this quite eagerly, for I found him most attractive. Soon we were lying side by side in the grass behind the log, kissing most passionately.

'Lord, Mary, but I did enjoy his kisses! Not that I haven't been kissed a dozen times before but only by shy, inexperienced farmboys or masters of the house who grope you all over with furtive haste, afraid their wives will catch them — or sailors, who are rough and stink of rum. This was kissing of such skill, caresses so gentle but assured that I wondered if all gentlemen are trained in the art of lovemaking as they are trained for politics, the Navy or the Church. It was difficult to pull away but I knew that if I did not it would be too late. My honour would be compromised, my hold on Captain Knatchbull would be lessened.

' "Oh no, please let us wait!" I gasped and sat up

beside him, straightening my bodice and removing twigs from my hair, which had become unfixed.

' "Wait? Why should we wait?" he demanded in a voice hoarse with passion. His face was flushed and his cream silk shirt-sleeves were stained with green moss. He composed himself with an effort for I could see that he was aroused. He seemed angry.

'My lower lip trembled and I barely whispered, "Do you not know?"

'Suddenly I flung myself away from him and cried, "Lord forgive me. What have I done?" And then began a most heartrending weeping — "Dearest, what is it? Please do not cry. What is the matter?" He held me close and stroked my hair. "We have done nothing except exchange a few kisses."

' "Yes, but I wanted to exchange more!" At this he embraced me with fresh vigour but I pushed him away. "My father would be shocked, my mother heartbroken if I should allow my love for you to run its full course before we are wed." And I stared so innocently into his eyes that his heart melted and he nodded meekly. "You are right, Maria. We must not be too hasty."

' "Then you do love me?" I whispered.

' "Of course I do." He kissed me gently.

' "And we shall be married?"

'He hesitated and looked a little shocked, but then he murmured tenderly, "Indeed we shall." And only then did I feel it was safe to kiss him back.'

At this astonishing news I sprang out of bed and hugged Maria.

'Oh, I am so pleased for you! Your wish has come

true. You'll be a lady and go to London, see operas and
wear fine clothes just as you dreamed!'

'And he will keep his word because he's a gentleman.
This he swore to me,' she replied, stretching across to
my bed and grasping my two hands in hers. 'You can
imagine what a happy mood this put me in Mary.' He
whirled me around like a dancing partner and together
we waltzed a few steps under the trees. We laughed as
we walked back along the path hand-in-hand like
sweethearts. At that moment I confess I felt more
hopeful of my future than I have in my whole life.'

'But why were you home so late?' I asked.

'It was not until we were in the carriage that I
noticed how dark it had become. I told Captain
Knatchbull not to drive me all the way home as the
gossips at Elmtree House would be watching. He
agreed that this was wise. He said we must keep our
love a secret from everyone until the time was right and
then we would elope. I said quickly this was the best
plan as my father would never agree to my marriage at
such a tender age. He seemed relieved to hear it and
laughed that he did not fancy begging a clergyman on
bended knee for the hand of such a precious daughter.
"What if he refused and broke my heart?" he said.

' "And mine as well," I added modestly. He kissed
me passionately again before we parted and vowed we
would meet again soon. I climbed the last of Elmtree
Hill as if in a dream. I did not even notice it was rain-
ing. As I reached the house I saw that the lights in the
dining room were blazing and the family awaiting my
service for their supper. I laughed as I saw them sitting
at table like stuffed dolls in a row, neither talking nor

smiling. What boring fools! Soon I will be far away from here, riding in a carriage beside a gentleman husband who is also a Captain in His Majesty's Navy and a hero of battles. The destiny I deserve has come at last. I only wish my wretched family could see me in the wedding finery I shall soon be wearing! What would my gin-sodden mam and the da who tried to crawl into my bed more than once think if they knew I had described them as a clergyman and his wife? They would kill themselves laughing. Witless fools. If Captain Knatchbull ever wants to meet them after we are wed I shall say they have died of the fever.' She pressed my hands in her strong grasp. 'So you must keep my secret, Mary. Never tell a soul even though you be tortured. Leastways not until I'm wed.'

'I have already sworn on the Holy Bible, Maria.'

# CHAPTER SEVEN

## Maria Falls in Love and I Introduce Her to Mr Wordsworth
### Elmtree House, August, 1819

Maria is gone again and it is not even her day off! She has been taking the most frightening risks lately and I have to cover for her in front of Cook, Mrs Burton, the Master, Mistress and the two young ladies. It is most vexing. I can manage to get through most of her chores without any of them discovering her absence, but today Mrs Burton said she was tired of hearing about Maria's 'indisposition' and was coming upstairs to drag her out of bed herself. I begged her to wait, saying Maria had been awake and coughing all night. Now she was at last asleep it would be a pity to wake her. Mrs Burton said I was too soft-hearted, but if I would start the washing on my own she would give her another half-hour. To my great relief, just as the half-hour was up, I saw Maria scuttle up the back stairs looking flushed and excited as usual. Although she tells me she and Captain Knatchbull are engaged, there is no date set for the wedding. They continue to meet in the woods and Maria certainly seems to be very much in love.

Every night she picks up my book of *Lyrical Ballads* and tries to make out the letters, but as hard as I try to teach her, she cannot learn them. Last night as we lay in our beds and the candle was beginning to flicker I took pity on her and asked if I should read aloud from the book. She agreed, which is unusual. She does not like me to draw attention to the fact that she is illiterate.

I began to read a very touching poem by Mr Wordsworth. It is one of my favourites. But it is also very sad, for it reminds me of my sister, Sarah. I am so fearful she may die, like Lucy —

> 'She dwelt among th' untrodden ways
>    Beside the springs of Dove,
> A maid whom there were none to praise,
>    And very few to love.
>
> 'A violet by a mossy stone
>    Half-hidden from the eye!
> — Fair as a star, when only one
>    Is shining in the sky.
>
> 'She lived unknown, and few could know
>    When Lucy ceased to be;
> But she is in her grave, and oh!
>    The difference to me.'

A tear came to my eye, but Maria did not think so much of it. 'I do not like that one. Read another,' she demanded. 'Something about love.'

'Here is one called "Love", I told her, turning to a

different page. It is written by Mr Wordsworth too.' I began to read again:

*'All thoughts, all passions, all delights,*
*Whatever stirs this mortal frame,*
*All are but ministers of Love,*
*And feed his sacred flame ...'*

'Yes, yes, that will do well enough,' Maria interrupted. 'I'll just learn that much. Now, start it again.'

I did so and we chanted the unfinished poem over and over until she had it word-perfect. Then she asked if she could borrow my book tomorrow.

'Well, yes — but you know that book is very precious to me, Maria.'

'I'll take care of it. Will you put a rose petal to mark the place where the poem is for me?'

'Of course,' I said. And then I guessed that Captain Knatchbull thought she could read. Maria has been so strange and unlike herself lately. I can only hope he is as much in love as she is.

# CHAPTER EIGHT

**Maria Spies on Two Gentlemen and Makes a
Nasty Discovery
Elmtree House, August, 1819**

An amazing coincidence today. Cook sent Maria on an
errand to deliver a brace of quails to the Hare and
Hounds in the village and as she was passing through
to the kitchen, who should she see in the dining room
but her beloved Captain Knatchbull eating lunch with
his friend Lieutenant Carmichael, another naval officer
who is staying at Mersham Le Hatch.

*Ah ha,* said she to herself, *here is a chance for some
fun!* Captain Knatchbull had introduced her to his
friend a few days earlier and the Lieutenant had seemed
almost as smitten by her pretty looks as the Captain
himself, so she said. Both the officers are waiting to be
called by some lord in the Navy to serve at sea again.
They are both restless and have been shooting some
game together. And here they were in their hunting
clothes, sitting in the ale house not ten yards from
where Maria unloaded her basket. There was a vesti-

bule close to the table where they sat and after delivering the quails she decided to conceal herself there and listen to their conversation. She was curious to know what they might discuss in private and hoped that she might be the subject of at least some of their chat.

At first they talked only of pheasant being rare in these parts and having to make do with one mangy fox. Then they complained about having to put up with living with dull relatives while waiting to go back to sea. After this, their conversation became more interesting to Maria. 'Your stepmother, John, seems a bitter whining woman since your father passed away. D'you know she warned me to keep my hands off the servants at Mersham?' Lieutenant Carmichael said indignantly.

'She did the same to me. To which I replied that her maids were all as ugly as sin!' The Captain threw back his head and laughed. 'She is not aware of my pastoral poetry readings with pretty Maria, however.'

'Maria is quite a beauty for a village girl,' his friend said as if he found this surprising. At this, Maria told me she found herself blushing. She then relayed to me the rest of the conversation, which did not please her at all.

'If she were not so lowly born I confess I could almost fall in love with her,' said Knatchbull quite seriously. 'Her innocence has caused me to behave with unusual restraint in seducing her. Damnably frustrating. Which is she, d'you think? A clever manipulative actress or the devout daughter of a clergyman? Her manners are quite refined but her speech is erratic, lapsing from genteel lady to modest serving girl. I've made inquiries in the village but no one seems to know

who her family is. She's not from these parts. At first I
thought she might be a coquette who had lain with all
the yokels hereabouts and now desired a gentleman, in
which case I would have been merciless. But I do not
think that is so.' He sighed. 'Come now,
Henry … you're an astute judge of character. Is it possible my pretty Maria could be genteel?'

Maria held her breath, although she said she was fit
to burst with outrage at the suggestion that she may
have lain with yokels.

'Don't be too swayed by her pretty looks, John,'
Carmichael replied, yawning. 'Perhaps you've been too
long in the countryside. Come and stay with me in
London. We'll go to Vauxhall Gardens, dress up in top
hats and hobnob with the pretty dancers, jugglers and
acrobats.'

'I should like that. But you haven't answered my
question.'

'About Maria?' Carmichael seemed almost to have
lost interest. He yawned again. 'My dear Knatchbull,
she is no lady. Her genteel accent and manners are pure
affectation. She has high aspirations for herself and
probably mimics her mistress. She's chosen you as the
means of realising her ambition to become a lady. Her
innocence is guile. If you are hoping for more than
kisses I should give up now. She is a pretty fortune
hunter who is withholding her virginity for the husband she plans to snare like a fox in a trap.'

'I have no intention of becoming that fox,'
Knatchbull replied quietly. 'I shall tell her at once that I
cannot marry her.'

'Do no such thing. I will reveal to you a way that you may have your bride without the trap of marriage.'

'Stop speaking in riddles, Carmichael. Come, let's get out of this place and shoot some more game. You have put me in a bad humour.' And then the pair marched out without another word.

Maria has been crying for an hour and says she will never see the wretch Knatchbull again. 'I should have guessed he was only playing with my affections when he refused to name the wedding day. Oh, how could I give him kisses of such passion when he was only mocking me!'

I held her close and let her weep but I was thinking of what she had told me. 'Listen, Maria, it sounds to me as if Captain Knatchbull does still love you. What does it matter what Carmichael thinks? But you must put the Captain to the test. Go to him and tell him you were so upset by his cruel words that you have decided not to marry him. If he truly loves you he will beg your forgiveness and set the wedding date. If not, then he's not worthy of your love and you must try to forget him.'

Maria sat up and dried her eyes. 'That is a bold plan, Mary, and very wise for one so innocent. I think that is exactly what I will do.'

# CHAPTER NINE

**A Wedding in London!**
**Elmtree House, September, 1819**

I am overjoyed that my plan has worked and the wedding date is set! Maria says she can hardly believe she is leaving her life as a servant for ever. Her valise is packed and tomorrow she will hide it in the woods at dawn before anyone is awake. At precisely midday she will walk out along the gravel driveway of Elmtree House for the last time, pretending to go on an errand to the village to collect the Mistress's new frock from the seamstress. But instead she will keep the money entrusted to her to pay the seamstress, hurry to the woods, retrieve her valise and there Knatchbull will be waiting in the carriage which will drive them to London. London! Yes, that is where they are to marry.

A few days ago she sent a message to the Captain to meet her in their usual spot in the woods. As she waited she was in a state of rage. All the joyful kisses they had exchanged in that mossy bower beneath the soft shadow of trees now seemed a mockery. When she saw him coming she ran towards him, threw herself into his arms and weeping all the while, told him that she could no longer be his love for she had learned what his true thoughts were about her character and her heart was broken.

He was shocked and embarrassed to have been caught out. She said a servant at the ale house had spied on him and Carmichael and revealed to her what had passed between them. Then Maria faced up to him and said: 'It is best I know the truth. I have come here to save you the trouble of telling me that you cannot marry me. For I could never marry a man who had even one doubt about my virtue, and you, I believe, have many.' And here she began to weep afresh.

Knatchbull looked aghast. Giving her his silk hand-kerchief to mop her tears he took her arm and shep-herded her to the log were they had passed so many happy hours. 'I am sorry I doubted you, Maria. Forgive me if you can.'

'Oh John, I am no fortune hunter planning to snare you like a fox in a trap. How could you ever have listened to such cruel lies?' she cried.

'There, there, I never believed Carmichael, not for a minute.'

'He is a wicked man. I am sorry he is a friend to someone as noble as yourself!' she burst forth.

She must have looked angry for Knatchbull smiled a little and said, 'I like you in this spirited bad humour, my dear. Come, I have something to ask you but first let us seal our love with a toast.' Then he produced a silver flask of liquor and two crystal glasses from beneath his cloak and poured them each a drink.

She dried her tears and smiled a little then. 'So you do still love me?'

'I do indeed,' he replied sincerely.

Their right arms entwined they clinked glasses, and sipped the wine gazing into each other's eyes, sending speechless messages. It was then that Knatchbull uttered the words she had hardly dared to hope for. 'Will you marry me, Maria?'

'I will, John. Oh, indeed I will.'

Now tears of joy streamed down her cheeks. They kissed tenderly and then with passion. She could hardly believe that her dream was about to come true after all.

Later, the Captain told her that Carmichael begged her forgiveness for his thoughtless words. He had been much in drink, and did not know what rubbish he was talking. To make amends he had offered them his lodgings in London for their wedding celebrations. They should be much obliged to him. He said he would invite Carmichael to be his groomsman if Maria had no objections. She agreed, and so the quarrel was resolved.

Maria told me she was sorry she could not ask me to be her bridesmaid. If I were to suddenly disappear from Elmtree House as well as herself, the cat would be well and truly out of the bag. I have agreed to cover for her for a few days, saying she is ill in bed again, so that she can make a safe escape.

All the arrangements were carefully made a few days ago at their secret meeting place in the woods. The

Captain has warned Maria they must be careful not to let people know where they have gone so that they have time to marry — then there will be nothing anyone can do about it.

Maria has told him that her loving parents sent her two sovereigns for her birthday, and she will use it for a wedding dress. But the Captain said that as it was to be just a small wedding at the Lieutenant's lodgings, with only a half-dozen of their friends, there was no need to buy a wedding dress. The marriage was to take place immediately they arrived. A clergyman had already been asked to perform the ceremony. Instead, the Captain suggested they might use the money for something else — some wine and refreshments, perhaps. Maria suddenly remembered that it is the bride's family that traditionally provides the wedding breakfast. 'Oh, John, you must think me very foolish. Of course the money must go towards food and wine for our guests.'

She tells me she still does not like Lieutenant Carmichael, but as he is the Captain's close friend and is allowing them to use his rooms, she feels obliged to be polite to him.

Maria is as excited as a child about her impending visit to London. Captain Knatchbull has told her that Lieutenant Carmichael's lodgings are near Piccadilly, not far from Buckingham Palace, where the Prince Regent plans to live after he ascends the throne. The Palace is being rebuilt so that it will be grand enough for him. They say his father, King George III, is very ill, so that day cannot be far off. Then the Prince (everyone calls him 'Prinny') will become King George IV.

# CHAPTER 10

## To Help Maria Elope I am Obliged to Become a Liar
## Elmtree House, September, 1819

When Maria broke the news to me that she was to be married to Captain Knatchbull after all I could hardly believe it! I can just imagine her dressed as a lady wandering through the gardens of Mersham Le Hatch with a parasol to keep off the sun. All she has ever wanted in life is to be a lady and now her dream has come true. She certainly has the airs and graces for it.

When I cried tears of happiness for her she thought I was sad to lose her, and of course I am. She swears never to forget me. 'Mary, when I am married I will come back to see you in my carriage and together we'll drive through the village splashing mud over everyone!' And then she laughed gaily and begged me not to cry any more or she would too and then her eyes would be red and ugly for her beloved.

'And do you and John Knatchbull truly love each other, Maria?' I asked. I have never before known anyone who has been madly in love and was curious to know how it was.

'Oh we do, we do! One day I hope you will be as happy as I am. I never thought I would truly fall in love. But it has happened.'

'And what does it feel like?'

'When you are apart it feels like an ache and when you are in each other's arms you melt with desire.'

'Desire. What exactly do you desire?'

'Oh Mary, you booby, why to make love to each other completely. Not just kissing and fussing about. The whole thing.'

'Ah,' I said, pretending to understand.

Suddenly Maria burst out laughing. 'One day you will feel it yourself, but remember, you must control yourself and not give in to him or you will never wed a gentleman.'

'I do not expect to wed a gentleman,' I said humbly.

'Then who cares? You may screw whoever you like!'

I covered my ears with both hands but I couldn't help laughing because Maria is so funny when she's wicked.

'Well, my innocent friend, what word would you prefer me to use? Swivel, tup, strum — take your pick! It all comes to the same thing: making the beast with two backs. Ah, I know which you'd prefer, the *elegant* phrase — "love-making". You may make love to who-ever you like!'

On our last night together we sleep side by side in my bed because I am afraid that I will miss her very much.

'Look, I will show you how it is to be in love,' she

says and kisses me slowly and deeply with her tongue inside my mouth. She asks me how I like it.

'I do.' I say.

Then she strokes my breasts. 'Do you like that too?'

'Not as much as the kiss.'

'That is what gentlemen must be prevented from doing. And this too.' She touches me between the legs. 'Never let them do that to you or you will be lost.'

'Lost?'

Maria sighs. 'Well, I have tried to instruct you but I must say, Mary, that you are not as quick at learning about love as you are at polishing silver.' Then we both laugh and hug each other and soon we are asleep in each other's arms.

In the morning, before we go downstairs to start our chores, I take my book *Lyrical Ballads* and write on the inside cover: '*To Maria, my dearest friend on the day of her most joyful marriage to Captain John Knatchbull, September 16th, 1819.*' Then I wrap it in my best handkerchief, which has an 'M' embroidered in one corner by my dear mother and give it to her. She hugs me close, sheds a few tears and promises to be able to read every poem in it by the next time we meet.

She has been up since dawn and is so excited she can scarcely do her chores without breaking things.

They are leaving for London at midday and will be married at five the next evening. Where will they live in London? How shall I know where to send letters? How soon will Maria be able to read them?

All these thoughts buzz in my head as I try to keep calm and pretend to Mrs Burton that Maria is dropping things because she is feeling ill again, and she may have to take to her bed as soon as she returns from the village on her errand to the seamstress. Mrs Burton sniffs and says she suspects Maria is malingering.

I hate telling falsehoods but today is so important for Maria that there is no help for it. When she walks out the gate at midday she turns just once to wave at me and then she is gone to a new life. I hurry inside and get on with the dusting but I can scarcely see the dust for my tears. I am so happy for Maria — and so afraid that I will be in disgrace and lose my job if the truth comes out. After an hour or so, when Maria is supposed to have returned from her errand, I tell Mrs Burton that she is indeed unwell and lying down. I say that she visited the doctor in the village and he has told her to rest for two days.

'And where is the Mistress's new dress, pray?' asks the Housekeeper.

'Oh, the seamstress took the money and apologised that it is not quite ready. She will deliver it here herself tomorrow afternoon.'

Another dreadful lie. (Maria says I must not be prudish and should say a 'lie', not 'falsehood'.) But at least by the time it is discovered she will be safely wed and there will be nothing anyone can do about it. I know she will repay the money as soon as she is married.

I ask Cook for some broth for Maria and take it to our room. I have to drink the broth myself and then report to Mrs Burton on Maria's progress — I say she is feeling a little stronger and will certainly be up by tomorrow evening. Mrs Burton snorts and says she is running a household, not a hospital. Cook gives me more broth. She is more tolerant of illness than Mrs Burton.

This evening there is a dreadful commotion. Miss Dolores has discovered that one of her fine kid gloves is missing and accuses Agnes of stealing it. Agnes asks what use is one glove. Miss Dolores takes Agnes by the hair and screams that she is insolent, a liar and a thief. Agnes howls. The mistress and Miss Lydia come running to see what the hullabaloo is about and then Miss Lydia cries out that she too has been missing something, a crimson ribbon that she brought back from Bath. Maria had been particularly fond of that ribbon: instead of returning it to Miss Lydia as she'd planned she must have decided to take it to London.

Suddenly Agnes points at me. 'Ask her where your pretty things have gone! If it ain't her what took them then it's her precious friend!'

Everyone stares at me. 'I swear to God I would never steal, Ma'am,' I say to the Mistress.

'Search her room!' cries Miss Lydia.

'Certainly, please do,' I reply as calmly as I can. 'But Maria is ill in bed. Could we wait until tomorrow?'

'By then you'll have hidden them somewhere else, you scheming pair of sluts!' cries Miss Dolores. 'No servant is to be trusted.'

'There, there, my dear. Are you sure you've looked everywhere for the glove?' her mother asks.

'Yes, I am sure.'

'And so am I,' cries Miss Lydia. 'It was Maria who stole the ribbon. I remember now. She was tidying my bureau where I keep it in a silver box. I'm going upstairs to search her myself!'

'Oh, please do not!' I plead. 'Her fever is contagious and you will surely catch it if you touch her, Miss Lydia. I myself have been careful to boil all her spoons and cups, even to cover my face with a kerchief when I bathe her hot forehead.'

Miss Lydia stares at me in fright. 'If she is so contagious why is she still in the house?'

'It is a fever that will pass, Miss, only dangerous for a day or two. So long as Maria does not venture downstairs she will not pass it on to anyone.' I am amazed at my own capacity for invention.

'Come, my dears, let me help you search for your things. Sometimes a new pair of eyes can find the most elusive trinkets.' And the Mistress escorts her grumbling daughters towards their rooms.

I could have hugged her.

# II
## To London

# CHAPTER 11

**My Life Becomes a Misery and an Apparition
Appears at My Window
Elmtree House October, 1819**

It is now two weeks since Maria left Elmtree House. I have not heard a word from her. I think of her almost all the time, no matter how hard I am working, and pray for her every night. I expect she is too busy going about London, seeing the sights. So much to see and do. She would be too embarrassed perhaps to ask her husband to write a letter to me — but oh, if only she would pay a scribe to send me a message.

I do hope they are happy. I imagine she has so much to buy — new clothes, furniture and household goods for their lodgings. I expect they have a servant or two to do the chores. I daresay Maria will order them about quite sharply. And what, I wonder, is it like to be a proper wife who melts with desire and then is allowed to be lost? There is so much I should love to ask her. I miss her so much, especially at nights when we would talk and laugh together no matter how tired we were.

Now I just pray, read my Bible a little because it is the only book I have, then try to fall asleep.

My life has not been a happy one since Maria left. The worst thing was having to confess to everyone at Elmtree House that I had lied about Maria's illness. On the afternoon of the second day, when the village seamstress did not arrive with the Mistress's new dress as I had said she would, the Mistress herself went in the carriage to collect it. She came back in a frightful state. The seamstress had indeed finished the dress the day before, but Maria had never called to collect it and she had certainly not been paid her money. At this dreadful news Mrs Burton was ready to storm upstairs and fling Maria out of bed, fever or no fever. I begged leave to speak with the Mistress first. I confessed that Maria had never been ill, but had run away I knew not where, and had asked me not to tell anyone until this evening. At this I broke down and wept for I was so ashamed. Not just about all the lies I had told but of not being able to tell the joyful truth, that Maria had run away to London to be married to a gentleman. She had made me promise not to tell about this but to let people find out for themselves when she returned one day as a lady in a carriage with her gentleman husband beside her. The surprise would be even greater and she would have more fun lording it over the village people, she said.

The Mistress was shocked and said she did not expect such deceit from a Christian girl such as I had pretended to be. At this I cried harder. She told me I was very wicked and she would have to consult with the Master as to whether I should be dismissed from my position without a reference. She said that as Maria had stolen the money they would send the constables after her and when she was caught she would be sent to prison or transported beyond the seas to a terrible place called Botany Bay where only convicts and savages lived.

At that moment the grandfather clock in the hall began to strike five. I put my hand on my heart and looked up to Heaven to thank God that the marriage ceremony would have begun.

'What are you doing, you foolish girl? Praying for forgiveness? Indeed you might!' cried the Mistress. 'Now get up to your attic and stay there with no supper until I have spoken to the Master and Mrs Burton.'

Since that afternoon no one has spoken one word to me. I have been allowed to stay on in my position but I have been punished by being 'sent to Coventry', as the Mistress calls it, for a whole month. Cook must point and make signs to tell me what she wants done and Mrs Burton sniffs even harder and turns away from me with a dismissive shake of her head when I ask if the sheets are to be taken to the drying room or left on the outside line for a while longer. Sometimes it is difficult to tell what she wants and I make mistakes. Then she points up to the attic with that sour look which means I am to go to bed without supper again. This is supposed to 'starve the deceit' out of me. Agnes sneers at me. The two young ladies do not look at me at all but hurry away with their noses in the air when I come to their rooms to clean, muttering about 'lying sluts' and 'low-born criminals'.

Cook saw me crying as I was on my hands and knees

scrubbing the kitchen floor yesterday. She pulled me to my feet and whispered, 'Not your fault, Duckie. That Maria was a bad influence, she was the real trouble.' Then she gave me a lamb bone which still had a lot of meat on it. I was grateful for I'd missed three suppers in a row and these were the first kind words I'd heard spoken for almost two weeks, ever since Maria left.

Being sent to Coventry is not as bad as the other two punishments — having my day off cancelled and being fined a month's wages.

I look forward so much to seeing the family, more so this month as I am so miserable. And they rely on my wages for food. Mother has sent word that Sarah is getting weaker but she cannot afford more medicine until next Monday, which is usually my day off. I must send word that I cannot come, but so far I have not had the heart to do so. If only Cook was allowed to talk to me I could explain how urgent my family's situation is and she might lend me some money. I feel she is my only friend at Elmtree House. The gardener, who used to give me a big bag of vegetables for the family every month, has gone back to Ireland to his family and the new gardener is a stern man who would not give one potato to his dying grandmother, as Maria might say.

Tonight I went to bed without supper again. I'd misunderstood Mrs Burton when she pointed at the henhouse and thought she had wanted the eggs collected this evening instead of in the morning. I thought it was odd, then remembered that the Master sometimes likes an omelette before his roast beef, and fresh eggs are better than those a day old. So I gathered them up and brought them to the kitchen.

Cook stared at them and then at me. 'Foolish girl!' she cried, forgetting the vow of silence. 'We never collect them till morning. It makes the hens cranky and then they won't lay any more. Take them back!'

'But Mrs Burton told me to collect them just now ...'

Mrs Burton stood in the doorway shaking her head vehemently. She grabbed me by the shoulders and shook me hard. I had never been shaken so roughly and felt as if my head might break off. She was spluttering in my face with the effort not to speak.

Cook dashed forward to save the situation. 'Ah, Mrs Burton, you meant she was to clean the fowl yard, not collect the eggs. Was that it?'

Mrs Burton nodded, her face squeezed into such a grimace that her lips and eyes seemed to disappear completely. Such was her relief at being understood that she did not notice Cook and I were speaking to each other.

'So off you go now, Mary, return the eggs before the hens notice and clean out the yard,' Cook said kindly.

'Yes, thank you, Cook,' I answered and gathered up the eggs. My stomach was growling. I only had a small bowl of barley broth and a crust of bread at midday. As I was cleaning out the fowl yard I even thought of stealing an egg and eating it raw, I was so hungry. I know Cook is sorry for me and will see that I get a decent breakfast tomorrow, porridge and even a cup of milk. None of this makes me feel any more sorry for what I did. But now I understand how it feels for my family, who go to bed hungry every night.

By the time I finished cleaning the fowl yards it was quite dark. As I was putting the bucket and rake away in the barn I heard rustling in the bushes outside and suddenly there was the Master standing in the doorway. He smiled, which surprised me. Everyone but Cook had done nothing but scowl at me since my disgrace. He put out one hand as if to comfort me, and in my misery, I stepped forward gratefully and allowed it to rest on my shoulder. In an instant he had grasped my buttocks and pressed himself hard against me. I struggled to push him off. He was panting like a dog on heat and I smelt his breath, which was fiery with spirits. I pushed with all my strength but he was a big man. 'Sir!' I cried. 'Please! Leave me be!'

'Come now, pretty Mary. I know you've been waiting for me, skulking out here in the dark when others are indoors.' His speech was slurred. 'You pretend to be a good Christian girl but no, tish, not the case. Not so pure you can't lie to protect that liddle slut Maria, eh? And not so pure you can't do shomething to pleash your master.' He began to propel me towards the straw. He was strong but unsteady on his feet and I was able to heave the rake between us and ward him off. Then I remembered that Maria had told me once to thrust any weapon you could find between the attacker's legs. I had not thought I could ever do such a thing, but now in my terror and rage I hit the Master with the prongs of the rake in just that place. As he fell forward, clutching his private parts, I fled from the barn. I heard him moaning but kept running until I reached the attic, where I rammed the chair beneath the handle and prayed that would stop him forcing his way in.

I lay in bed trembling at what I had done, listening for his footsteps on the stairs. Surely he would come after me, for I had not injured him badly. My heart beat fast with anger. How dare the Master, a gentleman I had respected until now, force himself upon me just because I was his servant? I had not believed Maria when she told me that he would. I vowed to run away the very next day — No, that would be no help to my family. I would wait until the Master was sober and confess to him how shocked I was at his behaviour and ask to be forgiven for the blow I had inflicted in self-defence. Then he would surely be ashamed and we could respect each other once more — 'Oh Mary, you innocent, of course he won't be sorry!' I told myself in Maria's voice. 'You must stay awake all night to guard your virtue.'

I waited. The hours went by and he did not come. Perhaps, after all, I had discouraged him. At last, in spite of my intentions, I fell fast asleep.

At first I thought it was a dream. Someone was banging on my attic window crying out for me to open it. I dreamed that the person was floating by, her face ghostly white against the casement. I sat up, thinking it must be the wind banging a branch against the pane. I lit the candle and then I saw it. A face at the window, white, pale and frightened. It was Maria.

# CHAPTER 12

### Ruined Maria is Buried and Alias Jane is Born
### Elmtree House, October, 1819

Maria said she thought I would never wake up. She'd been perched like an owl on the roof, knocking against the casement for an hour, it seemed (though I daresay it was only five minutes). The wind was howling and the elm tree bashing its branches against the house. It was a bitter night.

At last I lit the candle and ran to the window. She looked like a ghost. She was wet through, her face streaked with mud and scratched from climbing up the tree. I pushed open the window and helped her climb in.

'Oh Mary, never have I been more grateful to see you and our bleak little attic with its two beds so close we could hold hands as we dreamed.' She hugged me and then collapsed onto her bed.

I kissed her, held her cold hands in mine and wiped the rain from her face and hair. 'Maria, whatever has happened? Where is your husband? Have you run away from him already?'

She shook her head and turned her face to the wall.

'Are you ill, Maria? Shall I creep downstairs and fetch you some broth?'

'No, no. No one must know I am here.'

'If I am caught I will say the broth is for me.'

She shook her head weakly. 'I am past hunger, Mary.' Then she began to weep. I held her in my arms and stroked her hair and tried to soothe her. 'Tell me what has happened. Has there been an accident? Is Captain Knatchbull hurt?'

'Would that he were dead!' she cried out vehemently. 'He has betrayed me! And now he has thrown me out. I am ruined, Mary! Ruined!'

And so she related the tale of her disgrace, stopping often to weep as it was very painful.

Apparently Captain Knatchbull and his friends had been play-acting and the 'wedding' was nothing but a mockery. Poor Maria had no idea she was the butt of their amusement. She believed the chaplain who performed the wedding ceremony was a real clergyman, but he was only one of their friends dressed up, chanting rubbish, pretending it was Holy Gospel. Knatchbull had 'borrowed' a wedding gown for her from a pawnbroker, and the food and wine she had paid for herself.

After the marriage ceremony and the feast the guests stayed on for hours until midnight, drinking and carousing. Maria had eventually burst into tears and asked Knatchbull to send them away or else let the two of them leave and go to lodgings of their own to begin their married life in privacy. Quite drunk himself, he called her a prude and said they should not mind having a few friends present while they were consummating their marriage. And then he had taken her off to their bridal room to do so without delay.

'And did you melt with desire and become lost?' I asked, even though this did not seem likely.

'It was rather difficult with drunken guests banging on the door demanding to be let in,' she replied. 'But we got the business over with and then Carmichael burst in. "So has the filly taken the bit?" he shouted. At this insulting remark Knatchbull leapt up laughing, and looking most pleased with himself, announced to the whole company, who were huddled close around the door, that the bridle had indeed been fitted. There were some cheers, even from the ladies present, which I thought most indelicate. "Capital!" Carmichael cried. "Then pray let me take you all to supper to celebrate."'

Maria sighed as she went on with her woeful story. 'I did not wish to go out so late as I had already drunk a glass too many of wine and was feeling sleepy, but Knatchbull and the others all insisted, and still wearing my wedding gown I was bundled into a carriage which took us to Leicester Square,' Maria said. 'I was surprised to see the place crowded with fashionably dressed ladies and gentlemen, all arriving in carriages. Their jewels and costumes glimmered in the street lights and fair dazzled me. I thought it strange that such brilliant looking creatures should have such cunning faces. Perhaps they were not ladies and gentlemen at all but thieves and harlots in fancy dress? I put this thought out of my head as I was determined to enjoy at least part of my wedding day.

'As we climbed the stairs to the private dining room the smell of the ladies' perfumes mingled with the rich foods made me quite dizzy. Our party sat down at a long table and I stared in wonder at the roast beef, fruit tarts, custards and ices waiting for us on the sideboard. It made me feel ashamed of the poor wedding breakfast my money had provided. No wonder Carmichael had suggested we should go out to supper. More wine was poured into my glass. "Oh no!" I protested for my head was already spinning. "Be deuced, Maria. It's damned rude to refuse our host's Tokay," Knatchbull told me. It was the first time I had heard him use such language.

'We were joined at table by some other drunken gentlemen, who seemed to be military officers. One, very ruddy in the face and stinking of drink, lurched towards me and I shrank back against my husband's shoulder. I expected Knatchbull to push the intruder away but he just laughed and said, "This filly has just been broken in but I believe she already has a taste for a new rider." Then, to my horror, he stood up and walked out of the room.

'You can imagine my shock, Mary. I felt myself blush crimson with shame. And anger. I was very angry. The other ladies did not seem to find this behaviour odd. Indeed some of them were disappearing into secluded corners of the private room with some of the other newly arrived officers. Meanwhile, the gentlemen who remained at our table were grinning expectantly at me and the drunken officer. "Now Percy, there's a generous invitation if ever I heard one," said Carmichael. "I suggest you two make yourselves cosy."

' "How dare you!" I said to the officer who had taken the liberty of grabbing me around the waist and hauling me up to stand beside him. He leered into my face, clamped one hand on my bosom and grasped my buttocks with the other, while Carmichael and the other revolting gentlemen cheered him on. I pushed him away. "Step back or you'll regret it," I told him.

' "Come on, filly. This ain't what the gallant Lieutenant told me to expect." He made another grab and this time tore the bodice of my wedding dress. With all my strength I kneed him where I knew it would hurt him most. While he was bent double, gasping in agony, I ran out the door, down the stairs and fled across Leicester Square. I felt people staring and heard them jeering at me. I had left my cloak behind, my dress was torn and my hair had fallen down.

'Somehow I remembered the way back to our lodgings. Leicester Square is not very far from Piccadilly, and soon I recognised the entry into Grafton Street, and found the house where I had been married that afternoon. I rushed inside, ran up the staircase to our bedchamber, then threw myself down on our bed and howled. I felt so humiliated, Mary. Of course I knew that gentlemen could behave badly when they were in drink, but how could my husband allow such treatment of me? And on our wedding night! I resolved to have it out with him as soon as he returned.

'An hour or so later I heard him returning with Carmichael. Thankfully they had left the company behind. Draped in a shawl to cover my nightgown I sat primly on a chair beside our bed and waited.

'When Knatchbull came into the room he stared at me as if he'd seen a ghost. "What! Still waiting for a rider?" He threw back his head and laughed. "Henry!" he called. "Come in here. The filly has bolted right back to the stable!" Then he turned to me, "I thought you'd be halfway home to your scullery at Elmtree House by now."

'I was astonished by these heartless words but before I could say anything, Henry Carmichael appeared and gave me a look of such lechery that I recoiled. "Well, if this ain't a bit of luck!" he cried. "I take it the bride has returned to the bedchamber because she wishes to extend her favours to the best man." And he began to walk unsteadily towards me. I stood up. "Kindly leave this room," I said angrily. "I wish to speak to my husband alone."

'Henry pretended to look under the bed. "Husband? You have a husband hiding somewhere in here?"

' "Get out!" I cried and he fled in mock terror.

' "Dammit, Maria. Why are you in such a sulk?" Knatchbull asked me. "Henry is our host and he's treated us to a fine supper out with his friends. The least you can do is show a little gratitude." I stared at him in disbelief. "First you were rude to his guests who admired your looks and now, when all he asks is to share in your affections, you order him from his own bedchamber."

' "*His* bedchamber? But he has given it up to us for our wedding night!" I protested.

' "Yes, yes. He is generosity itself. So why should you

not allow him to return to it now that you and I have used it to our satisfaction?"

' "What! I most certainly will do no such thing. What do you take me for?" I shouted.

' "A shrew!" he shouted back. "And a coquette of the worst possible kind."

'I was silent as I took this in. Then I burst out, "If this is what marriage is all about you can keep it and be damned."

' "You have the tongue of a guttersnipe," he said and slapped my face.

'I threw my wedding ring on the floor at his feet and looked at him defiantly.

'He laughed. "It isn't worth picking up," he said coldly. "It's brass."

Maria hid her face in her hands for a moment before she could continue.

'It was then, Mary, that he told me the whole marriage had been a sham and everyone except me had known all along and wondered how long it would take me to discover it. He said it was all a prank, that I could not possibly have believed that he, a gentleman, would ever have considered marrying a servant girl.

'I was struck dumb and felt as if my heart was broken. Then I stared at him filled with hatred. But I would not let him have the satisfaction of seeing my tears. When he turned and walked out of the room I ran to the closet, dressed and packed my valise. Stifling the sobs until I got to the street, I ran from the house. As I passed him in the hall he said without bothering to lift his head, "Yes, it is best that you leave now. Saves me having to throw you out."

I drew back and covered my mouth with one hand. 'Oh my poor Maria, how could any gentleman be so wicked!'

Maria looked at me with tears in her eyes. 'There is nothing left for me in this life, Mary. Now that my honour is stained I am going to drown myself.'

At this I flung my arms around her and begged her not to think of such a thing. I told her she was worth more than a hundred gentlemen.

'No, I have made up my mind. It's taken me ten days just to get back here to say goodbye to you, my only friend in all the world. Tomorrow I will drown myself in the river that flows through the woods where we …' Here she broke off.

I held her close and rocked her like a child. I told her she had suffered most cruelly but that I had been praying for her and knew that God would protect her from now on. I told her that I loved her and would do anything to help her. She had only to ask.

At this promise her mood seemed to brighten and she soon recovered enough to sit up and allow me to take her wet clothes, give her my spare nightdress and cover her with my quilt.

'Mary, if I do not drown myself there is only one course I can take.'

'What course is that? Whatever it is I will help you, dearest Maria.'

'I must change into someone else. No longer will there be a Maria Wilkinson in the world who is shamed and broken, but a new girl, pure and innocent.'

I stared at her blankly.

'From now on you must never call me Maria. *She* is a

foolish, trusting thing, best buried with her grief. You must call me Jane, for I have always liked the name. It has a ring of quality about it. Jane Henrie, I shall be henceforth.'

'But can a person do such a thing? Just change into someone else?' I asked doubtfully.

'Of course. It is called an *alias*.'

I nodded uncertainly. 'And how can I help you with this new … alias?'

'I have some belongings I would like to leave in your care. Hide them for me, Mary. Guard them with your life. It would be safer to put them in your family's cottage than keep them here. The Master and Mistress may search your room at any time. It is in their power to do so.'

I nodded. 'Are they large things?'

She shook her head. 'Just some keepsakes, and my savings.' She produced a small leather bag and gave it to me.

'This is a fine bag, Maria. Was it a present?'

'You could say that. Now put it away very safely. *And do not call me Maria*. I no longer answer to that name. Now we must go to sleep. Tomorrow I shall return to London on the early coach from Sevenoaks.'

'But where will you stay in London? Surely it has horrible memories for you. Will you not stay here? If you were to return the money that was to go to the seamstress perhaps the Mistress would forgive you and accept you back at Elmtree House. It has been so miserable here since you left.'

She gave me a strange look, as if I was a feeble-minded fool, which hurt me a little. 'I can never return to this place. London is the city for me. I know I can find work in a house much grander than this. Until I do, I have the address of a decent lodging house where I can stay.'

'Won't you need your savings with you?'

'I may be robbed if I carry too much money. London is a den of thieves. I will send for them when I need them, Mary. Now, let me hear you call me Jane, for I must get used to it.'

'You are so brave, Jane, setting out alone on a new life. I would not have the courage to do so.'

At this she laughed and in spite of my fears for her, I had to smile for I could see that using her new name made her feel very satisfied.

'Cheer up, Mary. Life is not so bad. Knatchbull and his friends were bounders, certainly, but at least I got to know something of London and met a few people who may help me find a position when I return tomorrow. Who knows, in a few months time I may find a position for you! You should not stay buried here in the country all your life.'

I was about to say that I would be most excited to visit her in London and perhaps find a position there, when she thought better of her offer, 'Ah, but I know you'll never leave your nice secure place here in the village. It is probably better you stay here.'

As she was falling asleep I tried to tell her how worried I was about my sister Sarah being gravely ill, about having my wages stopped and being sent to Coventry. I also told her I'd taken her advice in defending myself against the Master with a garden implement. But she only muttered, 'I'm so tired after my long journey from

London.' But a moment later she said quite clearly, in a most refined accent, 'D'you know, Mary, that Jane Henrie will become quite an elegant young woman? I have seen a beautiful pelisse with a fur collar and hem in a shop in Oxford Street and I shall purchase it as soon as I return. I have enough money for a few luxuries for myself. I deserve them, after all I have suffered. One day I will get my revenge on that monster Knatchbull.'

She went straight to sleep then but I stayed awake, pondering. I was puzzled. At first she had seemed so distressed by the cruelties she had suffered at the hands of Captain Knatchbull, for she had truly loved him. I had been moved to anger on her behalf many times as she related her sad story. But once she had decided not to drown herself she seemed to recover quite quickly. She grew positively cheerful once she had thought of a new name for herself and seemed not to think any more about the disgrace she had suffered. I was at a loss to understand her.

Next morning I woke Jane at dawn as she had asked me to. She washed in my basin, dressed before it was properly light and again told me to guard her bag carefully.

'What is inside it?' I couldn't help but ask.

'My savings, and a keepsake from my beloved "husband", of which I doubt he will ever be aware.'

'Oh Jane, do please take care.'

'Don't fret, Mary. I am a careful thief. Swear to me that you will keep my savings close to you until I need them.'

'I swear.'

'You are my dearest friend, my only friend in all the world.'

We embraced and I could hardly bear to let her go. How would she making a living all alone in London? I had a half a mind to run away with her, but then what would happen to my unhappy family?

I crept downstairs to check that no one was about yet. All was silent. I was so afraid that someone would see her creeping out of the house and arrest her, for even though she says she has savings a-plenty, she declines to return the money she stole from the Mistress. I told her about being transported across the seas, but she just laughed and said they'd have to catch her first. She even took three ripe apples and a round of cheese as she passed through the kitchen, saying she'd need something to gnaw on the journey.

After she had left I wondered if she still had my book of poems. I hoped she had not left it behind with cruel Captain Knatchbull. I opened the fine leather bag she had left with me for safe-keeping and there at the top was the book I'd given her, still wrapped in its handkerchief with 'M' in the corner. I felt so pleased that she had thought to take it with her, even though she had been so upset when she ran away from Knatchbull. It meant that she valued it. I put it back, closed the bag and after much careful thought, hid it where I believed it would never be found by my employers.

# CHAPTER 13

## I Am Branded a Felon
## Elmtree House, October, 1819

Oh, my life is a misery. It is but four days since Jane's departure and I have reached such depths as I could not have imagined in all of my fourteen years. I can hardly believe I am the subject of such a sad story.

I must think straight and begin at the beginning. On the morning Jane left, the house was unusually quiet. Cook told me in a whisper that the Master was not well, had taken to his bed and wanted no noise or disturbance from the servants. Fearing the worst, I asked, 'So the doctor has been sent for?'

Cook shook her head. 'He was much in drink last night and remembers nought. His head is pounding and he was limping when he came downstairs to tell us to keep our noise down. He probably tripped over a bucket in the barn — I heard him moaning to himself out there when I took the scraps out to the dogs last night. The Mistress should lock up the brandy bottle.'

Then Mrs Burton came gliding into the kitchen and

caught us talking. She pointed to the box of ripe apples. 'So, Cook, you have discovered no losses this morning?' Cook went to look and said that yes, it seemed a few apples were missing. She did not seem to think it worth making a fuss over but Mrs Burton continued, 'And no other losses, Cook?' Her eyes rested on the cheese platter which is always covered in a cloth and left to stand overnight. When Cook lifted the cloth she exclaimed, 'The Stilton is gone!'

'Indeed.' Her beady eyes rested on me. 'And here is the culprit!'

I drew a breath. 'Do not speak!' said Mrs Burton.

'I am sure she would not steal a whole cheese, nor even a couple of apples. Even though she's weak with hunger from having had no supper for three nights,' said Cook.

But I interrupted her and mimed that I had taken them because I was famished. I thought it best to confess it, for they would never stop until they had found the culprit and I was feeling guilty enough about other things to accept the blame. What a commotion followed! The Mistress demanded the return of the cheese. She said I could not possibly have eaten it all no matter how greedy I was. I nodded that I had. By now I had told so many lies I'd lost count and felt that God would never forgive me.

The Mistress then shook me hard and shouted that I must tell her where Maria was run off to. She said she knew how untrustworthy I was and suspected me of knowing exactly where she was. She was so enraged that she commanded me to stop this foolish silence and speak to her — as if it was I who had imposed the silence on myself!

'Madam, I swear that I do not know where Maria Wilkinson is!'

This was not really a lie. Was she not Jane Henrie now?

'I don't believe you! My guess is that you're hiding her at your mother's cottage. I shall send a constable to search it and retrieve both Maria and the money she stole this very day.'

'Please do not, ma'am,' I pleaded. 'My family is troubled enough just now with my sister very ill and their debts mounting up. The bailiff would be sure to throw them out if he heard that a constable had been searching the place.'

'Very well. I will delay calling the constable to visit your home until I have searched your room for anything else you might have stolen.'

'Thank you,' I said humbly, but my heart sank.

Jane had only just left, so I had not been able to take her savings to my mother's cottage as she'd advised me to. Now they would be discovered. I could do nothing to prevent it.

Mrs Burton and the Mistress climbed the narrow stairs to the attic. I prayed for a miracle, but by the time I reached the open door they had stripped both beds, flung the bedclothes on the floor and were looking under the straw palliasses. When they did not find any money they wrenched open all the drawers in the rickety chest and threw my few possessions — spare petticoat, Bible, stockings, slippers, comb and handkerchiefs — onto the floor. At the back of the lowest drawer, which had been Maria's, they found one soiled kid glove. Mrs Burton held it up as if it were a dead rat. 'The first stolen article!' she cried in triumph. I did not think there was any point in denying that I had taken it.

They ransacked the room, even ripping the palliasses open so that straw lay everywhere, like a haystack exploded.

I was sure they would find that fine little leather bag but they didn't. I had hidden it rather well, if I say so myself. I had a mess to clean up when they had gone but I thanked God for His mercy and tried not to think about the morrow, when I would be forced to go with the constable to my poor mother's cottage and help to ransack that too.

As the Constable and I walked in through the gate in the picket fence that I had not entered for six weeks, I had mixed feelings — joy at the thought of seeing my dear mother, sisters and brother again, fear at what they might think I had done to cause a search of the cottage. I'd had no way to warn her I was coming.

Fortunately Constable Crimp is a man of middle age who had known us when my father was alive and we were in a better situation. I remembered him bringing a pony to be shod when I was a small child. Still, his duty was to be strict as he had heard from Mrs Robinson Doake that I was a thief. He did not return my smile when we met. As I walked down the path I noticed how full of weeds the garden was. I thought this unusual as our mother is so proud of her flowers and vegetable beds.

I pushed open the back door and what I saw made me draw a sharp breath. My mother sat alone by the bare fireplace in the only chair left in the room, rocking herself back and forth and moaning softly. She clasped a shawl close around her, shivering although it was not a cold day. There was nothing else in the room: no table, sideboard, chairs, ornaments, rugs or pictures on the walls. Even the cooking pots had gone, all but the ancient iron one we use for soup. My first thought was that we'd been robbed. I rushed to her and knelt at her feet. She cried out and held me tightly. 'Are you all right, Mama? Not hurt? Has someone gone after the thief?'

She shook her head and cried a little. 'There has been no thief, Mary. I had to sell everything. We have had almost no food this past week and Sarah is gravely ill. Oh, thank God you are here.'

It was then she noticed the Constable standing by the door. He shuffled uncomfortably and said he had known her late husband. I waited for him to explain his presence but he did not. We both looked at him inquiringly. He coughed and said he had heard in the village that things were bad with the family and asked what he might do to help. My mother shook her head and then looked up at him and said, 'Some food would be welcome, sir.' She said it as if she was begging and I felt a deep shame. I had never heard her speak this way before. Constable Crimp nodded and said he would bring some back directly. He turned back to us then and said, 'Your husband the blacksmith was a fine man. I am sorry for your troubles, ma'am.'

'Bless you,' Mother answered quietly.

When he had gone I hugged Mother again and took from my pocket some bread, cheese and pickles wrapped in a handkerchief that I had saved from my breakfast. 'Give it to the children,' she said and looked up towards the attic. 'They are all up there.'

'Why aren't they at school?' I asked in surprise.

'They have no strength to walk the distance when there is nothing to eat. Besides, how can I pay the schoolteacher?'

'What, they are starving! Oh Mother, why didn't you send a message to me? I would have begged the Mistress for some food for you!'

I raced upstairs. All three children lay in their beds in the middle of the morning. Charley and Meg shrieked when they saw me and flung their arms around my neck. Sarah, pale as a ghost, propped herself up on one arm and I hugged her too. Then I divided the food and even Sarah nibbled a little bread. It was pitiful to see them so hungry. I suddenly felt very angry at the unfairness of the world and vowed I would do something to change it. I began to understand why some people are driven to be thieves.

Constable Crimp was our salvation. He was back within an hour with a sack of potatoes, turnips and cabbages, a dozen stale currant buns from the bakery, a quart of fresh milk from the dairy and, best of all, a side of salted pork which would keep for weeks if the weather remained cool. My mother wept with gratitude. He said that he and the people of the village who had donated all this would see to it that she and the children did not starve. He said that if I was accused of being a petty thief in such a grand place as Elmtree House, then under the circumstances, he could understand the temptation. I could not help interrupting here to tell him that I had been wrongly accused. My mother, meanwhile, was staring at me in shock.

When he had gone I dashed upstairs to give the children each a currant bun and a cup of milk and to encourage them to get out of bed. Then Mother and I set about making a thick soup of the vegetables and pork. I thought I might never return to Elmtree House, I was so pleased to be at home.

Mother asked me about the accusation of thieving and I reassured her that it was all a mistake, but she asked more and more questions until I had to tell her that Maria had run away to London and it was she who had stolen the glove and the cheese and apples. Also a ribbon they had not discovered yet. I neglected to mention the money, as I did not want my mother to think too harshly of my friend. 'Mary, you must tell the Mistress the truth at once,' she declared. She was so insistent that I thought I must, for she told me that honesty is what our family is most proud of and none of us must ever lie, even to protect a friend. When I thought about the sorry state my family had fallen into simply because I had not been able to come home with my wages, and all because I had lied to protect Maria (or 'Jane' as I must call her) I thought that my mother was right. I hurried to the village to call on the dressmaker who had offered to accept me as an apprentice, for the time I had agreed to begin was only a few weeks off, and asked if I could earn some money as I trained by doing extra work at night. She said that recently my mother had admitted she could no longer see well enough to do this sewing so she would be glad of a young pair of eyes. If I worked hard and my work was satisfactory I could earn almost a pound a month.

I ran home full of joy and told my mother the good news. She was happy again and wept a few tears, and the children all danced about, saying that now we would be a whole family once more for I would be living at home. I said I would sew all night and earn enough for Sarah's medicine and the doctor to call regularly, to mend the roof and buy back our furniture. Mother laughed and said I must not work until I went almost blind like her, but I said my eyes were sharp as needles and I would grow carrots to eat so that my eyesight never failed, not even when I was an old woman of forty.

That was the happiest day I have spent in many weeks. I did not know it was to be the last I would ever spend with my family.


I left the cottage that afternoon to go to Elmtree House and hand in my notice. I knew that I should finish out the month there to give the Mistress time to find another servant, but it was only two more weeks. I hoped she did not ask more questions about Maria Wilkinson as I did not wish to lie any more, but if she did, I had decided to tell the truth. I had made up my mind that if the Mistress chose not to give me a reference, then it would not matter much for I had decided to become a dressmaker and work for myself once I finished my apprenticeship.

My heart was soaring and I smiled and sang an old

song my father used to hum as he worked at his anvil when I was a child: '*Down by the Sally gardens, my love and I did roam.*' I thought he would be proud of me if he could look down from Heaven and see me striding up the hill on this warm October day in 1819 with a plan to support the family, yet live with them and not be a wretched servant in somebody else's house. My father had never worked for anyone but himself and had the respect of both the village people and the gentry.

When she saw me returning to the house without Constable Crimp, Mrs Robinson Doake was most vexed. I explained that he had found nothing in our cottage and so had allowed me to walk back to Elmtree House by myself. This she took as a great insult. 'How dare a village constable defy my orders to watch over you closely! You are a thief, as you confessed to me yourself, and should not be allowed to wander the highways and byways alone.'

Then, very politely, I gave the Mistress my notice, explaining that my family needed me at home because my sister was gravely ill.

'Not so fast, Miss,' cried the Mistress and rang the bell for the Housekeeper. Mrs Burton appeared at once. 'The thief finds it convenient to quit this house now that the constable has let her off. She has given us two weeks' notice.'

'Two weeks! How dare you! You will have to work at least another month just to pay for the cheese you gobbled, two months for the gloves you stole and another two for the money my dressmaker never received. Insolent girl.'

I had never seen the Mistress so angry. Mrs Burton just shook her head and pursed her thin lips and narrowed her eyes to slits. 'Leave her to me, ma'am,' she said. 'You should not have to soil yourself with such vermin.' She pushed me roughly in the direction of the scullery where I suspected she meant to deliver me a good walloping with the broom handle.

'Wait!' I cried. 'I am not a thief. I did not steal anything and never have in my whole life. I was wrong to lie and take the blame. I see that now. The cheese, the apples and gloves and the money were taken by Maria Wilkinson, who is gone to London and will never return here.'

Silently I begged Jane to forgive me for this betrayal. I prayed that as she was no longer Maria they would never catch her.

But the Mistress was not satisfied with my confession. She told me to stay in my room while she called the constables from the town to come and question me.

As I climbed the narrow stairs to the attic the Master stood watching me from the landing. I had not seen him since that terrifying night in the barn. He had kept his distance. Although I felt a stab of fear at the sight of him, I gave him a steady gaze and did not drop my eyes in shame. It was he who turned away. I felt some small sensation of triumph then.

There were three town constables, two young, one old, so they must have believed they had a dangerous criminal to deal with. As they did not know my family, doubtless they thought I was a liar from birth. I sat opposite them in the parlour and the Mistress and Mrs Burton sat beside them, all in a row, as if they were the Inquisition.

The old Constable seemed kindly enough at first but when I repeated over and over that I did not know where in London Maria had gone, he became irritated and threatening. 'If you do not tell us all you know then you will be blamed for these thefts and sent to prison,' he said. I became frightened and begged him not to send me away from my family as I was much needed, both to earn wages and to keep their spirits up.

'But you earn very little. How do you expect to support a whole family on a pound a month?'

I explained that we were thrifty and grew our own vegetables and kept hens, but they had stopped laying at present and the garden had died because my mother was in a melancholic state about my sister, who was ill.

'So extra money would be useful for doctors and medicine for your sister?'

'Indeed it would, sir!' I said hopefully. I foolishly thought he meant to offer it to me, just as Constable Crimp had brought us food.

'So you stole that money from your mistress!'

'Oh no, sir. Never! I never would.'

Then he told the other two constables to search my room. They were more thorough than the Mistress and Mrs Burton, and found where I had hidden Maria's savings and keepsakes, under a loose floorboard under the bed which I'd covered with the chamber pot, which I'd hoped they would be too delicate to disturb. They bounded downstairs and presented the old Constable with the leather bag, which he emptied onto the table in front of all of us. There were gasps as a roll of bank-notes tumbled out and then a handkerchief with 'M' embroidered in one corner, wrapped around the book of poetry.

' 'M' for Mary. I suppose this is not yours either?' the old Constable asked sarcastically.

'No sir, it is not. I gave it to my friend Maria as a present on her ...' And here I stopped for I did not want to tell them of her wedding, but then thought they would see the inscription inside the book anyway.

However, they were not really interested in the book and handkerchief. It was the bank notes and the handsome leather purse that fascinated them. The old Constable counted out twenty pounds.

'Enough to hang you, pretty Miss,' he said, and turning the leather purse over and over he estimated that it would be worth another ten shillings and I must have stolen it from some wealthy gentleman. 'Do you have a sweetheart, Miss? Best to tell me all about it before you get in any deeper.'

I said that I did not have a sweetheart, nor had I ever met a gentleman who owned such a purse. I said the money was Maria's savings that I was keeping for her.

'Ah, then you do know where she is!'

'No sir, I do not. She said she would send for them when she needed them.' I knew I was letting her down completely, for now she would never be able to send for them without being caught. And I began to weep for the mess I had made for my dear friend.

The Constables left, taking away the money and the

purse, and instructed the Mistress to keep me well guarded until they returned. I was locked in the dark, airless scullery without water or food. There was only a rag to lie on and a chamber pot. I was there for a whole night and most of the next day.

When the old Constable returned late the following afternoon I was thrust out before him, blinking in the light and staggering against the chair they pushed me into.

'I have grave news, Madam,' he told the Mistress. 'Your servant here is not only a thief. The banknotes are forged. I am arresting her for the theft of a cheese, a pair of kid gloves, a leather purse, two pounds and for the forgery of twenty pound notes.'

'And the three apples? What of those?' said the Housekeeper sharply.

'Three apples as well, if you say so,' said the Constable, as if this were trivial.

'I would not want any of my honest staff suspected of stealing the apples,' she added, to explain herself.

I sat there in a daze.

'What have you to say for yourself, Mary?' asked the Mistress.

'Please, may I have a drink of water?'

# III
## Sydney Cove

# CHAPTER 14

**The Convict Ship *Medway***
**June, 1820**

After almost five months in a wretched cell in Middlesex Gaol, I was transferred to Newgate Gaol in London and thence to trial at the Old Bailey.

It seemed years to wait. Mother visited me as often as she could afford and always said I must plead guilty. Sad to say she believes that I did forge the banknotes. She says I am clever enough to know how to do such a thing or to make contact with someone who did. She says God will forgive me because I only did it to help the family and my poor sister, who is worse now and close to death's door. She begged me to plead guilty because then the Judge would have mercy because of my youth and I would not hang.

Having been found guilty — which all my fellow prisoners as well as the turnkeys had assured me I would be, though I had held on to hope — I am now aboard the *Melrose*, anchored offshore and ready to be taken to that strange land the Mistress at Elmtree

House once told me of, where there are only convicts
and black savages and from whence no one returns.

Such courage my poor Mother needed, to face this.

Elmtree House seems so far away. It is often in my
thoughts. The days I shared the attic with Maria are
some of the happiest I can remember. Yet they are
tainted with sadness because of the way she betrayed
me.

Sometimes, in the evenings on board this ship as we
wait to set sail, when the quarrelling and cursing is loud
around me, I let my mind drift away to that distant
land where Maria and I shrieked with laughter as we
played at dressing-up among the drying washing, and
forget about her betrayal. I have been reading my Bible
and the book of poems, which I was allowed to bring
with me, and asking God for strength to bear the burden of my future. But still, I am deeply frightened.

Cook has been kind over these past months and sent
little bundles of food quite often to the prison —
bread, butter, cheese, salt pork, even a pudding at
Christmas. Once she visited me herself and whispered
that she'd always known Maria Wilkinson was a dangerous friend for such an innocent child as me and she
prayed God that one day she would get her punishment.

When Jane came to visit me in Newgate Prison my
heart leapt for joy. Suddenly I heard a voice calling,
'Mary, Mary, is that you?' She was wearing a fine cloak,
with all but her eyes covered by a handkerchief to protect her nose from the prison stench. I almost did not
recognise her. She looked like a lady. Thank the Lord,

my dear friend has come at last to rescue me, I thought, and staggered towards her. She drew back as I reached the bars and stretched my hand out towards her. 'Oh Mary, you have aged ten years! What have they done to you?' she cried in alarm. 'You are like a ghost of yourself.'

'It is a touch of gaol fever, that is all.'

At this Jane drew herself up and moved further away.

I tried to smile at her, but she turned her face away. I must have looked like a grinning skeleton. 'Dear Jane! I knew you would come. I knew it!' And tears of relief sprang into my eyes.

'There, there,' she said, looking as if she wanted to run away.

'Mary, I want you to know that I had no idea the notes were forged,' she whispered urgently.

'So they were not your savings, Jane?'

'Of course not. I took them from Knatchbull the night he threw me out. I thought he owed me something for ruining my life — and now he has ruined yours as well. He is evil and we will be revenged on him, Mary. Oh, I am so angry at what he has done to you!'

I stared at her.

'It is not Knatchbull who has hurt me, Jane,' I said tonelessly.

'Well, it is certainly not me!' she protested. 'You could have said, "Wait, Jane. It is too dangerous for me to hide your money. Keep it with you." And if I had kept it I'd never have been caught. I'd have passed the forged notes off quick as an eel gets through a net, and been better off than I am already.'

'Perhaps,' said I vaguely, for I suddenly felt weak from the fever, as if I might swoon.

'Then I am forgiven?' Jane asked quickly.

I could not answer. She had no intention of trying to save me. Could I possibly forgive that? At last I nodded and hung my head.

Jane looked pleased for I know she does not like to be thought of as in the wrong, not by anyone, even such a sorrowful, pathetic creature as myself.

She passed me a scrap of paper with the address of her mother in Leeds on it and we parted in tears. 'Do not give up hope, Mary. You are still my dear friend and I have a feeling we will meet again.' Then she hurried away.

Some nights as the water ripples along the wall I cry when I think of the way Jane let me take her punishment for those stolen, forged banknotes. But I cannot believe she really meant me to suffer. I believe she meant to return for them. It was just bad luck that they were discovered first.

My fellow convicts waiting to set sail are good souls, although at first I was afraid of the roughest women who cursed my 'snivelling' and pushed me about. It is not their fault. They have led miserable lives and do not expect softness or kindness. When I shared my food with some of them in prison they stared in disbelief. I read aloud to them now. They prefer poetry to the Bible, and start cursing if I read more than a verse or two of Holy Scripture, saying it is a pack of lies.

Some know of other convicts who have been sent to the place we are going, this land beyond the seas, and tell tales of cannibals and mutiny. Others say it is not a bad place, a paradise for women — with ten men apiece to choose from and all of them able to make a fortune and own farms of a thousand acres each. I am confused. I cannot believe that in a few days I will be leaving England for ever.

# CHAPTER 15

## My New Master
## September, 1820

All I remember now of the beginning of our voyage is the sound of human moaning and high winds, the creaking of timbers, the smell of ropes, animals and vomit. It was hazy like a dream. I remember someone forcing water between my lips and sponging my hot forehead with a cloth drenched in sea water. This was Mary Jones, I found later.

We women were packed close together on sleeping shelves below decks where the air was foul. Many were glad enough to get out up top and share a bunk with a sailor. But Mary, my namesake, could see I was ill and afraid, and when one sailor came down below and announced I was his chosen girl, for I was surely too young to have the pox, she sent him off with a stream of curses.

She showed me how to vomit in a pail while the ship was pitching and rolling in a storm and not to spill a drop on those below. She bathed me all over in salt

water and lye soap, which was all we had, and when
that caused bad rashes, she waited till we came into
port then boiled fresh water, made soap from oatmeal
wrapped in muslin, and washed my body, hair and
clothes. In port she exchanged my hard biscuits and
salt pork for fresh fruit and vegetables. When I was able
to walk, she brought me up on deck to breathe the sea
air. Here I saw a woman seized with mania having a fit
and another being beaten with the cat-o'-nine-tails for
insolence to an officer. She was stripped of her upper
garments and tied so that her back took the lash. It was
a most horrible sight. But Mary told me she would
receive only six lashes, which she would survive well
enough.

Mary Jones explained that she was a prostitute who
had stolen a gold watch from a client while he slept.
Unfortunately he woke up just as she was hurrying to
the pawnshop with it to get money to feed her family of
seven, for which she was the only breadwinner. She
told me she was glad they did not hang her, for she still
had hopes of seeing her dear children and grandchildren before she died. Perhaps, she said, some of them
would be transported to Sydney Cove too.

Without Mary Jones I might not be here, safe and
sound as I am. I thank God for sending her to nurse me
back to health and for protecting me from the
unwanted attentions of the sailors.

The strange thing is that as soon as we came within
sight of this new land on the far side of the world, I
began to recover. The air was fresh as we drew near and
the water so green. The sun shone and we women came
up on deck and breathed the salty breeze deep into our-

selves. We laughed suddenly, as if it had gone to our heads like wine. It was then I began to regain my full strength. As we sailed through the tall, craggy cliffs they call the Heads and into Sydney Cove, I gazed at the shimmering water and thought it the most beautiful place on earth.

I thank God that I survived the journey here, which has taken months. There were some who did not and died at sea, to be buried in the waves.

So far I have seen no black savages although there are wisps of smoke from their campfires drifting up from the bush. I hear that many of them are sick with diseases they have caught from the white men, and are dying in caves along the shore.

The convicts I feared so much seem just to be prisoners like myself, hoping to make a better life for themselves. Though I did see a pitiful sight on my arrival — a gang of men chained together and swinging their picks in unison, cutting stone while a gaoler shouted at them as if they were beasts.

Sydney Cove is not so uncivilised as I had been told. As we sailed into Port Jackson I saw handsome buildings of yellow stone. One of these was the house where Lachlan Macquarie, the Governor, lives, I was told. I must try to remember his name. There is so much to learn.

As soon as we anchored, most of the male convicts were taken straight to a military barracks at Hyde Park, to be locked up until they are assigned to a work gang and marched to the stone quarry. But we females are in such short supply that we were to go off to our assignments immediately. I was glad of that. I do not like being locked away.

Mary gave me good advice for survival in Sydney Cove, saying I must put up my age to eighteen and call myself a dressmaker. 'Then you'll have a better chance. I have heard a girl can remain a skivvy in Sydney Town all her life, slaving in someone else's kitchen, or else underneath 'em, which is worse.'

I wish dear Mary could have stayed with me here but she has been assigned to a farmer as cook and housekeeper and left early this morning for the Hunter River, which is a long way off. She cannot write so I shall not learn what befalls her unless she can send me a message. It is like losing a mother for the second time. Mary said I must not cry about it. 'Just use your strength to find a good position,' she told me.

Mary Jones will be disappointed to hear I have not been assigned to a dressmaker, although I did take her advice. I said I was seventeen and had been apprenticed to one, which is almost true. I did not like to put my age up to eighteen as I have been told I do not look that old. I turned fifteen shortly before I embarked on the *Melrose*. I was still in Newgate Gaol. That was the very day Jane visited — at first I thought she had remembered and come especially for my birthday. But my fever was just beginning then so I was not quite myself.

I am told I will live at The Rocks. This is said to be a debauched and villainous place, yet from the vessel it seemed to be a harmless enough cluster of cottages, shops and public houses tumbling down the rocky hillside towards the sea, with a few narrow pathways like goat tracks running between the buildings. I could see a windmill and the spire of a small stone church. Apart from the huge rocks hanging right over the water's edge it looked a pleasant enough village to me.

I have been assigned as a servant to a Mr Andrew Frazier. He is aged sixty, a bachelor and an ex-convict who is much respected in the town. He owns a bakery, has ten servants and deals in exports and imports. This is all I know of him. I am to meet him later today.

I am very nervous. We women are all assembled on the dock, awaiting our new masters. What if Mr Frazier turns out to be a tyrant? Or a lecher? Mary Jones has given me advice on how to deal with this. But would I be brave enough to brand my master with a red-hot poker?

It is a warm day and my bonnet is not wide enough to shield my face from the hot sun. The sky is so high and wide with hardly a cloud in it. There are some large straggly trees around the shore and several sailing ships at anchor, and a few curious people staring at us as we huddle together awaiting our fate. When the first convicts came here thirty years ago they had to sleep in tents. I am glad that is no longer the case.

The muster has begun. Names are being called from a list held by a government official and women are walking off with their new masters like so many slaves at a market place. Some of them go obediently with flirtatious smiles, others drag their feet and lower their heads. A few are rebellious, struggling against their new master, yelling insults and reasons why they should not be parted from the sailors who have been their lovers on the voyage out.

I look about for a man who might be Mr Frazier. I imagine an elderly man with white hair, but the man who steps forward when my name is called is tall and striking, and dressed as a gentleman. He looks strong and has red curly hair with a bristling beard and eyes as blue as the sky above. He is courteous and offers to carry my bundle. I thank him but say I can manage it myself. I have learned to trust no one with my few possessions. We walk in silence up the hill to Cambridge Street.

When we are nearly at the house Mr Frazier says, 'I hope ye will be happy in my house, Mary. My servants are carefully selected. They are to be sober and to bring no children into the house. Do ye understand?' His voice is Scottish.

'I do, sir.' I would like to ask why he objects to children, but he seems a stern man and yet shy as well, so I do not ask.

'Please sir, what are my duties to be?'

'Ye must ask Flora, the housekeeper. She will be home directly. She has gone to Cockle Bay to gather shellfish.' He chuckles. 'D'ye like shellfish?'

'I do not know that I have ever had the pleasure of tasting them, sir.'

'Then pleasure ye shall have this very evening. Here in Sydney Cove we have the best oysters, mussels and cockles in the world.'

'I should be pleased to try them, sir.'

At Elmtree House we were never offered the same fine food as the Master and Mistress.

The house has a long passage with rooms opening off on either side. I can smell fresh bread from the bakery, which makes my mouth water. Mr Frazier leads me down the passage past a neat parlour and a breakfast room to a large, light kitchen and bids me sit at a table. He brings me a stoneware bottle and a cup, pours some brown fizzy liquid into it and says, 'Ginger beer, brewed here at The Rocks. Try it.' I sip it cautiously. It is strong and makes my nose tickle, but tastes good. Next my Master fetches a newly baked loaf, with butter, cheese and apricot jam. 'Eat up, miss. Ye must be famished after that voyage with nothing but bully beef and hard dry biscuits, eh?'

I eat hungrily. It is the most delicious meal I can remember. He watches me eat with satisfaction. 'We'll put some meat on those poor thin bones for ye, Mary, aye we will.' Then he calls loudly, 'Millie!'

A ruddy-faced servant girl appears in a huge white apron. She looks about eighteen, is stout, tall and has bright yellow curls tumbling down below her cap. She stares boldly at the Master. 'Yes?'

I am amazed that she doesn't call Mr Frazier 'sir' and that he does not correct her.

'This is Mary Jones, just arrived on the *Melrose*. Will ye take her to her room now, see she has all she needs, a warm bath and fresh clothes, before Flora gets back. Apron and cap too, Millie, and two towels of her own. Show her the house and introduce her to the others. Look around the neighbourhood. There's a good girl.'

Millie smirks at me in a not unfriendly way, 'Come on then,' she tells me.

The room I am to share with her and another servant named Bertha is large and airy with a window overlooking a garden with fruit trees. I can smell the apricots which must have been used in the jam. Perched on a tree are several large black-and-white birds singing in strange voices, like a gargling carol. 'What are those birds called?' I ask Millie.

'Magpies. And they'll swoop ya if ya get too near their nests. Peck ya eyes out. Make ya ears bleed.'

'Really?' I smile in disbelief.

'Lots of dangerous animals round here. Poison spiders. A girl died last week from a bite. And sharks. They found a man's arm inside one caught at Cockle Bay. And a whole dog too.'

I nod, but I cannot believe this. Millie seems to like dramatic stories. 'When ya've bathed and got the fleas off ya I'll take ya to see The Rocks. There's floggings at the market place on Wednesdays and hangings at the gaol on George Street, just behind the walls. People come from miles around to stand on our street to watch 'em. It's high up and you get a good view. Ever seen a hanging?'

'No.' I shake my head and feel my heart beat faster. 'I don't wish to see one, either.'

'Ah well. There's good times to have in the public houses, dancing, fiddle playing, brawling. Old man Frazier, he don't like us to go inside them, never touches a drop of rum himself though he sells enough, but we takes no notice of him after hours. He don't own us, do he?'

'We are assigned to him. We are convicts and if we displease him he can send us back to prison, can he not?'

'Aye, he can send us to the Female Factory!' Millie begins to laugh merrily. 'Sydney ain't like the old country, where servants and prisoners are scum, y'know. Here we are near as good as our masters. A convict can earn a ticket of leave and own a farm or a public house in a few years if she's clever. I learned a lot when I was in the Female Factory.'

'What is that?'

'The prison and lying-in place at Parramatta. I were there for months when I arrived, waiting to be assigned. Not a bad place to be. I caught on to the lurks. We 'ad some times there I can tell ya. And fights. What fights! The Matron had to bring the soldiers in. Constables couldn't stop 'em. D'ya like fightin', Mary?'

I shake my head.

'Ah well, ya'll have to learn. Have ya bath now so ya don't give us the pox and I'll show ya the town.' I am about to protest that I don't have the pox, but Millie gives me a wink which I take to mean she doesn't mean it. She takes me along an outside path to the washhouse where she has half-filled a deep wooden tub with warm water and placed a bar of yellow soap and a towel on the bench. 'I'll have to take ya clothes from ya and burn 'em,' she tells me. 'Old Frazier's a tyrant about cleanliness and disease from the ships. Says cleanliness is next to Godliness and doesn't let us forget it.'

'But these are all the clothes I have in the world!' I protest.

'I'll give ya new ones, much better than these rags.' And Millie begins hauling off my shawl and dress, stockings, bodice and petticoat. She is a strong girl and there is no point arguing any further.

I submerge myself in the tub and rub my whole body with the soap, letting my hair float about me like seaweed. When I look up I notice a curl of black smoke rising into the blue sky outside the high window. My poor rags are no more.

# CHAPTER 16

**I Become the Servant of Mr Andrew Frazier,
Ex-Convict, Respectable Baker and Friend of the
Governor
The Rocks, 1820**

There was a soft knock on the washhouse door and an
arm appeared around the edge of it to hang a colourful
assortment of clothing on a hook. 'I'm not peeping at
ya naked, mind, just bringing your new clothes. The
best part is the boots, if they fit ya. They're too small for
me and Mr Frazier says you're to have them.' The arm
placed a pair of fine leather lady's boots just inside the
door.

'Come in, Millie.' I was already wrapped in the
towel.

She sat down heavily beside me on the bench by the
tub. 'Ya smell real sweet now. Ya was a stinker when ya
got here.'

I blushed. 'There was only salt water to wash in on
the voyage and no proper soap or change of clothing.'

'Don't I remember it.' She pulled a face. 'And nought

but thin rags for the monthlies that ya couldn't get the
stink or stains out of though ya scrubbed ya fingers to
the bone. We had to rip up our petticoats to make do.'
She held up the boots. 'Rare quality, made in England.
These was bought from some rogue, by old Frazier over
the counter at his hotel, together with a shirt and stockings, for sixteen shillings. I was there and saw him count
it all out in copper coins. Being a Scot he's careful. Ah,
but he hummed and hawed before he decided to buy
them. And then, poor old sod, he was arrested for receiving stolen goods!'

'Mr Frazier was arrested?'

'Aye. The Constable told him it would be "a
fourteen-year business" if he was convicted, and
Frazier, being wealthy and afeared of losing his good
character, agreed to pay the Constable what he asked.
One hundred pounds.'

'A hundred pounds! For a bribe to let him off?'

'Just so. But before he could pay it, the owner of the
stolen goods showed up and seeing it was Mr Frazier
who was accused, he shouted, "How dare you arrest
such a respectable citizen. Let this man go at once! He
is innocent." So the Constable never got his hundred
quid and Mr Frazier returned the goods. The owner
said he could keep those boots because of the trouble
he'd had. Here, try them on.'

She knelt at my feet and I wriggled them into the
elegant boots quite easily. I walked about in them wearing my towel like a toga.

'Do they pinch?'

'Not at all.'

'So, Cinderella, ya get to marry the Prince!'

'What?' For one foolish moment I thought she must mean Mr Frazier. 'Who is the Prince?'

'Why, any man ya fancy in this fair city. There are five or six of them to every one of us. Take ya pick.'

'I am too young to think of marriage yet, Millie.'

'How old are ya?'

I hesitated, then said, 'Seventeen.'

'Ya never are. Ya couldn't be more than fourteen.'

I blushed and admitted, 'I'm fifteen, but I've heard it is wise to pretend to be older in Sydney Town. Mr Frazier thinks I'm seventeen, so please don't tell him my real age.'

'Secrets are safe with me. How old would ya reckon I was?'

'Eighteen?'

'Ya lying,' she scoffed, but looked pleased all the same. 'Sweet sixteen and never been kissed, ha, ha. And I'm strong. Feel my muscles.' She flexed an arm and held it close. 'There's plenty of beef to eat here in Sydney Town for girls to grow strong and hearty.' She pinched my puny arm and screwed up her face. 'Ya'll need to put on some weight before ya can fight.'

'Do we really have to fight here?' I asked in alarm.

Millie let out a peal of laughter. 'No, but it's the best entertainment on The Rocks. Come on, I'll show ya around. Tell ya all about the place.'

Mr Frazier's property included storerooms and warehouses adjoining the house as well as the bakery. He was a publican as well as an importer and exporter so there was a vast supply of spirits. Sacks of grain were piled high in one warehouse. In another, two workmen were stacking barrels against a wall. Millie called out to them. 'Will, Thomas, this is Mary Jones just arrived on the *Melrose* and assigned to Mr Frazier!' They turned, nodded their greetings to me, grinned in a friendly manner and went on with their work.

'No slacking in this household, let me tell ya,' Millie said. Leading me back into the house she introduced me to Bertha, who was down on her knees polishing the hardwood floor of the parlour, and to the cook, who was bent low over a huge wood-fired stove. 'Mrs Toomb, this is our new girl, Mary Jones.' The cook, an older woman whose face was red from the fire, shook my hand firmly. 'Welcome, Mary Jones.' Then she stared at me closely and her mouth turned down at the corners like a discontented baby. 'You look like a child. Is she of age?' she asked Millie.

'She's been ill on the voyage. She's old enough, ain't you, Mary?' She grinned at me and I did not know what I was meant to reply. So I nodded and curtsied to the Cook in my confusion, at which they both laughed. 'Pretty manners you have, Mary Jones,' said Mrs Toomb. 'We'll see if you can work hard by and by.'

As we walked down the steps and out the gate into Cambridge Street, Millie told me that Mrs Toomb had murdered her husband but they could not prove it so she'd been given a life sentence instead of a hanging. 'She did it with a carving knife.'

'How terrible. Does Mr Frazier know?'

'He knows about all of us. Every one. She did it in self-defence. The husband was a brute. She makes the best steak-and-kidney pudding I've ever tasted and she's been with Frazier over twenty years.'

'Is Mr Frazier a good master, Millie?'

'He's a wealthy old bastard but none too generous. He pays us what he should and no more.'

'Giving me these boots was generous,' I said.

'Ah, but that's for your welcome. To make ya grateful so's ya'll work ya guts out for him.' She grinned.

'He seems a good man.'

'Not too bad. Anyone who's been a convict theirselves is a better master than one what hasn't. He's strict, keeps the laws, works hard himself, but he can be violent if any of us upsets him. There was an assigned convict named Jex here a few years back who got horse-whipped out of this house.'

'What did he do?'

Millie shrugged. 'I don't rightly know. They say it was something to do with a woman's good name being slandered. Frazier's a respectable man. Ask anyone hereabouts. He'd make a good husband but is very particular. No sluts for Andrew Frazier.'

'Has he never been married then?' I'd imagined him a widower.

'Never talks of it if he has. Can't abide children neither. A girl who'd worked for him two years got pregnant to her man, who worked here too, and he told them to leave. No children allowed in his house.'

'He must be lonely,' I said thoughtfully.

'Aw, don't waste ya sympathy on old Frazier. He's almost one of the gentry. Gets invited to Government House, mixes with the toffs. He knows the Governor. Well, he would, wouldn't he? They're both from Scotland. And he's friends with the Government Arkyteck, name of Greenway, used to be a convict just like us.

Forger, he was. Macquarie gave him his 'mancipation and now he's designed the new Government House.'

'Is it very grand?'

'Four storeys high and posh as a palace, just like in England. Mrs Macquarie designed the gardens — and the new Orphan School in Parramatta, too.'

'Is Governor Macquarie much liked by the people here?'

'Well, he don't like us drinking rum. Tried to ban it, but who takes any notice? And he builds lots of roads and bridges and squares, what he names all after himself!' Millie laughed loudly. 'He cares about us convicts and believes we deserve our 'mancipation, which many don't. He tries to make this city safe and clean for us and the buildings as good as any in Edinburgh, Bath or London. But he's made enemies.'

We walked down Cambridge Street which had a fine view of the harbour. 'This is one of the best streets on The Rocks,' Millie said proudly. 'This and Cumberland Street, where some of the biggest two-storey houses are. Used to be just convicts, whalers and sailors round here, but now the swells are coming from over the other side of the Tank Stream. Must be they like the dancing and drinking.' Millie laughed. She seemed to know lots of people and waved and called to them as they stood at their shopfronts and doorways.

'Good day to ya, Jessy!'

'Good day, Millie.'

'Her husband William Wakeman used to be overseer at the Hospital, kept the patients clean, mustered 'em and locked 'em up at night but he took to drinkin' the spiritous cordial, lost his position.'

'What does he do now?'

'He's a Rocks constable.' I smiled at this but Millie did not seem to see anything odd about it.

'Good day, Mr Cribb.' A man wearing a butcher's striped apron passed us, carrying a sheep's carcass on his shoulder. He waved a bloody hand. 'Tell Mr Frazier I'm keeping the kidneys for him, will you, Millie,' he called.

'That's George Cribb,' Millie said. 'Owns a hotel what backs onto the yard where he slaughters his meat, and chucks the bones and offal into the cesspit, which ain't quite legal. Well, it used to be, but Governor Macquarie's trying to clean the place up, like I said. Says the offal and guts gets into the Tank Stream water supply and we'll all get sick. George still does it, but who knows except you and me, eh, Mary?'

We passed a public house called the Sheer Hulk. 'Good day to you, Poll!' called Millie to a woman washing clothes on the sunny steps in a wooden tub like the one I had bathed in. They chatted for a few moments and then walked on. 'Take my advice, Mary. Don't never work as a washerwoman. Poll gets one shilling and sixpence and her meals for working all day at that tub and her man, Mick, who's a labourer, gets three shillings for his day. Women's work is worth nothing.'

I looked at the sign where the licensee's name was printed. '*Sam Hulbert*,' I said aloud.

'Yes, that's the boss. How did ya know?'

I pointed to the sign.

'Ya can read then? Fancy that now. Old Frazier'll be pleased as punch. He's hardly literate himself. Ah, but you should see the Sheer Hulk when it's full of ragin' drunks! They let the male convicts out of the Hyde Park barracks some nights and where d'you reckon's the first place they come? Right here to The Rocks. I'll bring ya back on a Saturday night when the Sheer Hulk is burstin' with singing' and dancin'.'

I must have looked doubtful, for Millie dug me in the ribs with her elbow, linked my arm firmly in hers and said, 'Come on now, Mary, ya'll have some fun!'

In between the houses, up the winding streets, children ran helter-skelter everywhere. 'Don't they go to school?' I asked.

'Only if they can get into the Orphan School and that's only free for orphans. Others have to pay. But there's not enough places.'

'Are there many orphans?'

Millie shook her head. 'It's not like London where they beg on the streets. Families on The Rocks don't mind taking in an extra child or two if their parents have died of fever or been drowned. People have bigger hearts here than in the old country.'

She showed me the hospital and the gaol with its tall stone walls. 'Hope there's a hanging soon. Ya wouldn't believe how many people cram onto this high ground to get a look at what's dangling inside those walls. Takes six minutes for them to die. And they piss theirselves.' She lowered her voice. 'And worse.'

We walked on up Harrington Street, which was steep, and came to another public house, the Labour in Vain. The name was painted on a sign hanging from a pole at the front and beneath it was a crude drawing of a sailor scrubbing a Negro in a tub of water, trying to get him white. 'I've a friend in here,' Millie said. 'Come on in and meet him.'

We walked down stone steps and entered a fairly large room which was dark except for a window at one end just large enough to put your head through. The shutters were closed against the bright afternoon sunlight that slanted in between the slats, making golden ribs on a long wooden table by the end wall. There were two wooden benches for customers to sit against the walls. Opposite the door was a huge open fireplace, with a large cooking pot hanging above the hearth. I could smell beef and cabbage already cooked for the customers' supper. A large knife was chained to one end of the table. I stared at it, wondering if it was used as a weapon against unruly customers — 'Don't worry,' Millie said, 'It's just for cutting tobacco. Haven't ya never been inside a public house before?' I shook my head.

'Jem!' called Millie, and out of the gloom appeared a tall, lanky young man, puffing on a clay pipe and grinning at the same time. 'Here's our new girl up at old Frazier's. Mary Jones, fresh off the boat from London. Mary, this is Jem O'Connor. Say good afternoon to pretty Mary, now.'

The young man slouched against the wall and put out one hand unsteadily to take mine. 'Good afternoon, mish,' he slurred. Then he hiccupped and laughed, and the pipe dropped from his mouth to the floor.

'Easy now, Jemmie. Ya should stay off the grog till sundown at least or the publican'll give you a hiding.

Look what a bad impression ya making on Mary here. She's never seen a drunk before. Isn't that true, Mary?'

I shook my head uneasily. I would never forget seeing Mr Robinson Doake red-faced and swaying after he'd drunk too much brandy and how he'd made me the unwilling object of his affection. But I had never seen someone so drunk that they slid slowly down a wall, as Jem was doing now.

'Come on, Mary. We'll leave him to sleep off his lunch. Bye bye, Jem. See ya when ya's sober!' And we hurried out into the blinding sunlight.

'Pity about that. Jem is a wicked fiddler when he's sober. And dance? He's like a pixie with a spell put on him. Nimble as a flying fish.'

'Would you marry him, Millie?' I asked, surprising myself with my boldness.

'Marry him I would not! What a question. No, the man I'll marry doesn't know it yet but he will in time,' she whispered. 'And by then it'll be too late for him to get away!' She laughed, very softly for a change, behind her hand. 'Come on, we'll be late back. We'll have oysters to open for hours and the slut's wool to sweep up and water to carry. Oh, when does it ever stop!' But she laughed as if she did not care at all about the endless chores.

I felt happy to be a new friend of Millie, who seemed to look on her life in this strange land on the wrong side of the world as no punishment at all but an adventure.

# CHAPTER 17

**I Become a Respected Woman of The Rocks and
am Advised to Produce Bastards
The Rocks, Sydney, 1822**

It is hard to believe I have been here in Sydney Town
for two whole years. I have many acquaintances here
on The Rocks and several close friends. But the strangest
news is that I have recently changed my position
and become someone I would never have dreamed I
could be.

Just six weeks ago Andrew Frazier called me into the
room he uses as an office at the front of the house and
asked me to sit down opposite his desk, which was very
formal of him. He coughed, looked embarrassed and
then made a short speech. 'Mary, ye've been a servant
in my house for two years now.'

'Yes Mr Frazier.' I wondered if he meant to tell me
that two years was long enough and I should now look
out for another position.

'Ye're the most steady, upright and honest servant in
my house and ye're literate.'

'Yes, sir.' I did not usually call him 'sir'. He did not like it. But now he looked so grave, I felt it was appropriate.

'As ye know, Mrs Frith is leaving us to open her own public house. I would like ye to take over her position as Housekeeper. What d'ye say?'

I opened my mouth but no sound came out. Then I drew a deep breath and said, 'I would be honoured to be your housekeeper, Mr Frazier.'

'Good. Then move your things into Mrs Frith's room on Monday and I'll give ye a list of your new duties.'

He explained that I would be expected to manage not only the household of ten servants but part of the business as well. And I am only seventeen years of age! Mr Frazier thinks I am older, but I did not like to enlighten him, in case he reconsidered his decision. I will write to tell my mother! And I have vowed to myself that I will do my very best because I am so proud to have such a responsible position, and because I am fond of Mr Andrew Frazier.

Perhaps I do look nineteen or twenty. It is true I have filled out a lot since I arrived as a poor, skinny thing on the *Melrose*. I am taller and more womanly now and my complexion is rosier, although I try to shield my face from the hot sun. These days the men I pass by while I am shopping at the market and walking home along the shore give me admiring looks and pass comments, some of which I would not care to repeat, but all are complimentary in their way. I am no beauty nor ever will be, just a healthy, well-grown young woman with prospects, I believe.

As soon as Mr Frazier had finished talking to me I dashed off to tell Millie the good news. She was not as surprised about my new position as I was. 'Stands to reason, ya being literate and honest and all. Old Frith wasn't beyond stealing a bit of this and that when it suited her and Frazier knew it.'

'I can't believe she stole from him, Millie. She'd been housekeeper here for seven years.'

She laughed. 'I'll tell ya something. Ya'll be the first housekeeper in the history of Sydney Town that never stole a thing, Mary. They'll be puttin' bets on ya!'

Millie said that as it was my last Saturday night as a freedom-loving servant girl I must come to the Labour in Vain with her to celebrate. I was not keen to go but she insisted. 'Aw, come on. He'll have ya home every Saturday night from now on checking every bleedin' jar of preserved fruit and every bottle of grog and bag of flour. Put on ya dancing shoes and let's get out of here while ya still can!'

So that evening we waltzed down Cambridge Street arm-in-arm. The sun was just setting over Cockle Bay, as pink and gold as a ripe peach in syrup. We sang '*Cockles and mussels, alive, alive oh,*' as we fairly danced down the stone steps into the pub. I thought at that moment I had never felt so carefree.

'Good evenin' to you, Millie! Evenin', Mary!' There were welcome greetings from all over the crowded room. Jem was already playing his fiddle in a corner and Millie said that soon he'd be joined by other music-makers on washboard, tub drum, tin whistle and paper and comb. And then of course there would be singing.

Millie hurried across to the bar and ordered us a jar of rum each. I protested that I did not drink the stuff, but she only shook her first at me. 'Enough of ya puritanism, Mary. I'm giving ya a toast in the best drink in the colony! Now get it down ya gullet or else I'll force it down.'

We clinked our jars together and Millie downed her rum in three gulps. I sipped at mine. I meant to make it last all night — alas, that did not happen.

A couple of young fellows who must have been sailors from the vessel just arrived from Portsmouth had their eyes on us. I'd overheard them talking while Millie was at the bar. I looked away when they leered at us but Millie gave one of them a wink. I nudged her crossly. 'Don't do that. They'll never leave us alone now.'

'So? They've got cash to burn. Been at sea for months. They need some friends to show them how to spend it.'

'They're not that stupid.'

'Want to bet?'

Millie was swirling about, holding up her skirts in a coquettish manner and smiling at everyone around us. I wished she would stop.

Presently, as she intended, one of the sailors came over and asked if she'd like to dance. He seemed quite polite and was better looking than his friend, who looked pale and sickly. I supposed I would be stuck with the sickly one.

Jem was playing an Irish jig and Millie and her partner leapt into the throng of whirling dancers while I stood with my back to the dark wall, hoping it would make me invisible. But along came the pale sailor to me, to ask if I would dance with him. He looked so sickly I hadn't the heart to refuse. We did not prance as energetically as the others yet at the end of the jig he was breathless. He thanked me, brought me another jar of rum which I did not want, and said he was going out to get some air. I wondered if he had caught fever in the tropics or whether he'd just been very seasick on the voyage.

Millie came back then, perspiration making droplets on her brow. 'Why did ya let him go?' she asked. 'They are brothers and they're taking us out to their vessel by rowboat for a picnic lunch tomorrow. If you smile at yours a bit more sweetly.'

'Mine isn't well, Millie.'

'What's he got? Consumption or the plague?' She laughed and dug me hard in the ribs with her elbow. 'If ya think he's contagious I'll swap ya. I'm not fussy. Got the constitution of an ox.' She burst into raucous laughter and I knew she had downed a few more rums.

The music started up again and her young seaman reappeared. He and Millie whirled away.

I danced with Jem's brother, Seamus, this time, and because he had a keen sense of rhythm, I enjoyed myself. I was thirsty afterwards, but what with all the noise he did not hear me asking for a cordial and brought me rum again. That was my third and my head was feeling giddy.

I sat down on the bench and Millie came up to join me. We giggled together like children. I leaned against her and she said, 'Ya're having a good time at last Mary Jones, aren't ya?'

I replied that I was, and that she was a good friend to me and I would never forget her no matter what awful things should come to pass in the future.

'And what are these awful things ya predict, Mary?'

I said I did not know. And then I suddenly felt as if I might cry and could not help the tears streaming down my cheeks like a creek in flood.

'What, the rum has made ya maudlin, has it, Mary? That's a shame. Quick Georgie, get her a drink. A brandy, if you please, for she's just had bad news.'

The young sailor whose brother was sickly bent down beside me and patted my hand. 'Bad news?'

'Her mam died in England and she can't go home for the funeral,' said Millie gravely. 'Quick. A brandy. Get the best.'

'I'm sorry to hear it, miss,' said Georgie and dashed to the bar.

At this I began to sob in earnest, half-believing the sad news myself, I was in such a stupor.

'Rum's no good for ya, I can see that now, Mary,' said Millie consolingly. 'Brandy is expensive but we'll get him buying us both nothing but the best for the rest of the night, see if we don't.'

I shook my head. 'I should go home now, Millie. I feel quite strange.'

'Aye, and ya'll be stranger by and by.' Millie laughed. 'Here, this'll fix ya. Drink it up.'

I threw my head back obediently and drank the brandy in one gulp. Even Millie was impressed.

My memory of the rest of that evening is not clear. I recall a fight in which Millie was throwing punches at a smaller woman whose nose bled all over her bodice while the crowd gathered round them cheered, then more dancing, a quiet period when there was soft singing of Irish ballads, an argument about politics and then some jars of rum being thrown and fragments lying broken on the floor. Then all was quiet. I think I fell asleep on the sawdust behind a bench, for the last thing I remember was being gently lifted into a wheelbarrow by Seamus O'Connor, and Millie saying, 'Take her home now. She's not well. Wake Bertha up and tell her to put her to bed. And mind the Master don't see her. He thinks she's a teetotaller.'

Next morning my head felt like a suet pudding that will not rise.

I slept all Sunday, missing church, and only leaving my bed to race outside and vomit on the tomato plants. I vowed never to drink alcohol again. Millie came home that evening saying I had missed a lovely picnic on the *Belvedere*, which was anchored in Sydney Cove. She had been rowed there by Georgie and his brother John, who said he was sorry I had not been well enough to come too. John sympathised with me, however, for he had drunk too much rum himself the night before and was still recovering. 'He says the rum served here in the colony is the strongest he's ever tasted, even in the West Indies,' said Millie proudly.

And so ended my life as a carefree servant girl.

I feel proud to have the responsibility of Housekeeper. I know that I am one of the most fortunate young women in Sydney Town, to have a Master who trusts me and with whom I spend so many contented hours.

Andrew Frazier is an unusual man. When I first arrived I thought him stern but he is also shy and has suffered a great deal. He was very ill a year ago and I was appointed to nurse him. When he was delirious with the fever he ranted at phantom gaolers and pleaded not to be beaten any more. He has scars on his back which could only have come from the cat-o'-nine tails. Yet when he is well he never mentions the past.

He asked me to read to him while he was still too ill to get up and I read from *Lyrical Ballads*, the book of poems my mother gave me for my fourteenth birthday, which I once gave away to Jane as a wedding present. Later I told him the story of poor Jane's mock marriage because I thought he would be a sympathetic listener. He was. 'And where is your friend Jane Henrie now?' he asked. I told him I wished I knew. When I last saw her she told me she had a position as a maid in one of the finest houses in Mayfair, but she had not replied to any of my letters, sent to her mother in Leeds.

He smiled and said it wasn't likely she would be still there. When I asked why not, he replied that she seemed the kind of girl who would not be content to stay very long in one place. This surprised me, but when I thought about it, I realised it was true. He then said that I, on the other hand, was a young woman who would remain constant. I blushed at this and to show him that I too had ambition I told him that eventually I would like to make clothes for women and children and sell them in a small shop right here on The Rocks. 'There is a need for such a shop, and I would work hard to make it pay. I enjoy sewing, and have a gift for fashioning both pretty and practical garments out of scraps and fragments. I would enjoy serving the customers for people here are such open and friendly souls, even those who have troubled lives.'

Mr Frazier said he was sure I would do well in such a shop. He asked about my family and I told him how happy my parents had once been together, even though they had little money.

'Money is worth nothing without affection and constancy, Mary. Don't you agree?' he asked very seriously.

I said that I did. I told him more about my dear mother, brother and sisters, how Sarah had recovered from her illness, for which I thanked God, and how the village people were generous to our family after the day Constable Crimp found my mother sitting alone in the cottage with nothing to eat and not a stick of furniture left. I told him how pleased I was now to be able to send part of my wages home regularly, so that my brother Charley could finish school and be apprenticed to the village baker, and how I would love nothing more than to see them all again some day.

'It is not likely, I know, for even when I get my ticket of leave and am no longer a convict, the fare to return to England would cost more than I could save in a lifetime.' Mr Frazier was listening attentively, so I felt encouraged to continue and let him into a secret. 'I sometimes dream they all come here to settle, where the sun shines and there is enough food, work and land for everyone. When I suggest such things in my letters my mother thinks the sun has affected my brain! But she is relieved that I am not miserable living in Sydney Town. She just cannot understand *why* I am not.' I laughed out loud at this and Mr Frazier smiled and gave me a look of some affection.

Later I wondered about the 'constancy' in Mr Frazier's household. Millie and Bertha have each been here three years as assigned servants and Mrs Toomb has been Cook for decades. But there have been a lot of changes in the male servants since I took over as house-keeper. We have several newly assigned convicts who are troublesome and are suspected of stealing spirits from the warehouse. It is part of my job to catch them out.

My relationship with Millie has changed since I became Housekeeper. She is fond of Jeremiah, one of the troublesome new convicts, which makes it awkward for me. Yesterday I caught him hiding a bottle of brandy under his cloak as he stacked the shelves. I commanded him to open his cloak but he refused. I threatened to tell Mr Frazier if he did not put the bottle back immediately. He sneered, but did as I told him. Millie was watching and gave me such a look. She no longer gossips and criticises Mr Frazier when I am about, but turns to Bertha for her confidences. Nor does she ever invite me out to the Sheer Hulk or the Labour in Vain on a Saturday night to dance to the fiddle while she tries to get me drunk enough to accept the attentions of yet another young sailor with cash in his pocket. I am relieved in one way, but in another, I miss the confidences we shared.

About a year ago, to comfort myself and keep from being lonely I began to attend morning service at St Philip's Church every Sunday, just a short walk from the house. It was there that I made a new friend, Elizabeth Sibley.

Elizabeth is a woman I admire a great deal and yet feel sorry for. She is older than me, being thirty years of age, and has been living on the Rocks ever since she arrived here in 1813, transported for burglary. She is married to William Sibley, an ex-convict who is a mariner and property owner. They had a proper wedding in church and are not *de facto*, as husband and wife, as most convicts are. But they are not happy together.

A year ago Elizabeth lost her baby daughter, Sarah, aged just five weeks. Such a beautiful child. I was there at the baptism. Elizabeth was distraught. Since then she has had several miscarriages. Another child died about seven years ago, before they were wed. They have a son named Thomas, five years old, who is very dear to Elizabeth, but whenever she 'displeases' William, he threatens to send Thomas off to live at the Orphan School.

Elizabeth is a hard working, intelligent and generous woman, but after Sarah died she took to the rum. This makes her abusive and sometimes she is violent, smashing crockery and windows. She told me that William complains she has no respect for property and is without shame or remorse. But I can understand why she feels low sometimes. It is not just the loss of the babies. Last year she was granted a pardon for her crime, and now feels that as a free woman she deserves to own some of the property she has worked so hard for, but William will have none of it. 'He has his fancy women,' Elizabeth says, 'the trollops he meets at the wharf, to whom he gives presents. I don't ask for fine

bonnets and ribbons, just what is my due.' He calls
Elizabeth 'an emancipist', which is the worst insult he
can think of. I would think it was a title to be proud of,
myself.

Yesterday was a sad day for New South Wales because
Governor Macquarie and his wife sailed on the *Surrey*
for home. Crowds of people streamed down the hill
from The Rocks to King's Wharf to wave them goodbye. As I joined the throng I caught sight of Mr Frazier
striding just ahead of me. When he stopped to greet a
friend, I caught up with him. 'Ah, Mary, I'd like ye to
meet Mr Greenway, the Government Architect.
Francis this is Mary Jones, my Housekeeper and help-
mate.' He beamed at me as he said this. The Architect
gave an exaggerated bow. 'Delighted to make your
acquaintance, Miss Jones.'

'Mr Greenway designed our new hospital, Mary,
and most of those fine sandstone buildings in
Macquarie Street,' Mr Frazier explained.

'Alas, no more noble structures now that my patron
is leaving us,' sighed Mr Greenway. I thought he
seemed a little pompous and conceited for an ex-
convict.

'We are all very sorry to lose Governor Macquarie,
sir,' I said. 'It seems strange that he should be leaving us
when he's so popular.'

'He has no choice, young lady, no choice!' exclaimed
the Architect with passion. 'He's fought like a dog
against those skinflints in London to get the funds for
me to build churches, courthouses, barracks and a new

Government House. And now that wretch Bigge wants
to tear them all down!'

'Tear them down?' I asked in alarm. 'Surely not.'

'No, no, Mary. Mr Greenway does not mean it liter-
ally,' Mr Frazier said. 'He dislikes Bigge, that's all.'

'No more fine public buildings for this colony. No
more reforms. Keep the wretched convicts in their
place. Let 'em rattle their chains and suffer, says Bigge.'
Mr Greenway threw his arms about wildly as he spoke.

'Who is Bigge?' I asked Mr Frazier.

He lowered his voice. 'He's a Commissioner who
was sent here from London by the Colonial Office to
find fault with Governor Macquarie. He did his job
well.'

'Keep the convicts as slaves!' cried Mr Greenway.
'Let 'em work for the wool farmers like Macarthur who
will allow 'em no land of their own but keep 'em in
their place. Drive out the Governor who protects convicts and bring in one who'll crush them!'

'It's true, Mary,' sighed Mr Frazier. 'On Bigge's recommendation, Macquarie's budget has been cut to ribbons and he's been attacked until he's worn out. He's
been asking to resign for two years.'

'Who will be my protector now?' groaned Mr
Greenway.

'Come now, Francis. Bear up. We'll protect each
other. Isn't that so, Mary?' said my Master with a twin-
kle in his eye.

'Just look at the crowds rushing to the dock to wave
goodbye!' I exclaimed. 'Surely Governor Macquarie's
popularity must mean something to the Colonial
Office.'

'They don't give a damn what convicts want or think! They'll send some toady of the government in England, a flogger, a brute to replace that fine reformist Governor of ours.' Mr Greenway said this with such fury that I feared for the safety of the new Governor, whoever he might be.

As we reached the dock the crowds surged towards the vessel where Governor and Mrs Macquarie were waving from the deck. Mr Frazier and Mr Greenway bade me farewell, as they were to go on board and make their personal farewells. I thought it a sad day indeed for the Colony.

As the *Surrey* sailed out towards the Heads I walked slowly back up to The Rocks. I was pleased that it was Saturday and I could be alone that evening, for I was feeling melancholy and did not desire company.

I missed the friendship of Millie and our old friends at the Labour in Vain. I missed my mother, sisters and brother. And for all her wickedness, I missed Jane. I'd written six letters to her over the past two years but had heard not a word. Perhaps Mr Frazier was right and she had moved on long ago.

Saturday night is the time I balance the accounts in Mr Frazier's office. I enjoy sitting behind his leather-topped desk on his huge chair, working into the small hours. On Sunday I sleep in, having the luxury of being served breakfast in bed on a tray by Bertha (it would be too humiliating to expect Millie to do it, particularly when she often has a sore head after a long night out).

After church this morning I walk along Cumberland

Street with my friend Elizabeth Sibley towards Geranium Cottage, which is one of several she and her husband have built. This cottage is their home. She has told me it is her favourite. It has four rooms and a lot of land where more rooms could be built. Elizabeth has already purchased stone for such an extension and planted an orchard, which is flourishing because a little spring runs through it. There are stables and a well-kept kitchen garden. Geranium Cottage has one of the finest views of the harbour and Sydney Cove. As we walk we gaze down on the tall-masted ships at anchor and some native canoes being paddled slowly towards Cockle Bay. It is a peaceful setting. 'Geranium Cottage isn't a grand place but it has an air of contentment about it, don't you think?' Elizabeth asks me.

I nod and we smile and go inside. We sit in the back garden amongst the lavender and geraniums and Elizabeth makes a pot of tea and brings out pancakes she has heated on the stove, which we smother in honey and lemon juice.

'Where are William and Thomas?' I ask. I do not really want them here, it is so serene with just us and the bees buzzing and the smell of honey and lavender. 'William is at one of his committee meetings and Thomas is visiting the O'Haras, three houses away. They have a tribe of rowdy boys and stop him feeling lonely.' I nod with understanding, then say, 'I wish I had a child who loved his mother as Thomas loves you.'

'Even if he was the only one?'

'Even then.'

'You'll be a good mother some day, Mary.'

'I hope I can be as good as you.'

Elizabeth laughs. 'Tell that to William. He says that now I am emancipated I believe no punishment can be given me. I agree with him. I think my time as a dutiful wife is over.'

I frown and nod. I know William is a hard business-man. 'But he does value you as a wife, Elizabeth.'

'Not good enough! We've worked side by side these past eight years and now he is the owner of six fine cot-tages, all tenanted. But what do I own? Nought! Yet I am younger than he and have worked harder. What kind of law is it that is so unfair?'

I shake my head. 'It does seem wrong but it is the law, Elizabeth. If you rant against it or provoke Wil-liam by getting drunk and breaking up his property, he might petition the Governor to have you sent away to the Female Factory. Do be careful!'

To my dismay she suddenly cries, 'It's too late, Mary. He has already sent the petition. I expect any day to be carted off to that infernal place!' She turns away to hide her eyes which are filled with tears. 'And there is worse news. I didn't want to tell you because we have been so happy sitting here after church with our tea. William has advertised Geranium Cottage for sale! My beloved little house where I had such fond dreams of a big family. And while I'm away in the prison he'll send Thomas to the Orphan School. Oh, I'm so angry I could scream.'

I put my arms around my friend and hold her while she sobs.

'Never marry anyone, Mary. Never let them own you. Just work for yourself, become rich and produce bastards.'

# CHAPTER 18

## I Have a Joyful Secret Which I Can Scarcely Keep
## The Rocks, December, 1823

I have such happy news that I am bursting to tell everyone, to march along King's Wharf stopping seamen and their women to tell them, to walk by the quarry and tell the stonecutters, even to visit the sad-faced natives in their camp at Millers Point and let them know my good news.

But first I must go back a year and describe how my happiness came about.

Mr Andrew Frazier and I had been sharing confidences for many weeks and he seemed to want me near him more than was usual for a Housekeeper and her master. We would dine together in the parlour every evening and afterwards I'd read to him the books of Sir Walter Scott, of which he had several.

'I must confess to you, Mary, I am fonder of Scott than of your Mr Coleridge and Mr Wordsworth,' he said one evening.

I smiled at this. 'Then why did you allow me to read

you the whole of their *Lyrical Ballads* when you were ill?'

'I did not want to frighten you away.'

We began with Sir Walter's *The Lady of the Lake* which tells stories in verse about the battles between the Highlands and the Lowlands. But Mr Frazier could tell that these battles were tedious to me and suggested we move on to two novels called *Kenilworth* and *Ivanhoe*. These I enjoyed for they were full of romance and painted pictures of Scottish scenery so real that I could imagine the glens Mr Frazier told me he had roamed as a boy. The novels were humorous too, and I felt that by reading them together, and laughing in the same places, we were growing closer. Mr Frazier said that of course he could have read these books for himself, but his eyesight was not as good as it had been and he liked to hear my voice.

Often we would sit by the fire together talking late into the night and he would sigh when it was time to go to our separate rooms, and say that he had never felt such peace with anyone as he felt with me. One night he took my hand as we sat by the dying embers and asked in a hoarse whisper whether I would consent to be his … He hesitated, for he did not know how to put it.

I hoped above hope that he might be going to ask me to be his wife. But there are so few couples properly wed amongst the convicts in Sydney Cove. It is not the way of things. So when he whispered the word 'lover' I melted at the sound of it and comforted myself that this might be the first step on the way to holy matrimony. And to be honest I did desire him.

I looked at him, so shy and afraid of being turned down, and said, 'I would be honoured, Mr Frazier,' just as I had when he offered me the position of House-keeper. He smiled at me then, and laughed a little with relief and also because of the quaint way I had accepted. He told me that I was a fine looking young woman whom he admired and that he was a fortunate man indeed. I had never been called such things before and blushed at the compliment. He said that he had hesitated to ask me because he felt sure that I would prefer a younger man. I replied that I had been fond of him for a long time and there was no man I would prefer to him, young or old. He kissed me then and I saw that he had tears in his eyes.

We have been as happy as a newly married couple ever since. Andrew wanted to buy me a present but I protested that I did not need one as he was all I wanted. He went out and found an embroidered Cashmere shawl from India. I was so touched. When I wear it to church on Sundays and walk through the streets, people turn to look. It is too fine for me, I know. It should adorn some lady's shoulders, but because it was given to me by my lover I wear it often.

Andrew does not go to church with me, nor does he accompany me on walks. He has so much business to attend to, even on Sundays. Sometimes I think I would like nothing better than to walk arm-in-arm with him along the quay, alongside all the other couples prome-nading on Sunday afternoons in their finery, nodding to each other and smiling at the sparkling sea. But Andrew is a very private man and our evenings together are what he enjoys most.

It is no secret that we are a couple. I am known in the market place and all around The Rocks as Mr Frazier's common-law wife, and treated with respect. I would love nothing better than to be properly wed at St Philip's, but the subject has never come up between us. Andrew is content to have things as they are. In my letters I have not told my mother about my new situation as I know she would disapprove. She would not understand that customs are different on this side of the world.

Ah, but — here is my gladdest news — my dear Andrew is to be a father. And when I tell him I feel sure he will agree that our child should have the dignity of parents properly wed.

Elizabeth Sibley is the only person I have told about the child. She has advised me not to tell anyone else yet. It is well known on The Rocks that Mr Frazier has no love of children and has never allowed one into his house. However, I feel sure that once he hears he is to have one of his own, he will soften and change his opinion. Indeed, I think it will be a great joy to him in his old age to have a son or daughter. He has much property, and no one to pass it to.

Over the months we have spent happily in each other's company, Andrew has told me things about himself that few people know. He gives away much of his money to benevolent and religious institutions — the Bible Society, the Catholic chapel, the Scots church, the Sydney Dispensary and the Waterloo Relief Fund, to name but a few. Ten years ago, together with other emancipists who had made money since they were granted their freedom, he helped to fund a road to Botany Bay, a proper one of earth and stones. So he is keen to help this new colony and holds no grudges against those who brought him here in chains. He also sends money for charity back to Montrose, in Scotland, where he was born.

I have discovered that the Governors of this land have been served well by Andrew Frazier, too. Some years ago he purchased a hotel here on The Rocks which he named for Governor King, and just a twelve-month since he had the privilege of being part of the small group who welcomed Governor Macquarie on his return from Van Diemen's Land, and signed the address of welcome. Of course, he was often at Government House when Macquarie was Governor.

My dear Andrew wrote a memorial for me which he sent to the new Governor, Sir Thomas Brisbane (he is a Scot, which pleases Andrew), in which he recommended me highly and begged a ticket of leave for me, so that I could start my own small business, sewing and selling clothing here on The Rocks. The Governor looked on it favourably and I am now free to commence just as soon as I have saved enough money. Renting a shop is an expensive business and I still send a large portion of my earnings home to my mother, so I have a lot more to save before I become a woman of business. In any case, I no longer feel it is such an attractive idea, as I am much needed as Andrew's Housekeeper and his true love as well, not to mention becoming the future mother of his child.

Andrew is part of what I have heard called the middle class of society. He is said to be one of the wealthiest men in the colony and yet he lives simply, wearing well-made clothes but owning few, and more often eating at home with me than dining out. He drinks no alcohol, although he imports the finest Jamaica rum, French brandy, gin, whisky and Madeira wine. His carriage is a modest one. The presents he gives to me, apart from the shawl, have not been lavish. Sometimes I receive some imported English soap, Berkeley cheese or pearl barley for myself, but these I share with Elizabeth Sibley.

Last year poor Elizabeth spent a month in the Female Factory, where her husband sent her for 'misbehaviour'. When she came out she was most subdued. But because she ran off and stayed the night with a married couple nearby after an argument with him, William Sibley humiliated her further by putting a public notice in the *Sydney Gazette*. It read:

> I, the undersigned, do hereby caution all Persons from giving Trust or Credit to my Wife, Elizabeth Sibley, on my Account, she having left her home without just cause or provocation:- And I further caution all Persons from harbouring or concealing her, on pain of prosecution for the offence.
> William Sibley.

Anyone reading this would readily think Elizabeth a most disreputable woman, and sympathise with her husband. But it is an unfair description of the situation. I have observed the real events. It is true that Elizabeth sometimes drinks to relieve her sadness about her dead children and William's refusal to give her a share in the property, which I believe she rightly deserves. I try to comfort her so that she will not drink, but when she has a mind to it, she will not stop. I have seen her smash crockery, always her best platters, so it is she who suffers most, not William. She smashed three small windows in Geranium Cottage, which was her favourite, when her husband found a buyer for it. But I would not call that violent compared to what goes on regularly on The Rocks every night! Most times Elizabeth is a peaceful soul. She has not resorted to strong liquor for sometime now.

So when she warns me not to tell Andrew our happy news until I can hide my situation no longer, I take notice. I am only three months pregnant, which is not yet noticeable, so I have plenty of time to prepare him.

Friends on The Rocks tell me I am looking very pretty these days and it is hard not to burst into joyful laughter and tell them my secret.

Elizabeth and I went to the markets together yesterday but there was a public flogging so we hurried away. I felt quite ill at the sight of the lash on bare skin. She said it was the babe in my womb objecting to violence and predicted that it would be a girl, and a soft-hearted one at that.

Elizabeth is a stout woman and I had not noticed her own condition. She broke the news to me that day that she herself is six months pregnant! I was delighted for her. Our babies will be born within three months of each other and can grow up together as close friends. They will be true currency lasses or lads, free-born citizens in this colony, not transported to it against their wills. She is hoping that the birth of this child will please William as much as herself. Their marriage has improved since she stopped her drinking and he no longer pursues those saucy baggages who ply their wares along the quay after dark.

Elizabeth says she will introduce me to the midwife when my time is closer. I shall be able to visit her with Elizabeth and then the gossips will not ask, 'Why are *you* calling on the midwife, Mary?'

# CHAPTER 19

**I Receive a Great Shock**
**Sydney, March, 1823**

Elizabeth's baby boy was born March 1st and he is well! They have named him William Elias and his father is besotted with him. Young Thomas was allowed home from the Orphan School, where he has been boarding these past four months, so they were a family again. They plan to extend Myrtle Cottage, which Elizabeth has already made almost as pretty as Geranium Cottage, and for the time being at least she has forgiven her husband for not sharing the profits of the other cottages he rents.

Last night I walked up the hill to visit them and to bring a bonnet and shawl I had knitted for young William. They were all together in the front parlour, William and Elizabeth side by side on the sofa, young Thomas on his mother's knee, and baby William in his cradle being gently rocked by his father. I thought the Sibleys quite the happiest family on The Rocks.

This scene of domestic harmony gave me courage

and I hurried home to Andrew determined to tell him *our* good news. I am now six months' pregnant and amazed he has not noticed, in spite of my white lies about eating too much bread from the bakery. That evening he was busy checking lists of the latest goods arrived from London. 'Tea, sugar, oatmeal, split peas …' he said aloud, then turned towards me. 'Ah, my love, here ye are at last.' He held out one arm to me, bidding me sit down beside him, and pushed the list away. 'How is the new young Master Sibley?'

'He is beautiful! Oh Andrew, you must go and see for yourself.'

He shook his head. 'I'll leave the baby watching to you.' He frowned then and my heart thudded in fright, but I decided to rush on. 'Andrew, I have something to tell you. Good news.'

He looked at my face and his good humour crept back. 'What is it? Whatever makes ye look so radiant must be something worthwhile.'

'Guess! Can you guess?'

'Sir Walter Scott has written a new book.'

'No! But I wish he would. We've read *Ivanhoe* three times.' I moved close to him and put his hand on my stomach, where it was fullest. '*Guess*,' I whispered.

He did not move for about five seconds but stared straight ahead. Then he sprang up, flinging his hand away from me as though I had stung him like a scorpion.

'No!' He turned on me angrily.

I had never seen him like this — white with rage, and remembered the story of the convict named Jex, who had been horse-whipped out of the house. 'Ye've deceived me, Mary.' He spoke in a frightening low voice.

I shook my head. 'I thought you would be pleased! A child of our own to bring you happiness.'

'Well, I am not pleased. Ye have broken the most important rule of my house. Deliberately!'

'But surely rules do not apply to your own children!'

'I will have *no* children!' He shook his fist at me and I cowered away from him, fearing he would strike me. Here was a creature I did not know.

'But why, Andrew? Why?' I asked in despair.

'I have my reasons and they are nothing to do with ye,' he muttered darkly. 'Now get out of here.'

I stared at him in disbelief. 'What? Leave you?'

'Yes, at once. Leave my house.'

'But where shall I go?'

'I neither know nor care. I do not wish to see your face again, Mary Jones. Ye have deceived me. Tricked me, when I trusted ye. Ye're despicable. I thought ye were a better woman.'

'Please Andrew, don't send me away! It is *our* baby soon to be born.'

He glowered down at me and said, full of venom. 'How do I know that?'

I stared back in shock. 'Because you are my lover, my only lover in all the world.'

'Why should I believe ye? I've been tricked by a woman once before.'

I put my arms out towards him. 'Please, Andrew, I am not like that. You know I am not. Let me stay for the child's sake. I ask nothing for myself. No marriage. No money.'

He turned his back on me and said harshly, 'Go to the Female Factory! Go tonight. And have the child adopted. If ye dare tell a soul that I am the father, I will come after ye and destroy ye both.'

# IV
## The Female Factory

# CHAPTER 20

**My Daughter is Born and She is Perfect**
**The Rocks, June, 1824**

The greatest joy in my life at this time is my daughter, Harriet Jane.

On the night that Andrew Frazier threw me out of his house I could not bear to go straight to the Factory so I walked a mile to the cottage of the midwife, Mrs Figgins, who had become a friend since I began visiting her. She is a widow with no children left at home. I asked if I might lodge with her for a while. She kindly agreed, and when she heard that I had lost my position at Mr Frazier's because of a quarrel and had no possessions except a few clothes and books and a small amount of money, she asked why I did not go to the unborn child's father for help. Although I was distraught I told her I could not say who the father was. I think, from my tears, she may have guessed the truth but she did not push me further.

And so I stayed with Mrs Figgins, taking over the cooking and cleaning in her house, until my time drew near. I did not dare go out, even to the market, in case I should be seen and reported to Mr Frazier, who had ordered me straight to the Factory. I did not want my poor child to be born in a prison.

I managed to send a message to Elizabeth Sibley, telling her of my plight, and within a few days she came to visit me. She was most sympathetic and brought me baby clothes, a crib, and some money as well. She was furious at Frazier and said she had a mind to confront him, accusing him of cruelty, but I begged her not to, as then he might carry out his threat to come after me and the child and destroy us.

'What kind of a man is it, one of the wealthiest in town and respected by Governors, who will fling his common-law wife and unborn child out onto the street? His mind must be twisted. He will live to regret this folly, Mary, mark my words.'

I shook my head. 'He has been deceived by a woman in the past and is still bitter about it, I believe. Do you know anything about such a woman, Elizabeth?'

'William and I have lived close to Andrew Frazier on The Rocks for eight years and never heard a word of it,' she replied. At this I began to weep afresh. 'There, there Mary. Do not blame yourself. He is not right in his head.'

'If you could have seen the way he looked at me, Elizabeth, as if I were a slut,' I sobbed. 'He made me feel so ashamed and foolish.'

'You must not feel either. The loss is his, the cranky old moralist. What a hypocrite to give money away to "worthy causes" and turn his back on his own wife and baby! I've a mind to put a notice in the *Sydney Gazette* stating that he is a jilt and a miser!'

'No, no, that would ruin his reputation and he would think I had put you up to it,' I protested.

'I would phrase it cleverly and leave it unsigned.'

'Please do not even think of such a thing,' I begged.

Elizabeth shrugged and said he well deserved to lose his precious reputation and she would think of a plan of revenge. She can be dangerous when she is roused.

She came again a few weeks later when I was very large with child, but this time she looked miserable, haggard and had dark circles under her eyes.

'What is it my dearest friend? Are you ill?'

'I have not slept this past week. William Elias is ill, Mary. He hardly suckles and is growing weaker. The doctor is afraid we may lose him.' She began to cry. 'Why, oh why? I cannot bear it. Not another darling child!'

I held her in my arms and prayed to God to save young William.

Harriet Jane was born on June 30th and William Elias died on July 3rd. He had been baptised at St Philip's a few days before.

How I wished to visit poor Elizabeth! But Mrs Figgins forbade me to leave my bed, for I was weak as well as not wanting to be recognised by anyone on The Rocks. I knew that as soon as I was well enough I must go to the Female Factory, take my beautiful child in my arms and ride on the ferry to Parramatta, where I had been told I would be allowed to keep Harriet with me for as long as she suckled. She was already doing so with great enthusiasm. Most mothers believe their child is more beautiful than any other, but in Harriet's case it was true! She had a mouth like a rosebud, a finely shaped nose and eyes as blue as the harbour. Her hair was nought but some tufts of red curl at the back. Her tiny hands waved like sea anemones. She had shell-pink fingernails and she did not cry, but gurgled as if the whole world delighted her.

I had no intention of having Harriet adopted. I would find a position where a baby was welcome, and until that position became available I vowed I would remain at the Female Factory, keeping my child at my side.

Elizabeth came to see me again a few weeks later. Such a change in a woman I have never seen. Her grief had made her age ten years. She shuffled, instead of skipping along as had been her manner. Her face was shrivelled, her eyes red with crying. I let her hold my darling Harriet as long as she wanted and only when the child began to nuzzle for food at her bosom and Elizabeth made as if to feed her — for she still had milk — did I gently take her away and put her on my own breast.

Elizabeth stared at me then and said in a strange voice, 'You could give her to me, Mary. Then Andrew Frazier would forgive you. You could return to your old home instead of taking this innocent child to live in a prison. And you could see her at my house every day.'

I shook my head. 'No, Elizabeth. I could not do it.'

'But no one need know she is your child! I will say I have adopted an orphan to replace my poor dead William. Of course! It is what should be done!' And she leant across to take Harriet out of my arms.

'No! No!' I cried, for she was determined and half-mad with her grief. 'I am sorry but I could not do it!'

'Selfish woman! You care more for your own needs than your poor child's future. Do you know how many babies die in the Female Factory? Almost all! You will not be allowed to care for her yourself. She'll be given to some drunken slut in the nursery with twenty others to feed and if she is asleep when the dribble of milk comes round they'll miss her out and let her scream for hours before the next feed is due. She'll be piled in a heap like a puppy in a basket with all the other squallers, and if she doesn't die of starvation she'll catch the scarlet fever or the smallpox from one of them and die of that. I have been there and seen what happens.'

I covered my ears. 'I don't want to hear!'

'Instead of her dying, let her be my child. She will want for nothing, Mary. And you will be able to visit her whenever you like. I will tell her you're a cousin.'

I shook my head vehemently. 'Please, Elizabeth. Go home now and rest. I am deeply sorry for your loss. I will pray for you.'

'And a fat lot of good that will do!' She stormed off towards her home and I knew that she would get very drunk that night, and curse me as she hurled her best teacups at the walls.

I decided to leave for Paramatta the very next day.

# CHAPTER 21

## Harriet and I Become Inmates of the Female Factory
## May, 1825

Harriet Jane was born under the saddest of circumstances but now she is thriving, although we remain as prisoners at the Female Factory. Eleven months have gone by since I was ushered inside the high sandstone walls, carrying my bundle of clothes, books and Harriet wrapped in a shawl. I shuddered. It was not the cold, but the sadness of the place.

'Where is the Constable who escorted you here?' demanded the matron.

'I came alone, ma'am.'

'What have you done with the Constable, saucy wench?'

'There was no Constable, ma'am. I escorted myself.'

She drew back and blinked her small eyes as if I had played a new trick on her and she would soon get to the bottom of it. 'No Constable? Escorted yourself? What sort of convicts are they sending me these days? Give me the name of your vessel.'

'Please, Ma'am, I did not come directly from a vessel but have been assigned to Mr Andrew Frazier of Cambridge Street on The Rocks these past three years.' I said this with some pride.

'So he has sent you back because you are unsatisfactory?' she snapped.

'That is so.'

'He sent no letter to explain the details of your misconduct?'

'No, Ma'am.'

'Then we will just have to let time reveal the nasty side of your nature, won't we?' she said unpleasantly. 'What are your skills?'

'My skills, Ma'am?'

She scowled into the shawl at sleeping Harriet. 'Apart from lying on your back with your legs in the air. Can you cook? Sew? Launder? Make butter and cheese?'

'I can do all but make butter and cheese, for I was never a dairymaid. In England I was a maidservant in a large country house and was recently Housekeeper for Mr Frazier. I can make clothes and embroider well. Oh, and I can read and write.'

'Then you may be more useful than you look. I will put you amongst the first-class prisoners. If you disobey one rule, talk back or loiter, you will be demoted to second-class. Next to third, where you'll break stone all day in the hot sun, receive starvation rations and be beaten up by the sluts who work beside you.'

I nodded. 'Please, Matron, I would like to keep my

little girl with me as I work. She is very healthy and well behaved, as you see, and she is still being suckled so needs me close by.'

'What, and have you sitting down to feed her every half hour?' laughed the Matron. 'Not likely. She'll go to the nursery with the other babes that are more than three months old.'

'She is not yet six weeks, Ma'am. She is healthy and well grown. I do not mind her going to the nursery as long as I can be the one to look after all the babies.'

'So, you put conditions on your work, proud miss?' She squinted her eyes at me and seemed to be deciding whether to punish me at once or use my determination to her own advantage. 'The nursery is already staffed. But you say you can embroider. Do you have an example of your work to show me?'

I hastily drew back Harriet's shawl and showed her the fine needlework at the edges, then the embroidery on the front of her gown.

'You did this?'

'I did, ma'am.'

'Good. If you can produce work as fine as that and in quick smart time — for I have customers lined up for this kind of thing — then you may keep the baby with you and be paid a little as well. But if she howls or sickens or distracts you from your work in any way, into the nursery she goes. Do you understand?'

'Thank you, ma'am.'

That first night in the Female Factory I wondered what madness had made me come. Could I not have prevailed on the kind midwife to let me stay a little longer in her house? Or wandered the streets of The Rocks, in breach of my reassignment agreement, begging friends to take me in and hide me? Why had I been so foolish as to bear a child out of wedlock in the first place? Did I think I was beyond reproof? I prayed that God would not punish me by making me watch my innocent baby perish in a prison.

The first- and second-class prisoners slept in hammocks slung so close together that we could feel each other's breathing, smell each other's odours and hear every word spoken. And such words! I had travelled across the seas on a vessel full of convicts and heard bad language, but this was something different. The curses these wretched women yelled at each other! Elizabeth had never spoken about what went on at the Factory and now I knew why.

The worst thing was the neglect of the babies. Those who were very young, under three months, were allowed to be with their mothers. But did their mothers care for them? They did not pick them up when they cried, nor feed them, nor rock them. I have seen sows treat their piglets with more tenderness. This did not help the atmosphere in the closely packed dormitory.

'Shut that screaming bastard up or I'll come and throttle it!' yelled a large woman near me. The baby was only grizzling, not screaming, but after such a threat it seemed to take fright, and began to wail. The mother, a girl who could not have been more than fifteen, rolled over in her messy bed and yelled, 'Do whatcha like to it! Then you'll be a murderess as well as a harlot.'

To my horror the large woman rolled out of her hammock and marched towards the girl and her baby. But she didn't touch the child, just slapped the girl hard on the face. 'Put ya tit in its mouth!'

'Fuckin' cunt!' the girl yelled back. But she shoved her nipple roughly in the baby's mouth and soon it was quiet.

I kept Harriet very close to me that first night.

Next morning we were woken at dawn by a loud, clanging bell. Harriet took fright and began to cry. Quickly I held her to my breast. 'That's the way. Shut it up afore I eats it!' said the large woman. But she smiled at me as if she didn't really mean it. I smiled back anxiously and she asked my name and how I'd come to be at the Factory. I told her I was Mary Jones, who'd worked as a Housekeeper, but that I had quarrelled with my Master and been sent here to be reassigned.

'I'm Belle Marsh, business woman, arrested for hawking my wares after dark in a public place.' She took a clay pipe from under her petticoat and began sucking on it.

'What manner of goods do you sell, Belle?' I asked, trying to be friendly.

'Meself, my dear. What better goods?' And she threw back her head and laughed loudly. 'Trouble was, the Constable as arrested me wanted some for himself free of charge and I wouldn't oblige.'

I shook my head. 'That was corrupt of him.'

'Corrupt? Aye it was. And a fine word that is. Corrupt. I'll use it to describe the next constable as tries to arrest me.'

'So you will go back to your ... employment when you get out of here, Belle?' I asked in surprise.

'What else can I do to earn a living, dearie? It's me profession.' She said this with pride and a touch of resentment.

'I'm sorry. I didn't meant to sound ... disapproving.'

'I like them big words of yours, Mary. Whatcha do? Swallow a big book full of 'em?' She laughed some more. 'Now, what class are ye in? First, I bet.'

I nodded.

'Well, I'm in second. See me lovely yellow "C" on me sleeve? That means convict. If I was in third-class I'd have a big yellow "C" on me backside, which'd be worse. Ah, we wear a lovely uniform here. D'you like it?' She heaved a coarse cloth garment over her head. 'Paramatta cloth, they call it. All made here on the premises by us ladies ourselves. Ever see such fine gowns, Mary?'

I smiled and said that I never had.

'Youse in first class, you get to wear a better cloth. And eat more food. Beef on Sundays along with the prayers. And Bible readings every day. We all get that. You like the Bible, Mary?'

'I do, Belle, but I must admit there are other books I like more.'

'Oooh, a blasphemer. Did you hear that, Sal? The Reverend Marsden and Lady Darling will not be pleased to hear you say that.'

'Nor they will, Belle, but if Mary is nice to us, we won't tell them.'

Sally was the young girl with the baby. I was surprised to see her so cordial towards Belle after last night's violence.

As we went down the cold stone steps to breakfast and looked over the railing into the courtyard we could see a new prisoner arriving. I recognised her as Margaret Keeving, a resident of The Rocks. She had a pock-pitted face and had lost a good many teeth. She often used to drink at the Sheer Hulk.

Belle knew her too and waved and yelled out, 'Eh there, Margaret! Back for a spell with your old friends?' The Constable escorting her into the yard nudged her back to keep her moving towards the third-class section.

'Margaret's a regular at the Factory,' Belle told me. 'Last time she was arrested for using abusive language in a public place she fought so hard they took her off in a wheelbarrow!'

We sat at wooden benches at a long table. Each of us had a bowl of gruel, but only the first-class were allowed tea and sugar. I thought this most unfair and offered half of my tea to Belle. This caused an immediate outcry. Women all around me stretched their arms in my direction demanding tea as well. There wasn't enough and my mug was spilt in the commotion.

Suddenly there was dead silence. Matron and a slender lady in black walked to the front of the room. The lady opened a Bible and began to read. No one spoke another word, but the slurpings as the women ate their gruel grew louder and louder until the lady's voice could barely be heard. When the reading was finished Matron scowled horribly at us to show she was well aware what we were up to. But the lady seemed to notice nothing. Perhaps she thought all convicts ate like that.

The other women were ushered off to do their chores — washing clothes, weaving and sewing the coarse Parramatta cloth. I was about to follow them when Matron walked up to me and took me by the arm. 'Now you come with me, proud miss, and let's see if you're bluffing about what you can do with a needle and thread.'

Carrying Harriet in my arms I followed her to a small dark room near the office which seemed to be used as a storeroom. Inside was a hard chair and a mass of white cloth. 'I want fine shirts for gentlemen, dresses for ladies, nightgowns, baby clothes, all the best quality mind. And mind you don't get a speck of dirt on this pure white stuff.'

'How many of each do you want, Ma'am?'

'As many as you can make in a day. I have orders for dozens. There'll be more to make every day until you leave this place — which could be years if you disappoint me!'

'Slavery,' I said under my breath.

'What's that you say?' she snapped, coming so close that I smelt the onions and bacon she'd had for breakfast and the sour smell of unwashed flesh.

'Nothing, Ma'am. I was wondering whether I might work with a light. It is so dark in here.'

'John!' she bellowed. 'Fetch a candle for her ladyship.'

A surly fellow came to the door. I had heard from my fellow prisoners that he was her son, that he was a lecher and that he also stole provisions from the prison-

ers so that those in third-class in particular were close
to starving.

'If I were to leave the door open there would be
some light,' I suggested. 'Candlelight in daytime is
surely a waste, Ma'am.'

'Now it's a lecture on economy I'm getting, is it?
Leave the candle, John. Her ladyship will work by
God's sunlight. But don't let me see you leave that chair
till sundown, mind, or there'll be hell to pay. There's a
bucket in the corner for your bodily needs and John
will serve your bread and soup for luncheon his personal self, won't you, John?'

She winked at him and he gave me such a leer that I
held Harriet close to me for comfort and stared back at
him as coldly as I could.

# CHAPTER 22

**My First Visitor in Prison and a Letter at Last**
**June, 1825**

Today I received a visitor. My old friend Millie, who still works for Andrew Frazier, had come all the way by ferry down the Paramatta River on her day off with a letter for me. When she drew it from her bosom, I hugged her for her kindness. She told me she was soon to be wed to a blacksmith named Armstrong who had his ticket of leave. 'Ye'll not be surprised to hear that I'll be leaving Mr Frazier's house with no regrets, Mary.' While she cooed over baby Harriet she told me how sorry all the servants were that he had treated me so harshly. 'He's a cranky, moralistic old Scot with a bee in his bonnet about no babies in the house. He got burned once by some lass he fancied who tried to blackmail him, so Mrs Toomb says.'

Millie had brought me a jar of the apricot jam she knew I loved and a freshly baked loaf, and when I saw them, my eyes filled with tears. So great was my gratitude for these gifts and the letter that I read it aloud to

Millie while she played on the floor with Harriet. It was a very long letter.

> Chester Gaol, England, January, 1825
>
> Dear Mary
>
> Well, my friend, sitting here in Chester, I thought of writing to your Mother to see if she had heard from you lately. I have a fond memory of her reading a poem to us in her little cottage. I wrote to her using my new name, but did not tell her how I had come by it. To my surprise she sent a prompt reply. She said she was pleased to hear from me and that the family was well, even Sarah's health was improved. Sadly she could not say the same for you, who have quarrelled with your Master and been sent to a place named the Female Factory, taking your poor babe with you. She wrote: 'The Child, Harriet Jane, named after myself and you, is very dear to Mary. She does not say who the Father is.' She begged me to write to you to help lift your spirits.
>
> I am sorry for your unfortunate Situation, Mary. How could you allow yourself to fall so low? I pity you. I do not mind that you have named your Child after me, even though she will grow up Fatherless and no doubt suffer for it. But you must be miserable enough without my harsh words. Almost as miserable as I am.
>
> My life in London took a turn for the worse. Bad Luck is all it was. I deserve better after all I have suffered. I could have married, there have been plenty of offers. But I was never Desperate enough to accept Proposals even from Clerks (the handsome young Clerk who is writing this letter for me is most obliging). I still have Ambitions, in spite of everything. My looks are still

with me, although I grew pale and thin living in London. Country air is good for the complexion and there was always plenty to eat at Elmtree House, which now seems to belong to another Lifetime.

The London lodging I had last was very poor. I shared one room with three Sisters and their Brother who all work in the markets at Covent Garden. My fashionable Pelisse wore out. When Winter set in I did not know what I should do. Perhaps become a Whore, like the girl who had my bed before me. She drowned in the Thames. Oh Mary, I have had such sad Misadventures. I was persuaded to work as a Coquette with some Rascals who used to rob the tipsy Gentlemen I would lure into an alley at Covent Garden. One Gentleman was stronger and taller than any of the others I met. But he was very drunk, so I had no fear of getting away from him once my part was played. Alas, that night my Rascals did not show up to carry out their part of the Business. In spite of my struggles the Gentleman overpowered me. I shouted for help but no one came. It was a pitch-black night. He knocked me to the cobblestones and I could not fight him off. He took me by force and afterwards ripped open my Bodice and stole all the Money I had earned that night.

My cuts and bruises took a long time to heal. Oh Mary, I have not lost my terror of strong, dark men since that Dreadful Event. I prefer fair, slightly built men like my Obliging Clerk who writes this letter.

There seemed to have been a pause in the letter writing here. The letter continued on a second sheet of paper. Millie was absorbed by the words I read out, and even little Harriet seemed to enjoy the sound of my voice.

*I will continue my Unlucky Story. I found employment as a Hospital Nurse. The work was Demeaning — scouring chamber pots, scrubbing floors, bathing decayed bodies. I gave notice after a few weeks. I should have done so sooner. Too late, I realised I had caught Typhoid Fever from one of the patients. I was allowed to remain in the Hospital. Otherwise I would have died. When Summer came I was considered well enough to leave. I used to walk in some gardens nearby where I watched small Children playing while their Nursemaids ran after them to make sure they were warm enough, with their mittens tied on and woolly caps pulled down to their rosy-cheeked faces. It made me wonder how it must be to grow up coddled like that, with Servants paid to keep you warm and safe, well fed and well educated. No wonder Gentlefolk consider the world an easy place to live and believe they have the right to do as they please. How can it be that we, as their Servants, may be given a walloping with the broom handle or be allowed no time to eat? In one mansion where I worked I was lucky if I could run a piece of bread around the gravy at the bottom of the pan. Only the Upper Servants were given proper meals and beds. I slept beneath a thin blanket on a bench in the Scullery. Surely the Workhouse could not be worse.*

At this point the Clerk seems to have mended the nib of his quill, for the letter continued without the splattering of ink that occurred before. I went on reading:

*I now thought I might as well visit my Mother and her Family, and bought a coach ticket to Leeds. I had used my wits and been able to find some Money. I had forgot what a miserable place her cottage was, nought but wattle and daub set on a bare patch of ground. Even your Mother's cottage is better, Mary. My Mother was still with the useless Man she was living with when I left home two years ago, surrounded by their pack of brats. Only the oldest Boy and Girl, Will and Bridget, are my proper Brother and Sister. The other four are Stepbrothers and sisters I do not need to own. They are a poor looking lot with no wits between them. Soon they are to be sent out to work in one of the Cotton Mills.*

*When my Mother opened the door, blinking in the light, she looked quite old, with only three of her teeth remaining. When she threw her arms around my neck I recoiled, 'Ah, Maria, they said you had forgotten us, but I knew you never had!' she cried. 'It's our Maria come home from London!' she called out to the Children who were huddled around the hearth. The air was thick with smoke from the fire of dried dung. The sick, unwashed, flea-bitten little ones rubbed themselves against my fine cloak and gown. The smallest Boy, who was a mere babe when I left, cheekily held out his hand. 'What did you bring us t' eat?' he whined.*

*'Aye, what did ye bring from London Town for these half-starved little ones?' my sister Bridget demanded sharply. She is fourteen now and pretty beneath the grime on her face. Will is thirteen, but looks like a child of eight. He already works in the Cotton Mill, but that day he was home because of his troublesome Cough. They were all disappointed because I had brought no*

*presents. It was not enough that I had taken the trouble to travel all this way to see them! Fortunately my Stepfather was out. I took Bridget aside and spoke to her about him, telling her how he used to Molest me. She said she knew all about that and could take care of herself, no thanks to me. She had some spirit, I was pleased to see. I told her she could make her fortune in London. 'Get yourself a new life!' I urged her. 'Get away from all this.'*

*I was not pleased with her impertinent answer. 'What' she exclaimed. 'And leave these poor babies to starve? I am not so heartless as you.'*

*'If that is what you think then I will leave this minute.' I cried. 'Yes, leave now. Good riddance!' shouted my Sister. My Mother ran after me as I went out of the door. 'Oh Maria, we are worried sick about the children, what is starving, as you see,' she said pitifully. I handed her my Purse, full of the Money I had found. 'There, take my savings, and leave me be,' I cried. 'Bless you Maria! Bless you daughter! I always knew you was kind.' And then, Mary, I received all your letters at the same time! Mother had kept them all in case I should ever come back, and now she thrust them into my hands. I made my Departure, very thankfully as I must confess.*

The letter now continued on a third sheet, with the lines crossed over each to save paper, so that I had to turn it this way and that and it was more difficult to read. It seemed to be written in a different hand as well. Millie mimed to me that Harriet seemed to be falling asleep. Perhaps my reading sounded like a lullaby!

*A new Clerk has kindly agreed to take down my Letter,
for the former one has been told he is not allowed to visit
me any more. He bade me a sad goodbye and has sent
his fellow Clerk to me in his stead, who frowned when
he saw how much had been writ, and says we must not
use so much paper.*

*I now managed to find a position as Housemaid at a
big house outside Leeds, close to the moors. It is a cold,
windswept place. The work was irksome and the wages
poor, but I was given plenty to eat, and the fresh air, of
which there was plenty too, soon made my cheeks rosy
again. I decided to stay at Crag House until I had saved
enough to set off in search of a more exciting life. I heard
that the garrison city of Chester, near Wales, is full of
handsome military Officers just waiting to find pretty
brides. I was now over twenty years old and in danger of
becoming an Old Maid. If I could not get a Gentleman
then a well-paid Guardsman would have to do.*

*Well, as soon as I had enough saved I gave my notice
to my Master and received a most satisfactory reference
from him. What I did next was not wise — Oh, Mary,
how I now regret my foolishness. On the day of my departure the Mistress was away from home and on an
impulse I decided to take her new pelisse. It was fashionable enough, and its colour, Peacock-blue, looked
well with my dark hair and green eyes. So I concealed it
in my valise and went off in the coach to Chester. I had
not bargained for the jealous parlour maid, to whom I
had disclosed my destination. The Mistress returned the
next day, discovered her Pelisse had been taken, and the
parlour maid told her I had come to Chester. I had not
been settled in a lodging opposite the army barracks*

*more than two days before a Constable burst in upon
me, demanding to search my room. Of course he found
the Pelisse straightaway, and marched me off here,
where I was remanded in custody. The Master and Mistress
have brought the charge of theft against me and I
await my trial. So all my misdemeanours have finally
caught up with me. Here I sit, languishing in Chester
Gaol, hoping to God I may be acquitted of this pathetic
crime. A young Girl found guilty of stealing some
clothes from a drying yard is just back from Court in
floods of tears. She has been sentenced to five years in
prison and expects this to be changed to Transportation
Beyond the Seas. There are too many Felons, the gaols
here in Britain are filled to overflowing, so as many as
possible are sent to Botany Bay.*

*I am not feeling sanguine about my own case. (I had
wanted to write 'hopeful', but this obliging new Clerk
suggested 'sanguine' instead, a new word that I shall
make use of. You may remember how I enjoy using elegant
new words, Mary.)*

*Your most unfortunate but loyal and longstanding
friend,*

*Jane Henrie*

Millie and I sat quietly after I had read out this long letter.
I picked up Harriet and she fell asleep on my lap.
Some parts of the letter had made us chuckle, but
mostly it was sad. The beginning made me feel quite
angry. I do not need her 'pity' and do not regard my
position, however unfortunate, as one of 'having fallen
so low'.

I pondered on Jane. How could she be so foolish as

to steal a pelisse from a Mistress who seems to have treated her well? But I am truly sorry for her. The waiting is most miserable before a trial. I hope she has someone close she can turn to for comfort. If indeed she is to be transported she may come here, to Sydney Cove, and we may yet be reunited! But Jane is so clever, perhaps she will contrive to charm the Judge out of imposing such a severe sentence. Then I realised that Jane had written her letter four months ago. At this very moment she might be on the high seas, sailing towards Port Jackson!

# CHAPTER 23

**I Make an Offer to Matron and Andrew Frazier
Prepares to Take a Wife
July, 1826**

My daughter Harriet had her second birthday a few
weeks ago and a group of women in the dormitory gave
her a party. She is the only child within the prison walls
old enough to appreciate such a celebration. They had
saved their rations of sugar, bribed a turnkey for some
eggs and flour and even made her a cake! They played
simple tunes on whistles and with paper and comb and
then ran about playing Hide and Seek and Hunt the
Thimble. Harriet was in heaven. All that was missing
to make it a real birthday party was other children, I
thought sadly.

We had a shock in the Factory this morning.
Another baby died overnight in the nursery. His
mother, a girl of fourteen, told us she was glad. She said
she'd only come to the Factory to give birth. Now,
without a child, she'd have much better prospects for
reassignment and marriage. It is true that many

employers insist on taking only these women who are 'unencumbered'.

I was quite upset by this latest sad death and thought I would compose a letter to Governor Darling. I intended to get signatures (or marks from those who cannot write) from the women here who agree with me. I sat on my hammock and wrote a draft by candle-light, saying that if this Colony was to be populated with children who are free and hopeful, as the Governor said in a speech I read recently in the *Sydney Gazette*, then I believed their mothers must be helped to look after them. They had never learned how. And why should they try, when they are called harlots for giving birth in the first place? No one protects young girls from the masses of sailors who stream off the ships at the quay, or the drunken convicts allowed out of Hyde Park barracks on Saturday nights. I said I felt indignant about the Governor's noble words. If only the government would provide funds to help these young women bring up their babies, then I felt sure they would not leave them wailing or try to smother them and pretend they had died in their sleep.

Next day I took the letter to Matron, for I believed it would be in her interest to endorse it. But first I asked if I could read to her from an article in the *Sydney Gazette*, which she often passes on to me as she is no fluent reader herself.

*'Within the past 6 months 24 children have been born in the Female Factory and 22 have died in the same period. The Surgeon does not hesitate to express the belief that a part of*

*the deaths occurred because of inhuman treatment which the
infants experienced from their mothers.'*

'Inhuman is right!' Matron interrupted, nodding
vigorously. 'The lazy sluts roll over in their hammocks
and crush the poor little buggers. Still, that makes for
less bastards in the colony.'

'But Matron, some of the mothers are just children
themselves. What could they possibly know about looking after babies?' I asked, and then continued hopefully, 'I
would willingly teach them myself if you would allow me
an hour off now and then from my sewing.'

Matron shrugged and shook her head. 'Why do you
think the salaries of prison staff are so low? Because no
one could care less about convicts and their babies!
Take it from one who knows. If the mothers themselves
were given the choice between a lesson in baby care and
a jaunt to the nearest public house for a tot of rum,
they'd laugh in your face, Mary Jones.'

I knew what she was referring to and it made me
angry. Every few weeks Matron and her sleazy son,
John, would select a couple of new girls, tell them to
dress themselves in their best petticoats and drive them
outside the prison gates to some public house in
Parramatta where they would ply them with rum until
they were senseless. Then they paraded them through
the tap room like prize heifers, waiting for offers.
Sometimes the girls would not be seen again for days,
returning with glazed expressions and no memory of
what had taken place after the first merry drinks. And
often John would appear the next day with a self-
satisfied leer, as if he too had taken advantage of the

unfortunate prisoners. I have heard different versions of this story from half a dozen girls, all young and newly arrived at the Factory, and most of them ashamed and bitter. Yet until they can prove what they say took place there is nothing to be done. This makes me all the more determined to speak out against Matron and her son. But I must bide my time. I will try to speak to the Governor's wife next time she visits the Factory. She has complimented me on Harriet a number of times lately, which makes me feel great pride and happiness.

As for the letter to the Governor, Matron would never have signed it and would only punish those who did, so I kept it in my bodice.

Harriet has her own small hammock in the dormitory alongside mine. The women nearby do not mind her being there. Indeed she causes more smiles and laughter than I would have imagined possible in this sad place. She is learning to talk and sometimes imitates the filthy language she hears in the yard. I tell her they are bad words and I must wash out her mouth with soapy water if I hear them again. I teach her nursery rhymes instead.

However, most of the women are careful in front of my little girl. She has a dozen aunties to dandle her on their knees. While I am sewing she sits beside me and plays jacks with knuckle bones or listens to the stories I tell or sings her little songs. Of course I know I am privileged to have her close by. Matron constantly threatens to send her off to the Orphan School early if I do not perform my tasks to her satisfaction. But I am in a good bargaining position. She cannot afford to lose my needlework, for she is growing rich on selling christening gowns and embroidered shirts to the gentry.

I have just heard some news that distresses me a great deal. I should not be upset by it, for my life with Andrew Frazier is surely over but I still think of him fondly and hope that one day he will realise his mistake. As Harriet grows up I see flashes of him — his smile, the way he held his head on one side when he was trying to remember something and also his mass of red curls. She also has his deep blue eyes. She is the prettiest child. I would give a lot for him to see her because then he would surely know there is no doubt he is her father.

But this may never happen if what I have heard is true. Elizabeth Sibley has written to me that Andrew has become besotted with a convict girl of twenty named Eleanor Hatton. She arrived on the *Brothers* last year, transported for seven years for larceny, and has already had a proposal of marriage from a free settler named Thomas Powley, which she has refused.

'*She is a pretty girl but a hopeless servant,*' Elizabeth writes. '*She is assigned to a man named Goodwin on The Rocks. Seeing Andrew Frazier's wealth and respectability she promptly set her cap at him. She will not suit him I feel sure, for she is a flirt who prefers dancing, drink and dressing up to all the things he valued in you, Mary, like gentleness, hard work, intelligence and loyalty. But the old dogs are the silliest so they say and Frazier has applied for permission to marry Eleanor Hatton. The banns are soon to be read at St Philip's, so I hear.*'

At this news I felt quite faint. This morning I stayed

back in the dormitory. I swallowed my pride and wrote
to Andrew asking him to take me back as housekeeper,
nothing more. I had decided to lie to him, to tell him
that the child had been adopted and ask Elizabeth to
look after her for me, keeping her out of sight until I
had softened Andrew's heart. Once he set eyes on Harriet and saw his own likeness I felt sure he would realise
he had wronged me and forgive me.

Then I screwed up the paper and began again, but
my tears blotted the ink. I tried many different ways
of saying what was in my heart but the right words
would not come. Finally I scribbled just a few lines.

> *My dear,*
> *I hope you will not forsake the old one for the new one. Soon*
> *my time will be up and I will be coming out to my liberty. If I*
> *am guilty of any fault it is loving thee too well.*
> *Your ever loving and obedient servant,*
> *Mary*

Then I crossed out *servant* and wrote *wife*.

I hastily folded the letter and concealed it in my
bodice, then hurried downstairs to the yard where the
first- and second-class prisoners were doing the weekly
wash for the soldiers. This is the one task I am obliged
to take part in. It gets me out of my little sewing room
and I enjoy the company of the other women. They
had soapsuds up to their armpits and were squawking
and flapping like a flock of parrots in a pond. I waited,
concealed in the doorway, until Belle Marsh turned
and signalled to me.

Suddenly there was a shriek and Belle was pointing
as pretty young Sally O'Riley, whose baby had died a

year ago, lifted her skirts and showed off her fine ankles to the guards. She began to dance about, whirling a heavy wet soldier's cape around her like a partner. The women laughed and shrieked as she waltzed her 'partner' across to the drying line, kissed him farewell and flung him across it. The guards' attention being fixed on Sally I could dash across the yard behind them and take my place at the washtub. I took over the task of wringing out clothes, which is the most tiring job, but it was what I'd agreed I would do for getting ten minutes to myself upstairs without any guard noticing.

Belle Marsh and Sally O'Riley are two smart women well practised at causing distractions, and I am proud to call them friends. As I strained to twist the heavy cloth and squeeze the water out of it I was careful not to dampen my bodice where the letter lay. I wanted to get it to Andrew Frazier as soon as possible as I did not wish him to suffer by falling for a girl Elizabeth had described as '*smart as a barrel of monkeys and saucy with it, but who throws hard-earned money around like chaff in the wind*'.

If I was honest I would have to admit that I felt wildly jealous of the pretty creature. What right had she to be married to Andrew Frazier at St Philip's, which I had only dared dream of? As I wrung out the harsh cloth, twisting it tight so the moisture was squeezed out of it, I imagined it was Eleanor Hatton's neck.

# CHAPTER 24

**The Food Riot Results in Full Bellies and Bare Skulls**
**September, 1826**

Andrew Frazier has indeed married Eleanor Hatton, which breaks my heart, and makes me wonder what I have to look forward to in the world outside the Female Factory.

Belle Marsh and Sally O'Riley say I am a fool to pine over a man so hard-hearted that he would dismiss me just because I was pregnant. They have no idea that he is the father of my child!

Only Elizabeth Sibley knows the truth and she tries to console me by telling me the latest news of the newly-weds' quarrels. (She lives next door now so cannot help but hear them.) Andrew will not indulge Eleanor's taste for 'vanity' so she keeps absconding and drives him to distraction. They have only been married two months and have already been up before a magistrate to settle their differences.

Elizabeth has sent me a copy of an article written

about them by William Charles Wentworth, the young
editor of the *Australian* newspaper. He reports the incident as if it were high farce, which makes me very sorry
for Andrew. How he must hate such ridicule. The editor makes fun of Andrew's low status as a baker, even
though he is wealthy:

> *Her loving spouse, whose furrowed and care-worn cheeks be-
> tokened how much he was a stranger to those fond caresses
> which he vainly sought in the holy bonds of wed-
> lock … looked about him for one with whom he might di-
> vide his pillow and his cakes, and who might cheer his cot
> and warm him during the winter of his life — he saw Miss
> Eleanor … and became enraptured … but she put an extin-
> guisher on his hopes. He appealed to the worthy Magis-
> trates … His rib had taken all sorts of fine things, was fond
> of vanity, threatened to extinguish the flower of his profits
> and the profits of his flour …*

This kind of writing makes me angry. It is so conde-
scending. If Mr Wentworth is a typical example of a
young gentleman then I am pleased that I have never
met one.

A few weeks after this, Elizabeth Sibley wrote me
another letter in which she said that Andrew and Eleanor had separated again because '*Eleanor has begun to
keep a disorderly house where sailors get drunk and dance
and sing with the local sluts and Heaven knows what else.*'
She said that this house was quite close to Andrew's
business and people were surprised that he allowed it.
Andrew himself, who had never touched a drop before,
had begun to drink heavily and was neglecting his business.

I knew that he must be miserable. If only I could go to him I might help him to regain his composure and respectability. If only I had sent a note about returning as his Housekeeper instead of the one about loving him too well.

But now an event has taken place at the Female Factory that has changed my appearance, so that I do not wish to go anywhere, least of all to the man I still love.


I had left my sewing room on the first floor for a few minutes one morning to take Harriet down into the yard for some fresh air, when I was approached by Kate, one of the third-class prisoners, an emaciated young girl who was given a year's hard labour for prostitution. She had been breaking rocks in the yard with some other third-class prisoners. I felt sorry for them, wearing their unsightly Parramatta cloth with the large yellow 'C' in the middle of their backs. They were working in the hot sun without a bonnet between them. Some had fashioned crude hats by plaiting reeds together, but most of them had bare heads and their faces and necks were burnt red raw. Kate beckoned me closer and I walked towards them. The guards were off having their morning tea and rum.

'Our food rations have been cut again and we ain't gunna take it,' said Kate. There were mutterings of agreement from the other women.

'What will you do?' I asked apprehensively. Matron's office door was open.

'You'll see. Make sure you keep your little girl out of this yard about noon today.'

I nodded. 'Good luck,' I said and walked quickly away.

At precisely noon there was a sudden commotion down below. Screams, yells and howls of delight. The second-class prisoners on the first floor left their weaving and leant out of the windows to peer down at the yard. I ran to the windows too, Harriet clasped tight in my arms. About a hundred and forty women from third-class rushed into the yard hurling furniture so hard at the walls that it broke. There was a mass of movement like some violent dance. Suddenly they were out and away! How they got past the guards I do not know but they had it well planned. About forty of them took to the bush where it grows thickest near the prison. The other hundred headed for the Parramatta town. Matron and a small band of assistants ran in hot pursuit but the women only turned and yelled back insults. 'Git back or we'll fart in ya faces!' We cheered them from the first floor, waving and jumping up and down, laughing hysterically and calling out: 'Run, Kate!' 'Run, Sarah!' 'Bring us back some pork pies! Pickles! Cherries! Bread! Get some rum and beer!'

Soon constables were seen running in all directions outside the prison walls. Then came the soldiers, a captain, a lieutenant, two sergeants and about forty others charging in all directions, bayonets at the ready. They wore fur caps and many carried loaded muskets so they should have frightened the prisoners half out of their wits but they did not. We cheered them on. We did not think they would harm the escapees.

'They will fire! Don't run!' yelled Hatty, a girl who

had just arrived from London. But we just laughed and shook our heads and watched the third-class women run like Amazons. A few were caught and brought back by the soldiers. Then a few more. They fought and struggled in the soldiers' arms but the soldiers did not harm them. They were laughing!

Not half an hour later there was a shout from Belle and we all left our work again to peer over the balcony. 'Look!' cried Belle. 'They've brought back a feast!' And it was true. A mass of women came marching back from Parramatta with a military escort and their aprons full of bread and meat!

'But where did they get the money?' asked Hatty in disbelief.

'They'd have snatched the food off the stalls and run away, o' course,' said Belle, as if Hatty was an imbecile.

The women were shouting and cheering as they stuffed their faces and passed some to the soldiers.

Did they hang their heads and beg forgiveness now that they were captured? No! They hurled what was left in their aprons up to us on the balcony and we leaned forward, screaming with excitement to catch lumps of fresh bread and chicken legs and slices of beef. Then they started pelting the yard walls with stones and pieces of broken furniture.

The Superintendent of Police shouted an order. 'Take the ringleaders of this riot and confine them in the cells!' About six women including Kate were grabbed by the constables and roughly pushed towards the cells but the rest, in spite of the soldiers, rushed in to rescue their companions. 'If one suffers, all suffer! Take us to the cells! Take us to the cells!' they yelled, linking arms and violently kicking out at anyone who approached them, while we cheered them on from above. The constables fell back. There were not enough cells for one hundred and forty women, as every one of them knew. They had never seen such a display of mutual support. There was nothing they could do. They were powerless. The soldiers, far from being angry about this, seemed amused. They shrugged and laughed. Driven back to the walls by a group of chanting, dancing women, they turned on their heels and headed back to their barracks.

The food riot was a triumph for the Female Factory and the spirits of each woman were lifted.

But next day every one of us who had taken part in it, even those in second- and first-class who had just cheered them on, had her head shaved as punishment.

I cannot bring myself to touch my bare skull. My soft fair curls were my only good feature. Now I am as bald and ugly as a diseased monkey.

# CHAPTER 25

**The New Matron Arrives and I Hear News of Old Friends**
**December, 1826**

I have received another letter from Jane.

I am amazed to hear that she is across the sea in Van Diemen's land, in Hobart Town, and that she has escaped being sent to the Female Factory! It seems that on the journey from London she made the acquaintance of some free settlers, Mr and Mrs Officer, travelling with three young children. Mrs Officer was so ill that Jane volunteered to help. Soon she had been adopted by the family, invited to leave her hard bunk in the stinking orlop and sleep in an airy cabin above deck. '*I exchanged my convict rations of salt pork and rancid stew for roasted chicken and fresh fruit, so I did not get the scurvy like the other poor wretches, whose pustules grew like fungus and whose teeth rattled loose in their mushy gums,*' she wrote. When they arrived in Van Diemen's Land, Mr Officer declared to the prison authorities that Jane was a young woman of 'unblem-

ished background' and had her assigned to the family
as a nursemaid. She seems to be enjoying her new life as
'*almost one of the gentry*', as she writes. And already she
plans marriage!

I wrote back at once to tell her that I had received
her previous letter from Chester, and to say how happy
I am for her now — but also to say that I was hurt by
her suggestion that I should consider trying to escape
these walls, leaving Harriet behind. What a cruel
thought! I can only conclude that never having borne a
child of her own, Jane does not understand the over-
whelming love one feels. Yet again my old friend disap-
points me.

But since Elizabeth Sibley arrived back at the Factory, my spirits have lifted. She has been sent here once
again by her husband for drunkenness and disorderly
behaviour. It is a joy to be reunited after almost two
years. As soon as I could get her to myself at one end of
the yard, where we began sweeping side by side, I asked
her to talk about life on The Rocks. There are friends
and places and even sounds I miss very much. 'Are
there still rolling drumbeats at daybreak and day's end,
Elizabeth? When a new ship arrives does the boat-
swain's horn still call? Do the constables still call the
hours at night? And what about those out-of-tune bells
at St Philip's? Do they still ring on Sundays?'

'Yes, all of that, Mary,' she said with a sigh. 'And
there are still bloody floggings in the pillory at the market place. And mobs still jeer the condemned as they're
taken in carts to the hanging grounds. It isn't all sweetness that goes on, you know.'

The story of Andrew Frazier and Eleanor Hatton

grows worse. I delayed asking because any news of them was painful to my ears. 'She's made a fool of him in every way and boasts openly that she is spending his fortune and never cared for him in the first place,' Elizabeth told me.

'And Andrew? How does he take it?'

'He's drinking himself into ruin. His business is neglected and he now has debts that could land him in prison if he doesn't pull himself out of this sorry state soon. The bakery is closed, the imports sold off for next to nothing, the servants have mostly left the house and he wants to see no one, not even my husband, who claims he is a close friend.'

I shook my head. 'What can be done?'

'Nothing. He's brought it on himself.'

'I wrote to him but had no reply. If only I could see him, or let him see Harriet, I'm sure it would help.'

'Forget him, Mary! Like most men, he doesn't value the things he needs most. My own husband now cavorts with sluts who rob him. I predict it won't be long before he too is ruined.'

'So, is there no good news?'

She smiled. 'Not all is gloom. I have asked for a separation from William and he has agreed! He may even give me a cottage as a separation present, and when you get out of here you and Harriet can live with me on The Rocks and we will do all the things we used to enjoy.'

'That's wonderful news! Why didn't you tell me at once? You'll be an emancipated woman at last, Elizabeth, and I will sew to keep us all.'

'Don't get too excited. The miser hasn't yet agreed to

the cottage, but I've planted the idea firmly in his mind and hope he'll think it the easiest way to get rid of me. Now, tell me the news of the Factory. I read of the food riot in the *Sydney Gazette*. Everyone on The Rocks laughed about it for days. You were heroines, all of you.'

I shrugged. 'The third-class were the heroines. We just cheered them on, but then were punished just as hard. Head shaving is supposed to humble us and truly it's the thing we dread most. I would prefer the tread-mill.'

'You should've done what I did when my head was shaved for insolence last time I was here. I kept some curls and sewed them onto my bonnet front and back so no one could tell I'd been disgraced. Least not until I took a bath!' Elizabeth laughed. 'But no matter now. Your hair is growing back and looks pretty, though it's short.'

'Why, thank you. You're a dear friend to say so,' I ran my hand across the pale fluff that now covered my head.

'I hear that Matron was dismissed as a result of the food riot.'

Elizabeth gave me a quizzical look. 'And there are rumours that she and that filthy son of hers were repri-manded by the Governor's wife for exposing young women to moral danger within these very walls.'

I nodded. 'And exposing them outside as well.'

'I happen to know that the Governor's wife is not exactly a friend of yours, Mary, but that she is someone you trust.'

'That is true,' I said uncomfortably. 'But all that

about Matron and her son was common knowledge amongst the prisoners.'

'Ah yes. But who amongst them would have the guts to tell the Governor's wife?' She paused and eyed me steadily. I did not blink. She continued to probe. 'Why, such a woman would be starved and then flogged almost to death if she was found out.'

I felt myself turn pale but only said, 'I believe Matron Gordon will be better. She is more honest and seems content, for Governor Darling has promised to raise the salaries of all the prison staff, which should stop them stealing from the prisoners. Although this creates a small problem for me.'

'How's that, Mary?'

'Now there is less corruption at the Factory I can no longer spend my days sewing to make Matron rich, but must work at weaving and at the washtub like the other prisoners. For this I'm paid almost nothing, not enough for Harriet's food. I'm using my savings to support her now. I don't know how long they'll last.'

'You should apply for an assignment at once.'

'I have, but as I want only to go to a household where a child will be welcome, it's not easy to find a position.'

'There must be dozens of farmers who would welcome your skills as well as young Harriet.'

'Ah, yes, but you should meet them. They come here to the Factory to look us over. They're a crude lot! Most of them are men who make no secret of their intentions to use you as their whore as well as their housekeeper. If I met one I felt I could trust to respect me, I'd willingly go to live as far away as Bathurst or the Hunter River.

Although, of course, I would much prefer to return to The Rocks.'

'And does Matron allow you to pick and choose your employer?'

'So far she's been tolerant and understanding. She values me because I'm a trustworthy prisoner, she says, and a good example to the more violent ones. When she learned I was literate she asked me to become her monitor and help with the bookkeeping. She allows me to keep Harriet close by, but as soon as she is three, if I'm not gone from here, she must go away to the Female Orphan School.'

'I've heard it isn't such a bad place, Mary. Although my Thomas was glad enough to return home from the boys' school, I must say. Now the poor little devil is back there again. As soon as I get out of here I'll keep him safe beside me.'

We had finished sweeping and took our brooms back to the storeroom. Harriet danced along beside us, waving her little broom which had been made for her by Sam, the Turnkey, who sometimes brought his own small boy to play with her.

'Harriet and I would miss each other terribly if she went to the Orphan School, Elizabeth. We've never been apart for an hour and she is still so young. And that school is not a safe place. I read a report in the *Sydney Gazette* recently about the danger to orphans of loose bricks falling from an archway, and open drains that spread disease.'

'Ah Mary, you and your precious *Sydney Gazette*.' Elizabeth made light of my fears but she knew I had cause to worry.

That evening as we lay in our hammocks in the dormitory there was talk of the Female Orphan School again.

'It's not too bad,' said Sukey, an older prisoner who had just arrived at the Factory. 'When I visited my girl there a month ago they was feastin' on pork and plum puddin' and it weren't even Christmas!'

'Ah, but I've heard that once the visitors leave, the children are back to eating gruel and potato skins. They're left dirty and catch diseases,' said Catherine. 'Their eyes get inflamed because they all use the same water to wash in and the same towel. There are beatings and worse. Some of those in charge take advantage of the little girls' innocence. I know this for a fact. I've talked to two girls who ran away.'

Ettie agreed. 'My oldest girl, just eleven, complained that the Headmaster pulled up her clothes and was feeling all about her body. Another time he untied her frock and put his hands into her bosom. He told her he did this to warm his hands.'

Some women laughed. Others shook their heads. The cruder ones joked about whether it was better to let the Headmaster warm his hands or be thrown out of the school and let rougher men warm other parts of themselves on your body.

'A girl who is fondled by the Headmaster is just gettin' educated for later life!' declared Sukey. More laughter.

Elizabeth could see I was distressed by this talk. 'Nonsense!' she said. 'No young girl should have to put up with such humiliation. Not in the Colony. This is not England.'

'Indeed 'tis not! Here us women know our rights and won't be trodden down by any man who thinks that he's our better,' chimed in Margaret Keeving. Margaret was a servant who had lived on the Rocks for ten years. She regularly managed to get herself arrested so that she could come back to the Factory. I noticed she'd lost a few more teeth since her last visit. She was a spirited woman whom most of us admired. 'I were in Harrington Street the other night and had been in liquor with some sailors at a public house where we was dancing and singing as merrily as birds, doing harm to nobody. Then who should appear at the doorway but my mean-minded Master and his whining wife.'

'Oooh, Margaret, what had ye done to 'em, eh?' old Sukey asked.

'My Master stands there with his lip curling, commanding me to be quiet and come with him at once. It is past ten o'clock, so he says. I should be home looking after his children. I said I would not be quiet and I would not come to his house. The drink had given me courage to speak my mind, you see. At this there was a hush at the bar and all strained to listen. "I will neither work for you nor stay in your house, for I have lost more things there than I have gained," said I. At this his wife went pale for she knew my meaning. I folded my arms across my chest and said for all to hear, "If you do not send me back to the Female Factory I will go myself." As no one stirred, I left the pub, went into the street and began walking to their house to collect my clothes, which was few enough. There was some slags who followed me who was worse in drink then myself. I called them bloody whores and told them to go screw themselves, although I were laughing to myself, still thinking of the look of shock upon my Master's face. But a constable heard me swearing and arrested me. So here I am, back with me old friends in gaol and not a bit sorry for it!'

There were cheers.

# CHAPTER 26

**Matron Gordon**
**The Female Factory, June, 1827**

Next day as I worked in her office sorting the mail and accounts Matron Gordon watched me closely. This made me nervous. In the afternoon she came close to the desk where I worked and stared into my eyes.

'Mary, there is a lady who is a member of the Committee of the School of Industry for Girls who wishes to speak to you. You will go to meet her now at the Keeper's Lodge.'

'Yes, Matron.'

'Take Harriet with you.'

'Harriet?'

'That is what I said. Get along with you. Don't keep the lady waiting. She is a friend of the Governor's wife.'

My heart beat up high in my chest like a bird fluttering to get out of a cage. What could the lady want with me and Harriet? I hurried to the yard where Harriet was playing hopscotch with Tommy, the turnkey's son.

She was pleased to see me out of the office so early

and ran to meet me, flinging herself into my arms. 'Mama, Tommy won the game!'

She beamed back at her friend, then whispered in my ear. 'I let him win.'

The Keeper opened the door to his lodge when we knocked and ushered us into a small sitting room where he had lit the fire. A tall lady rose to meet us and held out her hand to me. It felt very soft and I was ashamed of my own coarse hand. 'You are Mary Jones. My name is Mrs Evans. My husband is Major Evans. We have recently come to Sydney and live at Potts Point.'

'And do you find it pleasant at Potts Point, ma'am?' I asked politely.

The lady looked surprised that I should have good manners.

'Quite pleasant,' she replied stiffly. 'You once lived on The Rocks, I believe, Mary?'

'I did, ma'am.'

I wondered what on earth such a fine lady wanted of me. She kept glancing at Harriet, who had perched herself on my knee and sat quietly watching the flames of the fire which seemed to delight her. I do not think she had sat beside a fire before.

'And was your little girl born there?'

'She was.'

'It was an easy birth? No complications?'

Suddenly I felt afraid. Was this lady sent by Andrew Frazier to check up on me? To make sure I had told no one that he was her father?'

'It was a normal birth, ma'am.'

'Ah. And who is your little girl's father?'

'I prefer not to say, ma'am.' I looked anxiously at Harriet who had turned her head to me inquisitively. 'I have sworn to keep it secret.'

'That is most vexing.' The lady looked about her and blinked her eyelids rapidly as if getting rid of a troublesome fly. 'What I want to know is whether he is healthy, and what manner of man he is.'

'He is healthy and was kindly when I knew him,' I replied quietly. I did not enjoy these questions.

'Speak up, Mary. Is he a convict?'

'No, ma'am. Not any more.'

'But he was one?'

'Yes.'

'Come here, little girl, and tell me your name.' The lady leant towards Harriet. She did not seem to be at ease with children. She spoke to her as if she were a little dog.

Harriet looked to me for guidance and I nodded. She walked obediently towards the lady and stood before her. 'My name is Harriet Jane Jones,' she said clearly.

'Turn around and let me look at you.' Harriet did as she was asked. 'You seem a healthy child and you are as pretty as the Matron told me. Do you like your life here in the prison, Harriet?'

'Yes. I play with Tommy and there are all my aunties here and Uncle Sam, and I have my own hammock next to Mama's.'

'So you sleep with the prisoners?'

Harriet turned to ask me, 'Are they prisoners, Mama?'

I nodded. 'We are all prisoners here but they like you to call them aunties.'

'Yes, aunties. And Mama and I play games and I can sing and say nursery rhymes and soon Mama will teach me to read books.'

'So you are literate, Mary?'

'Yes, ma'am.' I was finding these questions irritating.

'Open your mouth, child. Yes, you have good teeth.'

'If it is not rude to ask, ma'am, why are you so interested in Harriet?'

The lady opened her eyes wide and stared at me. 'Did the Matron not inform you? I am considering adopting her, that is why. I have been looking for a suitable child for some months and she seems by far the best I have seen.'

# CHAPTER 27

**Harriet is Saved by Her 'Bad Blood'**
**July, 1827**

I have been gravely ill with a fever these past weeks and can scarcely recall events or those who have looked after me. I am convinced distress was the cause of the fever. I could not believe that Harriet was to be taken from me. If I were never to see her again I would rather die.

Today I recognised Elizabeth Sibley, who was allowed to visit me. I asked her where I was.

'You are in the hospital here at the Factory, Mary. Thank God you are talking sense at last. You've been raving like a half-wit for almost three weeks.' She held my hands in hers and then soothed me by stroking my brow.

Suddenly I remembered Harriet and sat up with a jerk. 'Where is she? Have they taken her yet? Tell me quickly. Have they?'

'Calm yourself. She's in good hands.'

'Where? Oh, tell me where she is!' I began to weep.

'She is with me, Mary. She's been sleeping in her little hammock alongside mine these past three weeks.'

'With you? But how? Have you adopted her instead
of the lady?'

'No, no, Mary. She is not to be adopted by anyone.
She is your child and yours alone. I am minding Harriet for you, that is all.'

'But the tall thin lady said she had selected her. Like
a prize calf. She said it was all arranged.'

'She has changed her mind about the calf.' Elizabeth
smiled. 'If you promise not to start raving again I'll tell
you how it came about.'

And then my good friend explained, in a lowered
voice, how as soon as she heard the news that Harriet
was to be adopted without my consent and that I had
fallen gravely ill and could not be visited, she begged
Matron to let her take care of Harriet until the adoption took place. As the child was distressed because of
my sudden illness and had no one to look after her,
Matron agreed, provided Harriet was made clean and
decent every Friday afternoon so that she could take tea
with the lady at the Keeper's Lodge. Mrs Evans had
decided to take a month to make up her mind whether
or not Harriet was suitable for adoption into a
well-bred family. This was just a formality, Matron told
Elizabeth, as Mrs Evans was already sure that Harriet
was the right choice, and had booked her passage to
London so that she and her husband could show off
their new daughter to her grandparents.

'Harriet is a smart child for three and she understood what she must do to avoid being turned into a
lady and never seeing her dear Mama again,' Elizabeth

told me with a gleam in her eye. 'I taught her well and she was a quick learner. Next Friday we meet Mrs Evans for tea at the Keeper's Lodge and I wait outside as instructed. About five minutes into the meeting I hear a scream from the fine lady and out she rushes, rubbing her wrist and breathing fast as if she's having palpitations.

' "What is it, ma'am?" says I in all innocence.

' "That child. She has bitten me!"

' "Ah yes, so I see." For Harriet has done a good job and I can see the small teeth marks clearly, though she's not managed to draw blood.

' "She has been that way from birth, ma'am. Strange you were not told."

' "From birth! A *biter*?"

' "Indeed so, ma'am. She is also prone to nightmares and screams in her sleep. A difficult child, although she's so pretty. I have been a close friend of the family for many years and know it to be so."

' "Then you know what type of man her father was! Who was he? Tell me quickly, for the mother would not say," she demands most urgently.'

'Oh Elizabeth, you did not tell her, surely?' I interrupted in a panic.

She motioned to me to be quiet.

' "I knew him well, poor fellow," I tell the lady gravely.

' "A convict?"

' "One of the worst."

' "Not ... a murderer?" The lady blanches as she utters the word.

' "Strange they did not tell you, ma'am. He butchered five women, threw their bodies into a cesspit then dressed himself up in their clothes and paraded down George Street. He was hanged of course. But he couldn't really be blamed."

' "Not blamed for murder? Why ever not?" The lady's hands are now covering her face in terror.

' "Oh, he was quite mad. A homicidal maniac. Should have been locked away years ago. But like his little girl here, he was such a nice charming fellow on the surface. Except for the fits."

' "Fits? He had epileptic fits?"

' "Aye, he did. And so does she. Rolls around the floor foaming at the mouth. Nearly bit off her own tongue last night, she did. Never remembers a thing about it afterwards."

' "But this is shocking! Why was I told nothing of this?"

' "The little girl's mother would be ashamed to admit it, ma'am. That's why she's kept it from the Matron all this time. And now poor Mary is so ill it don't look as if she'll be in any condition to talk about it ever. We all know that young Harriet takes after her father. She's the spitting image of him, God rest his soul." '

In spite of feeling weak I was laughing helplessly. 'Oh Elizabeth, how could you? What if the lady discovers it was all a lie and comes back for revenge?'

'She never will. Ladies like that are frightened off fast. Bad blood is something that makes them run like the wind in the other direction. She's already arranged to adopt twin boys — currency lads, not convicts.' She laughed. 'And now, Mary, get yourself well as quick as you can, for I'm to leave this prison tomorrow morning and your little girl needs her mother.'

'Leaving, Elizabeth?' I said in panic.

'My time is up. William has agreed to a separation and handed over a cottage. I'll be an emancipated woman at last!'

I gave her a hug and tears sprang to my eyes. 'No woman deserves it more than you! But oh, how I shall miss you.'

'Get well, get out of here and you and Harriet can come and live with me on The Rocks.'

'If only we could. You are a free woman, Elizabeth, but I must still be assigned to a master before I can leave. Harriet is now more than three so I fear that if I don't find a master who will agree to let me keep her, they'll soon send her across the river to the Orphan School.'

'Once I tell them about her fits and biting I doubt if they'll take her at the Orphan School!' laughed Elizabeth. Then she became serious. 'Do you know a young man by the name of William Baxter?'

I nodded. 'He is one of the men in search of an assigned servant who has visited me here a few times. He works as a collector of insects and plants. A botanist, he calls himself. He is kindly and not unpleasant but he does not wish to take a servant with a child.'

'Since you've been ill, he has been asking after you every day and bringing little gifts. I have met him and I must say, Mary, he is most personable. I believe he may be in love with you.'

I laughed. 'You are mistaken, Elizabeth. What a foolish idea!' But I blushed a little for I was touched to hear of Mr Baxter's concern.

# CHAPTER 28

## Jane is Hurtful, I Meet My Ex-Lover's Wife and Mr Baxter Becomes an Attentive Visitor
### December, 1827

At last Jane has replied to the letters I sent to Van Diemen's Land.

*Hyde Park, Sydney, 1827*

*Dear Mary,*

*Well, it took longer than I had hoped for my husband, James New (who writes this letter for me), to get permission from the Governor of Van Diemen's Land to arrange passages for us both to move to Sydney, but here we are at last, settled in a comfortable house not far from the barracks at Hyde Park and the racecourse.*

*I find Sydney so different from Hobart Town, which I disliked for its gossips and cold weather. Here the sun shines and there is a bustle and style about the place that lifts my spirits. Why did you not tell me about the tropical flowers that grow wild amongst the rocks above the seashore — giant red ones that turn into mush when* they drop and tiny creamy things that smell sickly sweet like honey? Of course there are convicts everywhere about, as many as in Hobart, but they are at least chained together working in gangs building roads and bridges, whereas in Van Diemen's Land they mostly rot in gaol.

Although Sydney is a new town, there are a few fine buildings that remind me of the ones in London. I dislike the muddy roads here and the fact that it rains suddenly and violently in spite of the heat. On our first night here there was a terrifying storm such as I had never experienced in my life. Great sheets of lightning lit up the sky and thunder clapped so close I thought our house had been struck for certain. You did not tell me that Sydney is often afflicted by storms of this kind, Mary. This is the one thing I dislike about the town.

James has bought a public house on the Rocks with the money he made from the sale of his farm in Hobart. I shall be hostess to his clients, which we hope will be a better class of people from those I have seen straggling along the docks. No convicts will be allowed in of course, and only sailors with decent manners. We will serve proper meals with roast meats at noon every day. We expect some of the gentry to find us out soon and then, when we begin to make a profit, I shall encourage James to buy another public house. He is a good hard-working husband who is devoted to me and does whatever I want. He says he could not live without me, and even though his savings are gone now that we've also bought a fine cottage in George Street, he insists I must go to Madame Rous, who imports the best French materials, and buy all the silk I need for a new dress.

*She is an honest woman who will allow him credit until the end of the month. (Dear James is smiling as he writes this.)*

*You have written that you would love to see me and hope that I will take the ferry to Parramatta and visit you in the Female Factory. The journey would take most of one day, Mary, and I have so much to do ordering furniture and curtains for our new house that I must delay it for the present, although I am curious to see you and your child, of course. How have your pretty looks fared in this harsh climate? I take care to wear a bonnet always. James tells me I have the complexion of a lady.*

*Well, I must now attend to my social duties.*

*I am,*

*Your most affectionate and prosperous friend,*

*(Mrs) Jane New*

This letter, which I had opened so joyfully, left me quite despondent.

Then, a few days ago, it was with some shock that I heard who had been brought into the main yard of the Factory by a constable — none other than Eleanor Frazier! So I finally laid eyes on my ex-lover's wife. She was finely dressed and seemed spirited. She pushed the Constable aside when he tried to take hold of her by the arm and yelled at him. The rumour amongst the first-class prisoners around me was that she'd been arrested for running a disreputable house and for lewd behaviour and drunkenness. She is certainly very young and pretty. Matron was already making a fuss of her so I expect she will get plenty of privileges. When I saw how arrogant and foul-mouthed she was towards the Constable, an older man who was doing his best to control her, I could not help feeling sorry for Andrew. Oh, what a foolish man he was to choose her for his wife instead of me!

Mr William Baxter, the Botanist, has visited me regularly since I left hospital and I find him very pleasant company. I have told him that I would be interested to assist him with his plant collection, labelling and storing the specimens, as well as working as his Housekeeper if he could accept my daughter as well. But he says he has no suitable accommodation for a child, just a rough hut he has built on the Hunter River. He asked why I could not leave Harriet at the Orphan School, saying it would be safer as there are sometimes attacks by natives along the Hunter and we might have to flee into the bush. This alarmed me on my own account as well as Harriet's. I do not think I have the courage to accept Mr Baxter's offer, although I can see that he is disappointed.

Matron is becoming impatient with me. She says I must accept an assignment within a fortnight or Harriet will be sent to the Orphan School anyway. That will put a stop to 'all this nonsense' of hoping that my Master will take responsibility for a child as well as a servant. I am feeling in low spirits about the future.

Eleanor Frazier has been made a monitor of the third-class, although she's only been here a week. I saw her smiling and laughing with Matron this morning, as though they were old friends. I must say she looks even prettier when she smiles. I can see why poor Andrew would have become smitten by her. Old Sarah confided to me that Eleanor has been stealing meat from the other prisoners and even took some from Ann Hamilton, a girl who is so frail after five days in the cells that she cannot stand unsupported. I can hardly believe that anyone would be so cruel, but Sarah never lies to me.

As I was walking across the yard with Harriet to resume my bookkeeping duties in Matron's office I heard Eleanor shouting at the third-class prisoners breaking rocks for the new road in Parramatta. As monitor she is not obliged to do any work herself. She sauntered towards me and said, 'You are Mary Jones, are you not?'

I felt both rage and fear as I turned to face her. What did she want with me? Would she say something indiscreet about Andrew in front of Harriet?'

'Yes, I am Mary Jones.'

She looked down at Harriet whose red curls, blue eyes and shy smile are exactly like those of her father and said, with mock sweetness, 'I married the man who was once your employer.'

'So I have heard,' I said steadily, and made to move on.

'And what a mean-minded, dreary old fart he was!' she said.

Harriet giggled at the bad word and then looked up at me apologetically.

'Why did you marry him then?' I could not resist asking.

'For his money, of course. Why else?' She spoke gaily. 'But it's nearly all gone now and he's turned into a drunk.'

'You are pleased you have ruined him?' I said icily.

She stared at me in surprise. 'What, did you fancy the old codger? You're welcome to him! He got what he deserved for chasing a pretty young woman who could have had her pick of the young men.' She laughed. 'But that's not what I wanted to talk about. We have a friend in common, you and me, and she's in trouble, so I hear.'

'And who might that be?' I asked without much interest.

'Maria Wilkinson. Or Jane New, as she likes to be called these days.'

I stared. 'You are a friend of hers?'

She nodded. 'Our mothers knew each other in England. We were babies together, both neglected when our mams went to work in the cotton mill and started on the gin, but we survived. We used to play on the factory floor as happy as two larks, Maria tells me. I hadn't seen her since and wouldn't have recognised her as the fine lady I saw a couple of months back while I was out shopping. But she knew me at once. She invited me to drink tea at her house and she told me why she'd changed her name. A long story. That's when she mentioned you, Mary Jones.'

Eleanor looked to see that I was listening. 'Well, she's married now. She said it all took longer than she'd hoped — finding this husband, James New, and obtaining permission for them both to move to Sydney.

'We arranged to go shopping together another day, and I accompanied her to Madame Rous's establishment, where all the best people go to buy the finest French silks.'

I nodded. I knew Madame Rous's shop, and recalled Jane's mention of it in her letter.

'Well,' Eleanor went on, 'Madame showed her a great many silks, and at last Jane chose one of the finest, and also the most expensive. When she was told the price, she seemed surprised and raised her eyebrows, as though to imply that Madame Rous would not dare charge such a high price in France or England, but in Sydney Town the ladies are so desperate for fine material, they will pay whatever she asks. However, she was very polite to Madame. She told her that she did not believe in asking for credit, and that if Madame would put the roll of silk aside for her — all twenty-eight yards of it, which amounted to a very large sum indeed — she would return next week with the money. Well, Madame agreed to this and they parted on the best of terms.'

'But … you say she's in trouble?'

'She's been convicted of the theft of a piece of silk from that same Madame Rous where I met her. Imagine that. And because it's worth more than five pounds — a great deal more — she will get the death penalty.'

'I don't believe you!'

'Then read it in the *Gazette* for yourself. It's in Matron's office.'

Eleanor did not seem particularly upset about the fate of her childhood friend.

I hurried away, taking Harriet firmly by the hand.

'What's your little girl's name?' she called after us but I did not answer.

'Is that my new auntie?' asked Harriet innocently.

'No, she is no relation at all,' I replied firmly.

So Jane New had been arrested and, although she was out on bail, she was soon to face a trial. And if she was convicted of the theft she would be sentenced to death!

Though I was still hurt that Jane had never come to visit, I wrote to her at once, offering my sympathy and loving thoughts. I prayed that she would not be found guilty. But I feared things might not go well for her.

Mr Baxter came again today. He brought me some flowers which he tells me are called Frangipani, a plant newly brought into the Colony. They smelt so sweetly. He looked nervous and said he had been thinking things over. He said he had noticed how frightened I seemed when he mentioned the natives who some-times attack his property and that my fears were quite justified. He said that although he had hoped to live there, clear the bush and grow fruit and vegetables, per-haps he could just keep the hut for trips to collect his plant specimens, and rent lodgings closer to town. I told him this seemed a good idea.

He noticed that I seemed distracted and asked what was troubling me. I told him that my oldest friend was facing trial and might be hanged. He looked most sym-pathetic and this had the effect of making me more melancholy so that I began to cry. Mr Baxter then passed me his handkerchief and put an arm gently round my shoulders. It felt most comforting.

We sat in this way, side by side on the cold stone bench which is used for visitors, while I sobbed quite hard, my shoulders heaving and his arm never leaving me. After a while I felt better, as if a load of sadness about many things had slipped away from me. I stopped crying and Mr Baxter removed his arm. He is a shy young man and I felt that I might have embarrassed him.

'I am sorry to have bothered you with my problems,' I told him softly. 'I will launder this handkerchief and return it to you.'

'Keep it, Mary.' His voice was unusually hoarse and his face flushed quite pink. Suddenly he burst out: 'Will you consent to be my wife?' I stared at him. 'And bring Harriet with you? If you do we will live in town, I promise!'

Well, I have accepted Mr Baxter's proposal. It is a strange thing to have done, for I scarcely know him. Yet after his kindness to me the other day I feel I can trust him. He is not more than twenty-five and, as Elizabeth said, quite personable. He is quiet in his manner and seems gentle. He has been a convict but has earned his ticket of leave and been granted those acres of land on the Hunter River to make a farm. It is a big sacrifice for him to give up the idea of farming for a year or two until the natives move on and more farmers appear as neighbours. But he says he will be able to earn a small living collecting his plants and selling them to a gentleman in England who is a friend of Governor Darling.

I write my good news to Elizabeth, who is now settled in her cottage on The Rocks, and ask if she will come to my wedding, which is to be held in the church at Parramatta in a few months time. I am also inviting several fellow prisoners from the Factory, who have permission from Matron to attend. There is quite a commotion, with screams of delight, when they hear they'll be allowed to get out for a few hours. They will be well escorted by constables, of course.

I write again to Jane and invite her and her husband to attend. I tell her that I cannot believe she will be found guilty, and as the trial will be over before the wedding I beg her to come.

Harriet is as excited as I am. I have already begun sewing our dresses. Because the wedding is so soon and we will be leaving the Factory for ever, she does not have to be sent away to the Orphan School after all. It is a great relief to us both.

My good behaviour during the three and a half years I have spent in prison has meant that I will be assigned to my new husband for just one year; then, if my behaviour and work are satisfactory, I shall be granted my freedom. I write this good news to my mother, sisters and brother and say that by the time the letter reaches them I will no longer be Mary Jones but Mrs William Baxter!

# CHAPTER 29

**Two Deaths in One Day**
**The Female Factory, December, 1827**

This has been a sad day. When I woke this morning I heard the news that Ann Hamilton, the third-class prisoner whom Sarah swears had her meat supply stolen by Eleanor Frazier, had died, and there was to be an inquiry.

Poor Ann was not a popular prisoner. She wept and whined for food constantly and was fractious and often confined to a cell. I have seen her, while raking the gravel on the pathways, picking weeds to eat, even chewing on bare bones thrown to her as a taunt by her fellow prisoners. Perhaps she was ill. Or not right in her mind. We shall never know. She died quietly in her cell this morning before the sun rose. Eleanor was sleeping nearby keeping guard, as Ann had been trying to harm herself by beating her own head against the walls and had to be tied down.

Having heard of the tragedy, Lady Darling herself and some of her ladies' committee came to inspect the

Factory later in the day. I overheard them discussing the 'unsatisfactory conditions' and saying that the 'meat must have all boiled away in the soup' for there was none to see. I could have told them who has been stealing it and thickening the soup with flour, but I expect that will all come out in the inquiry. I also heard one lady say in disgust, 'The women are filthy and should be issued with towels and combs and allowed a weekly bath.' That would be a treat. I should welcome it but not everyone would, I'll wager.

Conditions in first-class are very different from third and since Governor Darling came we have the privilege of attending the parish church under supervision, being paid for the extra work we do and receiving visitors once a week. Our diet is a bit better than second-class and our dress too. I feel sorry for the misery I see in third-class.

I will be glad to leave here, although I will miss my friends.


When William came to visit me I told him the sad news of Ann Hamilton's death. 'Dry your tears, Mary, my love,' he said. 'This is a grim place and you've been here too long. You have a tender heart and suffer for other prisoners. It is not good for you.'

He gave me a bunch of jasmine and some cheese scones, still warm, baked for me by his landlady, and a bottle of blackcurrant juice, which he knew I liked to give Harriet for her health.

'Cheer up. The banns for our marriage will be read in church this Sunday and I want to see you there smiling. Otherwise the congregation will think I'm a cruel man and you want none of me.'

I laughed then and squeezed his hand tightly. I am so looking forward to being married to my dear William.

But he was obliged to break another piece of news. 'I'm sorry to be the bearer of sad tidings but there has been another death — someone you knew quite well.'

'Who is it, William? Tell me quickly,' I cried.

'I read about it in the *Gazette*. Your old employer, Mr Andrew Frazier, passed away yesterday. You have told me what a fair-minded Master he was. I thought you would want to know of his passing.'

He handed me a cutting from the newspaper. Andrew was described as '*an old and industrious inhabitant ... this wealthy baker who from the humblest circumstances in life, had by industry, honesty and continued sobriety for years risen to independence.*' I could read no more. My eyes were too blurred with tears.

'Oh Mary, what have I done? Upset you all over again.' William handed me his handkerchief. 'I'm sorry. I should never have mentioned it.'

# CHAPTER 30

## An Old Friend Gloats at Jane's Death Sentence
## The Female Factory, January, 1828

This morning as I worked in Matron's office I saw the *Sydney Gazette* open on her table, and almost fell upon it to see if the terrible news about Jane was true. Sure enough, there it was. Mrs Jane New of The Mermaid on The Rocks was sentenced to death for the theft of valuable silk from Madame Rous. The Magistrate John Stephen was petitioning for mercy. *To death.* The words made me tremble. I felt quite faint and fell back into Matron's armchair in a daze.

The news travelled fast. As I walked back across the yard I saw Eleanor Frazier with a crowd of prisoners round her. She is now monitor of the laundry and was telling the story of her friend's misfortune to a captive audience of women, all with mouths open and soap-suds up to their armpits.

'And will she be hanged by the neck until she's dead

so help me God?' asked one poor half-wit girl from third-class.

'Aye, she will. But she was always a thief. She used to thieve off me, her best friend!'

'Oooh. The slut! Did ya ever catch her at it?'

'I did. But she was a good liar. Innocent looks, she has. Like an angel. She charms the best of 'em. Gentlemen. Anyone.'

'Not the Judge though!'

'No, not this judge and jury.'

'She got what she deserved then, Eleanor, eh?'

'Aye, she did. Weeks I've been here in this rotten hole and has she come to visit me once? She who's sworn to be my closest friend. She has not! Quite the lady is our Jane. Wouldn't be seen dead near a prison.'

'Soon she'll be dead *in* a prison!'

There was laughter.

Eleanor is a hard-hearted young woman. The death of Andrew Frazier affected her not one jot. Earlier in the day I heard her boasting to the others that she was glad she'd got hold of his money before he'd 'carked it'.

I hurried by with my head bowed. I decided to write to James New at The Mermaid to see if there was anything to be done to help Jane. I knew no one powerful who might intervene on her behalf. I prayed that Mr John Stephen would be able to work a miracle with his petition for mercy.

# CHAPTER 31

**A Letter from Sydney Gaol**
**February, 1828**

*Dear Mary,*

*I cannot believe my luck. The sentence passed against me has been remitted! I believe it is all the work of Mr John Stephen, who, together with his learned father, brother and their legal friends has fought hard to save me from the gallows. It is all quite legal but I do not understand it fully as it is very complicated.*

*Unfortunately I am not free to go home to The Mermaid just yet. In fact I have to return to Van Diemen's Land. It has been argued in Court that the powers of a Lieutenant Governor of Van Diemen's Land do not extend to this Colony. Therefore I should never have been allowed to travel here. But since I did so, and committed a crime here, I cannot be punished for it in this Colony but must return to Van Diemen's Land to be judged again there. Mr John Stephen, a fine magistrate who has sympathy for me, assures me that once I get safely away from this Colony it is most unlikely that I will be tried for my crime again. He says I must petition Governor Arthur for my Emancipation and that he will help me to do so. He has already made contact with the Lieutenant Governor to plead my innocence.*

*The infuriating part of all this is that the court has ruled that I must be placed in the Female Factory, not for punishment but for safekeeping, until a vessel can be found to transport me back to Van Diemen's Land.*

*'But why cannot a vessel be found immediately?' I raged. 'If I have to be taken away to yet another prison I shall die of humiliation!'*

*'Calm yourself, Jane. It will only be for a few weeks,' said Mr Stephen, patient as always. (We are now on quite good terms as we have spent much time in each other's company over the past unhappy weeks and he has kindly lent me his Clerk to take down this letter.) 'Your husband has made every effort to find a vessel leaving immediately but his entreaties have been refused by the court.'*

*'I know and it makes me very angry. I think the court has a plot to keep me in prison much longer than they will admit,' I told him.*

*'Not at all, Jane. But if such a thing did occur I can get you out of prison, claiming you've been improperly detained, which I strongly believe that you have.'*

*I hung my head, Mary, and then began to cry. 'I am worried about having to leave the business I have worked so hard to build up and my new life in Sydney,' I sobbed.*

*'Jane,' he said, 'I will not let you down.' Then he left the cell quietly.*

*Then my husband James came to visit. I must say he*

*looked a sorry mess compared to the well-bred and re-
assuring Mr Stephen. He was no comfort at all to me
and only depressed me more with his whining talk of
having to sell our cottage and The Mermaid to pay my
Court costs. I know he has neglected the business while I
have been in Sydney Gaol. He says he has been too worried about me to concentrate on anything else.*

*'Oh Jane,' he started straight off, 'I didn't want to tell
you this. There have been rumours that you are guilty,
and you know how people gossip. Some of our best customers are staying away.'*

*'Well damn them! We'll see what Mr John Stephen
can do for me.'*

*I am to be taken to the Female Factory within a week
although I do not expect to be there long.*

*At least I shall see you again, Mary my old friend. So
start baking the sweetmeats, fluffing up the feather pillows and stashing away the rum, for I'll be there quite
soon.*

*I am,*

*Your disillusioned but still hopeful friend,*

*Jane New.*

*PS — One day, just before all this trouble, I was re-
turning home along Clarence Street when I saw two
constables riding past the Military Barracks. One of
them — I could almost swear it, Mary — was none
other than John Knatchbull! When he saw me he inclined his head towards me and nudged his companion
as if he would share some shameful secret. I hurried by,
pulling my bonnet down to hide my face. They seemed
to snigger together. I could not be sure it was him, but
the very thought of it put me into a severe state of agita-*

tion. Could he possibly have travelled across the seas so far of his own free will? To find him here after all these years, to have those horrid memories made real again was too cruel. I took a glass of brandy to revive myself and went to bed at once with the curtains drawn.

After an hour or so I got up, dressed myself prettily and — that was the day it happened — I went out to Madame Rous's place. I often find that shopping lifts my spirits.

# V
# Reunited

# CHAPTER 32

## I Am Reunited With Jane After Eight Years
## The Female Factory, February, 1828

I am beside myself with excitement. My old friend has always been a wonder at escaping her situation, no matter how grave, but managing to avoid the gallows is astonishing. I would like to believe she really was innocent of the charges but I am afraid I know her better than that.

Still, I know she is capable of charming gentlemen of even the most worldly type, and perhaps she has done the same to Mr Stephen. It is strange that she should be sent here. Perhaps the pardon is conditional on a period of confinement. I do not know. But soon Jane will be able to tell me herself.

It is almost eight years since we last saw each other, the day she came to say goodbye to me in Newgate Prison. I was already ill with gaol fever so my memory of that day is hazy. But I remember feeling two conflicting emotions — great joy at seeing her, for I believed she had come at last to confess that she, not I, was the guilty one, then shock and disbelief when she left me there to take *her* punishment after all. I was angry. How could my dearest friend betray me? She knew I was innocent and so ill I could scarcely stand, yet she let me take the blame for her crime and be transported across the seas away from my family for ever.

Ever since that day I have tried in vain to find a reason that might justify Jane's behaviour. Perhaps it's because, as she says, she came from a family who didn't love her, so she found it hard to love others. Or she may have thought I was so ill that day she saw me in prison that I would die anyway, and giving herself up in my place would have been a waste. No, these were not good enough reasons. I was angry with her for many years, but since she began to write to me I have been able to forgive her. Sometimes I wonder if Jane is right, and the best way is to fight against the rules and kick down the barriers. I do not have her courage for tough combat, although in my own quiet way I try to fight for what I believe in.

She is to arrive this afternoon about four o'clock, Matron Gordon tells me, and will be placed in second-class. Surely, if she is now free, she should be in first-class? I will wait a little until Jane has had a chance to make a good impression on Matron and then ask what can be done. Now that I am to be married to a free man I am back in favour with Matron.

I wonder what Jane will think of Harriet. I have told my daughter only good things about my dear friend. I know she has faults but it is best that Harriet does not hear of these. The child is so excited. For years I've told her stories of the happy days I shared with Jane at Elmtree House. Of course I've added extra bits to make it seem happier than it was. The story of Jane and Mary is like a fairytale to Harriet. I am sure Jane will love her on sight.

'Mary, how you've aged!' Jane says in shock. She picks up my hands and turns them over in hers. 'Such gnarled, hard-working claws. You poor girl. Life in the Colony and this horrid Factory has not been kind to you.'

Jane has altered her accent. She no longer speaks like a servant girl who grew up in Leeds, but more like a London lady from Mayfair. I pull my hands away, hiding them behind my back. 'Life here has not been too bad, Jane.' But I see that, compared to her soft hands and creamy complexion, I must look weathered and unkempt.

I take her arm and together we walk up and down the yard while she explains why she could not come to visit me at the Factory. 'I've been so busy at The Mermaid, fairly danced off my feet managing the place. We have excellent customers, currency people, not convicts.'

I laugh at her. 'But Jane, we are convicts, you and me!'

'Nonsense. We are practically free.'

'Now tell me all about your life since we last saw each other. Start with Mayfair. Was it very grand?'

She tells me it certainly was but she had to leave because a foolish footman fell in love with her and was trying to force her to marry him. She does such a convincing imitation of the lovesick young man, with pleading eyes like a beaten dog, that I cannot help laughing. It seems that this must have been the best of her jobs since last we met.

'Jenkins — that was the footman's name — asked to take me to Vauxhall Gardens. You can imagine, Mary, how I was longing to go there to see the jugglers, acrobats and fireworks, so I agreed.' Jane's eyes sparkle as she relates the story. 'Oh, it was a treat to wander arm-in-arm beneath the coloured lanterns in the trees and watch the fountains splashing and hear the orchestra play. I made poor Jenkins walk close behind a fashionable lady with her gentleman companion, so that we might be mistaken for gentry, but the lady spoiled my little game by turning round and saying loudly to her beau, "These servants with their sweethearts are everywhere this evening, Charles. Let us take some supper to escape them." ' She imitates the arrogant lady so well that I burst out laughing.

'They hurried ahead to an elegant restaurant beneath a painted awning with scenes of nymphs and maidens frolicking in the forest, where a band played pretty waltzes. I dragged Jenkins after them.

' "Let us view the fireworks elsewhere to escape these snotty minxes with their lily-faced fops," I said loudly as we passed them by. The lady heard me clearly and blushed. Jenkins turned to me in shock and then gave her an apologetic little bow. I shrugged and laughed at him. Then I propelled him quickly away so he could buy me an ice and a shot at the coconut shies.'

'Jenkins sounds a most agreeable young man,' I say encouragingly.

Jane shrugs and pulls a face. 'We had a pleasant evening pretending to be a courting couple, but I never intended anything more than friendship, for Jenkins, although handsome, would always be a servant. Oh, but the fireworks were magnificent, Mary! Rockets burst in the sky and spread whirling stars everywhere, snakes and dragons dipped and dived and explosions seemed to drop sparks right on our heads! I clung to Jenkins and it was soon after this that he did something I had never intended to let happen. He asked me to marry him and presented me with a gold ring that had belonged to his dead mother. He said he was very much in love with me and would be honoured if I'd consent to be his wife. Oh, but it was such a lovely ring, Mary, with a real diamond in the middle. Jenkins' mother had left it to him in her will, to be given to his beloved on their betrothal. Well, I didn't wish to hurt his feelings and lose the fun of wearing such a pretty jewel, so I said we could be engaged. I could always change my mind later, so I thought.'

'But you didn't marry Jenkins, Jane. What happened?'

She sighs dramatically. 'It's such a dreary story. Do you really want to hear?'

I know she is teasing. 'Of course! Tell me quickly.'

'Once I had agreed to be his bride, what a fuss was made in the household. I had no idea the Master and Mistress would behave as they did. Jenkins was a favourite and had been with the family since he was a child. His father before him had been footman to the Master's father and his mother had been parlour maid before me. The Master and his wife both kissed me (the

Master more enthusiastically than was proper), congratulated Jenkins and presented him with money to buy my dress and pay for a short honeymoon at Brighton. It was as if they owned us both! They gave a special party in the servants' hall with beer, cider, roast fowl, pork pies and a fruit pudding with a sugar wedding ring on top almost as if we were already married. It made me sick to look at it! My life stretched before me like a dull map. I would go on being parlour maid, loyal to the family until I died, then I would pass the same ring on to my daughter, who would marry the footman who would serve the Master's sons. I felt trapped and needed desperately to escape.'

'So what did you do, Jane? Return the ring at once?'

'What! And break Jenkins's heart? He wanted to publish the banns the very next Sunday in the church where his parents were wed!

'No, Mary. I told him I was so excited that I must take the coach to visit my family on my next day off and tell them the glad news. He begged to come with me but I said it was best I went alone as they were in ill health. The Master agreed to give me two days off to visit them. Jenkins gave me the fare for the coach, and I also took with me the money for our wedding he had entrusted to my care. I carried only a small bundle of my personal goods and a bag of my best clothes which I told Jenkins were presents for my younger sisters. When he waved me goodbye there were tears in his eyes.'

'What happened after you visited your family?'

'I never did visit them then, you ninny! I got away from Jenkins and never returned.'

'But you sent back the ring and the money?'

'Why should I? He'd entrusted them to me and I made good use of them.' Jane stares at me as if I am an imbecile. 'It's no wonder you've stayed so long in this prison, Mary Jones.'

I draw back from my friend and fall silent.

'What is it? Don't you want to hear any more of my exciting life? You said that you couldn't wait.'

I nod, for in spite of my disapproval I am curious. But I ask myself how I could have forgotten what different characters we two are.

'Jane, I am so selfish! I did not ask if you wanted to join the others for tea. I am not hungry myself but you must be.'

'Join that mob of cut-throats in that grimy mess hall? No, Mary. I have no need to do that. Matron offered me tea with her shortly before I came to meet you.'

'Oh,' I say in surprise. In all the time I have worked in her office and received praise for my efforts, Matron has never offered tea to me.

'Of course, you are not really a prisoner here, just waiting for a vessel, as you say.'

We walk up and down together, as close as when we were girls of fourteen and sixteen sharing confidences, although Jane asks me little about myself. I am delighted when I manage to make her smile mischievously just as she used to.

'Such a foolish thing I did, Mary,' she says at last.

'And what could that be?' I say it with a laugh.

'Why, meeting those ruffians outside Madame Rous's shop. But, believe me, I did not trust them to deliver me the silk unless I was there keeping watch. They'd have run off and sold it at a profit to some dealer in stolen goods if I had not been waiting.' Then she says in sudden fear, 'Swear you will never utter a word of this, Mary!' As she does so it dawns on me what she has admitted.

'Oh Jane, then it's true!' I clasp my hand to my mouth.

'Swear on your life!' she grips my arm fiercely.

'I swear.'

'It is all the fault of that cruel John Knatchbull. And now he is here in the Colony! Transported for theft. He is *here*! I made inquiries from a young lieutenant who comes to The Mermaid frequently. Knatchbull was caught picking pockets at Vauxhall Gardens, disowned by his family and transported here as a felon. He is one of the few "gentleman convicts" to be sent to Sydney Cove, and it seems he has quickly made use of his fine manners to be promoted to constable or mail carrier, so that he may ride out on a well-bred horse and give orders, not take them! He is still as crafty as ever, it seems.'

'Poor Jane. You must have been terrified when you saw him. Did he recognise you?'

'I am sure he did. And waved most cheekily and laughed, inclining his head towards his companion, no doubt to boast about our secret "marriage" and the way he had shamed me.'

At this moment the other prisoners appear on their way back from the mess hall. Sarah is bringing Harriet across the yard to meet Jane, as I've asked her to. I struggle to recover from the shock of what I've just heard.

Jane grips my arm so that it hurts. 'Swear!'

'I swear. I have done so already.'

Harriet breaks free of Sarah and runs towards us. She looks shyly up at Jane and then at me for reassurance. 'Harriet, this is Jane, who I've told you so much about,' I say with as much enthusiasm as I can muster. Jane is still staring fiercely at me, willing me to keep my mouth shut. Sensing there is some difficulty, Sarah nods to me and leaves us together. I lift Harriet up to give Jane a kiss, which she is in the habit of doing to all her 'aunties' at the Factory. But Jane turns her face away so that the child's lips barely brush her cheek. She gives Harriet a pained smile, then turns to me. 'It must be dreadful trying to cope with a child in a place like this, Mary. What a wretched life she must have had. Can she speak at all?' She stares at Harriet as if she is some ill-treated animal.

'Yes, I can speak and I have not had a wretched life at all. Mama and me and the aunties are quite happy, thank you,' declares Harriet with conviction.

Jane looks astonished. I cannot help smiling and give my clever child a hug.

# CHAPTER 33

### Jane Tells Me of the Way She Procured a Husband
### February, 1828

In the following days Jane told me many more of her adventures. She said that after the Assizes she was so distressed that she fell seriously ill and could not leave Chester for several months. Her sister Bridget had a change of heart, and with their mother came to visit her in prison with food and warm clothing, but Jane's spirits were so low that she took little interest in them. She felt her life was over.

Afterwards, her ship, the *Henry*, departed from London and sailed via St Jago. The journey took five months. There were seventy-nine female prisoners, two male prisoners and some families aboard. It was a cruel voyage full of rough seas and sickness, with the convicts battened down below decks whenever the weather was foul.

'Crossing the Equator it was so hot the tar melted off the timbers below decks and dripped onto the faces of some women as they slept,' she told me. 'I listened to their howls and rejoiced that I had skills to save me from such misery. Of course the women who had any brains found better beds for themselves with the sailors and officers. But the problem with this was that many of them did not bother to douche themselves with vinegar or seawater after screwing, so they fell pregnant and vomited with morning sickness as well as sea sickness. Most did not even leave their sleeping shelves to puke.'

I told Jane I remembered this well.

'The stench below decks was bad enough before, what with the dung from the pigs, goats, cows and chickens waiting to be slaughtered, but the vomit of the female convicts made it something terrible,' she said.

Then there were the storms. Most frightening, as I too recall, were those caused by the southeast trade winds and the Roaring Forties. Jane was sure they would sink one wild night. The waves, she said, 'were like walls of black water and the roar of the sea like some monster that never drew breath.' They were all much relieved to arrive in Van Diemen's Land.

According to Jane's account, Hobart Town is like an English country village, rather hilly with rushing streams and very green pasture land, although it is quite uncivilised beyond the main streets. The natives are ferocious, she was told, and there are many escaped convicts who remain in the bush and terrorise the island.

The house where she was assigned was not grand but quite large for Hobart Town and stood on a hill above the township. It had a well-planted garden, orchards, stables and a well. There was also a carriage in which she rode with the Master's children whenever it was too cold to walk. Jane seems to have enjoyed herself in Van Diemen's Land. She was the assigned servant of Mr Officer for over a year. Then things changed for her again.

'I first laid eyes on James New in the parlour of my Master's house in Hobart. They were discussing the price of grain, or some other farm product. I was struck by James's fair-haired good looks. I remember thinking to myself that with my dark hair we would make a handsome couple. But much to my dismay I learned that Mr New was engaged to be married to a Miss Johanna Scott, who was soon to arrive from England to stay with us.

'I was to be most attentive to her, my Mistress said, and act as her companion, if that was what she desired. I cleaned out the guest room, polished the floor and windows, swept the slut's wool from under her bed and put flowers on the dressing table.

'When this pale English rose went for fittings for her wedding dress I accompanied her to the dressmaker and held her petticoats while she stepped into the masses of white silk.' Jane's green eyes gleamed with mischief. 'I managed to find a number of unpleasant creatures that I would hide in her bedroom — spiders, a bush rat, a snake. When I heard her screams I rushed to her rescue, pretending this was an everyday hazard and begged her not to make a fuss or she would upset her kind hosts.

' "But the snake. Is it poisonous?" she wailed, as I smashed it with a garden rake.'

' "Most venomous," I told her. "If it had bitten you, you'd not have lasted five minutes." Actually it was a harmless carpet snake.

' "Oh, I cannot stay here. I cannot! I have night-mares every night," she wailed.

' "You will get used to it," I replied with a kind smile.

' "But perhaps I will never get used to it."

' "Then you should not stay," I said simply.

'Over the next week many unfortunate accidents happened to Miss Scott. She was taken riding on a horse that was supposed to be quiet and it bolted with her so that she fell and cut her head. She ate something that disagreed with her and took to her bed, vomiting every half-hour. Her beautiful wedding dress was attacked by an angry possum that tore the silk to ribbons with its claws and then pissed on it.

'I sat beside poor Miss Scott as she wept. "This last horror is a sign from God, I feel sure, Jane. You are right. I should not stay. I could not live here. This country and the people in it have suffered and understand each other but I do not want to suffer. I shall break the news to James this evening."

' "I think that would be best," ' I said consolingly.

'I paid the convict at the riding stables what I owed him and the old woman for the herbs she had mixed to provoke sickness and hid the scissors and threw out the jar of piss I had used to ruin the dress. As soon as Miss Scott had sailed I began in earnest to console James. I told him that during the weeks his betrothed had been in my care she had confided her doubts to me, and that although she was a sweet and pretty young lady, she would never have made him the wife he deserved.

' "But I have waited for her these two years!" he declared. "Built a home for us, worked hard on my farm to make it prosperous and now it is all for nothing! Why did she not tell me before she came here that her feelings had changed?" '

'He was in despair and it took all my charm and skill to comfort him. But I managed it and within three weeks we were engaged to be married.'

How far she has come from that point to her latest troubles when she found herself sentenced to death!

# CHAPTER 34

**Jane is Summonsed to the Supreme Court**
**Sydney, March, 1828**

Yesterday, as Jane and I were pacing the Factory yard together after muster, she wailed, 'I cannot abide this awful place another day! The stench, the food, the work, the beds. And the company! When John Stephen came to visit me this afternoon he said it was a disgrace that I am being kept like a common criminal amongst this low life.'

'I heard the conversation, Jane, for I was working in the office next to the visitors' room. That is not quite what he said,' I protested.

'Well, he knows I'm innocent if no one else does,' she replied haughtily. 'He's brought me gifts which I am able to pass on to Matron Gordon in return for special privileges but still the life here is unbearable.'

'So James has still had no luck in finding a vessel?'

'My husband is useless! He's lost the licence to run The Mermaid and continues to neglect the business, which he says must be sold as soon as possible. He is also selling our cottage, horses and household goods so that we may have money to pay the court costs and start all over again in Hobart. What a disaster!'

I knew Jane would be relieved today when the writ of Habeas Corpus came through and she was summonsed to the Supreme Court. Mr Stephen has assured her that the Judge in this court will not be prejudiced against her, as the last one was.

Matron saw to it that she had warm water for a bath and she was able to take off the coarse prison uniform she calls 'disgusting rags' and put on her own clothes again. 'I have a strong feeling I will not return here, in spite of what my husband says about there being no vessels available to take us to Hobart,' she told me thoughtfully as I helped her to dress.

'What do you mean, Jane?' I asked in surprise.

She shrugged as if she wished to say no more. 'I am so glad you are here to say goodbye to me, Mary. Your company has been the most comforting thing about my stay in this wretched place. You are the only one I can trust with confidences I've been bursting to unload for many years now. Even if you were tortured within an inch of your life I do not believe you would betray me. That's why I had Matron call you here to say goodbye in private.'

I felt deeply touched by these words, which seemed to be uttered sincerely. I handed Jane the marriage quilt I had made for her and also a fine white linen handkerchief with 'JN' in one corner, which I had embroidered. Then we embraced and I begged her to take care, for I sensed that she would take any risk rather than return to the Female Factory.

'Goodbye, dear Mary. I see you are weeping tears as usual. Oh, but you always were a sentimental thing.' She said this with a laugh. 'Don't weep. I'll write to you.' And with that she allowed the Guard to escort her to the high sandstone wall and out through the gate.

# CHAPTER 35

**Constable Cleme is Given the Slip and I Become Angry with Jane**
**The Female Factory, March, 1828**

*Jane New has escaped from custody and is free!*

The whole Factory is agog and the prisoners talk of nothing else.

I do hope she is careful. If she is caught it will be the worse for her.

Why, oh why did she not wait the few weeks until she could be set free legally? When she told me she would scale the walls of the Factory if she could not get out quickly I begged her to be patient. But Jane is wilful and determined.

There are so many rumours about Jane's whereabouts. Eleanor Frazier says she has been hidden by her gentleman admirer, the Magistrate Mr John Stephen, who had a horse waiting just behind the Court House to carry her off. She swears that Jane confided in her before she left the Factory. I do not believe this.

Another rumour is that she was rescued by her husband, James New, who has disguised her as a boy and taken her away to the Hunter River where she is working as a waterman. One of the turnkeys, who has just come from the Hunter River, is certain he saw her there. I do not believe this either.

The police are pursuing her and the newspapers make much of her escape. The Constable who let her out of his sight has been reviled as a drunkard.

My marriage to William Baxter is to take place in a few weeks. I have almost finished sewing the bridal dress and Harriet's dress as well. I have stayed up late and worked by candlelight for so many night that my eyes are red and swollen.

Sarah says I must stop or I'll look as if I have been crying for weeks and my bridegroom will be hurt and not want me in his bed.

What a shock we had today. Jane is back at the Factory! She was only a week at large and was caught about twenty-seven miles out of Sydney, at a place called Minto. She did not look sorry or ashamed as she was brought back into the yard by two constables, but held her head high and stared defiantly around her, although she was dusty and dishevelled.

To my surprise she is not to be punished by being demoted to third-class but is now in first-class! This is good news, although I do not understand how it came about. I have not had a chance to speak privately with her yet. All the prisoners are curious about how she escaped and gather round her as if she is a queen, but she will tell them nothing.

Only Eleanor swears Jane has confided in her and told her all about her lover, the Magistrate John Stephen, who lusted after her during the trial and hid her in his lodgings near Minto where they spent the week. She was only discovered after they quarrelled about their future. He wanted to continue their liaison and she wanted to return to her husband, so Eleanor says. I told her to shut her mouth and stop telling such lies. They will damage Jane's future, not to mention that of Mr Stephen, who has apparently been very kind to her.

At last Matron gave me permission to meet Jane alone and we walked up and down the yard in the twilight as we had done before she ran away.

She told me that on the day she left the Female Factory she had such high hopes of never returning that on the journey from Parramatta to Sydney she began to hum a merry tune as the ferry chugged down the river. 'I could sense my freedom in the very air!' she said.

'So you really thought the Judge would let you go free?' I said. 'Tell me what happened in the Court room.'

'The case did not take long. I was not called upon to say anything at all but just sat giving the Judge demure glances while others came forward with complicated legal reasons as to why I should never have been tried in a court in this Colony. Mr Stephen had done his work well. He told me he expected the case to be all over within a few hours, and it was.

'Finally the Judge announced: "Jane New is to be

discharged, but remanded in custody to be returned to the Factory *pro tempore*. Thus has terminated this long-pending and important case to the satisfaction of justice."

'What! Sent back to the Factory? I suppose I should have felt grateful to John Stephen for making sure I did not rot here indefinitely, but my disappointment about having to return to this wretched place, however temporarily, and then being sent on to Hobart where I am still regarded as a convict, was so great that I could not do more than give him a weak smile.'

'So how did you escape, Jane?' I was surprised at how urgent my voice sounded.

'I sat waiting in the rotunda beside the Court House to be transported to the Female Factory, guarded by about eight constables. It annoyed me that so many should be thought necessary to attend to my safe custody. I turned saucily to the senior man amongst them and remarked, "You must have a useless pack of men if it takes such a mob of them to guard one young lady." At which he flicked me with his stave, causing a spot of blood to appear on my forehead. At that moment, who should come out of the court building but John. "Mr Stephen, pray protect me from the brutality of these thugs!" I cried, dabbing at my head with the fine linen handkerchief you gave me, Mary. His eyes flashed with anger but he only said calmly, "It seems strange that it should require so many men to secure one female." He then asked for the man whose actual charge I was in, Constable Samuel Cleme, to take me to his office to wait.

'As I was being escorted down Philip Street by Constable Cleme, I put my hand to my forehead and made as if to swoon. It was a hot day and I asked the Constable if he would be kind enough to let me enter the house of an acquaintance that we happened to be passing just then, to get a glass of water. Seeing that I might faint and that my forehead was still bleeding, he agreed. We went in, I greeted my acquaintance, took off my bonnet and shawl, which I left together with your marriage quilt on the table beside the Constable and was given a glass of water. The constable received a small glass of brandy. I then signalled to the Constable that I was going to the privy and, being a man of delicate manners, and enjoying his brandy, he waved me away. I heard later that after about five minutes, when I had not returned, Constable Cleme became anxious and inquired of my acquaintance as to my whereabouts. They both searched the house, and, finding me gone, concluded that I had got away by the back door.'

I could not help but laugh at this brilliant piece of trickery and Jane looked pleased that I appreciated her deviousness.

'But what happened next? You were at large for a whole week, Jane. Where did you hide?'

'I cannot tell you everything, Mary. There may still be trouble. It is best you remain ignorant of some things.' She sounded agitated. Instead she said she wanted me to write a letter to her husband and smuggle it out to him.

'I will write it, Jane, but I cannot risk smuggling it out. That you must do yourself. What is it you wish me to write?'

'Dear Husband; I heard that you are in Parramatta; I

hope and trust that you will get an order to come and see me, for I am almost out of my mind at not seeing you.'

'Stand close to me in the shadows and I will write it now,' I said, fumbling in my pocket for the stub of a pencil and one of the scraps of paper I always carried. Many prisoners rely on me to write letters to their loved ones.

As I was writing Jane said, 'I want you to do something else for me, Mary. I need a man's clothing.'

I stared at her.

'Borrow some from your bridegroom for me. It is urgent.'

'What! Jane, I cannot! I am due to be released from here to be married in a few weeks. It would be madness to risk being caught doing such a thing. And William, too, would be blamed if we were caught. Don't you see that?'

She snatched the note from me. 'You have no courage, Mary, no loyalty to your old friend!' she cried. 'I expected better of you.'

I controlled my hurt at this insult and said calmly, 'You should not take such risks either, Jane. You will be free in a few weeks. Why not wait?'

'I cannot wait! I am not the waiting sort of person!' she cried. And then she turned on me a look of such hatred that I drew back in shock. 'I am not gutless like you, Mary Jones, to wait over three years in prison without one attempt to get out. You could have helped me but you won't! You are a selfish, spiteful woman and the worst friend in all the world!' She almost spat the words at me and at first I was struck dumb. Then a

slow burning anger came over me and I began to speak
to her in a low voice.

'You are wrong, Jane. It is not I who am the worst
friend in all the world but you. I know that you
betrayed me and let me take the blame for the forged
banknotes when we were girls. How could you do such
a thing? I loved and trusted you and tried to protect
you after your mock marriage to John Knatchbull. But
now I am beginning to doubt that even that really happened. Did it, Jane? You don't have to lie to me for I see
you clearly for what you really are. A betrayer of
friends.'

Jane gasped. She had never seen me so angry and yet
so controlled.

She cried out passionately, 'John Knatchbull
betrayed me and I betrayed you!'

'But why, Jane, why?' I asked. 'I did nothing to
harm you. I loved you dearly.'

'And I loved him, the evil wretch. Work it out for
yourself,' she said brokenly. 'If you do not believe that
he tricked me into a false marriage, then go and ask
him. He is staying in Clarence Street and goes under
the name of John Fitch here in the Colony.

I shook my head. I did not want to upset her further.
But I still did not see why she would betray me because
she herself had been betrayed. 'Is it true what Eleanor
Frazier is saying about where you have been hiding this
past week?' I asked her gently.

'It is a pack of lies,' she retorted.

I sighed with relief.

'It is my husband who hid me, Mary. He loves me
dearly and has just opened a subscription for me. I will

tell you no more.' Then she smiled and a queer look came over her face. 'But if Eleanor wants to lay the blame on John Stephen, who is a gentleman with a fine reputation to uphold, although he did seem to fancy me at the trials, then who am I to say it never happened?'

I stared at her in astonishment. 'But which is the truth, Jane?'

She smiled and shrugged. 'Let the clever ones find out. I'm sure you must know.'

# CHAPTER 36

**A Nightmare of Jane**
**The Female Factory, 6 April, 1828**

Last night Jane escaped again from the Female Factory.

This afternoon a number of us were lined up in Matron's office to be questioned by two Constables. Only Eleanor had anything to say that interested them. I stood in silence waiting my turn, and listened with distaste to what Eleanor said.

'Yes sir, she was my dearest friend. Our mothers knew each other in England and we've been close since childhood. Jane New told me of her plan to escape from the Factory on Sunday night while the others were at muster. She had borrowed men's clothing and was wearing them as a disguise. Her husband was meeting her outside the prison walls with a cart.'

'Most helpful, Mrs Frazier. And what do you know of her previous escape from the Constable in Philip Street?'

'She told me she was helped to escape by the Magistrate Mr John Stephen, sir. I believe they were lovers and he hid her in his house in Minto for the week she was missing.'

The constables looked impressed and exchanged smiles of lewd satisfaction. I felt ill and wished I did not have to take part in this cross-examination.

Matron Gordon was questioned too, but looked as puzzled as the rest of us about how Jane had escaped. She seemed afraid that she might be held responsible so did her best to lay the blame on the prisoners. 'Talk to Mary Jones again. She often talked alone with Jane New. I'll warrant she knows more than she will tell.'

And so the tedious questions continued far into the night. 'What exactly did Jane New tell you about her intentions to escape?' they asked me.

'She told me nothing, sir.'

'But you were her closest friend. If she confided in Eleanor Frazier, whom Matron says was not as close to her, then surely she must have told you more.'

'She only told me that what Eleanor had said about Mr John Stephen hiding her when she escaped from the Constable was a pack of lies, sir.'

This made Eleanor toss her head angrily. She give me a withering look. 'What would you know, you poor innocent slag?'

One of the constables then took Eleanor out. The other continued to question me until I thought I would fall asleep where I stood. I did not tell him what Jane had said about her husband hiding her, for I was not sure whether it was true.

'We have reason to believe that Jane New escaped wearing men's clothing. How did she come by such clothing?'

'I do not know, sir.'

'You have a male friend who visits here regularly and has been seen to hand you packages. Did he provide the clothing?'

'No, sir. Mr Baxter and I are to be married. He would never threaten my chances of getting out of here by doing such a thing.'

'We will question Mr Baxter.'

'You will find him innocent, sir.'

Finally I was allowed to go. I prayed that William would acquit himself well. My mind was turning over and over the last thing Jane had said to me: '*Let the clever ones find out. I'm sure you must know.*'

Was Eleanor right to call me 'innocent'? Did Jane really mean to let John Stephen take the blame for hiding her, to protect her husband and herself? Did she take him as a lover so that he would do everything in his power to protect her? I had known Jane long enough to believe this was possible.

And was Jane telling the truth about John Knatchbull being in the Colony?

I dreamed a most disturbing thing. Jane New was standing at the top of a well, poking something far below in the water with a long staff. She was dressed elegantly and laughing to herself as she leaned over. In the water a face appeared. It was John Knatchbull's. He was drowning and crying for help. Jane poked the staff into his face until it disappeared. Then another face appeared. I knew it was John Stephen's. He too cried for help but Jane only laughed and pushed his face under the water. The next face that appeared was my own. I cried out to Jane so she would recognise me and pull me out. But she pushed me under too and water filled my lungs so that I could not breathe. I awoke in a sweat, panting and afraid.

'What is it, Mary?' whispered Sarah at my side. 'You were crying out "No Jane, don't, don't! Don't kill me. I'm your friend!" '

# VI
## The Rocks

# CHAPTER 37

### I Receive a Most Unexpected Wedding Gift
### Female Factory, April, 1828

Nine days passed and there was no news of Jane. Her husband James New had disappeared as well. Her name and description were printed in a list of escaped convicts that appeared in the *Sydney Gazette*.

> *Henrie, Jane, alias Wilkinson, alias New, Medway, 20, Dressmaker, Leeds, 5 feet 3*$^1$/$_2$*, black eyes, dark brown hair, fresh ruddy comp. From Female Factory.*

Not all of the details printed there were true. Jane was more than twenty, she was no dressmaker and I would never describe her complexion as 'ruddy'. More like roses and cream. Her eyes were green as a cat's, not black. She liked to spell Henry with a 'y', at the end. She seldom wrote her name, but still made her mark after someone took down a letter for her; this would not have seemed important to a newspaper. Oddly, I felt indignant on Jane's behalf about these mistakes.

I felt sad, too, that we had been so angry with each other the last time we were alone together in the Factory yard. Yet I was not sorry I'd told her of my true feelings about her betrayal. She was right when she told me that she was not the sort of person who could wait to be released; I saw now that she was desperate to escape and did not mean the hurtful things she said about me. If only I could have told her that in my heart I wished her well and hoped that she would never be caught.

My wedding day is here at last! Elizabeth Sibley, who is to be my matron of honour, visited early this morning to help me bathe and dress my hair. She brought presents too, wrapped in a cloth, telling me I must not look at them until after the ceremony. Then she handed me a sealed paper and said secretively, 'But this you must open at once.'

It seemed to be an official letter of some kind. I hoped it was not a summons to Court to be cross-examined again about Jane New's escape.

There were two letters inside, one from a solicitor. The other was written in a hand I recognised immediately. It gave me quite a start. 'But he is —'

'Read it!' said Elizabeth.

It was Andrew Frazier's last will and testimony. He had left all his worldly goods, his property and his money to me, '*Mary Jones of the Female Factory, late of my employ.*'

I was speechless.

Elizabeth smiled broadly. 'So you see, Mary, the old rogue came to his senses on his deathbed and has finally given you what you deserve,' she said. 'There may not be as much money left as he had before he married Eleanor, but at least there'll be enough to set you up in a cottage on The Rocks so you can start that little clothing shop you've been dreaming of for years.' Then she hugged me. 'Happy wedding day!'

# CHAPTER 38

**I Am Married to William and Become a
Rockswoman Again
The Rocks, July, 1828**

It was indeed a happy wedding day. The sun shone and
a small breeze ruffled our skirts as we walked to the
church — Harriet, Elizabeth Sibley and I, completely
without escort, like the free females we are. My friends
Sarah Carter, Sally O'Riley and Belle Marsh from the
Factory followed in the company of Matron Gordon
and a constable. I was sorry not to have more wedding
guests, but those of my friends who were not allowed to
attend for reasons of being third-class or having committed some recent misdemeanour assured me they
would still be able to hear the bells pealing from the
Factory.

The Reverend Samuel Marsden, who officiates at
many convict weddings, was there on the doorstep to
meet us. I have heard him described as a dour, humour-
less man, but today he was smiling. As we passed into
the church porch and waited to walk down the aisle, he

said, 'I wish to compliment the bride and her maids on their appearances.' Matron overhead this remark. Beaming like a proud mother, she told the Reverend Marsden, 'Mary is a talented seamstress, you know.' He gave me a surprised, questioning look and I smiled and nodded. Did he think that because we convicts sewed coarse Parramatta cloth into uniforms all day we could make nothing else?

I peeped into the church and saw William standing at the front near the altar with his back to me. He was dressed in a neat dark suit and his ears were bright red, so I knew that he was as nervous as I was. His friend, Martin Crisp, whom I had not met, stood beside him as groomsman. They had both got their tickets of leave at the same time, I knew, and been granted land on the Hunter River together.

When the Wedding March began to play I walked forward on Elizabeth's arm, with Harriet walking behind holding the train of my dress. It was a joyful moment I shall never forget. As I stood beside William and heard the words of the marriage service and we made our vows together I thought my heart would burst with happiness.

After the ceremony we walked in a small procession towards a public house nearby and people came into the street to cheer us and throw rice and rose petals. This was quite unexpected and I held out my hands to catch the floating petals while Sarah, Belle and Sally, still wearing their convict uniforms, caught the rice and shoved it greedily into their mouths, pretending to be starving. This play-acting made the people laugh and some ran into their houses to get bread and apples to throw to the women, who caught them neatly and shoved them in their pockets with toothless grins of thanks before the Constable could stop them.

As we reached the public house Matron signalled to the Constable that he should escort my convict friends back to the Factory, so after many embraces and a tear or two we parted, but not before I had thrown my bouquet to Sally, who also hopes to marry one day.

Matron and the Reverend Marsden also took their leave. Neither wished to be seen to enter a common public house where grog is drunk, although I happen to know that Matron has a generous supply of gin hidden in her office.

Elizabeth, Martin, William and I drank a wedding toast in mugs of ale, while Harriet had ginger beer, and we all ate some fine pork pies and slices of cold mutton with pickle. Then a fiddler appeared and played us a jig.

'Dance! Dance!' cried Elizabeth. 'First the Bride and Groom!'

So William and I danced together for the first time in our lives, for a merry few moments that left us both breathless and laughing. Then Elizabeth danced with Martin Crisp and I caught hold of Harriet's hand and brought her onto the sawdust-covered floor to dance with me and William. The fiddler played on and was soon joined by a customer who produced a tin whistle, and then by a young man who played the spoons. Other people joined in the dancing and wished us well on our wedding day, and so it seemed that there were many guests after all.

It was the happiest party I'd ever had and when we

were all too tired to dance another step Elizabeth told William and me that our 'bridal chamber' awaited us at the top of the stairs. She took Harriet off to sleep in another room with her, and Martin went back to his lodgings in Parramatta.

At last William and I were alone. Our marriage bed was a large four-poster which took up almost all of the room. Suddenly I felt shy. Turning away from it, I walked to the window and looked out through the lace curtains. I could see the high sandstone walls of the Female Factory clearly in the moonlight, and sighed. The women would be side by side in their hammocks whispering and laughing, cursing and crying.

When I turned round William had his back to me and was undressing quickly. I sensed he felt as shy as I did. I turned my back to him and did the same, hanging my dress on the only chair. Then we both ducked under the covers, still with our backs to each other. Neither of us said a word. I began to laugh softly, partly out of nervousness and partly because it seemed so stupid to hide from each other when we had longed for this moment for months. William leaned over and kissed me gently. I returned his kiss with passion. It was over three years since I had lain with a man I loved and I was more than ready for it.

That was three months ago and we are now settled into our new home in Cambridge Street on The Rocks. I must say we are most contented. Elizabeth says everyone on The Rocks can tell we are newlyweds because of the way we walk along the wharf on Sundays arm-in-arm, not looking where we're going but gazing into each other's eyes.

After poor Andrew Frazier's debts were paid there was just enough money left for me to buy a cottage and the small shop next door, which has yet to be repaired. William told me that he would not touch a penny of Andrew's money but it all must be used to fix up the shop, which will become my seamstress business eventually.

The cottage has four rooms as well as the kitchen so we have plenty of space. William uses one to lay out his specimens and there are two bedrooms and a parlour. In the evenings we sit on our small veranda and watch people strolling home down the hill or to the public houses for their tots of rum. We are already well known to the neighbours and they call out and wave to us. I have started a kitchen garden full of vegetables and herbs at the back and in the front a flower garden. The cottage is not new and has needed some repairs. Now it is as neat as a new pin, with crisp curtains, fresh paint, scrubbed boards and shining windows.

Harriet thinks it is like heaven here, where she can run about freely and chatter to other children. She is very trusting and calls all the women in the street 'aunty', even the drunks who yell abuse at her. I have warned her to stay clear of these, and of some of the men. She has almost no experience of men.

William is absorbed in his work much of the time, which I do not mind as I have been busy myself. He has already been away at the Hunter River twice, to live in his hut with his friend Martin Crisp and clear some of the land, as well as collect specimens. I have a feeling he is anxious to settle out there in spite of his promise to live in town for a few years. He does not talk of it but often seems distracted when he returns, and tells me with longing how Martin will soon be moving there to start his farm. I try to cheer him up by preparing his favourite dinners — steak-and-kidney pudding and toad-in-the-hole. He kisses me then and whirls me round the kitchen, saying I am the dearest little wife in the whole Colony.

I must say I like being married. I enjoy it when the butcher or the baker respectfully call me 'Mrs Baxter'.

Last Sunday I suggested to William that we should hire a rowboat and go at low tide to collect cockles. It was a fine sunny day and I wanted to show him a part of the harbour that I loved. William agreed and Harriet was so excited at this idea that she skipped up and down the passage chanting, '*Cockles and mussels alive, alive oh!*' over and over. I prepared a picnic lunch of fresh bread, tomatoes and cheese while William collected a wooden bucket, sharp knives, and hats to keep off the sun.

We rowed slowly out amongst the barges and ferries and barquentines with sails tied to their masts, around the orange-coloured rocks covered in bright green weed and past the mangroves, along the shore beyond Soldiers Point to Cockle Bay, where we anchored the boat and clambered out onto the rocks to gather our cockles. The only sound was the gentle washing of waves on a small white beach. Harriet soon forgot about the cockles and dashed into the water to paddle and splash. A tall white heron stood still on a rock. A blue butterfly floated by. Cicadas screeched from the bush above us.

Across the harbour on the north shore faint smudges of smoke drifted into the sky from tiny settlements. It was so peaceful. After we'd filled the bucket with cockles William and I sat close together on the sand and stared towards the setting sun. 'Do you like being married, Mary?' he asked me.

'I never believed I could be so happy,' I whispered to him.

Not everyone is as fortunate as we are. Elizabeth Sibley is pleased to be no longer 'Mrs Sibley'. She insists on being called by her maiden name, Elizabeth Male. But on The Rocks, where she has lived for fifteen years, she is always called 'Elizabeth'.

She and her young son Thomas live not fifty yards from us in Cambridge Street, which is a blessing. Originally her husband was going to give her a cottage in Essex Street next door to Thomas Hughes, the Hangman, where nobody would live, not even the poorest tenant. But she shamed him out of that.

A few days ago Elizabeth told me she wanted to introduce me to a friend of hers, a wealthy widow named Sarah Wills. 'Sarah lives near Dawes Point at the foot of The Rocks and owns a great amount of property — her house, a warehouse, two farms, and a brig with cargo valued at £2,500.'

'Heavens! What's in the cargo? Gold?'

'Elephant oil.'

'Ah.' I was not sure what elephant oil would be good

for. 'And how did she come by such wealth? Did her husband leave it all to her?'

'Not all of it. She is a business woman in her own right, which is rare enough in these parts. We should learn from her, Mary. Put on your bonnet and we'll pay her a visit this very afternoon.'

Sarah Wills was a large, impressive-looking woman. She welcomed us into the parlour of her beautiful house and asked us to sit down. It was quite a formal atmosphere. We felt as if we were being interviewed for positions in her household, rather than paying a friendly visit. But she had understood perfectly what we wanted to know, and over tea and scones she told us with a smile that in 1812, when she married George Howe, who was the Editor of the *Gazette*, husbands on the Rocks still referred to their wives as 'my woman', by which they meant 'my property'.

'Oh my goodness! Things have improved a lot since then, Sarah,' said Elizabeth. 'The Rocksman will now wait for his friends to refer to his wife as "Jack's woman", then smile at her possessively.'

They both laughed. Then Sarah said seriously, 'As soon as I married and before I had any of the six children, I had a Deed of Trust drawn up.'

We looked at her attentively but remained silent for this was the advice we were anxious to hear.

'This meant that when my husband took it into his head to go off with another woman and have five children by her, neither I nor my children lost anything. By then I was running my own businesses anyway, but without the Deed of Trust, the other woman and her children would surely have got the lot!'

We thanked Sarah Wills for her advice and Elizabeth cursed all the way home that she had not had a Deed of Trust before William Sibley made off with all the money they had both worked for, leaving her to support their young son as well as herself.

'At least you have the cottage, Elizabeth,' I said consolingly.

'Not much for fifteen years of misery married to that philanderer. Did you see in the papers a few months back how one of his fancy women — Charlotte Beeby Walker, that's her name — robbed him and he had to bring charges against her? I'll bet *she* doesn't get three months in the Female Factory for misbehaviour!'

As we walked Elizabeth kept insisting I should draw up a Deed of Trust immediately.

'But I do not believe I would ever need one,' I protested. 'William is the gentlest, most fair-minded husband. He has insisted I keep what is left of Andrew's money for my shop.'

'Yes, at present he seems generous. But just wait and see! My guess is that after a year or two he'll want some cash himself and his mates will say, "She's your woman and her property is yours. Take what you want!" '

'What nonsense, Elizabeth! William is quite different from other men.'

Elizabeth almost collapsed with laughter. 'Wait and see!' she cried. 'Sarah Wills drew up that deed while her husband was still besotted with her, and just as well she did, or she'd have been out on the street with her six children. She should be an inspiration to all women on

The Rocks, and you are a silly goose, Mary, if you think your husband is better than hers was.'

I felt disgusted with her words and for the first time, I decided not to speak to my friend for at least a week — until, hopefully, she had come to her senses!

# CHAPTER 39

### Eleanor Frazier Seeks Me as a Friend
### The Rocks, September, 1828

There is still no word about Jane New, who has now been at large five months. There are plenty of rumours about what has happened to her. She stowed away to New Zealand dressed as a man. She is back in Van Diemen's Land living as a respectable married woman. She drowned trying to board a vessel near Bradley's Head. She is living with her mother, who was transported here as a convict and is now a free woman, and her new stepfather. Together they run boats up and down the Hunter River and Jane is disguised as a waterman.

I read in the newspapers that Eleanor Frazier gave evidence in court about Jane's escape from the Female Factory and then said that Mr John Stephen helped her to escape on the first occasion and hid her in his house in Minto for a week. Mr Stephen described Eleanor as 'the most notoriously abandoned prisoner in the Factory, whose profligacy is notorious thoughout the Colony.' Eleanor is mischievous and can be mean, but I have met far worse prisoners than her in the Factory.

I hear that Mr Stephen has lost his job as Magistrate and is in disgrace. I wonder if he did help Jane to escape. She can be very persuasive and I would not be surprised if even he succumbed to her charms. Wherever she is, I do hope Jane is safe.

I had quite a shock today. William was away at the Hunter River, Harriet was playing with friends next door, and I was hard at work sewing a bridal gown for a customer, when there was a loud knock at the front door. My neighbours never knock, just call out and then come in, so I wondered who it could be. When I went to open the door there was Eleanor Frazier herself standing on the front porch. My first thought was that she too had escaped from the Factory. But she looked too well dressed and self-satisfied to have just clambered over a wall. 'Well, Mary, aren't you going to invite me in? I'm your neighbour now,' she said jauntily.

I ushered her inside. 'Well, well, very nice cottage indeed,' she said, taking everything in. 'Don't worry. I've no hard feelings about Andrew Frazier's will. You were a better friend to the old man than I ever was a wife to him.'

I was speechless.

My silence must have shaken Eleanor's confidence for she hastened to offer me some juicy gossip. 'I have the latest news on Jane New, for your ears alone.' She lowered her voice. 'She and her husband James New stole clothes from their friend, a sailor named James

Middleton, and Jane, disguised in them, sailed all the way to New Zealand. She is now settled in Hokianga and keeping a house of black savages as prostitutes!'

'I don't believe a word of it, Eleanor.'

'Then I'll introduce you to a sailor who swears it is true. He saw her there,' said Eleanor indignantly. She sniffed. 'In case you're wondering, I'm a newly married woman myself now. Remember that shy young clerk in the office at the Factory? Mr Turner?'

'I do.' He was afraid of most of the prisoners and looked awkward whenever one of us came to his office on an errand.

'Well, it's him I married. I'm Eleanor Turner now. Wed at Scot's Church, Parramatta, just like you. Being assigned to him I was allowed to leave the Factory immediately, of course, and now we've moved to The Rocks, just up the road.' She pointed. 'I heard you lived here so thought I'd best pay a neighbourly call. You look surprised, Mary.'

'I am. I had no idea …'

'Just shows how cut off from the real world you Rockswomen are!' She laughed. 'How's Elizabeth Sibley? And old Margaret Keever? She got out just before me and lives hereabouts.'

Politely I offered my best wishes on her marriage.

'Oh, don't mention it.' She settled herself into the most comfortable chair. 'Mr Turner is a harmless rabbit with little twitching whiskers, who is very nervous around me, but at least he got me back my freedom. I don't think I'll keep him long.'

'You are not in love with him then, Eleanor?' I asked.

She roared with laughter. 'Have you seen him?'

'Yes. He is shy but not unpleasant.'

'Oh Mary! You're still so innocent. I'd have married him if he was an imbecile. He was the only man I could get in the Factory.'

I gave her a disapproving look. 'Does he love you?'

'No, I don't think so. I haven't done anything particularly nice for him. Though I did tell him once I was grateful.'

'And is he content with that, Eleanor?'

'He wanted a wife and now he's got one. Isn't that enough? There's five men to every woman in this Colony. Half his luck!'

I turned away, shaking my head.

'Don't be such a judge of others, Mary. I wanted to be your friend in the Factory but you were always so standoffish and superior, you made me want to puke.'

I turned back and stared at her.

'You probably think I couldn't have cared less about ruining Andrew Frazier. You're wrong. He was a good man. But he was too old. And he was strict, like you, always judging me, criticising me for wanting to have a dance and wear pretty clothes. He could afford them. Why wouldn't he give me some? The first time I fought with him about that he lost his temper, called me a slut and struck me. I hated him after that. When he still wouldn't buy me anything I stole his money, as much as I could get hold of, and squandered it. He came after me with a horsewhip once but I hid in a friend's house. Then he begged me to come home, saying he would buy whatever I wanted. I told him he was a disgusting old man and I'd never loved him. That's when he broke down and didn't care what happened any more.' She sighed. 'I was sorry afterwards, for I saw how fast he sank into the drink. He took a slut to live with him and she helped herself from his purse when he was sleeping. She boasted in the Labour in Vain how easy it was. She lived with him for eight months, which is why he sent me to the Factory. It was her that finished him off, poor devil, not me as you imagined. I wanted to explain it all to you. But you'd never let me talk to you for longer than a minute, except about that Jane New. Otherwise you'd be off with your nose in the air, looking furious.' She hung her head.

'It wasn't just Andrew Frazier you stole from. You took food from a prisoner in the Factory who was sick and starving. That's what made me really angry with you,' I said.

'Ann Hamilton was a whining bitch. Everyone hated her!' she burst out. 'I only took her food once. At least I didn't hit her like the others did.'

'Did you feel any remorse when she died, Eleanor? Or when Andrew Frazier died of a broken heart?'

'Yes! Yes, yes, yes,' she cried out in earnest. 'But I've never said it, not to anyone till now.' She looked up at me. Then she burst into tears. 'God forgive me, but you make me say the truth, Mary Jones!'

'Well, what is the *truth* about Jane New?' I asked, showing her no mercy now. 'Did Mr John Stephen really help her to escape?'

'I don't know. He might have,' she wailed.

'But you gave evidence in court that Jane told you he did.'

'No, she didn't tell me nothing. I wished she'd talk to

me but she wouldn't say a word. Even though we were friends as children she wouldn't talk to me. Only to you. It broke my heart!' The wails grew louder.

'Eleanor, you have perjured yourself in a court of law and caused Mr John Stephen to lose his position. That is a serious offence.'

'What do I care! He's a gentleman. He can get another job. For once I had people listening to me, hanging on my every word. Not judging me and telling me I was no good, like you and Andrew Frazier!' she cried angrily.

Suddenly I felt a wave of compassion. This weeping woman was hardly more than a girl and yet she'd suffered a hard life. Her brazen manner was to keep up her spirits and cover her loneliness. She had as much remorse as anyone, including myself. I *had* judged her and not wanted to hear her side of the story about her relationship with Andrew Frazier. I too had seen him angry and knew how terrifying it was.

I put my arms around Eleanor and held her while she cried.

# CHAPTER 40

## A Gentleman Makes an Unexpected Visit to My Humble Cottage
## The Rocks, December, 1828

My little shop is almost finished and next week I shall move all my sewing into it. It will be a relief not to have half-finished gowns, shirts and baby clothes all over the parlour. Eleanor Turner has been helping me to line the new shelves and stack them with neatly folded quilts and petticoats and to display the gentlemen's wear at the front of the shop, along with the ladies' frocks. She is quite artistic and has an enticing way of arranging things. It is a surprise to me to see how well we get along together since her visit here a few weeks ago when she broke down and cried. She has worked hard for me ever since and refuses any payment, although she accepts the petticoats I make for her. As we sat sewing side by side one afternoon I asked her, 'Did a sailor really swear to you he saw Jane New in New Zealand, Eleanor?'

She shrugged. 'He did, but I must confess he was much in drink.'

I nodded, relieved that the rest of the story must certainly be false as well.

'Damn, I've pricked me thumb again and there's blood dripping onto this baby's nightgown. I reckon I'm better at arranging things than sewing 'em, Mary.' She put her sewing aside and prowled about the new shop with a critical eye. 'You know what's missing?'

'Tell me.'

'You need a sign above the door outside saying "Mary Baxter: Seamstress". Let me paint it and hang it out for you!'

I wrote out the words and Eleanor copied them carefully, working on the sign all afternoon. When it was finished we stood outside admiring it.

Later that evening Elizabeth Male came by to look at the almost finished shop and made a further suggestion. 'Why not hang up a painting of yourself sitting on a cushion sewing a fine seam, like Curly Locks?' she said with a mischievous smile.

'What do you mean?' I asked, puzzled.

'Don't you know that nursery rhyme, Mary?' She recited:

*'Curly Locks, Curly Locks,*
*Wilt thou be mine?*
*Thou shalt not keep chickens,*
*Nor yet feed the swine,*
*But sit on a cushion and sew a fine seam,*
*And feed upon strawberries, sugar and cream.'*

She burst into a peal of laughter. 'I think that is just how William sees you. Long may it last!'

I frowned. I still had done nothing about the Deed of Trust.

'Is William still away up on the Hunter?' she asked casually.

'You know he is.'

'Strange that he spends so many weeks away at a time.'

'He has a lot of specimens to deliver before Christmas and he and Martin are hurrying to finish another room on Martin's hut.'

'Have you ever been up there, Mary?'

'No. What use would I be to men clearing land and building all day?'

'You might be company for William.'

I sighed. 'I have so much to do here and it isn't really safe for Harriet.'

'Why not leave her with me for a day or two and go by yourself?'

I felt uneasy about leaving Harriet with anyone, even Elizabeth, although I knew that what she was suggesting was probably a good idea. I had been lonely and ill at ease lately. During the past few months William had been away more often than he'd been at home, and he'd been sending fewer and less affectionate letters. Mostly he just asked me to send on more money. I had always known that he earned very little from his botanical collections but lately he had seemed to be particularly needy.

'Thank you, Elizabeth. It is not good for a husband and wife to be apart so much. I'll travel there next week just before the shop opens. And you are right about drawing up a Deed of Trust, too. Do you still have the address of your lawyer?'

She smiled and handed me a piece of paper. To my surprise the name on it was Mr John Stephen.

So it was that just a few days after I'd written to him, there was a knock on the door and on the porch stood the young gentleman himself. I recognised him at once from the cartoons in the newspapers. He introduced himself and apologised for calling on me instead of replying in writing. I invited him in and offered tea, which he accepted. He was a most polite and pleasing young gentleman and I was intrigued to meet him after all the rumours I had heard. He told me that the Deed of Trust I had requested could be drawn up immediately, and asked where I had heard about it. When I told him it was Sarah Wills who had suggested it he raised his eyebrows and said that she was a most successful business woman. He asked if I too was interested in going into business and I said that it was my ambition to do so. He tactfully inquired whether my husband was in favour of this. I told him that he was, and that he had insisted the money I had inherited be used to start my shop. Mr Stephen said it was fortunate that he was such a reasonable man.

'Mrs Baxter, I confess there is another matter on which I would like to speak to you,' he said, looking anxious. 'I have heard that you are an honest and reliable woman and that you were a close friend of the escaped prisoner, Jane New.'

I drew a deep breath and held his gaze steadily. 'Yes

sir, I knew her years ago in England and met her again recently at the Factory.'

'Are you aware of the allegations being made against me in regard to Jane New, Mrs Baxter?'

'I have read about them in the newspapers, sir.'

He coloured slightly, then said briskly, 'I am anxious to clear my name of these allegations. They were made by a notorious and unreliable prisoner named Eleanor Frazier, who is now married to a Mr Turner. Do you know her?'

'I do, sir.' I said this guardedly. Although I had reservations about Eleanor, I felt myself rising to her defence in the presence of this confident, indignant gentleman.

'What do you think of her character, may I ask?'

'She has a lively character and has been known to embellish the facts, sir, for she enjoys a dramatic story. But she is kind to her friends and is not an absolute liar.'

'Well, she has lied most convincingly about my part in Jane New's escape and I have lost both my position as Magistrate and my honour,' he replied angrily. 'Governor Darling has chosen to listen to the evidence of a convicted criminal above my own, apparently believing that I was infatuated with Jane New, when I was only trying to defend the wretched woman.' He looked quite upset and I felt sorry for him. He apologised for the outburst, then said quietly, 'I wonder if you would be kind enough to help me to trace Jane New, Mrs Baxter.'

'I would if I could, sir, but I've not heard a word from her since the escape,' I replied honestly.

He looked disappointed. He was about to take his leave when I said, 'All I have heard about Jane's whereabouts are rumours and hearsay, but there is a waterman you might speak to, name of James Wood. He says that about five weeks after Jane's escape from the Factory he rowed James New to a vessel that was lying to below Bradley's Head, and he swears he saw Jane New on board that ship dressed in sailors' clothes. She knew him from when she and her husband kept a public house, The Mermaid. She called to him, "Goodbye Jem." '

Mr Stephen became quite excited by this news. 'Did the waterman say what ship it was and where it was bound?'

'He did not, sir. But Jem might tell if you asked him.'

'Do you know where Jane New stayed after her escape, while she was waiting to board the vessel, Mrs Baxter?'

'I do not, sir.' I hesitated and then said, 'There is a man by the name of John Jobbins who says he lent money to James New to pay the passage for himself and his wife on a vessel about to leave the Colony. He has a box of Jane's clothes still, so I hear — perhaps by now he has sold them off to pay back the debt.'

Though this could all be just more rumours about Jane, I told Mr Stephen where he might find Jobbins and Wood and he thanked me profusely, saying that if they would give evidence his case could be well advanced.

He promised to return with the Deed of Trust for me to sign in a few days' time.

# CHAPTER 41

## Jane's Daring Escape and Adventures in a New Land

*The Bay of Islands, New Zealand, 1828*
*My dear Mary,*
*Only now do I feel it is safe to write to you. It was an adventure getting here, I must say. You would have been too much afraid to try such a daring escape so I will tell you about it, as now I am far enough away from the law to be out of danger. At last I have shaken off my shackles and begun a new life.*

*I have employed a young Scotchman, a runaway convict himself, as a clerk in my business — he writes all my letters as I dictate them. Perhaps I will never have to waste time learning to read and write.*

*Now to my tale. After I escaped over the Factory wall (Yes, I managed without your husband's clothing, dear Mary) I hid in lodgings for five weeks until James found a ship for us. We could not go directly to Hobart Town — no ship's captain in Port Jackson would risk taking a* 'felon' on board. Instead we planned to sail to Batavia in the Dutch East Indies, where no one would know me, and from there, some time later, board a vessel bound for Van Diemen's Land. We certainly had no wish to live in such a steamy, disease-ridden hole as Batavia, which is well known as a sailors' graveyard.

We chose a day to embark when no less than five vessels were sailing from King's Wharf, in order to confuse those who might pursue us. The 'Mary' sailed for Batavia between six and seven in the morning. The 'Cumberland' and the 'Guide' were bound for India. 'Resolution' and 'Henry' (yes, Mary, the very same transport that brought me from England) both sailed for Launceston, and our would-be captors no doubt deduced we were on one of those two vessels bound for Van Diemen's Land.

I took passage aboard the 'Mary' in disguise, as Midshipman James Middleton — you would have laughed to see me swaggering as a sailor — and James assumed the name of William Burke. At dawn we were rowed out to Bradley's Head where our ship was lying to. I would have liked nothing better than to return with Jem Wood, the Waterman, to Port Jackson, to hide away a few months until the constables stopped looking for me, and then, with a change of name and hair colour, resume my life in Sydney, which is the sort of town that forgives reformed criminals. Hobart Town is a dull backwater where my convict origins would hang round my neck like an iron collar for ever. But I could not tell James that. He loved the place.

I stayed below decks for most of the voyage as I felt low in spirits and was seasick. The Master of the 'Mary' *had been well paid and asked no questions about the pale figure wearing a sailor's garb who sometimes prowled the deck after dark.*

*When at last we anchored off Batavia and were rowed ashore I felt great relief. James set off to find us lodgings near the port so that we could organise our departure quickly.*

*The Dutch build their colonial houses of wood with wide verandas and small windows to keep out the tropical heat. I went into such a house, an inn, to get out of the sun. As I was now dressed as a female again, I was soon approached by a pleasant enough Dutchman who introduced himself as Willem Blok, a trader. I told him my name and said I was a traveller, with plans to start a small business.*

*'Not much scope for your business here in Batavia,' said he, looking me up and down. 'Unless you want to grow coffee, tea, indigo or tobacco. These crops bring good profits for our treasury — the Indies are seen as the cork on which the Netherlands floats!' He gave a cheerful grin. He was not exactly handsome but I could tell he fancied himself. He soon began boasting of his friends in high places. 'The new Governor-General, Johannes van den Bosch, I know well. I could introduce you to him,' he offered. I declined his offer in a civil manner. I did not want him to become too friendly too fast. Then, giving me a sly look, he said quietly, 'No scope for your business in Batavia, but I can tell you of a place not far from here where a woman with your looks could make a fortune.'*

*Just at that moment I looked out of the window and saw James returning so I bade my new friend farewell, but not before we had arranged a time to meet again to discuss the business he had in mind.*

*James had found lodgings in a small wooden house with a floor of dried mud. It was clean and smelt strangely of hops, perhaps because of its grass roof. Brightly hued flowers and plants poked their heads in the windows — crimson and purple and smelling of honey. A woman brought us coconut milk to drink. It is not milk at all, but a clear liquid, quite refreshing. She cooked fish on a fire of coals and served them wrapped in palm leaves. 'This must be what it is like to be a savage,' I said to James. — 'Don't fret, Jane. There will be a vessel leaving for Van Diemen's Land before long,' he told me. 'And I will move heaven and earth to get us on board.'*

*I wished he would not trouble himself.*

I read on eagerly, as though Jane's letter was a chapter in some wild romantic novel. I could not guess what would happen next.

*I met Willem again that evening and he told me about a place called Kororareka. 'It is off the north coast of New Zealand, at the Bay of Islands. The most beautiful wilderness imaginable. That is where you will make your fortune, my good woman.' By now the astute Dutchman had guessed I was a runaway of some kind. 'There are no laws there to hold smart people back. No Governors, not even a constabulary. And the whalers who come into the Bay of Islands after spending a year at sea are rich beyond imagination. They have money to burn and are desperate to spend it. You'll make a fortune if you play your cards right, pretty lady.'*

*'I hope you are not suggesting anything improper, sir,' I said in a tone of wounded dignity. — 'Beg pardon, ma'am. I would not dare insult you with any such suggestion. I got carried away with the romance of the place, that is all.'*

*We talked a long time about this strange part of the world and I wondered how I might get there. 'You will need money to start with. Don't go there empty-handed,' Blok told me. 'If you buy good muskets you can sell them to the natives for profit or exchange them for land or timber. The natives are warlike and will exchange anything for muskets. You could make your fortune in less than a year.'*

*Over the next few weeks I had several more meetings with Willem Blok. Eventually he introduced me to a ship's Captain who owed him a favour. This Captain happened to be sailing in a week's time to Hokianga at the Bay of Islands to get a load of timber, and he agreed to take me on board, although the fee he asked was high. I decided to leave it until the last minute to tell James, for I knew he would not approve of the plan I had now set my mind on.*

*On the evening of my departure, when my bundle was already on board the vessel bound for Hokianga, James came rushing up from the port shouting, 'Jane! I have found a ship for us! We sail for Hobart Town in three days time!' He swung me round on the mud floor of our little house, where we had in truth been happy these past weeks. 'James, I cannot go with you,' I told him gravely. — 'But it is all arranged!' he protested. —*

'No, you must go alone. In Van Diemen's Land I will not be a free woman. There will be another court case. I shall be thrown back into prison. I would rather die. I have made up my mind. I am not going back there.'

James was terribly upset. He could not believe I was leaving him on his own. 'It's that Dutchman, isn't it? I've seen you with him. He is your fancy man, isn't he?' I told him it was nothing so sordid. I had a plan to start a business and Mr Blok had encouraged me, that was all. 'I must sail to New Zealand as soon as possible. I shall stay a few months and when I've made my fortune, who knows, you may want to join me. I shall be a free woman by then. I could even return to Hobart Town if you wish. Now I must hurry, for the vessel sails tonight.' — 'Tonight?' He staggered as though he had been punched. 'We cannot part, Jane. I'll come with you!'

I flung myself into his arms. 'You are my own love,' I told him. 'I shall miss you terribly. But you must not come. I will succeed in business and win back our lost fortune, and you will be proud of me.' I covered his face with kisses. 'I am going now, James, but I need some money to survive. We'll meet again soon. I will write to you. When it is safe I will join you in Hobart Town, I promise.'

James handed me his money purse. 'Take it all!' He covered his face with one arm and sobbed, holding me close with the other. 'Oh Jane, you have broken my heart!'

'Have courage, my love. We won't be parted long. Kiss me goodbye.' I twisted my head to look down at the vessel at anchor close by. 'The wind is coming up fast to fill the sails!'

*I tore myself away from him and almost leapt out of the door. As I was rowed the short distance to the ship I watched the sad figure of my husband standing alone on the wharf. I was sorry to leave him so miserable, but lately he has been more of a burden and I knew the time had come to make a clean break. I may see him again, I may not.*

Goodbye for ever, James, I thought to myself as I read this. Ruthless, ambitious Jane!

*After some weeks at sea I landed at Hokianga, a rugged harbour settlement on the west coast of the North Island. You would be frightened out of your wits by the natives here, Mary, who look so fierce and give blood-curdling war cries. They are so savage I have been told that they eat their enemies. Our old friend the Reverend Samuel Marsden, who has been in New Zealand for some time, is trying to tame them with Christian teaching but I think he has had no more success than he did with us Females at the Factory!*

This made me smile. I remembered how the Reverend Marsden had complimented me when I arrived at the church in Parramatta for my marriage. How complicated life was, with laughter and tears all mixed up together. I read on.

*Why did I decide to escape the Factory? I never believed that Judge in the Court who said that when I returned to Van Diemen's Land there would be no more trials. If I had waited in the Factory for a vessel to take me back to Hobart Town I'd be in prison now. A lamb to the slaughter — that I would never be. So here I am, alone in this wild, windy land where the cliffs are sheer and tall forests grow right to the water's edge.*

*Well, it is not quite true that I am alone. There are several other runaways like myself living here amongst the natives. Such a warlike race they are! The men are strong and tall, built like giants. They disfigure themselves with tattooing that covers most of their bodies. The women are beautiful but they too have tattoos on their chins and upper lips. It is a horrid blemish. Still, they are friendly enough to us, calling us 'Pakeha'. They live in villages like forts that they call 'paa', digging into the sides of steep cliffs to protect themselves from their enemies. Their war canoes are huge and long and ornamented with carvings. It is not difficult to believe the tales the missionaries tell of slaughter and cannibalism, but so far they have shown only kindness to us poor castaways living along the shore. Some native girls showed me how to cook their food, sweet potatoes, fish and pigeons, by burying them in earth ovens. It tasted very good.*

*After a time I decided Hokianga was too rugged a place. I had had no choice of landfall. I heard there was a better settlement across the bay called Kororareka, where whaling ships from England, France and America anchored offshore and where some almost respectable white people were settled, ships' captains and so on. This is the place where Willem Blok told me I would make my fortune, and I decided to go there as soon as the stormy seas were calm.*

*So now I live in Kororareka, a busy place with grog*

shops galore. The missionaries disapprove of these and of the native girls who 'have no morals'. However, the Reverend Gentlemen are kept too busy trying to stop the battles between native chiefs on the beach and in the Bay to attempt to do anything about such evils.

I have a thriving business which I will delay writing about until I hear from you. You would smile if you could see me in this remote part of the world greeting my customers in a gown made of the finest silk, courtesy of Madame Rous! I could never have worn it in Sydney Town for fear of a noose around my neck. I carried it across the seas with me rolled in a bundle, and one of the 'savages' the missionaries' wives have taught to sew made it up into a passable gown. Fat Madame Rous would gnash her teeth if she could see her precious green silk shimmering in the moonlight as I promenade along the shore at Kororareka!

Your humble servant, dearest friend, and soon to be very rich Jane New

PS Congratulations on your marriage, which must have taken place months ago.

# CHAPTER 42

**Mr John Stephen Becomes a Friend and My Foolish
Husband is Jealous**
**The Rocks, December, 1828**

I was relieved to hear Jane was alive and well, but disturbed to hear that she had gone so far away! I had imagined she was in Van Diemen's Land, safe with her husband, not alone in New Zealand. It sounds a frightening place, full of savages and tribal wars that not even the missionaries can stop. Why are there no constables, I wondered? It seems there is not even a Governor of the country. Jane is brave-hearted to stay in such a place.

I admired her boldness for all the risks she had taken — the escape from the Factory over the wall, the disguise onboard ship, living on a wild beach with castaways and savages. She was right. I could never have done what she did.

But I was shocked to hear that she had abandoned her husband, James, and broken his heart. How could she be so cruel? He was devoted to her. He had taken great risks to get her out of prison and hide her, and had almost ruined himself with debts fighting her case in the courts and paying her passage to Batavia. How could she then leave him and take the last of his money? I felt angry and outraged with Jane for the second time in six months.

I do not know why she is so secretive about the kind of business she is engaged in and why she would not allow poor James to assist her in running it. He has ever been her loyal business partner.

I was in a quandary. Should I tell Mr John Stephen I had heard from Jane? Just knowing where she was might put his mind at rest.

For a week I worried and wondered about Jane and about Mr Stephen, and for all of that week Harriet was ill with a cough. She was still lying on the sofa by the fire the morning Mr Stephen called with the Deed. I introduced him to Harriet and he asked if I had sent for the doctor.

'I have tried, sir, but he is busy and cannot come,' I told him.

'Then let me send for my own doctor, who will come at once, I assure you.'

'I could not afford such a doctor as treats the gentry, sir,' I said quickly.

'It is no matter. I will see to it. The child seems very ill.' And he hurried out. He has a kindly manner and I trusted him. I was most relieved his doctor was coming, for Harriet had been coughing and wheezing so hard that at times I thought she would not draw another breath. I had tried all the herbal remedies I knew but nothing eased her dreadful cough.

In half an hour Mr Stephen returned in a cab with a gentlemanly doctor dressed in black. He examined Harriet, who weakly submitted to all his requests, and then he turned to me and said gravely, 'Your little girl must go to the Military Hospital in Fort Street, Mrs Baxter.'

'But there are infectious diseases running rife at the hospital!' I said in alarm. 'Could I not nurse my daughter at home?'

'Rumours, just rumours,' he said, dismissing them with a wave of his hand.

But Mr Stephen could see how distressed I was. 'Dr Balmain, I too have heard about the danger of infectious diseases at the Military Hospital. Why not prescribe medicine for Harriet and call on her regularly until her condition improves?' he suggested most reasonably. The Doctor shrugged. As long as he was being paid by Mr Stephen he did not seem to mind doing this.

He wrote out a prescription, and a messenger boy, such as are plentiful on The Rocks, was sent directly to get medicine from an apothecary. I marvelled at the power of wealth and connections to get things done in a hurry.

As soon as the Doctor had gone I thanked Mr Stephen with all my heart. After such kindness, I could not do other than tell him I had received a letter from Jane New and I copied out her address. He was deeply grateful for this. 'It will be of immense assistance in my case. I am grateful to you.'

There, I thought, I have been disloyal to Jane at last! And I felt a certain relief at it.

Mr Stephen was curious to learn more about Jane than just her address. 'What sort of clothes did Jane New arrive at the Factory in?' he asked.

'Very fine clothes. Jane always dressed like a lady. In truth, when she arrived at the Factory some prisoners mistook her for a member of Lady Darling's committee.'

Mr Stephen smiled broadly at that and almost laughed out loud, as if he admired her spirit, but collected himself just in time. He produced a letter from his pocket and gave it to me to read. 'This cheeky note was sent by her to my brother Mr Sydney Stephen, the Judge, whom she treats like a servant,' he said.

I read the note, which listed Jane's clothing, down to the last stocking, then added: *I authorise you to get my property that Mrs Gordon, Matron of the Factory has, and if she refuses I give you full authority to bring action against her.*

I smiled. 'Will your brother do it, sir?'

'Certainly not. I had forgotten about the list until now. The letter is sent from Hobart Town in June, so she must have asked her husband to post it to confuse the authorities as to her whereabouts. Her plan of deception worked well.' He re-read the note, shaking his head. 'She is amazingly sure of her rights for a convict who has so recently abused the law and all those who would have helped her.'

I could scarcely contain myself for wondering how

much he had helped her. I thought that if he was in love with her once, he was evidently sorry for it now. 'Jane is certainly a pretty young woman and had many admirers even when she was in the Factory wearing her unbecoming uniform, sir.'

He turned on me with some irritation. 'Do you think I have an interest in discussing Mrs New's looks and her admirers, Mrs Baxter? I tried merely to give the unfortunate woman a fair trial. I swear to you, I did not help her to escape nor did I harbour her in my house. I would have been mad to do so. My brother is a Judge and my uncle holds the most senior position in the judiciary of the Colony. I myself believe wholeheartedly in the legal system and until recently had a promising career in it. Why would I risk everything for an infatuation?'

'Sir, I accuse you of no such thing! Pray forgive me if that is what I have given you to understand. But I know Jane New and have seen her bewitch the most intelligent of gentlemen, friends of the Governor visiting the Factory to inspect the inmates. She has a rare charm and an innocence about her that I fear is misleading.'

I knew I had rattled on and said far too much, perhaps to save my own embarrassment and Mr Stephen's feelings, but he just nodded thoughtfully. Then he turned away and said quietly, 'Misleading, indeed.'

He called several times over the next week to see if Harriet's cough was improving and seemed almost as relieved as I was that she grew steadily better. He often thanked me for my help. Both Jobbins and Wood had agreed to testify to Jane's escape from Sydney Cove and had passed on further contacts. He did not mention Jane again. He told me he was leaving soon for England to plead his case there. 'Governor Darling has given me no choice,' he said bitterly.

The next time he visited I took the opportunity to ask him if, in his duties as a magistrate, he had heard of a gentleman convict named John Knatchbull.

'I have heard there is an educated convict in the Colony, a brother of Sir Edward Knatchbull. He was transported for picking pockets in Vauxhall Gardens in London,' he replied. 'Why do you ask?'

'Because Jane New once told me she was married to him in a mock ceremony. He deceived her cruelly, so she said. She was only sixteen and he took advantage of her innocence.'

Mr Stephen looked sceptical. 'Do you think that is true, Mary?' (We were no longer so formal with each other. He now used my first name and I had stopped calling him 'sir'.) 'I did once, but I have had doubts,' I replied. 'I would like to know the truth of it. It has affected my own life as well as Jane New's.'

He looked curious but asked me no more questions. He said he would try to find out more about Knatchbull.

He paid us one last visit before leaving for England. Harriet was quite well by then and was able to thank him herself for all the care and attention he had arranged for her. She had sewn him a little purse embroidered with forget-me-nots. It was not entirely suitable for a gentleman to carry but it was her own idea, so I allowed her to present it.

'Why, Harriet, this is splendid! Did you really make it all by yourself?'

He was good at play-acting, I thought. Perhaps he had learned to do it in court.

'I did, Mr Stephen. I would like you to take it to London.'

'I most certainly will. And carry it with me on Bond Street, where some of the smartest shops are, so that people can see what fine purses we have in the Colony!'

I laughed. He was going too far. Harriet only smiled and nodded. 'I would like you to do that,' she said gravely.

When Harriet ran outside to play, he told me he had found out a little more about the convict Knatchbull. 'He goes under the alias of John Fitch. Last year there was a letter from London of dubious quality sent to the Colonial Secretary, Alexander McLeay, apparently on behalf of a woman claiming to be his wife. As there is no record of Knatchbull or Fitch ever having been married, I would guess that the intention of the letter was blackmail.'

'Then he may have tricked another poor girl into believing he had married her,' I said grimly.

'It is possible. Or the girl may have been trying to cheat him out of some money. He still has connections with his family, in spite of his disgrace.' He paused, then added, 'I hear that when he was in the Navy he accumulated debts with fellow officers which he refused to pay. And in the Colony he was not much liked by the other convicts. He gained his ticket of leave in record time, so I hear, by betraying plans of escape to the authorities.'

'He does sound like the sort of man who would ruin a young girl's life,' I said thoughtfully. 'I hope that I never have the bad fortune to meet him.' (Perhaps even then I had a strange foreboding about John Knatchbull.)

John Stephen nodded absent-mindedly. I could tell he wasn't really interested in the subject. As he was leaving he said, 'Mary, if you have any further news or information about Jane New while I'm away I would be obliged to you if you'd pass it on to my father, Mr Justice John Stephen, at his town residence at Ultimo House. And if you need any further assistance from our family doctor, please don't hesitate to contact my father also. He is such a hypochondriac Dr Balmain practically lives in his house!' He smiled. 'My mother is a sensible, compassionate woman. You may trust her completely.'

I suddenly felt extremely grateful to him and said, with some feeling, 'Mr Stephen, you are a very kind gentleman.'

He only laughed and shook his head a little sadly.

At the door, just as he was leaving, I said on an impulse, 'Are you and the Stephen family admirers of Governor Darling?'

He gave a short, harsh laugh. 'It is surely no secret that we are not. Why do you ask?'

'I have read articles in the newspapers by Mr Wentworth, who is often critical of Governor Darling. The Governor is said to disapprove of certain judges, and I thought perhaps one of them might be your father.'

'You are most perceptive, Mary, and have analysed the situation well,' he replied. 'We Stephens are opposed to militaristic authoritarianism and Darling believes that is the only way to govern.'

I did not entirely understand what he meant but thought that the Governor must be too much like an army general for the Stephens.

'When I was at the Factory, Governor Darling made some changes and improvements there, getting rid of a corrupt matron, raising the salaries of the staff and feeding us better. That was good. But I was always a bit afraid of his wife. She had a grand lady friend who was most determined to adopt Harriet.'

I told him the story of how the lady was eventually dissuaded by Harriet's biting her and he laughed out loud. He congratulated me on my daughter's cleverness and said I had brightened his dull mood. I too felt brighter after his visit. I shall miss him when he goes to London.


I had to delay going to the Hunter River to see my dear William because of Harriet's illness. Now he has written that he has heard I receive frequent visits from 'a gentleman' and sounds angry. Foolish man! We have been apart far too long. I must go there directly and surprise him, explaining that Mr Stephen has been kind to us and he has no reason at all to be jealous.

William also wrote that he would be too busy to come home for Christmas. This cut me to the quick. Being apart on our first Christmas as a married couple would be just too bad, I thought. William's recent letters have been brief and a little terse but I imagined this was because he'd been working too hard. Although I had mentioned the Deed of Trust to him I did not feel I should yet ask him to sign it, as his humour has not been good these last weeks. Perhaps he is right to feel hurt that I am not more often beside him, I thought. So I packed a hamper with a ham, some freshly baked loaves, cheese, a chicken, a plum pudding and some fresh vegetables from my garden, closed up the shop and the very next day Harriet and I took our places on the coach that drives there once a week. It was Christmas Eve. We were excited. It was the first time we had journeyed so far outside Sydney. I hoped that the road would be safe, as I'd heard there were bushrangers and escaped convicts who'd gone wild and dressed like the black savages, with spears and red mud painted on their faces. I had decided to take Harriet with me, as it had been so long since William had seen her.

Harriet, unaware of possible dangers, was in high spirits and chattered all the way, pointing out creeks and logs blocking the narrow road, and keeping the other passengers amused. 'We're going to visit my Papa who lives on the Hunter River in a hut he made all by himself,' she boasted to a farmer's wife.

'Are you just? Up on the Hunter we all builds our own huts, did you know that, Missy?'

Harriet shook her head. 'But on The Rocks Mama and I did not build our cottage for it was builded already, while we was in the Factory.'

The farmer's wife opened her eyes wide and said knowingly, 'Ah yes, the *Factory*.'

I tried to hush Harriet but she was enjoying the attention of the other passengers too much.

'And what sort of life did you have in that bad place called the Factory, young lady?' asked a rugged-looking man with white whiskers.

'It were not a bad place for I had all my aunties to play with!' Harriet replied with pride. There was loud laughter from all the passengers.

I looked out of the window at the straggly gum trees and smiled to myself. I was a free woman with a clever, healthy child, I had a business of my own and as was on my way to spend Christmas with my dearest husband. Life could not get much better than this, I thought.

# CHAPTER 43

## I Am Sadly Surprised and My Life is Changed
### The Rocks, April, 1829

My situation has changed a great deal in the past few months. When Harriet and I travelled to the Hunter River in high spirits to visit my dear William for Christmas, we were unpleasantly surprised to find that he was not living alone. The sun was just setting as we clambered along the path from the road where the coach had set us down. In the distance we saw the hut he had so often described to me, and there outside it was a young woman cooking on an open fire.

'Who is that lady, Mama?' asked Harriet brightly.

'We will soon find out,' I said, tight-lipped. I put down the basket of food and our bundle of clothes, which were heavy, and stood watching from the shelter of the bush. Presently William came out of the hut and, walking up behind the woman, he folded her in his arms. She turned to face him and they embraced for what seemed a long time.

Harriet turned a questioning face to mine. I shook

my head, for I could not utter a word. My heart was pounding and I felt dizzy with shock. My first impulse was to turn and run. But where would Harriet and I sleep in this darkening bush full of snakes and natives? We waited and watched.

The woman extricated herself from my husband's embrace at last, and he sat down on an upturned crate while she ladled food from the pot on the fire onto plates. Stew or soup. It smelled good.

'Will they leave some for us, Mama?' asked Harriet hopefully.

I shook my head as if I could not tell and tried to smile to reassure her.

'Let's go down there and ask for some. I'm hungry,' she said.

'Just wait a little. We have food of our own in the basket.'

'But I want some of Papa's dinner. Why is that lady eating it all up?'

'Sssh,' I said gently. 'We'll go down there soon.' And I handed her part of the loaf I had baked that morning and a leg of chicken.

They looked the very picture of a domestic couple, sitting side by side in the firelight on their upturned crates eating their supper.

Why, oh why had I not realised what would happen if I stayed on The Rocks for so many months, leaving him alone? I had selfishly wanted to open my shop and not listened to his yearning for a farm of his own on the land he had been granted when he earned his freedom. I was a foolish woman. Elizabeth Male had been right to mock me by calling me 'Curly Locks' who sat on a cushion all day sewing a fine seam. If only I had taken her advice and come here weeks ago when she first suggested it. But how could I have left Harriet when she was ill, and the shop, which had only just opened?

When they had finished eating the woman took the plates into the hut and William lit his pipe. He sat back, enjoying the evening.

'Now we will go and see Papa,' I said cheerfully. 'We did not want to interrupt their supper, did we?'

Harriet gave me a look which showed she couldn't see why not and we picked up our bundles and set off down the track. It was almost dark now. As we came close to the hut our feet cracked some twigs and William sprang up. He leapt towards the hut and grabbed his gun which he pointed in our direction.

'No! No!' cried Harriet. 'Don't shoot us, Papa! We've brought your Christmas pudding!'

He seemed to freeze, a black silhouette in front of the fire. Then he put down the gun and walked towards us. At the same moment the woman came out of the hut and called, 'Who is it, Will?' He made no answer.

When he reached us Harriet threw herself into his arms, laughing with relief. 'We thought you were going to shoot us like savages!' she cried. 'But you were only joking, weren't you, Papa? We've brought lots of food for you' — she looked anxiously over his shoulder — 'and for the lady too.'

'What are you doing here, Mary? You didn't write that you were coming,' he said tensely.

'We came as a surprise. For Christmas,' I said bitterly. I turned towards the young woman who had

come forward, looking curious. 'You had better introduce us to your friend.'

Next day was the worst Christmas I can remember. I
was too miserable to eat a morsel. William too ate very
little, but he made up for it with rum. Most of the rich
food was eaten by Harriet, Alice Wilton (that was the
young woman's name) and Martin Crisp, who had
been groomsman at our wedding and now, just eight
months later, seemed to be presiding over our
separation.

After the meal William and I went for a walk by the
river to try to talk through our differences. I was
already feeling numb and did not hold out much hope
for our future together. The night before he had told
me he was in love with Alice. After he had walked her
home to her father's farm nearby, Harriet and I slept
together in the bedroom while he slept alone on a narrow bed in the kitchen. I saw female garments under
the pillow in the bed he usually shared with Alice.

Alice was eighteen, he told me as we walked, the
daughter of a hard-working sheep farmer whose wife
had been slain by natives a few years back. In spite of
the shocking death of her mother, Alice was 'a fine bold
girl who loves the land and would like nothing better
than to be my wife and live here with me,' he said. 'You
are a town woman, Mary. You want to be in business.
You have gentleman callers who help you draw up
Deeds of Trust to make yourself independent of your
husband.'

I was hurt and shocked. I had no idea that he

resented my shop and the Deed, which I had been careful to tell him about well before I drew it up.

'But William, I thought you were proud of my independence. You told me you were.'

'Well, I lied. If you think I'm going to sign that damned Deed then you're mistaken. I want a wife who admires me, not herself. And I want children that are not the bastards of some other man.' He had never been so belligerent.

'Harriet adores you. She thinks of you as her Papa. How could you say such a thing?'

'Who is Harriet's father? Why the secrecy? Tell me now!' He grabbed my arm and shook it.

I wrenched myself free. I was angry. 'I made a promise to him not to tell anyone and I will keep that promise,' I replied.

'It's no wonder I've grown to despise you! You keep a promise out of respect for a man who gave you a bastard and yet you have no respect for me!'

I had never seen William in such a mood. 'But I do respect you! I love you, don't you see? Of course I admire you, much more than myself, but I have respect for myself. Surely that is not a bad thing?'

'You have more than respect for yourself. You worship yourself! You and your convict friends, the women on The Rocks, think you can do what you like!' He was shouting now, whacking at trees with a stick as if he wished it were me he was beating.

'William, don't say such things. You have drunk too much rum. It is not like you to say such things.'

'Shut your mouth, woman. I will say what I like! I have spent a miserable time with you — I was a fool to take pity on you enough to ever marry you. All convict women are sluts and whores. I should have listened to my friend when he told me that. But now that I've found a pure woman I will marry her instead. And don't try to stop me!'

I stood still, allowing this to sink in. 'Your friend Martin Crisp told you all convict women were sluts and whores?'

'He did and I didn't listen. But now I know he was right.'

I let him walk on alone. I did not think there was much point in continuing our talk.

Early next morning Harriet and I took our leave. Martin Crisp had offered to drive us in his horse and cart some ten miles along the main road so that we could meet a coach on its way to Sydney.

I sat up beside him and Harriet stayed behind us so that I could speak to him in private.

'Martin, tell me frankly, when you were groomsman at our wedding, did you really think that I was a convict whore and slut?'

He blushed for he had not heard me use such words before. He turned his head away, not wanting to answer, then said quietly, 'It is a common belief in the Colony this is what convict women are.'

'But when you met me and saw how much in love with William I was, and he with me, and when you danced with me and my friend Elizabeth that evening, did you yourself believe we were sluts and whores?'

He shook his head.

'Then why, Martin Crisp, did you poison my husband's mind against me?' I said angrily.

He had no answer and we drove in silence for the last few miles.

It is now four months since William and I have seen each other. He has sent me one letter but that was a legal one, with nothing personal in it. He has petitioned for a divorce and I shall give it. I feel deeply sad and a failure, in spite of the fact that my little business is doing so well and soon I will have my ticket of leave.

Harriet is five and at school now and does well at her letters. She reads and recites verse and sings as happily as a young magpie, but she too is sorry not to have her Papa with us. 'Why did he not want to be with us any more, Mama?' she asks over and over. 'Was he angry with us? Why did he like the other lady better?'

It is too painful for me to explain, so I shrug and say that men are strange creatures. 'You and I have been happy, just the two of us, for many years. Let's not think about Papa.'

'But will we get a new Papa by and by?'

I say I do not think so and she looks sad. 'Who would you like for a new Papa?' I ask jokingly.

'I have not found one yet but when I do I will tell you.' She says this very seriously.

I hug her and give her a ha'penny to buy a toffee apple from the sweet seller at the other end of Cambridge Street.

The other night, when I had given special permission for Harriet to stay with her great friend Polly round the corner in Harrington Street, I thought I would close the shop early and call on Elizabeth Male. I was feeling melancholy and needed to confide in a good friend. But Elizabeth was not at home. I went on to King's Wharf, as I enjoy watching ships on the harbour. It is something I do when I am feeling lonely or homesick. As I was returning, climbing the narrow goat track to the Rocks, I was hailed from a rickety little house perched on a boulder. 'Mary! Why so glum?' called Eleanor Turner. 'Come on in!'

I had never been inside Eleanor's cottage. It was a mess, with windows smashed and no paint or curtains, but she made me welcome and showed me around as proudly as if the place was a palace. I did not see any sign of her husband. 'Is Mr Turner not at home this evening, Eleanor?'

She sighed, like a heroine in a tragic story. 'Mr Turner is not at home this evening nor will he be on any other evening.' Then her face crinkled up with laughter. 'He's left me and good riddance! He was boring me to death! What a dull man!' She gestured at the broken windows. 'I gave him a good send-off as you see. Apart from the breakages, what do you think of my cottage?'

'Why, it's very … promising,' I said tactfully. I wondered at this tradition of smashing windows on The Rocks whenever husbands gave trouble.

'Ha, Mary, you are the very soul of charity. Yes, it is promising. It belonged to a waterman who died. Right there, in that chair you're sitting in.' She laughed as I jumped up. 'Stay there. It's the best chair in the house.

He left the cottage to his son, who doesn't need it for the moment so he told me to stay here as long as I like.'

'Very generous of him, Eleanor. Is the son a good friend of yours?'

She laughed again. 'No, he's in prison. On Norfolk Island. He won't be needing the house for five years or so. Come, I'll take you to my local, The Whaler's Arms, for a rum or two with my friends. That'll cheer you up.'

I was about to protest that I had to go home to Harriet when I remembered that I didn't. 'And don't say you've got a pile of sewing to do, for you work far too hard as it is and all good Rockswomen need a treat on a Saturday night!' With that Eleanor grabbed my arm and dragged me off.

As I sat in the public house drinking rum with Eleanor and her raucous, lively friends I wondered what William would say if he could see me. 'Convict whore, with her sluttish Rockswomen friends.' I could feel my mood turning maudlin. A tear ran down my cheek.

Then a fiddler started up and Eleanor grabbed me and whirled me onto the floor. I had not danced since my wedding night and the memory made me sadder. I whirled around faster and faster, grinning through my tears. No one seemed to notice I was crying and after a while I stopped and began to enjoy myself. A few more rums and Eleanor and I were staggering.

'Come on home and I'll cook you a feast!' cried Eleanor. 'They don't serve proper food here, just sawdust and offal.'

We clambered the short distance home to her cottage, slipping on rocks and laughing wildly. Inside I slumped into the chair the waterman had died in. It suddenly seemed rather funny that he had dared to die in my chair. I had a short sleep and was woken by the delicious smell of kidneys and bacon frying. Eleanor served them to me on a tray with a napkin and good silver. I did not ask where this had come from. We sat in the derelict cottage eating our elegant supper and sipping glasses of sherry, which Eleanor had magically produced from a shattered sideboard in the corner.

Suddenly I remembered that one of William's favourite suppers was kidneys and bacon and I began to sob.

'Oh Mary, stop your snivelling!' cried Eleanor. 'I know you miss the wretch, but believe me, you're well rid of him. He was probably just after your money!'

'No, no. He wasn't. He told me to keep it for myself.'

'And when you did, he hated it! He expected you to say, "Oh William, please take my inheritance for yourself!" '

'Do you think so?'

'Yes, Mary, yes! Why are you so stupid? Sorry, my dear. You aren't stupid, just far too trusting.'

'It's all my fault he found someone else, Eleanor. I refused to live on the Hunter River with him.'

'Ooh. How awful you were not to go and get butchered by the savages just to please him! What a shameful wife! Listen, Mary, he's found a silly young girl who worships him blindly but you are a clever woman with plans of your own.' She stood up and gestured wildly to make her point stronger. 'He's jealous of your life here on The Rocks, of your cottage and your friends, your customers, your smart little daughter and your emancipation. You'll be wealthy by and by and he'll be just another battling farmer scared out of his wits by the savages and bushfires and his sheep dying in the drought.'

She raised one arm in triumph and proclaimed: 'You'll be a true woman of The Rocks!'

I hugged Eleanor. She had made me feel much better. After some more sherry she said she would escort me home in case I lost my way. She picked up a full bottle of rum, just in case we should need it, and we had a merry walk home under the stars, singing happily all the way. The Rocks clock struck midnight as we came in sight of my cottage. It seemed a pity to end our joyful evening so soon, so we danced and sang a little longer in Cambridge Street, a fine new song we had composed, which repeated the refrain, '*We are Women of The Rocks, Oh no we do not have the pox. For we are Women of The Rocks, Oh yes and proud of it!*'

Suddenly a Constable appeared and said he was arresting us for causing a riot.

Next morning this Constable was mysteriously found to be drunk. No charges were pressed. Eleanor had gone back to the station with him and plied him with the whole bottle of rum.

# CHAPTER 44

**Jane Takes on a Dubious Business and Survives a Maori War**

> *Kororareka, 'Hell Hole of the Pacific',*
> *The Bay of Islands, 1830*

*Dear Mary,*
*Well, I have seen more than enough bloody warfare. 'The Girls' War' as it is known in these parts, was enough to make me a pacifist for life. It was fought on the beach here at Kororareka and went on for days. A hundred were killed including Chief Kiwikiwi's daughter and at the end of it all, in honour of the dead Chief Henghee of the Ngapuis, both tribes set fire to our town!*

*But let me go back a few months to my arrival in Kororareka and the setting up of my thriving business.*

*On the opposite side of the harbour, about two miles away, is Paihia, a neat little settlement where the missionaries live. The Reverend Henry Williams, who runs the Mission Station, is not a bad fellow. He is trusted by* the natives and has even made some converts. The Whalers call Paihia 'Heaven side' and Kororareka (which they much prefer) 'Hell side'. Kororareka was once a Maori 'paa' but now it is a collection of huts where we Pakeha deserters from ships and runaways from the law get along well enough with the natives. They have moved only a little distance away and provide us with kumara, potatoes, fish, pigeons and wild pigs. There is a cluster of grog shops along the shingly beach, along with a carpenter and blacksmith, and two whaler captains have cottages here where they stay while their boats are being repaired.

When I arrived here I was not well. A kindly settler and his native wife, Lydia, took me in and nursed me through my illness, which lasted a few months. I recovered and was soon in the best of health again. I was able to get close to Lydia, who introduced me to her friends. Native girls are full of laughter and don't need much of an invitation to keep the sailors company on their ships. The sailors invite the girls to clamber up the side of their ship until it is time to sail. Here, I thought, was an opportunity for me to do some business. The 'ship girls' are a scandal to the missionaries. Over in Paihia the Mission women take native girls into their homes and try to teach them to be good housewives. They teach them to cook, clean and sew, even to read and write. But as soon as a ship appears on the horizon the girls drop their mops and kettles, needles and thread and race to the beach where there is always some cousin or aunty willing to paddle them out to the Bay. Even before the ship drops anchor it is surrounded by laughing girls climb-

*ing aboard to meet old friends. In return for a few coins or a battered musket they will stay on board for weeks.*

*What a waste of capital, thought I.*

*The Chiefs do not appear to mind the girls of their 'paa' behaving like this so long as they bring back muskets. But, I thought, what if the muskets they got from me were superior to those the whalers give them? Why, then the chiefs would insist the girls should work for me!*

*I decided to meet with the only Chief I knew in Kororareka and come to an arrangement. In the meantime I hired a carpenter to build a cottage on the waterfront made of native materials so that the girls would feel at home. Finally, I used almost all the money James had handed over as we parted to buy twelve fine muskets. Ten of these I locked away in the gunpowder store at the end of the beach and two I kept locked in a chest.*

*As soon as the cottage was completed I invited Chief Kiwikiwi of Kororareka to afternoon tea in the front parlour. The invitation was delivered by a native girl who worked for me as a cook. She returned in her canoe the same afternoon and told me the great Kiwikiwi would come in three days time to talk business with the Pakeha woman, but he did not like tea. Instead we prepared a small feast of pigeon-blood soup, baked fish and kumara.*

*We sat in my small garden at the back of the cottage and after Kiwikiwi had eaten I showed him one of my prize muskets. He examined it carefully and pronounced it better than the 'sham damn iron' weapons offered by the sailors on board the ships. I explained there were many more just like it for the Chief if he would allow me to employ the girls of his 'paa' to work* only for me, instead of going freely to the ships. The Chief thought hard for a while and said it would not be easy to stop the girls climbing aboard the ships. It was a thrill for them to see a white sail in the distance and then to paddle out in a fleet of canoes and surround it. He said it was like a war, except that the sailors were kind to the girls and welcomed them. He explained that these were not 'fine girls' who would become wives of the tribe but war captives who did the hard work in the village. Allowing them leave to work for me would mean they were unavailable to work for the tribe. He suggested it would be better for me to give him two muskets to settle such a difficult contract, not one.

He is a clever Chief. I had foreseen he would not be content with one musket, which is why I had a second one in the chest. I said that he could take one now and the other when he had delivered the six girls I would need to open my business. They need only stay three days each, I said. Then they could return to their 'paa' and six more girls should come. In this way they could all enjoy the novelty of meeting sailors and feeling they had helped purchase muskets for their 'paa'. Of course they would be fed on the freshest food and no grog, I reassured.

The Chief nodded gravely. To save face he insisted on the last word. He said it would be no disgrace if the girls were given presents to take home to the men of the tribe. I agreed. He also requested that the girls should take herbal steam baths, made by putting certain plants and water on hot stones, to prevent any Pakeha diseases being brought back to the tribe. Many other tribes had suffered after their war captive girls had lain with the

*Pakeha, he said. I assured him that we had more mod-*
*ern methods of preventing venereal disease and even*
*pregnancy. He looked surprised.*

*Only then did Chief Kiwikiwi rise with dignity and*
*take his leave. 'That's probably the last I'll ever see of*
*Kiwikiwi, the musket or his girls,' I thought to myself.*
*But I was wrong. The very next day he arrived with a*
*small fleet of canoes paddled by some native men and*
*containing six of the prettiest girls I had seen. A pity*
*about their facial tatooes. They looked excited and*
*fairly danced over the shingles to my cottage where they*
*ran from room to room shrieking with delight at the*
*beds covered in white nets to keep out mosquitoes. They*
*bounced on the beds and tore off the nets, draping them*
*over themselves like brides. I clapped my hands crossly*
*like a schoolmistress and gestured for them to put the*
*nets back. But they took no notice whatsoever, appar-*
*ently deciding they were far better as veils, sashes and*
*fishing nets. I decided to let them use them as they*
*wished, at least for the moment. Kiwikiwi took his sec-*
*ond musket and departed with dignity and not one*
*word.*

*And so my more than profitable business began.*

*On the first night the girls sat outside on the veranda,*
*draped in their mosquito nets, giggling and talking*
*softly to each other. They looked like a cluster of virgins,*
*though I doubt that they were. When the first customer*
*came to the front steps they fought over him! I had to in-*
*tervene and speak firmly to them.*

*By the third night we had more business that we*
*could handle. I took bookings. The customers were de-*
*lighted by my pretty girls in their demure white veils*

*and by the end of the first week they had given us a name — 'Brideshouse'.*

*During the day the girls slept, swam, played, ate, carved wood, made baskets or went hunting to amuse themselves. The whalers paid me well for their services and appreciated the grog I served as part of the hospitality. I did not allow drunkenness and my cottage was always kept clean and neat. When the third day came and six more girls arrived, none of the first girls wanted to go home. They liked the freedom, the atmosphere, the harmonicas and fiddles and tin whistles the sailors would play and the little presents they brought them — whale's teeth, shell necklaces and foreign coins.*

*I sent a message to Kiwikiwi to say that if he was willing to accept another musket I would keep all twelve girls but for the moment he was not to send any more.*

*There was a squabble between the girls who had mosquito nets and those who had none. I had no more nets to give the new girls. I settled the matter by cutting the original nets in half, now that they were not being used to keep out mosquitoes. A bit more fighting went on about this but it stopped when I threatened to send the troublemakers back to their 'paa' immediately. I began to feel like the Matron at the Female Factory! I had to employ an extra cook and the carpenter began work on extending the cottage.*

*At the end of three months I had made enough money to buy twelve more first-class muskets and had made a handsome profit for myself as well. So I did not welcome the disruption of a war.'*

In past letters Jane had related other adventures, misdemeanours and daring exploits that had amazed me, but this letter from Kororareka contained the most astonishing news I had ever heard. Her daring schemes and extraordinary tale made me feel that my own bid for an independent life was a very small achievement by comparison.

Eagerly, I read on:

*How did the Girls' War start? Who knows? It doesn't take much to start a war. The natives just love fighting and will seize any excuse. In this case the Reverend Marsden blames Captain Brind, whom the Missionaries regard as a depraved villain. Two of his girls, one from the east side of the Bay, the other from the west, quarrelled on board his ship. The captains rarely come to Brideshouse. They prefer their own cabins, which the lesser ranks do not have. Who can imagine either of those young girls wanting an old ruffian like Captain Brind with his bloodshot eyes? The muskets he offered were rusty, almost defunct. Perhaps the Chief of their village was not as fussy as Chief Kiwikiwi. At any rate, the two girls continued their quarrel on Kororareka beach by trying to drown one another. Soon all the other native females, including my girls, joined in.*

*Brind, realising that a full, scale fight was likely, and knowing that the people of Kororareka were not prepared for it, offered them muskets and then sailed away! Then another ship's Captain named Duke offered muskets to the other side, just for a bit of sport.*

*The girls who started the fight were both related to*

*chiefs. Pehi was the daughter of the Hongi Hika. She is also related to the chiefs Titore and Rewa. Morewaka, a Ngupphi, was related to the Kororareka chief Kiwikiwi; some said she was his daughter. So the fight was serious. Chiefs and warriors kept arriving in war canoes for weeks before the battle began but the Missionaries still hoped for some reconciliation (they call it a 'korero', a kind of conference) and believe me, the settlers in Kororareka hoped for the same thing. For once we all supported the missionaries, even the roughest whalers and grog shop owners.*

*Who should arrive on a peace mission in the middle of a mass of war canoes but old Samuel Marsden, just back from Sydney Town. He must be sixty-five if he's a day and yet he had the guts to clamber down from his vessel, the 'Elizabeth', in his hot black clothing, and sit on the beach beside the Chiefs, tattooed and scowling, for a 'korero'. War dancing went on all around them and the odd musket shot was fired but Marsden didn't flinch and then, to the great relief of us watching from our flimsy houses on the waterfront, it seemed than an agreement had been reached.*

*But it didn't last! The war canoes kept arriving at our little bay for another week. It was almost a relief when the battle started. It began at ten o'clock in the morning and went on until past midday.*

*We, the white Pakeha setters, lay flat on our faces on the floors of our small wooden houses and hoped to God we wouldn't be struck by a stray bullet.*

*We saw the body of Moewaka, Kiwikiwi's daughter, being carried with some of the wounded on board a ship, the 'Royal Sovereign', anchored in the Bay. Poor*

*Kiwikiwi! I felt deeply sorry for the dignified Chief who had helped me go into business. Later a coffin was made for Moewaka and she was returned to her people.*

*The other dead on the beach were not so fortunate. For days they were left where they fell, to be eaten by dogs. They stank so badly they had to be burned. They had bloated to twice their size and been blown by flies. Some had their entrails out where the flesh had been devoured and were in a state too horrible to describe. Young boys were harpooning them with sticks for sport.*

*On Saturday, as the battle was ending, the Reverend Davies and the Reverend Williams came over from Paihia and did what they could for the wounded.*

*On Sunday we hoped it was all over, but no! At daylight they started again and this time the great Chief Henghee of the Ngapuis was killed. The beach was declared taboo in his honour and both tribes then set fire to the town. Then they left the dead lying on the beach and fled in their war canoes. We saved ourselves by running up into the hills, where there is a stream. Fortunately, the ground being damp, the fire did not travel past our poor village.*

*We have been struggling to rebuild our wooden houses these past weeks. My remaining girls all fled back to their tribes, so business has ceased. Such is life on this island paradise of Kororareka, which since the Girls' War has been christened 'the Hell Hole of the Pacific'.*

*Thank you for your letter which reminded me how peaceful life is in Sydney Cove. I am glad you have an honest little business of your own, Mary. Pray do not be* shocked at the immorality of mine. It is all destroyed now in any case.

I am,
Your exhausted but still hopeful friend,
Jane New

# VII
## Prosperity and Tragedy

# CHAPTER 45

**Harriet Learns Bad Language from Mr Wentworth and I Await the Homecoming of Mr Stephen**
**The Rocks, June, 1834**

Although I have written many letters to Jane I have not heard from her in more than three years. I have read in the newspapers that the natives in New Zealand are very fierce and that ships avoid the Bay of Islands because it has become a battleground between warring tribes. I do not hold out much hope that my poor dear friend is still alive.

My daughter Harriet is now ten years old and has almost completed her schooling. She is a clever girl, with high spirits and a gentle nature and is as pretty as a picture. I hope to find a good position for her. She has no talent for dressmaking, I am sorry to say, as she does not have the patience, so I will have to find some other skill she can learn to earn a living. She has had lessons on the pianoforte and practises every evening in the church hall at St Philip's. She says she would like to be a singer, a dancer or an acrobat but this is just a youthful fancy, I hope. There is little scope for paid work as a performer in the colony and such people are not regarded as respectable, although whenever travelling players come to town they do attract a great crowd and seem to be enjoying themselves.

I have been divorced from my husband William Baxter for almost five years now. I hear that he married Alice Wilton and they have two sons. He is farming sheep on the Hunter River and scarcely ever comes to Sydney. The pain in my heart has dulled with the years and I think of William less and less. We came to an amicable ending, and he signed the Deed of Trust before our divorce, I think out of fondness for Harriet. But I am not inclined to marry again, and keep my distance from men who would tempt me.

My dressmaking business has expanded so that now I have two shops on The Rocks and have had to take on extra staff to run the second one. I am sentimentally attached to my first shop on Cambridge Street with my cottage next door, so I have stayed here and manage it alone. The larger shop on George Street, which attracts fashionable customers from Potts Point and the eastern part of Sydney over the Tank Stream, is managed by my friend Eleanor Turner. She does a fine job of flattering wealthy customers, and so long as I can keep up with the demands for silk frocks and ruffled shirts, I shall continue to make a profit.

For several years now I have been visiting the Stephen family at their home in Ultimo House. Harriet's cough returned every winter for three years and I was often obliged to ask for help from Dr Balmain. Mrs Stephen was always most kind to me and in return for medical help I was able to do some sewing for her. Her husband was always ill, so the Doctor seemed to be often at their house. One afternoon Mrs Stephen confided to me, 'The Judge is infirm in body and memory yet he refuses to retire.' She made a tut-tutting noise and shook her head.

A few days later I overheard her son Francis complain to his friend Mr Wentworth, 'Father is incompetent in the discharge of his public duties. He suffers from gout and is off the bench for months at a time. It is scandalous.' So I was not surprised when Mr Stephen at last tendered his resignation.

This meant he had more time to dote on his illnesses. He is prone to rages, mostly about money. As I passed his room on my way to deliver some altered garments to his wife one afternoon, I heard him yell: 'I retired on condition I received an allowance of £750 a year and by God I will *not* settle for a measly 500!'

Mrs Stephen, realising I had overheard this outburst, invited me to stay for tea. She sighed. 'He is very obstinate, my dear husband, and I daresay he will persevere until they give him what he wants.' Hoping to brighten her mood I asked for the latest news of her son, John Stephen Junior. She told me sadly, 'After all these years of effort he is making little progress with the case in London and thinks it better to return to the Colony to fight it here. My poor son is entirely innocent of the accusations made against him by Governor Darling. He feels the stigma of them deeply and is keeping his distance from our family and friends in England until his name is cleared. Nor will he accept any financial help from the family. I have had several letters from him at a place called Gray's Inn, which I believe is a cheap lodging, quite spartan in its apartments. John is owed over £1000 in salary and if even a portion of this sum were paid he could meet the heavy expenses he has incurred while pleading for justice in London.' The poor woman drew breath. 'John has written so many letters to Sir George Murray and to Under Secretary Hay and of course to Governor Darling himself, begging for a personal interview so that he might defend himself against the accusations, but so far he has been refused. That man Darling is no friend of ours!'

'Is Mr Stephen still accused of concealing the convict Jane New?' I asked.

'Indeed he is, Mary. They say he hid her under the name Frances Dixon, in lodgings taken by him after she escaped. But Mrs Dixon is quite a separate person from Jane New ... although apparently they looked very alike. Mrs Dixon worked as Housekeeper in the lodgings my son used at Minto for his shooting expeditions. He was able to get proof of this before he left for London, but it made not a bit of difference to Governor Darling, who dismissed him from his position.'

'He was very kind to me and my daughter Harriet,' I said, by way of consolation. But still I wondered whether in Jane's case his compassion had overcome his better judgment.

'And you apparently have been helpful to him, Mary. I expect John home very soon, for he says that at last he has enough evidence to mount a case to plead his innocence.'

'Oh, I am pleased!' I cried, and then blushed, for Mrs Stephen was looking at me with a knowing smile.

'I am sure he will call on you as soon as he arrives,' she said.

I hurried home with my heart beating fast and began thinking of the design for a new gown I might make for myself. By the time I reached Cambridge Street I had come to my senses. 'What makes you think that such a gentleman would ever allow himself to be anything more than a friend to a woman of your class?' I asked myself. 'You are a foolish, deluded woman, Mary Jones.'

But when I went to sleep that night I was still designing the gown in my head.

Mrs Stephen has asked me if Harriet would like to come to Ultimo House to help out in the dining room during her school holidays. The Stephens entertain a great deal and are always looking out for reliable maids. I replied that it was a kind offer and I would ask Harriet, although I did think she was too young.

Privately I thought that a servant's life was the last thing I wanted for my only daughter. But when I mentioned it to Harriet, she jumped at the offer.

'I would get to meet all the ladies and gentlemen at the Stephens' dinner parties. There is music and even dancing sometimes. I have read about it in the *Sydney Gazette*,' she said excitedly.

'But you would not be dancing, Harriet. You would be clearing plates from the dinner tables and scraping them in the kitchen.'

'Well, I would see the dancing and hear the music. Oh, do let me go, Mama!'

'All right, but just for the holidays,' I said. 'You can do better in life than become a servant to gentry, even such an agreeable family as the Stephens.'

'Perhaps they would like me to play to their guests sometimes, or sing to them,' she said hopefully.

'Indeed they would not! A servant is not an equal. Remember that.'

'But the Stephens are our friends, Mama.'

'They are kind to us but I would not presume to call them friends. They are upper class and we are not.'

She looked puzzled. She was a child of the Colony and had not experienced the class differences of England that I had grown up in. I was pleased she was free of it but felt apprehensive for her.

After the first dinner party Harriet came home full of stories.

'There were twelve people at dinner and I had to learn how to take the plates away from the right side and not spill a drop of gravy or do it too roughly so as to make people notice me. I had a smart cap and apron just like a real maid and had to scrub my nails clean first and let the Cook inspect them.'

'And were you able to do it all correctly, Harriet?' I asked anxiously.

'Oh yes, it was easy. There was no dancing but two ladies played a duet and then one sang by herself, but her voice was all quavery and I did not think she should perform unaccompanied.'

'You did not say such a thing I hope, Harriet?'

'Oh no, I wouldn't be so rude. Perhaps she was just nervous.'

'Perhaps.'

'They have a most beautiful pianoforte. A much better one than in the church hall.'

'And were the guests polite to you?'

'Oh yes, polite to me — but not to each other! There was a gentleman called Mr Wentworth who said insulting things about almost everyone. And the other guests just laughed!'

'Really? What did he say?'

Harriet was a clever mimic with a sharp memory so she was able to re-enact the conversations most convincingly. She puffed out her chest and became an arrogant gentleman with an upper-class English accent: 'This Busby was a nobody in Sydney and now he's been promoted to Governor of New Zealand! *Haugh, haugh, haugh!* Governor Darling recommended him. Let's hope he can put an end to the Maori massacres.'

Then Harriet changed herself into a shy young lady. 'I should think Mr Busby has a very difficult task ahead of him,' she simpered. Back to being blustering Mr Wentworth, she roared: 'Difficult? It's impossible, my dear young lady. If he and his wife aren't shot with arrows and eaten in the first year they'll be cooked and eaten in the second. Poor bloody fools!'

'Stop, Harriet! What language is that?' I cried.

'It's what the gentleman said!'

'No matter. Gentlemen are allowed to swear if they have a mind to. But we are not.'

'Why not?'

'Because gentlemen have other means to gain

respect. Working-class people must mind their language or they'll end up in the gutter.'

'Why won't Mr Wentworth end up in the gutter too?'

'Because of his money, connections and class.'

'So gentlemen are allowed to swear if they are upper-class, and ladies are allowed to sing badly. Class is bloody stupid!'

'Harriet! I forbid you to use that word. You will not be going to the Stephens' house again, I can tell you that.'

'Oh but I will, Mama. Mrs Stephen has invited me to come there to practise on the pianoforte whenever I like.' Her eyes were shining and I had not the heart to forbid her to go, but I did put a stop to her waiting on table at their dinner parties.

The mention of Maori massacres had sent a chill through my bones. It would be a miracle if poor Jane had survived … And there can be little hope for Mr John Stephen if she is gone from this world and cannot write to vouch for him.

There was another reason I did not wish Harriet to become a servant at Ultimo House which I found hard to admit to myself. I did not want John Stephen to come home and see my daughter as the servant I had been not so many years earlier.

I was now a business woman of independent means. Certainly, I had been a servant and a convict and had been helped to start a business with money left to me by an ex-convict, my *de facto* husband — but perhaps, as his mother often told me, Mr John Stephen was a compassionate man. Whether he was also one who did not believe in class barriers I did not know.

# CHAPTER 46

**John Stephen Returns and Jane Confides She Has a Strange Attachment to a Savage**
**The Rocks, July, 1834**

I have had a most disturbing few weeks. When Mr John Stephen arrived home he greeted me warmly, holding both my hands in his and saying, 'My dear Mary, how good to see you.' He seemed both excited and nervous about his case, which is to open in a few weeks' time. He asked if I would be interested to attend the Court and follow the proceedings. I said that of course I would. He then smiled affectionately at me and said, 'That gown is most becoming, Mary.' I could not get out a word of thanks for the compliment.

Then, on the same day, I had a letter from Jane.

*Kororareka*

*Dear Mary,*
*Yes, I am still alive, though you must have been wondering all this time. Not just alive but prospering! Yes,*

*your old friend the escapee has become a woman of
property.*

*You would not believe the changes in our little settle-
ment in just three years. It has become almost respectable! The natives, which we now call the Maori, even
have the New Testament translated into their own language. And they are about to get a printing press to
print the scriptures so they can read them! Who would
have thought that such warlike savages would come to
such a state? There has not been a Haka war dance on
the beach for over a year.*

*I hear that people in Sydney are very afraid of the
Maori. No captain in Port Jackson wants to sail within
fifty miles of the Bay of Islands for fear of being hunted
down by a warrior, shot with a British musket and then
eaten! These fears are quite amusing to us locals. I think
of myself as a New Zealander now. I speak some of the
Maori tongue and respect their customs enough to be
able to live in harmony with them. Well, most of them
— some are impossible. But then there are bastards in
every race.*

*After the Girls' War I gave up my Brideshouse and
became a trader in flax, but I made a loss on that so
moved into sealskins. That was better. But better still
was kauri pine, which I predicted would become the
next big export. I was right. I made a tidy sum from
kauri which I have invested in my latest business, a grog
shop with a small hotel attached. This hotel I am truly
proud of. I intend to make it the finest Public House on
the Bay of Islands.*

*One night some years ago I met up with Johnno
Johnson, a settler who had bought land on the water-*

*front here and wanted to build an inn. 'A nice place,
where ladies like yourself would feel at home,' he explained. 'Not a rough blood house like this!' And he gestured rudely at the grog shop we were obliged to drink
in. I encouraged him to build this inn. He did and
called it The Duke of Marlborough.*

*It became well known as a place that ladies could
safely visit, and a year ago, when Johnno was thinking
of selling, I offered him my price. At first he refused for
it was not high, but then, with no other offers, accepted,
and now The Duke is mine!*

*How I love playing the grand lady hostess to my
guests. I'm a natural, so the local traders say. They laugh
a bit at my airs and graces (no spitting in the bar, no
bare chests, no brawling or loud singing and shoes to be
worn at all times) but I watch them looking at the
grandfather clock in the hall and the French chiffonier
and the polished brass aspidistra with its ferns and lilies
lushly blooming, and I know they admire my style, although they pretend to be ruffians.*

*I have had foreign dignitaries stay in my hotel. They
always remark on the 'opulence' of the Bay. I've had sea
captains from America, Britain, Australia, even
France. They stay here with their wives, who are pleased
to escape the confines of the ship for a few weeks. They
stroll along the waterfront, take tea in my parlour and
talk about the new church that is being built. Yes, we
are soon to have a Church of England in Kororareka
and I shall go there every Sunday. Who would believe
that I have become so genteel!*

*Of course I am a landowner myself now, having pur-
chased five hundred acres from the Maori. It is at pres-*

ent heavily timbered but one day I will clear some to grow wheat or vegetables. My remaining few muskets took care of the land purchase and Chief Kiwikiwi was well satisfied. I would not wish to displease him for he is a useful ally and I am fond of him, in as much as a white woman can permit herself to feel affection for a Maori. There are many liaisons between Maori women and Pakeha men but none that I have noticed between Maori men and Pakeha women. I know for a fact that this is not because they find our pale skin unattractive.

I must say that I enjoy my new life here and do not miss poor James New or the institution of marriage one bit. I have many friends amongst the settlers — whalers, traders, and ship's captains and their wives and am much respected in our little town as a trader and business woman. Even the Reverend Williams seems to have forgotten about my earlier life as a convict and brothel keeper, and visits The Duke to chat with me about various things.

The latest amazing news here is that the powers that be in London have sent us a Governor! Mr James Busby and his young wife. Why? We have managed well enough without so much as a constable for as long as anyone can remember.

The Reverend Williams called into The Duke about two weeks after the welcome ceremony. He told me that Mrs Busby was with child. 'It is a lonely place they live in up there on the bluff at Waitangi. I wonder if you, Mrs New, as one of the most respectable ladies in the Bay of Islands, might visit Mrs Busby to see if there is anything she needs?'

'I should be glad to, Reverend Williams,' I replied

*graciously. 'If a boat could be arranged by the Mission people to take me across to Waitangi I would be most obliged to you.'*

*And so a week later I was paddled across in a long canoe towards Waitangi, on the opposite side of the Bay, by a strong young Maori named Kawatai who worked at the mission. The journey took some hours. When we landed I was appalled at the rough, steep climb that lay ahead. But Kawatai offered to escort me up the cliff and carry my gifts, then wait for me below. When we arrived at the top I was quite breathless, although I am not a weak woman. It was a bleak place, with hardly a tree in sight, but had a most splendid view of the Bay in all directions. The cottage, set back some hundreds of yards from the cliff, stands all alone. It is constructed of fine cedar with a handsome front door. They must have transported the timber from Australia instead of using our own fine kauri, except for the kauri shingles on the roof. I thought the use of foreign cedar a foolish indulgence.*

*Mrs Busby smiled shyly and showed me into the parlour which was simply and sparsely furnished. She made no apology for this. She will be dazzled by the luxurious sofas and pretty lamps at the Duke of Marlborough, thought I.*

*We talked of the baby, due early in the new year. 'Do you have children, Mrs New?' she asked.*

*'Sadly, no,' said I. 'My husband was taken from me a few years ago and since then I have led a single life.'*

*She expressed her sympathy, assuming of course that he was dead.*

*'You must feel lonely at times in a wild foreign coun-*

try like this,' she said, expressing her own feelings rather than mine.

'Oh no, Mrs Busby, for I have friends aplenty and my work at the inn keeps me too busy to mope. You must bring your husband and come across there to stay for a few days. I have comfortable rooms and a fine cook. It is quite an elegant inn for these parts and most entertaining in the evenings. We have a fiddler and a flautist and there is dancing on Saturday nights. I hope you will come.'

She sighed and said she would love to but her husband was kept at his desk with his documents and reports to be sent back to London until late at night. 'He is most conscientious,' she said. She made it sound as if it were a disease.

'Then you must come alone, Mrs Busby!' I cried. 'Be my guest at any time. I will arrange for the Missionaries to send a boat for you. It is not good for you to be so alone up here with only the Maori yowling in the forest behind you for company.'

'No, it is not good,' she said quietly, as if to herself. Looking out the window with an anxious expression, she asked, 'Mrs New, are the Maori likely to attack us here, do you think? The Missionaries assure us there is no danger but I have heard their war cries at night and they do prowl about. Things have gone missing from the outhouses, garden implements and an axe. Two chickens have disappeared from the larder — our servant is sure the Maori stole into the house while we slept and took them.'

I was about to try to reassure her that they would not

*dare steal from the King's Representative when a Maori face appeared at the window. Mrs Busby screamed.*

*I leapt up and put my hand on her shoulder. 'Don't be frightened! It is only Kawatai, who paddled me across the Bay, come back to fetch me.'*

*The poor young woman was trembling all over like leaves in a gale. I went to the door and asked Kawatai why he was so early. He pointed to the sky and told me a storm was coming and we must leave now. Although I could see no black clouds, I nodded and went back inside to bid Mrs Busby goodbye. Her husband had appeared, alarmed by her scream. He had his arm protectively around her shoulder. I apologised for Kawatai frightening her. I let the Busbys know that most of the Maori were harmless and they should try to be friendly to them.*

*Mr James Busby shook hands with me and thanked me for my visit and for the presents. He did it rather formally and I could not help thinking that he blamed me for his wife's scream and did not really welcome a woman of my class into his home.*

*'Don't forget now,' I called out gaily to Mrs Busby as I hurried down the hill with Kawatai, 'The Duke of Marlborough in Kororareka!'*

*Mrs Busby stood beside her husband at the front door and waved. Kawatai shook his head at me and looked bemused. 'You think they will come to your Duke, Mrs New? Never, never, never,' he muttered.*

*When we reached the canoe he began paddling in a different direction from the way we had come. We seemed to be heading towards Hokianga and away from Kororareka. 'What are you doing, Kawatai?'*

*He did not answer. I looked at the sky and saw there was no sign of the storm he had warned me about. I panicked a little then for I had heard stories from the Missionaries about the sudden treachery of Maori they had trusted for years.*

*'Take me straight home at once,' I commanded. But he looked into my face as if he were carved of kauri wood and understood not one word. I began shouting and pointing in the direction of Kororareka. When I had shouted myself almost hoarse he said with dignity, 'Waka Nene is waiting.'*

*This silenced me.*

*During the journey we spoke not a word.*

*The seas were calm so we had no trouble landing by the river beneath the cliffs covered in forests. I looked up at the immense kauri pines in awe. This was the place I had come to as a runaway convict, knowing nobody.*

*It looked more serene today than I remembered it. There was no sign of anyone at the place where we left the canoe. Kawatai beckoned me to follow him and we set off inland along the river bank through the forest.*

*I knew we were approaching the house of a powerful Chief, which was ornamented with the heads of his enemies killed in battle. I had first been to this house almost four years ago. I had not been frightened then for I was being proudly presented to the Chief by his son, Nene, a handsome young warrior who had saved me from a terrifying experience that I have never described to anyone. The Chief had received me into his 'paa' and given me his blessing. I had been grateful then, but later I had betrayed both Nene and his father by leaving suddenly without saying goodbye. I had often wondered*

*why Nene had taken this insult without pursuing me.*
*Now I asked myself why he had waited so long to bring*
*me back and what he might wish to say to me.*

At this point I laid the letter down for some moments. It occurred to me that my dear friend could have dictated wonderful tales to her loyal Scottish clerk that would keep readers turning the pages until they came to the last word. Novels almost as enthralling as those of Sir Walter Scott that Andrew Frazier and I had read together so long ago. Except that Jane was relating her own experiences. A line from Lord Byron's poem *Don Juan* came into my mind (yes, I still open a book of poetry occasionally) — '*truth is always strange, — Stranger than fiction*'. Jane's life was so extraordinary that she had no need to make up imaginary tales. Although I had often wondered whether she were telling the truth in times gone by, this account of her adventures in New Zealand rang true and held me spellbound.

I went on reading:

*As I followed Kawatai along the bank of the wide*
*fresh-water river at Hokianga I began to feel a sense of*
*peace. It was quiet, except for the cry of birds in the*
*reeds, birds so tame that they would wait until we were*
*close enough to touch them before they'd sail off proudly.*
*I remembered the names of some of them — 'tuuii',*
*'huia', 'kookako'. Mosses, shrubs, ferns and climbers*
*tangled together beneath the giant kauri trees. And the*
*flowers had such fragrance as I'd forgotten in my years*
*away living amongst the grog shops and the cursing*
*whalers of Kororareka.*

*I had no presents to give the old Chief, I realised. Except a bunch of lavender I had picked from my garden and pinned to my cloak. He would not think much of that. I supposed I must offer him the cloak. I wondered if he would still be angry about my sudden departure four years ago.*

*But I was wrong about being taken first to the Chief's house. Before we reached the clearing where the 'paa' was, before we even came to the sloping gardens dug into the hill where I had helped the Maori women tend kumara and yellow gourds, a figure stepped out of the forest in front of me. In the dying light I could not tell who it was. Kawatai suddenly disappeared and I then knew it must be Nene.*

*I stood quite still and waited.*

*He was tall and as dignified as I remember. He wore a cloak, his hair dressed with red earth and fish oil, combed into a knot on the crown of his head and decorated with feathers, shark's teeth and pieces of bone. He carried a green adze. To anyone else he would have looked fearsome.*

*He walked towards me slowly and stopped a few feet away, never taking his eyes off mine. He was six feet tall and I almost a foot shorter so he was gazing down at me when he spoke.*

*'You are well?' I had forgotten how deep and soft his voice was.*

*'I am in good health. And you?'*

*'I also.'*

*There was silence. I wished he would smile and make a joke as he used to.*

*'The Chief is well?' I asked, as it is polite to do.*

*He inclined his head. 'But he is old.'*

*I nodded in respectful agreement. 'Kawatai said you wished to speak to me.'*

*He beckoned me to follow along a narrow path through the forest. We reached a clearing where an old man stood silently waiting. He was wearing a war mat, woven very tightly, and his body was painted in red ochre. Nene introduced him as Te Mahanga, who had once been a warrior. To my astonishment the old man came forward and shook my hand, saying 'How do you do, my boy.' Then he grinned broadly at his cleverness.*

*I laughed.*

*But Nene remained serious. 'Many years ago Te Mahanga sailed in a ship to London,' he said.*

*The old man began to gabble excitedly in Maori, telling how this came about. He made gestures but I could not make out his meaning.*

*'He says the ship was named 'Ferret' and he left New Zealand when he was young because he wanted to be a man,' Nene translated.*

*'Missa Savage was the captain and he was a good man.'*

*Then Nene turned questioningly to me. 'He says many things about London that I cannot believe, Jane. You will know if he speaks the truth. It is your country.'*

*'You want me to hear these things?' I asked.*

*'Yes.'*

*I felt a bit disappointed. I had wondered if he wanted to see me for other reasons. But I turned my attention to the old man who was saying, 'Pai ana uta nui nui toki.'*

'He says London is a very good country with plenty of iron.'

'That is true,' I agreed.

'Pai ana whare, nui nui haere.'

'He says he went inside a house and it walked.'

I shook my head. 'He is lying.'

The old man became passionate and gabbled some more, gesturing wildly until I understood. 'Ah, he went inside a hackney coach and a horse pulled it along.'

'He says it was a very good house. It walked fast.'

More gabbling. 'He went in a house that went up in the clouds,' said Nene in disbelief.

I thought about this. 'He might have climbed a tower, or been inside a church with a steeple.'

'Nui nui tungata, nue nue wurri, ittee ittee eka, ittee ttee potato,' cried Te Mahanga.

'He says in London there are plenty of men, plenty of houses, but very little fish and very few potatoes,' Nene translated.

'True,' I said.

By now Te Mahanga was dancing around Nene waving his arms in triumph.

Nene just nodded humbly, accepting his mistake. I felt quite sorry for him. Then, regaining his dignity, he ushered me away from Te Mahanga and into a secluded part of the forest where we sat down on a fallen log. 'There is more I must ask you, Jane.'

Here comes the real reason for our meeting, thought I. I knew better than to be coy with Nene so I looked directly into his eyes and waited. But again I was wrong in my expectations.

'The great King William of London sent a message to

*the Chiefs to come and hear what he had to say.' He paused, then said sorrowfully. 'I did not go for I had first to go to a meeting with Chief Reti from Waitangi, who is angry that the King wants to buy land there.'*

*'I wondered why you weren't at that ceremony a few weeks ago.'*

*'To stop Reti and his followers going to war I have missed the words of King William so I learned nothing of his special powers.'*

*'Don't worry, Nene. It was nothing important.'*

*He shook his head. 'To me it is important. You must tell me the words of this William and what powers he has.'*

*'He didn't come in person, just sent a letter. Writing, like you learned at the Mission.'*

*'Writing,' Nene repeated, looking disgusted.*

*'The letter was read by Mr Busby the new Governor, who is here to keep order. King William's writing promised there would be goodwill between the Pakeha and the Maori. If the whalers get drunk and take Maori women by force or take land or anything else from the Maori without payment, or harm Maori people, they will be punished.'*

*'King William will make the Pakeha pay utu?'*

*'He says so.' I shrugged. 'But that was three weeks ago and although we've all been waiting for these great powers to take effect, nothing whatever has changed in the Bay of Islands so we're all just carrying on as usual.'*

*Nene was thoughtful. 'Tell me about King William's governor, the great Missa Busby who wants to buy land from Reti at Waitangi. I have heard he is your friend.'*

*I felt awkward. Of course I was ambitious to have*

the Governor as a friend but Nene might see this as a further betrayal of mine. 'I visited him today but his wife was friendlier to me than he was.'

'Will he want to have power over our people?'

'I don't think so. But he doesn't like them stealing his chickens and spades.'

Nene looked surprised. 'But that is utu for his people cutting our trees and taking our river water.'

'Perhaps you should explain utu to Mr Busby. In the meantime tell your people to stop stealing from him or there'll be punishment.'

'From King William?'

'Yes.'

'But what punishment can he give in writing? He is not here. He cannot use muskets to shoot us even though he is a great king!' Nene began to smile at last and then to laugh in the way I remembered. He thought the whole Pakeha idea of power ridiculous.

'He can get other people to punish you.'

'Who? Missa Busby? I have seen him being paddled in his canoe. He is small and white like a dead fish. Very weak man.'

'He can get the Missionaries to punish you,' I said without much conviction.

Nene laughed loudly, shaking his head. 'Missionaries need us to protect them from tribes outside this bay who would fight and kill them. And they like to teach us. We like to learn about God a little bit but more we like to learn to speak and read their language so we can trade with the Pakeha. Then we can travel to far lands like Sydney and London.'

'As Te Mahanga travelled?' I asked, for I sensed that Nene was jealous of the old man's strange experiences.

He did not deign to answer.

Nene was right of course. The Pakeha had no power over the Maori and Mr Busby would soon discover this for himself.

I began to smile in agreement with Nene but then he looked serious and said, 'You left us suddenly, Jane. You ran into the forest and paid the relatives of Heke, my enemy, to take you across the Bay in his canoe to Kororareka. Why?'

I hung my head and said quietly, 'I missed my own people.'

'Then you should have told me. I was angry that you left without saying a farewell. I nearly came after you, to bring you back.' He put his hand across his heart. 'You hurt me.'

'I am sorry, Nene.'

Nene nodded gravely. Then he picked up my left hand. 'So you have a husband now?' He held the finger on which I wore James's wedding ring. I had not worn it for a year after I left him in Batavia but now, as a re- spectable owner of The Duke of Marlborough I had thought it best to put it back as any grieving widow would do.

'I had a husband once but he is dead.'

'When did he die?'

'Four years ago,' I said, without thinking.

Nene stood up. 'He was not dead when I met you?' He looked at me angrily.

'No, no, he was already dead then.'

'But four years ago you did not wear this ring of his. Why do you wear it now?'

I shook my head. 'For vanity. It is gold.' I smiled. 'I'll take it off and put it on the other hand if it offends you.'

'Yes, take it off.' He turned his back on me as if I'd shamed him.

'You live with Pakeha people at Kororareka and never visit us here. You do not pay your respects to the Chief of this 'paa' even though you lived here, once under his protection. You were not happy here Jane?' he asked softly.

'Yes, yes! You know I was, Nene. I am sorry!' I felt a wave of emotion and choked it down. 'I am sorry I haven't visited. Will the Chief see me now?'

'Not today. He is old and needs time to prepare himself. Another day. I will send a canoe for you.' Then he added very softly, 'I will not come to Kororareka as I think you have Pakeha friends who would talk mischief.'

I nodded and looked away.

'You have a new life now, Jane. I see it in the way you turn your head to the ground.'

I could not raise my head or he would have seen my tears.

'You have not told me all that is in your heart,' he said gently.

I shook my head and wiped my eyes quickly with my sleeve as I used to when I was a child and had no handkerchief. 'I cannot tell you everything, Nene. Not yet.'

'But you will one day, Jane.'

'Yes, I promise.'

*Later*

*Alas, dear Mary, it is many months since I began to write. But I have been so busy with guests at The Duke. I have furnished my grand hotel much as I remember Elmtree House, where we had to scrub the wretched flagstones in the courtyard and fetch and carry, polish and skivvy for that useless family. Oh, those two daughters, one fat as a pig and the other dried up like a walnut. But all that is long ago and the only good thing about slaving there is that I took note of which were the finest clocks to buy, which lamps, settees and sideboards. And now, in my own fine establishment, even the silver has been copied from Elmtree House! And I glide around giving orders in a flowing gown, just like Mrs Robinson Doake, only grander.*

*Of course there are no elm trees surrounding the house, but giant fig trees with gnarled roots and thick shiny green leaves to give plenty of shade. Some afternoons there are up to three hundred people strolling along the path by the beach outside my hotel and many of them stop to take tea here — ships' captains and their wives, officers and their ladies, retired whalers and their families, even clergymen!*

*Although there are plenty of offers I do not feel inclined to marry again just yet. I am more interested in becoming a successful trader, respected in the Bay of Islands. I export flax and kauri boards as well as running my hotel and grog shops ('saloons' we prefer to call them these days). And now that I have befriended the new British Resident, Mr James Busby and his wife, who is still rather timid and much afraid of the Maori, I am considered most respectable. The traders here treat the*

*Busbys with coldness and jealousy, not to say rudeness, so Mrs Busby is most grateful for my company. Only the Paihia Missionaries are kind to them.*

*Mrs Busby gave birth to her first child, John, prematurely due to an attack by the Maori. A group of them robbed an outhouse and fired eight or ten shots at the Residence. As Mr Busby came to the front door one shot struck it and sent a splinter into his cheek. A chief named Reti was the main offender. Some of the other Chiefs, one of whom I know well, decided to punish him by banishing him and forcing him to give up two hundred or three hundred acres of his land to King William of England. Of course this decision was never enforced. How could anyone force a Chief like Reti to do that without starting another war?*

*If you are ever inclined to take a journey to New Zealand, bring money to buy cheap land. I would be pleased to entertain you here at The Duke of Marlborough and introduce you to certain Maori Chiefs who will sell you whatever you need. I am a trusted friend of several of the most powerful Chiefs, one in particular who was educated by the Missionaries and speaks perfect English. A noble warrior who once did me a great kindness. I confess to you Mary that if I ever came close to being in love ... but I must not burden you with shameful secrets.*

*You said in one of your letters that you and your husband are now separated and that you have a prosperous business in making and selling clothes.*

*Hoping that you and your daughter, whose name, I regret, I have forgotten except that the second name is Jane, are both well.*

*I am,*
*Your friend the teller of true stories,*
*Jane New*

Finally I laid down the letter. 'Your friend the teller of true stories' … it was almost as though she had divined my thoughts!

I wanted to write back to her at once.

# CHAPTER 47

## Jane and I Quarrel over Mr John Stephen's Innocence

*Cambridge Street, The Rocks, 1834*

*My dear Jane,*

*How wonderful to hear from you at last and to know that you are well and safe! As I heard more and more reports of violence and the wars with the Maori in New Zealand I was most troubled and concerned for you. But as usual Jane, you have used your courage and wits to defeat the odds and have survived very well. I am greatly relieved.*

*You are to be congratulated on your success as the owner of a fine hotel and as a trader. Also on your new friend Mrs Busby who must find you inspiring as well as a great comfort. As for your 'shameful secret', I am not sure what to think. Surely you do not mean to tell me that you once had a liaison with a savage? Forgive me if I misunderstood you. My life is very steady and un-*

*eventful and I have no experience of foreign customs.
You lead such a strange and different life.*

*I should love to travel to the Bay of Islands some day
although it does not seem it will be possible for some
years yet. Perhaps when Harriet is grown and settled in
a position. You might remember how she loved to sing
and dance (even though you have forgotten her name,
dear Jane). She has developed her talent for these things
and has set her heart on becoming a performer, which
gives me some concern. Performers are not respected in
the Colony and she is a clever child who could do better
for herself.*

*I was sorry to hear that you and James are now sepa-
rated. He was always so loyal and loving towards you. I
hope he is not too desolate without you.*

*Mr John Stephen has a case about to open in which
he is hoping to prove his innocence of the charges
brought against him by Governor Darling. I shall attend the court as often as possible and will no doubt
find it hard to hear evidence against those I would
trust. As you and Mr Stephen are both my friends I wish
the whole sad business could soon be resolved. Mr Stephen still has a long way to go before his name is cleared.
He has worked hard to do this for the past five years. If
you have anything you wish to say, Jane, I am sure he
would welcome it. And I would too. If your conscience is
clear then I beg your pardon, but if not I beg you to act
quickly and send a written statement to the Court at
the address I have enclosed. This would bring peace of
mind to so many people in the Stephen family, not to
mention the judiciary and Mr John Stephen himself.
You are far enough away never to be troubled by consta-*

bles of this Colony again, so I beg you, Jane, for the sake
of our old and dear friendship, to examine your
conscience and act as you see fit.

The matter is urgent as the case is soon to be heard.
I am,
Your obedient servant and dearest friend,
Mary Jones

PS Since separating from my husband William Baxter
I have reverted to my maiden name.


                  The Duke of Marlborough, Kororareka, 1834
My dear Mary,
I am surprised that you should think I would have anything to say to Mr John Stephen that might help prove
his innocence.

On the contrary, he is guilty of all he is accused of
and more besides. As I have told you before he is a gentleman who, like the rest of them, believes he is above
the law. Of course he helped me to escape and hid me in
his lodgings at Minto. We spent a week in bed together
which was pleasant enough and got me safely away
from the constables. But then, when I was tired of it
and wished to return to James, who'd sent a message
that he had been making arrangements for our passage
on a ship to take us away from the Colony, the sensitive
Mr Stephen protested that he was in love with me and
could not bear to lose me! What did he think I would
do? Remain hidden away at Minto as his mistress to be
visited whenever he was free of court duties in Sydney?
We quarrelled and your new friend called me names
that would have shocked you, gentle Mary. Then I dis-

*guised myself in men's clothing that I borrowed from his landlord, Mr Crisp, and at last, after a lot of shouting and tears, I persuaded him to drive me in the gig to Sydney, where James was waiting, innocently unaware that the 'gentleman' had become smitten by his wife and tried to keep her as his prisoner.*

*So if you think I would ever say anything other than what a liar and a hypocrite Mr John Stephen is, then you are greatly mistaken, Mary. For his sake it is better I keep silent.*

*I am shocked that you should take the word of a spoilt, whining 'gentleman' against that of your oldest friend, who, like you, has suffered at the hands of the upper class all her hard-working life!*

*I am,*

*Your obedient servant and disillusioned friend,*

*Jane New*

*PS Think no more about my 'shameful secret'. I was a fool to mention it to one who has lived such a sheltered life as you have.*

At first I felt shocked at Jane's angry denial of Mr Stephen's innocence. And then I realised she was lying. Her hard life amongst the savages must have increased her fury at gentlemen like him, who she believes have all lived soft lives. It hurt to think that Jane could not even tell me, her oldest friend, the truth.

The Court proceedings have now been going for almost two weeks and I know I should get back to my shop or the business will be in a bad way. But I find myself so caught up in the case that I cannot bear to miss a minute of it.

Elizabeth Male says I am obsessed by it and I should leave the gentry to their own mad pastimes. 'Fancy someone spending almost five years of his life gathering evidence just to prove that he is innocent of sleeping with a convict girl!'

'No, Elizabeth. It is much more than that. Mr Stephen lost his position as a Magistrate and his honour because of Governor Darling's unproven accusations.'

'Well, I myself and almost everyone I know has lost a job and a reputation at least once in their life. What we do is find another job and to hell with our reputations.'

'It is different for the gentry, Elizabeth. They feel great shame.'

'They are fortunate to be able to afford the luxury. But what has all this to do with you, Mary? You were a friend of Jane New's. Are you hanging around in court just waiting to hear the Judge call her a liar and a cheat? We know that already.'

'She is innocent until proven guilty,' I said firmly.

'You are beginning to sound like a magistrate yourself, Mary.'

That night, I dreamed of being in a windswept, primitive settlement, sleeping in a hut with the sound of surf pounding just beyond. There was a man with me. Protective, loving and gently spoken. I felt safe with him. Suddenly, just outside the hut there was a disturbance and a woman appeared. She flung me away from my lover and clasped him to her. Now he held her close and said the same gentle things to her while I was forgotten. The woman was Jane. I could not tell who the man was. When I woke up my cheeks were damp and I realised I'd been crying.

The day after this disturbing dream I dragged myself down to the Court House feeling weary and ill at ease. I had not been sleeping well and was worried about Jane and Mr Stephen and what was the truth of it all, and not being able to free myself of my obsession to attend the Court.

The trial had arrived at the question of whether Frances Dixon and Jane New were two separate people or one and the same. After Jane disappeared, constables had been sent in the middle of the night to search the Minto premises. They did not find any woman, or Mr Stephen, but the bed in his room was still warm.

Warm! I saw John Stephen sitting up suddenly in bed at the sound of the constables' horses, gently shaking Jane awake, then leaping up and ushering her quickly outside, shielding her, holding her close as he guided her to a safe hiding-place in the bush.

The constables had opened all Mr Stephen's boxes and trunks in his house at Minto and taken certain papers away to give to the Governor. One of these was a letter stating that a Frances Dixon was a free woman.

To my surprise, after discussion about this Frances Dixon, Matron Gordon of the Female Factory appeared in the dock. She looked older and more florid. I thought the drink must be getting to her.

Mr Stephens asked her questions about the clothing Jane New left behind the night she escaped. Matron produced a list of them and read aloud: 'One gown, one petticoat, one shift, one shawl, two handkerchiefs, one pair of black silk stockings, one pair doe-stuff shoes, one cap, one black satin bonnet, one pair tortoiseshell side combs, cash, three shillings and fourpence.'

I remembered the clothes well. Jane had arrived at the Factory wearing them. That was when many of the prisoners mistook her for a member of Lady Darling's committee.

Then John Stephen asked Matron Gordon, 'Was there anything peculiar about her escape?'

'Not that I am aware of, for I don't know how she escaped unless it was over the back wall.'

'Could she have escaped without assistance either from within or from outside?'

'I think she could without assistance from within. But I don't know whether she could have succeeded with no one to help her outside. The prisoners frequently escape without assistance. I have seen women with their ankles cut and their legs broken from dropping down the walls.' She did not sound as if this bothered her too much.

'Is it probable then that there was assistance from without when Jane New escaped?'

'I could not say, because some women have frequently escaped unhurt.'

'In which class was Jane New?'

'In the First.'

'Is the First-Class allowed the use of pen, ink and paper?'

'Not without my approbation.'

'Were you ever asked to give paper to Jane New?'

'Not that I recollect. I am most sure that I was not asked and I am sure I never did.'

'Are you not aware that Mrs New did write a letter in the Factory?'

'I am not.'

Here I held my breath. Of course it was I who had written it for her, if it was the one to her husband.

'Supposing it to have been to the Colonial Secretary, would it not have been sent through you?'

I breathed a sigh of relief.

'Certainly it ought. Any letter written by a prisoner is supposed to go through my hands.'

'Suppose that any person had brought you an order signed Jane New, directing you to deliver up those clothes, and a list of them corresponding with that you have produced, should you have thought the order, being dated Hobart Town, was any proof that Jane New was at Hobart Town?'

'I don't know,' said the Matron, looking confused, 'but I should not have acted upon it without the approbation of the Members of the Committee.'

'Might she have been in this Colony when she sent you such an order, dated Hobart Town?'

'Yes, she might. I think it likely she might.' Matron sighed. She was used to conducting her own cross-examinations and clearly did not enjoy having the procedure reversed.

'Had you in your establishment in the year 1828 a female prisoner named Eleanor Frazier?'

'I had.'

'Do you consider that woman worthy of credit?' As he put this question John Stephen did not permit himself even a hint of the distaste I knew he felt for my friend Eleanor.

'No.'

'Would you believe anything she stated?'

'I don't think I should.'

'Did she not hold some responsible situation?'

'She was monitor of the laundry.'

'Do you pick but a worthless character for that situation?'

John Stephen had trussed up the Matron nicely. I could not help but smile.

'No, but I was not aware of her character at that time, as I have been since.' She was flustered and began gabbling — that the prisoner was a monitor but not a paid one, and that although she had a bad character out of doors she was well behaved in the Factory.

Naturally Matron did not mention that clever Eleanor had succeeded in bribing her so that she was able to do pretty much what she liked in the Factory. If she felt like it she'd change from laundry monitor to supervising third-class prisoners breaking rocks, or hang about the office flirting with the shy young clerk, Mr Turner.

I could see that John Stephen wanted to find out how close Eleanor Frazier and Jane New really were, to show that Eleanor might have helped her to escape.

So perhaps he could do without 'the truth' from Jane New, after all.

# CHAPTER 48

**I Rejoice that My Daughter is Luckier in Love than
I Have Been
The Rocks, January, 1840**

My darling daughter Harriet was married today in St
Philip's Church just as I had always wanted to be. Her
husband, Thomas Craig, is a free man, kind, steady
and considerate, a seaman born in the Colony and as
loving a husband as any girl could hope to find. She is
not quite sixteen and he is nineteen. They seem like
children to me.

Such a pretty bride she was, with a gown of cream
lace I had made for her and a veil to match. She carried
orange blossom and her red curls were twisted into an
elegant coil on top of her head, though many curls
escaped after the ceremony when the two of them ran
hand in hand, laughing and hugging each other, all the
way to their new little cottage that had been my wedding present. They left the church covered in rose petals and ran down Charlotte Place, with the guests
following. The piper and fiddler could hardly keep up

as the wedding party skipped and danced along Kent Street, past the quarries, and at last came to the tiny stone cottage on The High Rocks.

Elizabeth Male, Eleanor Turner and I had prepared a wedding breakfast in the parlour and as each breathless guest burst in the door we passed them a glass of cider. Such excitement as the bride and groom explored every inch of their new home that I had kept a secret until that day. 'Oh Mama, what pretty cups and saucers! Look, Tom! A dresser for the plates. A quilted bedspread of our very own! Oh, and a mangle for the washing. My mother is ever practical.' The cottage was simply but tastefully fitted out, with a sunny courtyard at the back where Elizabeth and I had already planted shady fruit trees and a little kitchen garden growing parsley, thyme and rosemary. 'Oh look Tom, herbs! I shall make you an omelette full of them every morning of your life!'

Tom swept her up into his arms and swung her round the apple tree. 'And I shall never complain, my darling, even though eggs make me bilious!' They laughed and kissed and darted back inside to chatter to their guests. Everyone seemed very young, like children playing at a wedding. They sang songs to the bridal couple, toasted their good health and danced until after midnight.

Over the past months I have watched my daughter fall in love. It was a touching experience for she is very close to me and I could feel her every emotion.

It all began when I gave in to her great ambition to join a group of travelling players. For years I tried to

interest her in every other job I could think of, from
governess to dressmaker to owning a flower shop. But
her heart was set on just one thing. She had been taking
lessons in pianoforte and singing for many years, and
could pick up the steps of any dance in no time, so it
should not have surprised me. In spite of my hopes that
Harriet's love of theatre and performance would disappear, on her fifteenth birthday she joined a troupe of
travelling players and that very day burst in the door to
tell me the good news.

'Mama, you'll never guess! They have accepted me!
We're to tour the whole Colony! I am to have not one
job but four. Dancer, singer, acrobat and stage hand.
We leave by coach next week. Oh please let me go,
Mama. It is all I have wanted in life. Ever!'

Although I had great misgivings, and even considered travelling with the troupe as their seamstress to
keep an eye on her, Harriet's strong will prevailed and
she went off alone.

A memory had flashed across my mind as Harriet
burst in the door. Myself on my fourteenth birthday
bursting in at the door of my mother's cottage in Kent
with the glad news that I had been accepted as a maid
at Elmtree House, and my mother, instead of being
proud, bursting into tears and saying, 'Oh Mary, you
have broken my heart!'

So I gathered myself together, held up my head and
said, 'Harriet, I wish you a safe journey.' At which she
flung her arms round my neck and almost squeezed the
life out of me.

It was on this tour that she met Thomas Craig,
whose ship was anchored at Newcastle harbour when

the troupe performed in the only theatre in that town. He and some friends watched the show and afterwards he came backstage to see if the singer was as beautiful as she had appeared onstage. 'He thought it might be a trick of stage lighting or makeup!' laughed Harriet when she told me about it later. 'He did not come to congratulate me on my fine voice, mind, just my looks,' she said indignantly. 'So I sent him off with a flea in his ear, thinking I would never see him again. But the next night he was back. It was the same for three nights, until the troupe was ready to move on. On the last night he brought flowers and was very bashful. He said he hoped I would not be offended if he told me that my voice was as sweet as a lark's.

' "So you are English then?" said I.

' "Oh no, I'm a colonial lad through and through," he said quickly, for many of the songs in our show poke fun at the English.

' "But if you are not English you could never have heard a lark sing, for we have none in the Colony," I replied.

' "Oh." He blushed in confusion, then said, "A magpie, then. You sing as sweetly as a magpie."

'I burst out laughing. "So you think I warble, do you?"

' "No, no, never warble, I meant to say —"

'I cut him off with a loud magpie warble, a most horrid noise. He stared at me and blushed some more, looking most ashamed of himself. I think it was then I fell in love with him, Mama.'

'Poor Tom,' I said. 'You are a saucy thing, Harriet. Were his feelings badly hurt?'

'Only for a minute. I forgave him instantly and we became the best of friends.'

So they wrote to each other for six months and met whenever they could, which was not often while the tour went on and his ship sailed further north. But it was enough.

As I have sat up late sewing Harriet's wedding gown these past weeks, I have thought of John Stephen. In spite of being born a gentleman he is different. He talks to me like an equal. We have shared confidences. I have seen him at his most vulnerable and been able to comfort him. I know he feels affection for me. And this was a new country where the class system was being broken down. Why should we not allow ourselves to fall in love?

Six years ago, on the night that his case finished and he was pronounced not guilty of all the accusations that had taken him five years to fight, he did not go out celebrating with his witty friends and brothers, Mr Francis Stephen, Mr Wentworth and the others. He came to my cottage.

It was dusk and he looked weary and hollow-eyed. I thought at first that the news must be bad and he had lost. I had not expected the case to finish for weeks yet, and when he came to the door looking so exhausted I feared the worst. He came into the parlour and sat in the armchair opposite me and sighed deeply. Then he rose, took both my hands in his and said, 'It is finished, Mary. We have won.'

I put my arms around him and kissed him. It was quite spontaneous. He looked surprised. He blinked and smiled, then held me close. I pulled gently away and we talked of the case by lamplight for perhaps an hour. He told me that he had been dreadfully afraid he would lose. Even now he could not quite believe he had won, and was no longer regarded as a disgrace to his family.

I felt that anything might happen that night. He was waiting. And I was waiting. For what? I sigh even now as I think of it. I was waiting for him to say some words that would give me hope. He said other things of course. Kind words. Words of gratitude. Appropriate words for a man in his position towards a woman in mine. — 'I trust you so completely, Mary. You are a true friend.' That was all.

He left soon afterwards and I have seen little of John Stephen in the long time since that evening. I avoid going to Ultimo House and send one of my staff to deliver Mrs Stephen's gowns or to collect them when alterations are needed. I think she understands why I no longer visit her. I have not been lucky in love.

So I am full of joy at the sight of my daughter who at not yet sixteen believes she is the only woman in the world who has loved her husband so much. And he, the dear boy, returns it.

I felt sad about my old friend Jane New. The court proved John Stephen innocent, so there is no doubt she was lying about their love affair. I am relieved about that. Why did she do it? Because she is still angry with all gentlemen? Or just to amuse herself by shocking people?

I could not bear to imagine them in each other's arms. I like to think of John Stephen as a faultless gentleman.

# CHAPTER 49

**Jane Faces New Dramas in New Zealand and Promises to Visit Me**

*Kororareka, February, 1840*

*My Dear Mary,*

*Are you still sulking because I told you the truth about Mr Stephen? I heard that he won his case anyway, so lies must be the fashion in Sydney Town. Not much has changed since I left eleven years ago, it seems.*

*I thought we should make up our quarrel before I come there to visit. Ah ha! What do you think of that? Bold Jane risks arrest to return to the place where they judged her a criminal but let her escape from their clutches not once but three times! (Once from the Constable in Philip Street, once over the wall of the Female Factory and once in a vessel that landed me here safe and sound in New Zealand, in case you've forgotten.)*

*As I shall be risking my neck by returning to Sydney Town, I shall travel under a false name and look very different from the Jane New you remember. Let's hope you recognise me when I arrive on your doorstep, for I expect to enjoy your hospitality for at least a week and to select some gowns from your dress shops, and of course to meet that daughter of yours. Perhaps, if I am not too weary after all that, I shall go out and about on The Rocks and renew old acquaintances. I can see you trembling, Mary, and asking yourself, 'But will she be recognised and shall I be thrown into prison for harbouring a criminal?' Never fear. I am a mistress of disguises.*

*We have had some new dramas here in New Zealand this month. The ceremonial signing of the Treaty of Waitangi with the Maori has taken place, and New Zealand is now a British Colony under the rule of Queen Victoria. The unfortunate Mr Busby has been dumped in favour of Captain William Hobson, who now has the title of Lieutenant Governor.*

*But I predict trouble brewing. Mr Busby may not have been perfect but he did good things for which he has never been thanked. When Missionaries and others came to him with a proposal to ban the sale of liquor in the Bay a few years ago, he said the matter was outside his jurisdiction. Three cheers for Busby! If the Temperance Society had got its way, every grog shop would have been closed and most of us leading business people in Kororareka would have gone broke. He also designed New Zealand's flag and made the whalers pay tax to enter the Bay. He persuaded the Maori chiefs to sign a declaration that made us independent, and called us 'The United Tribes of New Zealand'. Your Governor Bourke, back in Sydney, was not too pleased about that, so it was only a matter of time before he sacked poor Busby.*

*At least Busby took the trouble to push back some of*

*the greedy gentry from New South Wales who came here to buy all the Maori land they could get. And he stopped one tribe selling off land that belonged to another tribe! Hobson, the new man, is such a weak specimen that I doubt very much that he will care what happens to the small amount of land still owned by the Maori. Once it is all sold off and the Maori have spent the payment, they'll want their land back. They are not like Europeans: if the Maoris' land is lost, then so are they. There will be wars, I know it and God help us settlers then!*

*Anyway, although I was asked last month, as a 'respectable person' of Kororareka, I refused to sign a proclamation saying that New Zealand came within the boundaries of New South Wales and that Her Majesty the Queen was the only one who could recognise valid land titles. What nonsense! We should be able to make our own rules here and our own arrangements with the Maori, as we have always done.*

*I confess I have bought land of my own from the Maori at a cheap price, but then I count myself as a friend, one who speaks some of the language and understands their ways. I find them very mischievous and funny when they are bored and trying to stir up trouble with the pompous British. I don't think I abuse them.*

*Now, I hope for the better, we have the Treaty of Waitangi. At least it may stop those land-grabbing Sydney swells coming here and buying up everything! (As you can see I've become a passionate New Zealander.) The Maori were given just one week to think about the Treaty and consult with the few Pakeha they trusted, such as the Missionaries and Mr Busby. I played a small part in all this, for I am trusted by one of the most influ-*

*ential Chiefs, a young warrior called Nene — I have mentioned to you before. He is a powerful speaker to his people and he also speaks good English and can write. There are many things he doesn't like about the Pakeha. Even I come in for criticism from him sometimes, which I dread. I have known him for many years. I will not tell you more of this just now as you once wrote you found it hard to understand how I could have a 'savage' for a friend.*

*Instead, let me tell you about the Signing of the Treaty. At Mrs Busby's kind invitation I went to the Ceremony. It was quite impressive I can tell you. The hillside at Waitangi was a moving mass of Maori people, led by the Chiefs and a handful of Pakeha. I could not help thinking that to wipe out the whole 'respectable' Pakeha population of the Bay of Islands would have been so easy for the Maori that morning. Later I heard there were one thousand five hundred Maori people walking up that hill. Down below you could hardly see the blue of the water for the red of war canoes. There were also small canoes, sailing boats, row boats, whaleboats and a larger vessel named the Herald, which had brought the new Governor to New Zealand.*

*We all walked towards a huge tent made of sails and spars on the lawn in front of Mr Busby's house. There was room for less than half the crowd inside the tent, but as I am a friend of Mrs Busby I was escorted to a seat near the dais. The rest of the crowd waited in smaller tents outside.*

*Governor Hobson stood up to address the vast meeting in English and the Reverend Williams translated. He said that Queen Victoria wished to protect her sub-*

jects in New Zealand, giving them rights and property and holding back the trouble-makers, but this would not be possible unless the Chiefs granted her sovereignty. This meant that they must give her power over their territories. They could keep their land, forests and fisheries, but if they chose to sell them, they must do so at prices agreed on by people appointed by the Queen.

He then read out the Treaty. The Reverend Williams explained each part of it very carefully to the Maori and asked them to consider it cautiously before agreeing. He told them that the Missionaries approved of it, and then called for discussion.

This 'korero' and the feast that would follow was really what most of the Maori had travelled so many miles to take part in.

An old warrior named Te Kemara stood up first. Facing the Reverend Williams, he roared out at him: 'Thou, thou, thou, thou bald-headed man, thou hast got my land!' Mr Busby looked most embarrassed, for he guessed that he'd be the next to be accused, and he was. Both men tried calmly to explain, as they must have done often before, that they had paid well for the land.

I could see that the new Governor and his staff had seen nothing like this before and their self-satisfied smirks soon left their faces as one by one the Maori Chiefs rose, dignified as lords in their frightening tattoos and cloaks of animal skins, to ask questions. A Chief named Wai spoke thus: 'To thee, O Governor! This. Will you remedy the selling, the exchanging, the cheating, the lying, the stealing of the whites?' The Reverend Williams managed to translate this as quite a polite question, to which some of the Maori who spoke English objected.

There were interjections, jokes, arguments and dramatic, passionate speeches. Nobody was in a hurry to come to a decision and the new Governor had to be more patient than he'd probably ever been in his life. Some speakers shouted that they did not want either a Governor or a Treaty. They would not be tricked out of their lands by anyone! They were the Chiefs!

Rewa, one of the Kororareka chiefs, stepped up to the table and said in perfect English, 'How d'ye do, Governor?' Everyone burst out laughing, including the Governor. He shook hands with Rewa, who then announced that he would not sign the Treaty!

By late afternoon it looked to me as if the Treaty was a lost cause. The atmosphere was hostile and Governor Hobson looked pale, sickly and defeated. Then in came two Chiefs who changed the mood of that place completely. One of these, Patuone, I had not seen since I was a castaway on the wild beach at Hokianga over ten years ago. The other Chief was Nene.

It was Nene who came forward to speak. I held my breath as I listened, for he was still as eloquent and impressive as he had been one stormy night when I was afraid and went to him for protection. That is another story. I may tell it to you one day. Or I may not.

What Nene said to the six hundred in the tent I shall not easily forget. He first spoke to his own people, asking them to remember how their country had improved since Europeans came and how before this time they had fought many wars and shed so much blood. He became angry with them. He then told them more quietly *that they should receive the Europeans and believe their promises. He turned to Governor Hobson and said, 'Thou must be our father! Thou must not allow us to become slaves! Thou must preserve our customs, and never permit our lands to be wrested from us!'*

*This is what changed the day. The meeting closed, leaving one clear day for the Chiefs to consider whether or not to sign. On Friday, 7th February at eleven o'clock the Treaty was signed by forty-six Head Chiefs with about five hundred others watching.*

*I have seen this Treaty. The signatures vary from diagonal crosses to serpents, swirls, and horizontal marks. All are distinctively different, most being copies of the Chiefs' face tattoos, which they call 'moko'. But Nene signed his name in English.*

*My clerk, Mr Macrae, tells me his hand aches from writing all this so I will spare him by finishing at once.*

*So far there have been no war dances on the beach at Kororareka, so I am hoping I will get on board my vessel for Port Jackson before the Chiefs decide they are bored and set fire to our little town again. I may bring someone with me. A young person. No, not a suitor, as you might expect of me, Mary. But still someone quite dear to me. Ah ha. I see you are in suspense already.*

*I am,*

*Your obedient servant and dearest friend, who forgives you at last for your foolish suspicion of me over worthless John Stephen.*

*Jane New*

# CHAPTER 50

## I Become a Grandmother at the Age of Thirty-five
## The Rocks, June, 1840

Today Harriet gave birth to a baby girl. She is perfect. Harriet has just had her sixteenth birthday, but even so young she shows all the signs of becoming a devoted mother. Thomas Craig has been granted leave from his ship to spend the first week with his new family, and a more doting father I have not seen in all my days.

He took the tiny bundle from the Midwife as soon as the babe was swaddled in a shawl. Such an expression of loving pride passed over his face as he looked from child to mother that I felt the tears spring to my eyes and thanked God that Harriet had what I had never had — a man to adore and protect them both.

'Oh Hatty, she is beautiful,' he said and kissed his daughter's soft skull covered in downy fair hair.

Harriet sat propped up against her pillows, took the little girl from him and said dreamily, 'She is called Mary, after my mother.'

'And shall her second name be Rose, after my

mother?' whispered Tom, for he did not want to wake his daughter.

'Yes, Mary Rose is her name,' whispered Harriet, without taking her eyes off the child.

'And shall her third name be Victoria, after the Queen?'

I smiled to myself. Tom has always been loyal to England.

'The Queen of England?' Harriet looked puzzled, then shook her head slowly. 'It is rather a lot of names. Mary Rose Craig is simpler, don't you think?'

Tom turned his gaze back on the child as if he might ask her opinion. Then he nodded. 'Yes, Mary Rose Craig is simpler.'

The Midwife and I crept out of the room to leave the young family alone together.

And so at the age of thirty-five I am a grandmother. And my mother Harriet is a great-grandmother at the age of fifty-three! I must write to tell her the good news. She is well and living with my sister Sarah in the same cottage that I grew up in. They keep each other company, and live a quiet, contented life, so my mother says. My sister Meg has married a merchant and they live not far away in the next village and have three young sons. My brother Charley grew bored with his work in the village bakery and went to sea as a cabin boy. He has since been promoted and wrote to me a year ago that he would sail all the way to Port Jackson if he could find a vessel bringing cargo to the other side of the world, but so far none have offered him a position. I would dearly love to see any member of my family again, but particularly Charley, who was so close to me when we were children. Our mother used to say that we were headstrong and would both come to bad ends.

Jane New would laugh to hear me described so. Compared to her I am meek and have led a most uneventful life. It is four months since Jane told me she was setting off to visit me and I have not seen sight nor sound of her. I hope she is safe. Most likely she changed her mind about coming at the last minute and forgot to let me know. I am deeply disappointed. The guest room has been ready for months with fresh flowers changed twice a week. I arranged to employ someone to take over my shop for a week so that I could show Jane the sights, and borrowed a rowboat to take her for picnics but I have had to cancel all that. Why is Jane so thoughtless?

Harriet would stay in bed only two days and then she was up in spite of the soreness she felt. She said it was good to feel her body slim again and she wanted to move about and go out to her little garden, carry Mary Rose into the sunshine and let her smell the lavender. It was here, sitting under a shady gum tree, with the baby in her arms and Thomas close beside her, that I found them as I came from my cottage with a pie I had baked for their supper. As I hurried down the path towards them a gentleman stepped out from behind the tree, where he'd been looking out across the quarry. 'Mama, look who's come to visit us. Mr Stephen!' cried Harriet happily.

I stopped and stared and my mouth fell open. At least I did not drop the basket. John Stephen came forward smiling and held out both hands to me. 'Mary, my dear,' he said. I took his hands. 'It has been so long since I saw you. Forgive me. I have been abroad. How are you?' His voice was the same. Rich. Deep. Very warm.

I spluttered some nonsense in reply. I was most disconcerted, but nobody seemed to notice.

'Mr Stephen came to see Mary Rose and look what he's brought her!'

Harriet held up a white satin box. I came closer to look inside. A beautifully embroidered lace gown lay there. It looked like a family heirloom.

'A christening gown, I believe,' he said. 'It belonged to my mother and we were all christened in it, so I imagine it's almost worn out!'

'But it belongs to your family!' I protested.

'No, no. We've finished with it. My brothers and I are mostly resigned to be bachelors. My mother would be honoured if Harriet and Thomas would accept it as a gift for Mary Rose and whoever might follow her.'

Harriet laughed. 'Oh yes, we'd be delighted to, wouldn't we, Tom? Tom wants at least three daughters and three sons but I'm going to ask him to wait a while!'

Now she was lifting the tiny bundle into Mr John Stephen's arms. He took her carefully, not looking embarrassed or awkward as some gentlemen would, but gazing at her little face in wonder. After he had looked a good long time and even made clucking noises, he handed Mary Rose to me. The closeness of him did not make me melt as it had the last time I saw him. But it was as dear to me, and as familiar as ever, as if we had never been apart these past five years. He turned to me and said quietly, 'I think Mary Rose has her grandmama's fine eyes.'

I did not even blush, but replied just as quietly, 'I think it is too early to tell, John.'

To my surprise it was he who blushed this time. I had not used his Christian name before, although he had in the past invited me to.

# CHAPTER 51

## A Broken Promise

*Kororareka, February, 1841*

*Dear Mary,*

*Unfortunately I have had to postpone my journey to Sydney yet again. I am sorry that you have been disappointed not to see me as I promised, but life here has been so busy since the new Governor came.*

*Kororareka is full of new settlers, land speculators, surveyors, lawyers, hoteliers and shopkeepers, all of us busy from dawn to dusk. We are quite the progressive town. Now we have a Harbour Master and Pilot, a Port Doctor and Police Magistrate. Even the flagstaff, which stood in front of the Busby's residence at Waitangi for so many years has been transported across the bay to Kororareka to stand on the hilltop above our town.*

*Who would have thought that Governor Hobson and his entourage would be lodged here in Kororareka? They complain bitterly about not yet being in the new capital, a town five miles up the harbour named Rus-*

sell. But what is there at Russell? Nothing but plans drawn up, so I hear. We hope the Governor will be obliged to stay here and that this will become the seat of Government. What a transformation that would be for our riotous old town! Why, just a year ago we still had the notorious Kororareka Association which protected our goods and property from thieves by punishing them in our own way — locking them up in a sea-chest or tarring and feathering them, marching them up and down the streets, then drumming them out of town!

Now everything is ruled by Government officials.

And what is the most popular place for these new Government officials and their assistants to visit? Why, The Duke of Marlborough, of course. I declare that if I were to leave here even for a few weeks to go to Sydney, there would be riots if the place was not open for business and running as smoothly as only I can manage it. Such is the life of a devoted business woman in a capital city. Well, dear Mary, you have your own small business so you would have some idea of what I mean.

Kororareka has become a boom town in just one year. Huts, tents and thatched cottages have sprung up all over the place to house the population, which has increased ten times over. Will it last? Who knows? As long as it does, we are making our money as fast as bees make honey!

Give my best wishes to your daughter, Harriet. Expecting another child so soon after the first, is she? Well, the Colonies must be populated I suppose and who better to do it than the daughter of a moral ex-convict like yourself? Ha, ha.

I am,

*Your obedient servant and weary but increasingly wealthy friend,*
Jane New.

# CHAPTER 52

**Harriet, Still Suffering from Shock, Exerts her Independence**
**The Rocks, June, 1843**

The worst news possible for my daughter Harriet arrived just one month ago. Her husband Thomas Craig drowned when his ship hit a storm off the coast of Queensland and he was thrown from the mast while climbing it to free a sail.

Harriet let out a wail like a woman possessed when she heard this. Then ran to their bed where she lay for many days just staring at the wall and sobbing quietly. I took the children, Mary Rose, who is three, and the twins Andrew and Will, who are not yet two, to my cottage so that she could be peaceful. Elizabeth Male and I took turns to watch over Harriet and mind the little ones, who were better off away from a mother so filled with grief. For the first week she would take nothing to eat and said she did not want to live. I told her she had the children to think of. She stared at me blankly. I had never seen her so low.

I called at Ultimo House to ask my friend John Stephen if he would send the family doctor to attend Harriet and he came immediately. He gave her a sleeping potion and recommended beef broth, rest and care.

She has been too tired lately, what with Tom so often away and three small children to care for. They have had all had bad illnesses this winter. Young Will was almost carried off with the scarlet fever and then Andrew broke his leg when he fell down some steps in their garden. Finally Mary Rose caught the chicken pox and now, in spite of Harriet having bound her hands in cloth so she could not scratch the scabs, her pretty face is badly pockmarked. Of course Harriet blamed herself for this. It has been a bad year for my daughter. She was already pale and much thinner than she should have been. And now the spirit has gone out of her, she is like a ghost herself. I asked some of her old performing friends to visit her but when they came she refused to see them.

I devised a plan to put managers into my two shops and take Harriet and the children to the mountains for a change of air. It was not healthy for her to be still distraught after so many weeks. But when I mentioned this scheme to her, she cried out that she did not want to leave the house where she and Tom had been so happy all their married life. She talked as if he was still alive and sometimes I heard her murmuring to herself behind the closed door, as if she was talking to him. I began to fear for her sanity. I felt sure she believed that if she just waited long enough he would come home.

This afternoon when I came to their cottage I let out a small cry of shock. There on the peg in the hall hung Tom's greatcoat, just where he had always hung it. And his boots stood beneath it.

I ran into the bedroom. Harriet was not there. The bed was neatly made and all was in order. I ran to the kitchen and there she sat by the window, dressed at last and drinking a cup of tea. Her hair was neatly coiled on top of her head and a little colour had come back into her cheeks.

I embraced her and said I was happy to see her so much better.

She smiled and offered me tea. After a while she said, 'A seaman was here this morning from Tom's ship. He brought me Tom's things.'

'Ah, that was good of him Harriet.'

How I wished she could have attended a funeral for her husband. Then she might have believed he was really dead. But I knew that the body had not been found and that a ceremony had been held at sea to commemorate Tom Craig, as is the custom for drowned seamen.

'I have put Tom's trunk under the bed where he always puts it when he comes home from the sea, and now that I have his clothes as well it is almost as if he is home for a visit, Mama,' she said serenely.

Oh, it was a pitiful thought!

'But my darling, he is gone. You must face it and let me and your friends comfort you.'

She looked away, out the window into the garden. 'I will face it, but let me have these imaginings for a few days yet.'

I nodded. After a silence she said, 'The seaman who came was an older man, a gentleman and very kind. He stayed to talk with me and said that although he did not know Tom well, he knew him to be a brave and competent young seaman and that he fell through no fault of his own.'

'Ah, that is a great comfort to hear,' I said softly.

'Yes, it is. And Mr Fitch — that was his name — promised to visit me when he is ashore, as he lives nearby, and tell me more about Tom's life at sea, for I knew so little about it. He said he would often talk to Tom and other sailors on the *Windlass* when their vessels were in port together and that is how he knew him.'

'And how did he come to bring Tom's things to you, Harriet?'

'The captain of the *Windlass* is a friend of Mr Fitch's and when he found that Mr Fitch lived near to us in Kent Street, he asked if he would kindly deliver them here. See? He has brought back the miniature picture of me and the children that Tom kept by his bunk. He told me that Tom was fortunate to have such a beautiful wife.' Here she paused and shook her head sadly. 'He says that Tom's wages for the month will arrive by post in a few days' time. He seemed concerned that now I am a widow I might also be a pauper, and asked if I had relatives to help take care of me and the children.'

'And I hope you told him that you had a mother who would sell everything she owns to keep you all safe and well beside her,' I said.

'No Mama, I did not, although I know it is the

truth.' She turned to face me. 'You have worked hard all your life to support me and now, as you grow older, you must think of yourself. I am perfectly well able to take care of myself and the children.' She said this with pride.

I smiled indulgently and asked what she had in mind.

'I will take a position as a servant in a house not far from here where I can live in with the children. Then this cottage can be let to a tenant and that money saved for our futures.'

'What!' I protested. 'But this is your home! What house will you take a position in? You have told me nothing of this.'

'It is all arranged. Mr Stephen has friends with a large house in George Street who would be glad to offer me a position as Nursemaid to their two young children. They have no objection to me bringing my own children there and will even provide a small cottage behind the main house for us to live in.'

'But this is so unnecessary, Harriet! And so sudden. When did you arrange it?'

'Mr Stephen has been visiting me every week for the past month, as you know, and when I told him I did not want to burden you with responsibility for us but felt too weak to go looking for a position, he suggested his friends.'

'Well!' I was quite taken aback. 'I wish he had bothered to discuss it with me first.'

'Why should he discuss it? I am a grown woman, Mama, not still your little girl who must ask your permission to earn her own living,' she replied evenly.

I stared at this suddenly changed, independent young widow. Was she the same girl who had lain weeping on her bed for over a month? She seemed to read my thoughts. 'Thank you for allowing me time to grieve, Mama. I will never recover fully from losing Tom, but at least you gave me the time I needed to be alone with him in spirit, and now I feel strong enough to do what he would have wanted me to — not to be a burden on you any longer.'

'You are no burden!' I cried.

'You brought me up to be strong and independent and you have suffered enough to give me everything I wanted in life. Now I want to make my own way.'

'Oh, Harriet!' I flung my arms around her and wept, for she had rewarded me too much for the little she'd been given. I was so very proud of her.

# CHAPTER 53

## Harriet Becomes Romantically Entangled with the Worst Man Imaginable
### The Rocks, October, 1843

Harriet has made a great effort to be independent. For four months now she has battled to do two difficult jobs — one as full-time Nursemaid to the rather spoilt offspring of Mr and Mrs Harcourt in George Street, the other as the only parent of her own three children. She is worn out, but refuses to give up. I tell her she has proved she can be financially independent so why not go back to her cottage now and let me help her? She says she cannot do that. The rent the tenants pay for the cottage will be used for her children's education. She is a proud young woman who will allow no one to help her.

Did I say no one? Not quite. Mr Fitch, the gentleman who says he knew Tom at sea before he fell to his death, is a regular visitor to her lodgings behind the Harcourts' house. She says that he helps her. I know very little about him so this makes me uneasy.

I have met the gentleman only once. He is past middle age, of medium height and well built. He seems kind enough, but I fear it is unhealthy for him to call on her so often to remind her of her dead husband, telling her anecdotes about him and his fellow sailors when their ships were anchored in the same port, which she, apparently, never tires of hearing.

Last Sunday, when I took the children to my cottage as I always do, so that Harriet may rest on her afternoon off, she surprised me by saying that she and Mr Fitch were 'walking out' together. Rather a formal term for a stroll along the wharf, thought I, but I was glad that she was getting some fresh air at last. The Harcourts' house is dark and stuffy. They seem to regard sunlight as harmful, and do not like Harriet to take the children out walking on The Rocks for fear of disease or bad company. They are over-protective, in my opinion.

Imagine my surprise, when I was walking back to George Street to return my grandchildren to their mother, to catch a glimpse of Harriet and Mr Fitch walking together up ahead, arm-in-arm, she leaning close to him as she laughed affectionately into his eyes. Why, he is fifty-six years old, so she says, and a gentleman! He should know better than to play on the affections of a recently bereaved young woman. I felt outraged.

As soon as he had gone I confronted Harriet with this. She turned to me with the dignity of a queen and said, 'Mama, I must tell you that John Fitch has proposed marriage to me.'

'What!'

'I have told him that I don't wish to contemplate it so soon after becoming a widow.'

'I should think not!'

'But that I will consider it after a year has passed.'

'But that is only eight months away. You hardly know him, Harriet.'

'Ah, but I do. He has confided in me very often. He is the kindest of men. He has had a miserable and unlucky life but now he says he has found true love for the first time ever and wants to devote the rest of his life to looking after me and the children.'

'But Harriet, he is older than I am! And what do you know of his character? If he is really a gentleman, why does he wish to marry you?'

'Because Mama, he loves me! He was abandoned by his English family and lost his fortune after he was unfairly arrested for stealing and brought to the Colony as a convict. Next he was falsely accused of forgery and sent to Norfolk Island where he worked as a sail-maker in such bitter conditions that his legs became paralysed and he had to walk on crutches for two years. But now he has earned his freedom, as you and so many of your friends did, Mama. He is Master of his own ship which runs between Sydney and Port Macquarie. It is a cutter and what do you think it is called? The *Harriet*!'

I shook my head. 'What a coincidence,' I said, pretending to be impressed. My daughter was so weary and so in need of comfort after her sad loss that I feared her judgment had gone. To be swayed in the direction of a stranger because his ship was named the *Harriet*? I ask you! But all I said was, 'I am glad you've decided to wait a year before considering marriage to Mr Fitch.'

'He has agreed to be patient, although he'd much prefer to marry me at once. When you get to know him better you will see what a loving man he is, Mama, and how gentle with the children. He has suffered terrible injustices and yet he bears no grudge against anyone. He's a truly remarkable gentleman.'

'Hmm. There is something about him that sounds familiar and it makes me uneasy.'

'Oh Mama, you are so cautious! I'll invite him here to tea next Sunday and you will see for yourself what a charming, admirable person he is.'

I awoke suddenly that night and sat bolt upright in my bed. John Fitch! Wasn't that the alias used by John Knatchbull when he became a convict? John Stephen had mentioned it to me years ago. Could it be that my daughter's suitor was none other than the man who had so cruelly deceived Maria Wilkinson and changed her from an innocent girl into the hardened convict, Jane New?

I could not sleep but got up and dressed and paced the floor until it was light, when I hurried to Ultimo House to check with John Stephen whether my belief was correct.

He was at breakfast, surprised and mildly alarmed by my appearance so early. But once I had explained that Harriet was considering marrying an ex-convict whom I considered dangerous, he sprang into action and we hurried together to the law courts, where we looked up the details I needed from a comprehensive record of convicts in New South Wales.

'Yes. John Knatchbull whose alias is John Fitch, was the third son of the late Sir Edward Knatchbull, Baronet, of Mersham Le Hatch in the County of Kent ...'

'Are you sure there is only one John Fitch? Could it possibly be someone else?' I asked.

'I can't be certain, Mary, but I would be surprised if there were two convicted John Fitches in the Colony.' He pulled out more papers and read aloud: 'As a boy he was educated for the Navy — midshipman, lieutenant, commander by 1813, saw service in several theatres of war — Boulogne, the Azores, North America. On reduction of the Navy in 1815 he was put on half pay. He served in South America. In 1818 the Admiralty removed his name from the list of commanders for failure to pay a private debt.'

That would have been just before he met Maria Wilkinson, alias Jane, I thought to myself.

'Ah, here it is! In 1824, under the name of John Fitch he was convicted of stealing a pocket book containing a blank cheque and two sovereigns at Vauxhall Gardens. Sentenced by Mr Justice Burroughs to transportation for fourteen years.'

'I wonder why he changed his name in court?' I said.

'It happens frequently in England when the accused wants to save his or her family from disgrace, particularly if they belong to the aristocracy,' John Stephen replied.

He read on, abbreviating the details for my benefit. 'Arrived in Sydney on the *Asia*, 1825, spent a few weeks at Emu Plains, transferred to Bathurst. Appointed a constable and carried the mail on foot once a week between Bathurst and Mount York — must have been trustworthy,' he remarked, 'or appeared to have been. Captured eight runaways, which shortened his time for a ticket of leave, which he was granted in 1829. He sounds a smart fellow.'

'Yes, he was smart all right,' I said grimly.

'You have known him before, Mary?'

'No, not I, but a friend of mine.' I did not want to mention Jane New, for I knew John Stephen loathed her. He seemed to have forgotten that fourteen years ago I had asked him to find out if Knatchbull was in the Colony and had even mentioned the mock marriage in which he had deceived Jane. Perhaps he had not believed in her story enough to bother remembering it.

At about the time Jane had told me that she had seen Knatchbull riding with a friend near the Hyde Park Barracks — and she had seemed genuinely upset by it — I had not known whether to believe her, but as he already had his ticket of leave by then, it could well have been him.

John Stephen continued, 'In 1831 he was charged with forging the signature of Mr James Dowling to a cheque for six pounds, ten shillings.' He interrupted himself. 'That would have been when I was away in England, but I remember mention of it. Dowling is a friend of my family. In 1832 he was tried and found guilty, death sentence commuted to transportation for seven years to Norfolk Island.'

'Harriet told me he spent years on Norfolk Island,' I said. 'I am sure that is the same man.'

'Shall I continue reading?'

'No. But thank you, John. It has been a great help.'

'The man is well bred, has been punished for his crimes and does not appear to have committed any more for the past twelve years. He may be a reformed character,' he said.

I nodded, although I was not convinced of this. I said I would take my leave, as John had to hurry off to his duties in court. He asked obligingly if there was anything else I needed and I said there was not. I decided that I should go at once to warn Harriet that John Fitch was not to be trusted.

'Oh Mama, I refuse to listen to such gossip!' Harriet cried, as I helped her dress the children. 'At least come and meet the man before you pass judgment.'

It was cold and damp in her lodgings. 'Is there no fire here, Harriet? The children's hands are like ice.' I began rubbing them.

'Pray do not fuss. They are well rugged-up and fires burn in every room in the big house. We will soon be cosy enough.'

'But why doesn't Mr Harcourt provide coal for a fire for you here? It's been unseasonably cold for weeks and Mary Rose still has her cough. It must be freezing in the evenings.'

'If I want coal I must pay for it. Please don't fuss. We'll have a fire on Sunday when John comes to tea. Now, Mama, I must ask you to go as I'm late to get the Harcourt children's breakfast.' She gathered her small brood in front of her, urging them along like a mother goose with a flock of goslings. They waved to me and called out goodbye, and after I had waved and blown kisses I turned my face into the sharp wind to hide my tears.

# CHAPTER 54

**Jane Will Be Here for Christmas!**

*Kororareka, December 1843*

*My dearest Mary,*

*Your sorrows are at an end. I am on my way to Sydney at last! My ship leaves the Bay of Islands in a few days time and I shall disembark in Port Jackson in time to spend Christmas with you. What a thrill that will be! You can start pouring rum into the pudding and brandy into the sauce right now.*

*I shall be in need of cheering up as my life in Kororareka has been dismal since the capital was shifted to Auckland. Now that the Colonial Secretary and his department have all gone most of the shipping bypasses the Bay of Islands so there is almost no trading at all. We have become a ghost town and I have lost a fortune. There is also no law and order. The land speculators take no notice of the Treaty and cheat the Maori of their land. The Government exercises its right to Maori land by paying sixpence an acre for it! Corruption is everywhere. Hotels which can't be sold even at rock bottom prices are advertised to let and houses and gardens are being given free of rent to any tenant who will take care of them.*

*Yes, Kororareka has changed in three years from a prosperous community to a shabby colonial township dependent on nothing but what is left of the whale trade. The Police Magistrate and his men turn a blind eye towards trouble. I wish the old days of tarring and feathering the law breakers were back! There are ruffians amongst the new settlers who show no respect for the Maori.*

*Chief Hone Heke, who is supposed to be civilised and a Christian, objects so much to the British flagstaff high on the hill above our town that he has chopped it down three times! He says this flag takes away the authority of the Chiefs and all their lands. Chief Waka Nene, who I know well, has sided with the British against Heke. I feel sure that Heke will keep on chopping down the flagstaff just to infuriate the British. It is only a matter of time before there will be another war. Then all our property will go up in flames and I do not think I could bear to see it.*

*What better excuse for me to come to visit you at once!*

*Your most loyal and oldest friend,*
*Jane New*

*PS. I may be bringing the young person I mentioned earlier.*

# CHAPTER 55

## In Spite of Good Intentions I Deliver My Daughter to a Monster
### The Rocks, December, 1843

It will be a relief to see my old friend after so long. I hope she doesn't let me down and change her mind about coming at the last minute. Broken promises mean nothing to Jane. I am so in need of an ally against John Knatchbull. And who could be better than Jane? I would love to see her confront him and make him confess to the mock marriage that ruined her. Then Harriet would see with her own eyes what kind of man he is. At present she sees only his virtues and when I beg her to wait a little longer before accepting him, she regards me as far worse than just a mother who is making a 'fuss'. I fear that she now sees me as her enemy. It is heartbreaking.

I went to tea a few Sundays ago to meet John Fitch, as he calls himself, At first, I admit, I was favourably impressed. I thought that perhaps my friend John Stephen was right to believe that since his punishment Fitch has become a reformed character. I gave him the benefit of the doubt.

He greeted me with great charm and wholesomeness. No sign of condescension or arrogance at all. He is obviously deeply fond of Harriet. I saw that she trusted him and how she blushed when he took her hand. He was, as she had told me, gentle and patient with the children, who also seemed to like him.

He was open with me when I asked questions about his employment. 'Yes, it is true, Mrs Jones, that I have a ticket of leave and until recently was the Master of the *Harriet*, a coaster which ran between here and Port Macquarie. But my dearest Harriet implored me not to go to sea any more as she was naturally very anxious about my safety after the loss of her late husband. So I am now a landlubber, waiting to get the vessel sold.' He smiled and said confidently that he would have no trouble at all finding another job.

'And where do you live at present, Mr Fitch?'

'I am renting lodgings in Clarence Lane from a Mr Charles Hollowell, ma'am.'

I felt some relief when I heard this. Mrs Hollowell is a respectable woman and one of my most valued customers. I would make discreet inquiries of her about John Fitch.

'Will you tell me a little about your family in England, Mr Fitch?' I asked pleasantly. At this Harriet frowned. She no doubt thought I was being too inquisitive, but I was determined to draw the man out.

John Fitch gave me no sign that he resented my question, however. 'I should be glad to,' he said, and settled comfortably in his chair ready to begin his history. 'I was born at Provender in the County of Kent and lived at my father's residence, Mersham Le Hatch. I was one of eight children born to his second wife. My mother departed this world when I was a young boy. I shall never forget my poor broken-hearted father placing me on his knee and telling me my Mama was gone to Heaven.' Here he paused as if overcome with emotion and Harriet placed her hand in his for comfort.

He continued, 'I was placed under the care of a governess, Miss Verney, together with the rest of my brothers and sisters. She took as much care in our education and morals as if she had been our mother. My boyish days were spent in riding my pony and occasionally spending a week or two at my grandmother's, where I was indulged in every way.'

'Your childhood sounds a happy one except for the loss of your mother,' I said sympathetically. 'And did you go away to school?'

'I did. Ah, but we were not always good fellows. We got up to tricks!'

The children gathered close to their mother and Mary Rose turned her little face up to his. 'What tricks did you do?' she asked.

John Fitch laughed at this and set her on his knee. I did not care for this intimacy. The child was smiling at him in expectation. 'Once a parcel of us boys got around an old woman who kept an apple stall and had an iron pot for the purpose of roasting apples. One of the boys threw a cartridge of powder into the pot. A few minutes after, the explosion took place. *Boom!* Away went pot, apple stall and old woman, heels up!'

He burst out laughing. 'We boys lost no time in making a noble harvest of the apples.'

'And what happened to the old woman?' asked Mary Rose gravely.

He shrugged. 'Why, we set her upon her legs again, much better than before. All we wanted was some fun.'

Mary Rose scrambled down off his knee and came to sit by me. I nodded but said nothing. I remembered that Maria Wilkinson had been a little shocked by the heartless mischief performed by John Knatchbull as a schoolboy, and had told me other stories of cruelty he had proudly related to her.

He talked on about his career in the Navy, often dropping the names of important commanders who had praised him for his bravery in battle. If one could believe the half of it he should have been an admiral by now, knighted by the Queen, thought I, not an ex-convict hoping to marry a poor young widow with three children.

I poured cups of tea for us all and passed around a cake I had made with apricots, almonds and cream.

'Why, this is a splendid tea!' said John Fitch. 'When we are wed, Harriet, we must invite your dear mother to perform this service every Sunday.' He laughed at his own little joke.

I smiled my thanks and asked with feigned innocence. 'And how do you get along with your brother Edward these days, Mr Fitch?'

His expression changed. He looked at me with a hard, clenched face. 'It seems you may have heard how he tried to cheat me out of my inheritance,' he said tightly. 'It is well known in England, but I did not think the news had reached the Colony.'

'I have a friend who knew your family many years ago,' I said casually. 'She mentioned to me that you and your brother had quarrelled.'

He wrinkled his brow for a few seconds, wondering who that friend might be, then evidently decided to let it pass. 'It is no secret to those who knew our family that the present Sir Edward Knatchbull was a cruel and barbarous brother to me. He tried all he could to wrong me out of that property which my father left me by will. He forced me into law, which lasted four years and at last was settled by arbitration in my favour.'

'Not satisfied, he formed a plan for my ruin and so well laid it out that by the assistance of emissaries of his, he got me apprehended and convicted for a piece of blank paper. Yes, it was nothing but a blank cheque I was supposed to have stolen from some fop at Vauxhall Gardens that ruined my life.'

Here he grew so agitated that he stood up and began pacing the room. Harriet gave me an angry look and then pleaded, 'John, there is no need to talk about all this if you do not want to. The subject is painful to you, and Mama should not have asked about your brother.'

'No, no, Harriet. As I am soon to be part of your family she has a right to ask.' He sighed and continued, 'I was tried at Guildford and got transferred to this Colony for fourteen years. Lost my rank in His Majesty's Navy, my pay, and pension, and after serving King and Country with honour, having bled for my country in numberless actions ...' Here he stopped and smote his head with his hand in a dramatic fashion.

'Enough, John! You upset yourself!' cried Harriet, running to his side. 'Mama, I beg you to stop torturing him. Can't you see he has suffered enough?'

'No, Harriet,' he said firmly, suddenly recovered and bearing the look of a martyr, 'let me go on.'

Harriet resumed her seat and he his pacing. 'The Judge, on passing sentence, said he "knew all about me". How was he to know this? — Had not my brother biased his mind and prejudiced him against me, no doubt telling him tales of my unpaid debts and my bullying of younger officers. Lies! All lies. The verdict delivered by the jury was guilty with a strong recommendation for mercy. But was any mercy shown by the Judge? None at all.

'Still, my brother persecuted me. Fearing that some of my friends would take up my case — for the papers were full of it, crying shame on the Judge — and to get me out of reach, I was peremptorily ordered to leave for Sydney Cove. This was my deathblow, my downfall, my ruin …'

'But look how well you have recovered in spite of all that persecution, John!' cried my sweet Harriet. 'You have your freedom, a new life in a better country and a woman who loves you dearly. You are far from ruined!'

'You are right, my love.' He put out his arms and she came to him gladly. 'I am a fortunate man, indeed.' And he buried his head in her shoulder like a child to be comforted.

Finding the sight a little sickening I hurried to take the dishes out into the washhouse, and while I was attending to them Harriet began putting the children to bed. Soon he wandered outside and as it was a fine night, sat down on the well beside the washhouse. Now was my chance to have a word with John Fitch alone.

I finished my chore and came absent-mindedly into the twilight to stand beside him.

'I must thank you, Mrs Jones, for having brought such a fine daughter into the world.' He paused, waiting for me to acknowledge the compliment, but I remained silent. 'I have not yet done you the courtesy of asking for her hand in marriage, but now that you have satisfied your curiosity as to my background, I would very much like to do so. Is this a good moment, just after sunset on a pleasant Sunday evening, for me to go down on one knee and beg for the hand of Harriet Craig?' He did not go down on one knee but smiled in self-congratulation at his own charm and wit.

At that moment I despised the man.

'My curiosity as to your background is not quite satisfied yet, Mr Fitch,' I said, keeping my gaze steady. 'The friend I mentioned earlier, who knew of your quarrel with your brother, was named Maria Wilkinson.'

He raised his eyebrows. 'I'm afraid I do not remember her.'

'On the sixteenth of September, 1819, you were married to her, sir.'

A look of pain and puzzlement came over his face and he shook his head. 'I was never married to anyone, ma'am. You mistake me for somebody else.'

'I do not, Mr Fitch. My friend Maria Wilkinson was but a girl of sixteen when you tricked her into believing

she was to be your wife. You and your friend Lieutenant Carmichael drove with her to London where a
mock ceremony was held in your friend's lodgings.
Other friends dressed up as a preacher and wedding
guests. Rings were exchanged and vows spoken. There
was a party and a wedding night. Maria Wilkinson
believed it to be real.'

'Ah!' He closed his eyes as if better to picture the
events of so long ago. 'That wedding. But my dear Mrs
Jones, that was nothing but a young man's prank!
Maria was as well aware of it as any of us.'

'Indeed she was not! She spent a miserable time in
those lodgings behaving as your wife, putting up with
the unwanted attentions of your so-called friends, and
when she discovered the whole marriage was a sham
and a mockery, and that she was a ruined woman, she
wanted to drown herself!'

'Surely not. She had fun, as we all did. And as for the
attentions of my friends being unwelcome, she positively encouraged them! She was a country girl, bored
with her life as a servant, who begged us to take her to
London, and the "marriage" was only a small part of a
party that lasted several days. There were plenty of
other young ladies present who enjoyed themselves
thoroughly, dancing, drinking champagne and flirting
with us eligible bachelors. The only unpleasantness
happened at the end of a dinner in Leicester Square
generously given by my friend Carmichael, when
Maria fled into the night, having stolen a substantial
amount of money from me and my friends as well as a
small leather bag that had been a present from my
father.'

'Why didn't you send the constables after her if she had robbed you of so much?'

'Too soft-hearted, I expect. She was a naive girl and my friends and I took pity on her. She would bore me to death reading the same poem over and over, but she did amuse me. I admit that I was fond of her for a few weeks.'

'Is this the book she read to you, John Knatchbull?' I asked, and here I produced from my apron pocket the poetry book that she had left with me for safekeeping at Elmtree House all those years ago. I showed him the inscription: *To Maria, my dearest friend, on the day of her most joyful marriage to Captain John Knatchbull. September 16th, 1819.*

He stared at these words in silence and then said dully, 'I believe it is the same book. But she lied to you if she told you she was to be married. The poor girl was deluded. A liar and a thief.'

'You did not send the constables to retrieve the banknotes she stole, sir, because they were forged!'

'What!'

'She hid them in the attic I shared with her at Elmtree House, where we were both servants. I was blamed for that theft and the forgery, which is how I came to be transported to the Colony.'

'But how dreadful! I assure you, Mrs Jones, I had no idea that any of the banknotes were forged. Could it be that some of those she stole from my friends …? No, no, I hardly think they would forge notes. They were well off. Maria must have got the notes from some-where else.'

'No, sir, she did not. She was heartbroken when she

returned to Elmtree House. As I have said, she wanted to drown herself.'

'I can't imagine why. She'd had a splendid time. She was probably play-acting. She was quite a clever actress.'

'What do you mean by that?' I asked indignantly.

He shrugged, then gave me a shrewd look. 'She could fall into a flood of tears at the drop of a hat if she wasn't getting what she wanted. It fooled me at first but Carmichael saw through it.'

'And what caused her to fall into a flood of tears, may I ask?'

'Oh, any small slight. I can't remember exactly. She was a fanciful creature.'

'Was it when you told her that the marriage had all been a mockery?'

'No, no, I never told her that. Believe me, she knew it from the start. It was a prank, a bit of play-acting. Good Heavens, it all happened so long ago …'

'And so Maria never believed you were really going to marry her? Do you swear to that?'

'She may have imagined, at one time, that I would. But it was all romantic nonsense, a fantasy she had concocted. How could a gentleman in my position ever have considered marriage to a servant girl?'

I smiled in quiet triumph. 'But isn't that exactly what you are considering now, John Knatchbull?'

There was silence.

Then he burst forth in rage. 'You are a mischievous woman, Mary Jones! You have led me nicely by the nose into condemning myself. As you well know, my circumstances have changed a great deal since I had such arrogant thoughts. I am a changed man! Can you not see that? Don't you think I have suffered enough?' He was passionate and uncontrolled, his face red and his arms swinging wildly. I kept well away, as I thought he might strike me. It was a long time since I had seen a man so threatened by the truth. 'I tell you, if you dare stand in my way by trying to stop my marriage to Harriet I will do you an injury!'

He sat down on the curved stone of the well with his head in his hands, the very picture of self-pity. After a minute he lifted his head and looked at me with feigned sadness. 'Forgive me. I spoke foolishly. Harriet is as virtuous a woman as ever walked. There is not a blemish to be found in her character and I do not want to quarrel with you, her mother, whom she loves. Will you forgive me?'

I nodded but still kept my distance. I was not afraid of John Fitch but found it repulsive to step too close to him.

'Shall I tell you what she told me when I first asked her to be my bride?' he asked.

'Please do,' I said calmly.

'She said to me, "Dear John, do nothing hasty that you may be sorry for afterwards. My deceased husband, not long before his death, spoke to me upon the subject of again marrying and placing a father over his children. He told me that if I found a man that would make me a good husband and not ill-use the children, not to continue in the state of widowhood. From what I have seen of your behaviour, I think you will make me a good husband and a father to my children. At present I cannot give you a decisive answer further than this: if

I do not see in your conduct anything that might tend to prevent it, and after I have remained in widowhood a suitable time, I will become your wife; but I do not promise." '

He stared at me. 'You see how easily you could prevent this marriage from taking place, Mary?' I flinched at the use of my Christian name on his lips. It was as if he used intimacy as a weapon. 'If she sees anything in my conduct to give her doubts she will not marry me. And you could so easily plant the seed of doubt. She has made me no promises.'

'So you would prefer that I did not tell her the story of my friend, Maria Wilkinson?'

'I would be deeply grateful if you did not.'

I nodded thoughtfully. 'I will think upon it.'

'Whatever happened to Maria?' he said, by way of lightening the conversation.

'She changed her name to Jane Henrie, worked as a servant in London for some years, was arrested for theft and transported to Australia for seven years. She married, separated, then went to New Zealand, where she is now a successful business woman, and she will arrive in Sydney to stay with me in a few days time. Would you like to meet her again?' I asked sweetly.

'Wretched woman!' he exploded. I was not sure whether he meant Jane or myself, but I took the opportunity to hurry inside and bid my daughter and the children goodnight.

As I was readying myself to leave, Harriet whispered, 'I am glad you asked John some of those questions, Mama, although it was painful for me as well as for him, and at first I was embarrassed. He is so kind and gentle, but I must tell you that he does have odd moods. It is because he has suffered so much in prison and been so ill-used by his family. All he needs is a loving wife and family and he will forget his anger.'

'Has he been angry with you, Harriet?'

'No, never! But he often rants about the wickedness of others, those who pretend to be your friends but then betray you. He describes the way he would like to punish them, which is quite horrible. He is a very moral person and a good man really, Mama.'

'I hope so. You are quite right to take your time to get to know him before rushing into marriage. He respects you for telling him that.'

'Does he? Did he say so?'

'Yes, he did. He told me you are virtuous and without a blemish, so please continue that way.' I smiled and kissed her goodnight.

'Thank you Mama.' She gave me an intimate smile in return. 'I will send him home at once.'

But as she walked with me to the gate, Harriet told me, 'Mama, I want, above all else, to make him a happy man and a good father to my children. I may decide to marry him earlier. And I do not want you to interfere with that decision.'

'Earlier than next May? That would be most unwise, Harriet!'

'Why, Mama? Why?' she demanded.

'Because you would not have had time to find out all about the man. He may not be quite what you think.'

'And what, pray, have you been able to discover in one meeting with John Fitch that I have overlooked in months of meetings?'

I could control myself no longer. 'Oh Harriet, he is a violent man! Can you not see that? He could be dangerous to you and the children.'

'How dare you say such a thing! He would as soon lay a hand on me or one of those little children as fly to the moon. You are cruel to say such things. Cruel!' And her eyes filled with angry tears.

'There, there, my darling. You said yourself that he had odd moods and described the horrible things he would like to do to those who betrayed him.'

'Yes, but I will not betray him! Never. I want only to make him happy,' she sobbed.

'Of course you do. But what if some time in the future you should fail, through no fault of your own, to live up to his high moral standards? He would be revenged on you as he threatens to be on others who have displeased him.' I sighed. 'Harriet, it breaks my heart to see you crying, but I have met men of this kind before, quick to judge others, with fiery tempers, and I tell you that I do not trust him.'

'Then you had best leave at once, Mama, for I am in complete and utter disagreement with you.' And with that she turned around and hurried away.

'Lord, now see what I have done!' I moaned as I turned towards home. 'Delivered my only daughter to a monster.'

# VIII
## Visitors From New Zealand

# CHAPTER 56

**Reunited With My Oldest Friend at Last**
**The Rocks, December, 1843**

'Oh, how changed Sydney is after fourteen years! Or perhaps it is that I have forgotten the bustle after the peace of the Bay of Islands.' Jane sat on the sofa in my tiny parlour, her eyes shining as she bounced up and down and threw her arms about, gesticulating.

'What a crowded harbour, full of coastal vessels loaded with coal, cedar, whale oil and wood for the clipper ships to take to England. And on the wharf such stinks and noises, such strong breezes from the sea and yells from the Town Crier and hawkers screeching out their wares, selling baskets and old clothes, haddock, chitterlings, baked potatoes and cockles, and a hundred people hurrying along, chattering and shouting to each other.'

'Well, yes, we have become a busy town since you left.' I could not take my eyes off my old friend. I had forgotten how excitable she was and how full of the joy of being alive.

'I have just walked down George Street. Such a noise of traffic — horses and drays loaded high with produce, a fire cart with horses galloping and bells ringing while men cling to the sides, smart carriages clip-clopping by and slow, grim processions of convicts still dragging their chains.' She gasped for breath. 'And on The Rocks, Mary, there is such a mass of new cottages and public houses, shops and grain stores tumbling down the steep slopes!'

'Yes, yes, it is all quite changed. But Jane, I wish you had let me come to meet you at the wharf.'

Just a few minutes earlier I had heard a knock at the door, and poking my head out of the upstairs window I had seen two sailors. 'Wait! I am coming!' I cried in excitement, for I suspsected that one of them might be Jane.

Flinging open the door I recognised her immediately. 'Welcome, dear Jane! Oh, how good to see you!' And I hugged her hard against me.

'But how did you know me?' she demanded. 'For I am well disguised.'

At this I laughed out loud. 'Come in, come in, and the young boy as well.' I put out my hand to shake his, and now it was their turn to laugh.

Once inside they had both taken off their sailor's caps and two masses of black hair tumbled down.

'Oh!' I cried out, my hand to my mouth. 'I was quite deceived by the young lady's disguise.'

'Meet Miss Eliza Jane Wright, daughter of Captain Wright of Kororareka and his Maori wife, Lydia, both great friends of mine. Eliza is my God-daughter, and I have brought her to Sydney so she can see how the rest of the world lives. And of course to meet my dearest friend Mary Jones.'

'You are very welcome, Miss Wright,' I said, looking from one to the other of them.

'The young lady is thirteen years of age and in search of a wealthy husband; is that not so, Eliza?'

'Why yes, Mrs Jones.'

'Bur surely thirteen is a little young ...' I stammered.

'In New Zealand the Maori custom is to marry early, so I hope you have a good list of suitable young men, Mary. We thought we might conduct interviews here in your house.'

I must have looked shocked for Jane and Eliza could sustain their prank no longer and both burst out laughing.

'No, no, she is teasing. My Godmother is telling lies!' cried Eliza, collapsing onto a chair and pulling off her shoes. 'I should hate to be married to anyone just yet. I have lots of exploring to do first. I should like to travel in a ship right across the world.' And then she began chattering to Jane about the details of this in what I took to be the Maori language. Jane interrupted her to say that it was rude to speak in a language I did not understand and Eliza quickly apologised to me.

Now I took them upstairs to the pretty guest room overlooking the street and the harbour below and then offered everything at once — a bath, tea, a rest, cool drinks, a tour of The Rocks. I was so delighted to see Jane and over-anxious to please that she had to laugh. 'We will accept all of these things in due course, but first let's just have tea and a talk,' she suggested.

Eliza said that if I did not mind she would miss tea and go for a walk around The Rocks 'to explore'. I told her to take my umbrella, as it looked as if a summer storm might blow up and to take care not to talk to strangers or to go near the public houses.

At this cautious advice Eliza and Jane both laughed. 'She has seen storms and strangers and grog shops all her life and she is a sensible Christian who will come to no harm, Mary, not some scatterbrain from a heathen country,' said Jane.

'Oh, I did not mean to say —' I protested, and then I saw that Jane was teasing. I smiled. 'Well, take the umbrella, anyway.'

And off went Eliza Jane as happy as a bird free of its cage.

'She is a most beautiful, proud-looking child,' I said when she had gone. 'Is she a half-caste?'

'Yes. Her ancestors were warriors. She has been educated by the missionaries but has many relatives who are still warlike. The Maori are different from the natives here.'

'I believe they are more warlike. Our natives are dying of the white man's diseases and no longer fight. At least not near the towns. I hear they are still quite fierce in the bush.'

'Perhaps that is because they do not want white people on their land without a treaty,' Jane said.

'Perhaps,' I agreed. 'The Government has not offered any treaty that I have heard of.'

'Then they should take a lesson from New Zealand,' she replied.

I laughed and said she had become most patriotic and Jane said she had indeed.

We could hardly drink our tea for telling each other news, though the first hour was spent in Jane telling me hers. I told Jane that she was a brave, adventurous woman. I admired her for achieving all that she had in a strange new country. 'But now that Kororareka is abandoned for the new capital, Jane, and there is the danger of war between the Maori and the settlers and you have lost so much business, will you not move to Auckland?'

'I have thought of it, but I am too much attached to my little town to abandon it just yet. All my friends are there and I am much respected, even by the clergy in the Bay of Islands. It is a most beautiful place, Mary. And there is Eliza Jane, of course.'

'Your Godchild. Yes, of course.' I felt slightly puzzled by the deep attachment and would have liked to ask her more, then thought better of it.

'And how is your daughter Harriet and her little brood?'

I then told Jane the story of her husband's drowning and that she had a new suitor determined to marry her who was most unsatisfactory. 'Oh Jane, I cannot tell you how glad I am that you have come. You must help me put a stop to it. The man Harriet intends to marry is none other than John Knatchbull!'

'What!' Jane stared at me as if I had produced a knife and threatened her. 'You cannot mean it, Mary. That man is evil, the very devil. Can't the foolish girl see that? Have you not warned her? Told her what happened to me?'

'She won't listen to a word against him!' I cried. 'I've done everything in my power to dissuade her but Harriet is determined to marry him.' I threw up my hands in despair. 'He seems to have cast a spell on her.'

Jane shook her head slowly and was silent. Then she began pacing the floor. 'I knew he was here in the Colony, for I saw him once. And the Colony is so small that it would be unusual not to meet him here eventually. But to *marry* the scoundrel. A spell, you say. Huh! We'll soon see about that.' Jane's green eyes flashed angrily. 'Damn his manners and his charm! I can't believe there are still women fool enough to fall for them.'

'Oh Jane, if you would talk to her, tell her of your painful experience, I feel sure she would change her mind about the man.'

'I will call on Harriet first thing tomorrow morning,' she said grimly.

'Oh thank you, my dear friend. I am half out of my mind with worry.'

'Calm yourself, Mary. This marriage will never take place, I swear to you. If I'm wrong I'll give you a half-share of all I own in the Bay of Islands.' She laughed. 'Not that it's worth much any more.' Then she shuddered. 'How does Knatchbull look these days? He must be old.'

'He is fifty-six and looks well enough. He behaves as a gentleman, tells dramatic stories, half of which I don't believe. He says he owns a cutter. He has the air of a seaman, but he is working at nothing at present. I believe him to be a violent man with no control of his temper. He threatened to do me "an injury" if I should try to prevent him marrying Harriet.'

'Why, he is old enough to be her grandfather! There are plenty of eligible men around. What does she see in him?'

'He is a gentleman and she has always trusted them, for when she was a child one gentleman was very kind to us when she was ill, and when she visited his house later on his mother made her welcome and let her practise on their piano.' I felt myself blushing as I babbled. 'And perhaps, as she never knew her father, she is attracted to this older man.'

'Who was the gentleman who befriended you and Harriet, Mary?' Jane asked, as if she already had her suspicions.

'You know who it was, Jane.'

'Yes, I suppose I do,' she sighed. 'And is Mr John Stephen still your close friend?'

'He is a friend to me, though not as close as I believe he was once.'

'What are you telling me, Mary?' she asked in surprise. 'That you fancied him once?'

I blushed more at this. 'It was foolish of me. He did not return my feelings and I am well over it long ago.'

Jane realised this was a painful subject for me so she did not persist, although she was much intrigued. She could not resist one question, though. 'Did you sleep with him?'

I stared back as if she had struck me. 'I did not.' I shook my head adamantly.

'But I bet he tried hard to get you into his bed.'

'He did no such thing. He is a gentleman.'

'Oh, Mary!' Jane flung her head back and stared at the ceiling. 'Gentlemen are lechers as much as any man. They just have better manners.'

'Then I suppose he did not find me attractive enough to bother trying.' I turned my head away to hide the fact that I was still much affected by his rejection.

Jane came to my side and put an arm around my shoulders. 'There, there, Mary. You missed out on nothing. He was not such a great lover as all that. If my memory serves me right his passion was spent in a few minutes and then he would lie snoring for the rest of the night with a contented smirk on his face while I tossed and turned in a state of great dissatisfaction.'

I burst into sobs and buried my head in her bosom. My old friend had always been a convincing liar. This time she was doing it to console me. 'Oh Jane, it is good to have a cry about it at last!'

She patted my back and seemed pleased for once to take the role of comforter. 'And as for not being attractive, Mary, it is nonsense. If you are worried about your sunburnt complexion and the few lines of sorrow on your face, those can soon be fixed. See what I have brought you!' And she fumbled in her pocket for a jar of poultice. I saw that it was almost finished. 'This was brought to me from France by a ship's captain I am friendly with. Take it!'

'Oh Jane, I could not.'

'Do. I have many more at home. I buy them by the dozen.'

'Is that why your complexion is so youthful and

unblemished?' I asked in wonder. 'You look no more than twenty-five, yet you must be thirty-seven.'

'Ssssh, no talk of age. Now, tell me more about Knatchbull so that I may be well prepared when I confront him after Harriet has rejected him. I do not relish the thought of facing the wretch, but I am prepared to do it for you, Mary, as my dearest friend.'

I imagined that Jane was in fact quite looking forward to a stoush with her old enemy, for she said with some satisfaction: 'I have nothing to fear from him now.'

# CHAPTER 57

## John Knatchbull Turns My Daughter Against Me
## The Rocks, December, 1843

I called on Harriet early this morning in her lodgings behind her employer's house in George Street to tell her the glad news that Jane had arrived and was seeking a meeting with her and then with John Fitch, whom she had known in England many years ago. I wanted to find out what time and place suited them both.

But I did not get as far as making any suggestions. Her lodgings were in frightful disarray. Boxes and a trunk of clothes half-packed lay on the floor, rugs were rolled up, crockery piled on the chairs and the children were running about in a state of undress with the little boys yelling at the tops of their voices.

'Harriet, what has happened?' I exclaimed.

She stood in the middle of it all looking distracted. 'I am moving out of here, Mama. That's all.'

'But why, my dear? What has happened?'

She shooed the children into the other room, gave them toys to play with and a hunk of bread apiece, closed the door and sat down wearily. 'There has been an unpleasant incident.'

'What? Have you quarrelled with John?' She shook her head. 'With your employer then?'

'No, no. I am leaving my position but not because of that.'

I waited. 'A man came here uninvited last evening …' She paused, for she was much distressed.

'Who? A thief?' She shook her head.

'Did he harm you, Harriet? Tell me, please,' I said urgently.

'His name is Boyle and he works in the Commissariat stores. He told me soon after Tom's death that he had been his bosom friend. I thought it strange, as Tom had never mentioned him, but I did not wish to offend him, so allowed him to visit me here a few times.'

'You did not tell me about this.'

'I do not tell you everything I do, Mama. He seemed harmless enough. He is a married man and he knew that I intended to marry John Fitch, so I did not suspect him. He would stand by the well out there and say how much he missed Tom and tell me what a good man he was. If it was a hot afternoon I would offer him a glass of cider. One day he told me how they had once gone drinking together and he'd had to help carry Tom home. I thought this odd as Tom was not a drinking man and I had never smelt rum on his breath. I began to doubt Boyle then, and asked him not to visit me again. He stayed away for a month. Then last night he came back, much the worse for drink. John had been here earlier but he had left. The children were asleep and I was just about to go to bed myself. When Boyle came to the door I asked him to go but he pushed his way into the house. He lunged at me and held me in an embrace that almost choked me, and put a question to me of the most degrading type. I told him to get out and he used the language of the gutter. I grabbed the poker and struck him with it with my full force. He cringed on the floor and I cried that I would tell his wife and the whole world of his behaviour. Again I told him to go. But he would not and crawled after me, grabbing at my legs as if he would pull me down with him, all the time using expressions that disgusted me. I took an ounce weight from the shelf and threw it at him, which scratched his lip, and he left the house with a curse.' Harriet was breathing fast like a bird caught in a net. 'I cannot stay here alone any more, Mama,' she said.

'Of course not. What a horrible experience! You must all come to me!'

'No, I am going to Mrs Hollowell's in Clarence Lane. She has room for me and the children in her lodging house. It is all arranged.'

'What! Pay rent when you could be living free of charge with your own mother?'

'You have only one spare room, Mama and the children would disturb you in the shop. Besides, I prefer to be near to John. My feelings have been much hurt by the episode last night ...'

Here she jumped up to close the shutters lest anyone in the main house should overhear, and burst into a flood of tears. I held her close as she wept as if she could not stop.

When she lifted her head she said, 'I fear the world is

talking about me and that I should not be living alone, tempting strange men to take advantage of me. I have changed my mind about waiting until May to marry John. I shall do as he wants and marry him on the first of the New Year. Then the world may talk as it likes. They say we are living together now, but God is the best judge of that.'

I was in despair. I did not want to add to my daughter's sorrow by arranging the confrontation between Jane New and John Fitch. But how else could I prevent this wedding? 'And what does Mr Fitch say about Boyle?' I asked quietly.

'He knows nothing of the visit or he would surely tear Boyle limb from limb. I want no violence. My life is hard enough.'

'My darling girl. Then who else knows about Boyle?'

'Only Mrs Hollowell. I ran there earlier this morning. I had not slept for fear of the brute's return and she could see the state I was in. Fortunately John is away for a few days seeing to the sale of his cutter. Mrs Hollowell has promised to tell him nothing. She is sending a cart to take us and our things to her house later today so I must make haste and pack.'

'I will help you, Harriet.' I said, jumping up. 'Mrs Hollowell is a good soul. But how will you afford the rent at her house?'

'John has often asked me to move there and said that he would be pleased to pay our rent. He has some small embarrassment about my being a servant, you see, and would prefer that for the few weeks before our wedding I did not live as a servant in my Master's house.'

'Oh, and why is that, Harriet?' I asked, keeping calm with an effort.

'He intends to tell his family about our marriage and would prefer that they did not know I had been a servant.'

'I see.'

'Mama, I know that you have some differences with John, but I should like this Christmas, my first with him, to be a happy one. It is his birthday as well, you see. So I hope you will not mind if I spend Christmas day with him and the children at Mrs Hollowell's. She has already invited me. The children are very excited about spending Christmas day with their new father. John has made the boys hobby horses and carved a wooden doll's cradle for Mary Rose. I know you have your friend Jane New for company this Christmas so I hope you won't mind if we don't invite you.'

I felt as if a knife had entered my heart. Not only was this scheming man taking my daughter from me but my grandchildren as well.

'Of course you must do as you think best, Harriet. I shall bring the presents I have for you and the children to Mrs Hollowell's on Christmas Eve.'

'Oh no, that would be too much trouble for you,' she said quickly. 'I can come and collect them myself. Will you be at home early in the afternoon?'

'I shall make sure that I am. Will you bring the children to see me?'

'I cannot say … they may be having their naps.'

'But it is Christmas! Am I not to see them at all?'

Harriet let out a deep sigh. 'What am I to do? If I try to please you, then I displease my husband to be.'

'What are you saying? That John Knatchbull *alias* Fitch does not want me to see my own grandchildren and daughter on Christmas Day? Why, we have never once been apart on that day, you and I, in your whole twenty-one years of life!'

'Exactly, Mama. Which is why he thinks it is time I grew up and made my own choices.'

'And your choice is to be with him and exclude your own mother?'

'I am sorry to say that it is.'

# CHAPTER 58

## My Old Female Factory Friends Offer Me Comfort
## The Rocks, December, 1843

Jane's interview with Harriet was not a success. Although they met in private, away from Hollowell's where John Fitch might have burst in upon them, Harriet was not convinced that anything Jane told her about him was the truth. He had already warned Harriet that her mother was scheming to blacken his character by sending her old friend Maria Wilkinson, alias Jane New, to tell 'filthy lies' about him, and even before Jane could get a word out, Harriet burst forth angrily, 'I know all about you, Mrs New. Do not dare to speak ill of my beloved John Fitch, for he is far superior to you in every way and I will not listen to anything you say!'

'Ah ha, I see that John Knatchbull has taught you well, Mrs Craig. I too would not hear a word against him once,' said Jane with a sly wink. 'If not for my sake, hear what I have to say for your mother's and your own. Come, it is Christmas. Let us be generous of spirit.'

'No, I will not, for John warned me you had a wily tongue. He said, "My dear, I pray that you will not damage your pure soul by heeding any word this outrageous female may utter, for she is deluded and the worst kind of low criminal. She has changed her name often to escape her crimes, and even when I took pity on her and did not pursue her after she had stolen from me and my dear friend Lieutenant Carmichael, she spread cruel rumours about us both." '

'How dare he! The coward. It was he and Carmichael who abused me after he had lied to me about our marriage. I was but sixteen and a virgin. Did he tell you that?'

Harriet put both hands over her ears. 'No more! John warned me you had a hot temper and used the language of the gutter.' And she turned and ran out the door.

'Goose! Fool! Imbecile!' yelled Jane. It was hard for her to have to come home and tell me she had failed. And she had taken such a risk by going out in broad daylight without her sailor's disguise to meet Harriet at Elizabeth Male's cottage.

Well, we have had our rather sad little Christmas dinner this evening with me trying hard to be jolly, but all the time holding back tears because I had not seen Harriet and the children. The presents I'd prepared so lovingly were collected by an errand boy with a note from Harriet apologising that she was too busy to come herself and a white rose for me that had wilted in the heat.

Jane told me she could not care less if she was caught by a constable; she'd storm around to Knatchbull's lodgings at once and expose him for what he was in front of Harriet, Christmas or no Christmas. I begged her not to.

Later in the evening I tried hard to be cheerful when Elizabeth Male came by with Eleanor Turner. Eleanor gave Jane such a warm welcome that Jane seemed to forget how much she loathed her. Perhaps it was the Christmas spirit. Both women had dined well in some public house nearby and were well into their cups and singing merrily. They'd brought presents and a bottle of rum which had given them good cheer on the journey. They were carrying a strand of mistletoe they had stolen from a gentleman's carriage parked in George Street outside some grand house, so they said, and draped it festively over my doorway.

When they heard the sorry tale of Knatchbull stealing my beloved daughter and grandchildren, they too offered to march up to his lodgings and abuse him soundly, then escort Harriet and the children home to me.

Again I begged them to leave my daughter in peace, for she had made her own choice.

Jane's God-daughter Eliza Jane was much intrigued by Jane's old friends from the Female Factory as they made a jolly night of it reminiscing about fights in the yard over food, bribing the Turnkey to smuggle out letters and stealing grog from under the very nose of Matron.

'And do you recall Matron's looks the night a group of us bared our backsides to the whole Board of the

Factory, including the Governor and his Lady?' screeched Elizabeth.

'Ah, I wish I'd been at the Factory then to be part of that show!' sighed Eleanor.

'Now Jane, tell us the truth,' cried Elizabeth. 'I've never understood how on earth you got over that fourteen-foot sandstone wall.'

It seemed that Eliza Jane had heard this story many times before and it was one of her favourites. 'It was simple,' she told us. 'She got her husband James to hang a stout rope down from the other side and then she climbed up it to the top, dragged the rope after her and jumped into his arms.'

Elizabeth and Eleanor marvelled at the simplicity of the act and wondered aloud why they had never thought of such a thing.

'Because you had no one you could trust to get the rope up there in the first place!' Jane boasted.

Elizabeth said that was true in her case. 'Imagine William Sibley rescuing me from the Factory! Why, it was always him as put me in there!'

Eleanor said she'd had to marry a boring fool to get out of there and they laughed about this too. But I could only smile sadly and stay silent.

After we had kissed each other goodnight under the mistletoe and Eliza and Jane had staggered upstairs to their beds I felt free to cry softly in the parlour downstairs. It was a relief.

I was startled when Jane appeared on the stairs in her nightgown, holding a candle. 'Mary, I vow to you that I will get revenge on John Knatchbull and shall do it without anyone suspecting a thing,' she said grimly.

# CHAPTER 59

## Jane and I Set Out to Confront John Knatchbull
## The Rocks, January, 1844

Today I had good news. The wedding of Harriet to John Knatchbull has been put off for a week until January 8th. I am grateful for even this short delay.

Harriet called on me for the first time in weeks today to thank me for the Christmas presents. Jane and Eliza had gone out, disguised as sailors again, to shop for souvenirs to take back to friends in New Zealand. They wanted painted emus' eggs in particular and the skins of kangaroos.

Harriet and I sat together in my little garden behind the cottage with a cool glass of cider each and listened in silence for a few minutes to the rumbling of thunder across the harbour. 'I used to be so afraid of storms when I was a little girl in the Factory, Mama. Do you remember?'

'Yes, the women would scream and go wild. I tried to explain to you that they were excited by storms, not afraid of them. Storms caused a break in our tedious routines.'

'But the women would run out into the yard until they were soaked and scream at the sky. They turned into demons in a storm.'

'They were daring the lightning to strike them dead. It was a diversion, one might say.'

'You would hold me close and tell me that storms always passed and the women were only playing a game, they were *enjoying* the storm!'

'I believe they were, Harriet.' I smiled at her.

'This disagreement we have had about my intended husband, do you think it will pass like a storm?' she asked sorrowfully.

'I hope so, Harriet. I do hope so. I am sorry you did not trust my friend Jane.'

'No, I did not trust her,' she said and quickly changed the subject. I thought she seemed tense and very nervous for a young woman about to be married to the man of her choice. I asked about the children and she said they were well and promised to bring them to visit me after the wedding. I asked about her new lodgings and the landlady, both of which she said were most satisfactory. She seemed preoccupied with plans for the wedding and told me her dress was now almost finished and was very beautiful. As soon as John had paid for it, which he planned to do tomorrow, she would bring it home, she said, but no one must see it before the ceremony. After she had described it in detail I expressed some surprise that a widow should wear a white wedding dress with a veil but she said that John had wanted it so. It hurt me deeply that she should choose a dressmaker other than myself, especially as I know I am by far the best seamstress hereabouts, but I supposed John would have objected. She told me with some bashful pride that the dress had cost six shillings, which was more than the cost of board and lodging for a month for her and the children at Hollowell's.

'John has insisted on paying for both dress and lodgings, although I have told him I would gladly contribute. He is so generous.'

I was comforted that I had not been invited to attend the church; for I could not, in all faith, have wished the bridal couple well.

Harriet told me that John had not much money left after all their wedding expenses, although he expected some to arrive from his family as soon as they received his letter telling them of the marriage.

'John has as yet been unable to sell the cutter and he is vexed by the fact that people who owe him money have not repaid loans he made to them.'

'That is too bad,' I said softly. I had no intention of offering money to assist this man I did not trust, although I sensed he may have sent Harriet here to ask for some.

'And where will you live once you are married?' I asked.

She hesitated. 'We are not sure. We may stay on at Hollowell's but John would prefer to have a house of our own. We thought we might put the tenants out and move back to my cottage in Kent Street.'

I drew in a sharp breath. 'That cottage was my wedding present to you and Thomas Craig.'

'Yes, Mama, and a most generous one. But it is mine now and surely I can do what I please with it.'

I turned my head away to hide my anger and sorrow. 'And so you can, Harriet. But I should be distressed to think of you sharing that cottage, where you were once so happy, with John Knatchbull.'

'Pray do not call him that!' she cried. 'He changed his name to Fitch even before he came to this Colony. I shall be Mrs Fitch and the children's names will be legally changed to Mary Rose Fitch and Andrew and William Fitch. There is nothing you can do to change that, Mama. I have given him my promise.'

'And what else have you promised him?' I asked bitterly. I found it impossible to hide my feelings any longer.

'Not to speak ill of him to anyone, particularly you, as he believes you wish to poison my love for him. He told me that when you came to tea with us you put such impertinent questions to him about his past that you caused him to lose his temper, something no gentleman should ever do.'

'Then maybe he is no gentleman. Can't you see, my darling, that he is so damaged that no wife, however loving and devoted to him, can repair him? He is a violent man! There, I have said it. Harriet, I fear for you and the children.'

'Then don't, Mama! It is only you who cause him to feel violent. He said that your accusations incensed him so much he feared that he might strike you.'

'You see!'

'He said it was only the thought that you were the closest relative of his beloved that stayed his hand.'

'Just what I told you!'

'Why is it that you make him so furious? He says you have a tongue like a viper and should be kept well away from me and the children or you will destroy our innocence.'

'What! How dare he say such things! He is afraid of me because I tell him the truth about himself. No "gentlemanly" mask can hide that man's cruel nature from me.'

Harriet shook her head. 'I believe John is right about you, Mama.'

She turned away sadly. Then, looking dreamy, she said, 'To me he is the kindest and most romantic of men. Why, he told me only yesterday that from the first time he saw my miniature portrait that poor drowned Tom Craig had he vowed he would meet me and wed me if he could.'

'So that was the reason he offered to bring Tom's possessions to you,' I said knowingly. 'I wondered why the Captain of his ship did not do it as is usual and proper.'

'You are full of suspicion, Mama. John persuaded the Captain that as he was a close friend of Tom's, it would be less painful for me to receive his things from him than from a stranger. And that is how he came to call regularly on me and why I soon began to ask his advice on every subject.'

I sighed. I doubted the scheming Knatchbull had ever been a close friend of Thomas Craig at all. Why had Tom never mentioned him to either Harriet or me? We had heard stories of his other seafaring friends.

They were young and cheerful, not old and full of self pity and hatching plots like Knatchbull.

But Harriet was enjoying reciting the wretch's virtues so I held my tongue. 'Nearly three months passed from the first of our meetings before one day, for the first time, I allowed him to seal our mutual pledge with a kiss upon the lips. He was happy with this partial promise and said, "Harriet, I vow to you that I will put my shoulder to the wheel to bring up your young family." '

Harriet sat well back on the garden bench, smiling and hugging her knees just as she did when she was a little girl and feeling pleased with herself. I confess I was torn between wanting to disillusion her and letting her enjoy this fantasy.

'He told me that although I had been a servant and a performer in a travelling troupe he knew from the first time he saw my portrait that I had the grace and bearing of a lady and could well be trained to behave as one,' she continued happily. 'He said that I was already virtuous and modest. He believes that his family and even his brother, the unkind Sir Edward Knatchbull, might accept me in time and that once we are married, his lost inheritance, which was so unfairly taken away, will be restored to him.'

'I see,' said I as evenly as I could. I was incensed by Knatchbull's condescension towards my daughter. Before she met him she had been proud of her achievements as a performer and of her job as a nursemaid. 'And why has John never married before this?'

'Perhaps because he is solitary by nature and grew accustomed to keeping his own company. Even in His

Majesty's Navy, surrounded by fellow officers, he said he often felt alone.'

This question seemed to intrigue Harriet, for after a pause she said thoughtfully, 'He told me that when he was a prisoner at Norfolk Island he applied for permission to occupy a solitary cell in order to guard himself from the resentment of other prisoners who accused him of betraying them to the authorities.'

I nodded knowingly. I could well imagine him needing the protection of a solitary cell after such betrayal.

'He has admitted to me that he has been a lonely man all his life. When he was first transported to the Colony, he was offered the duty of carrying the mail once a week on foot from Mount York to Bathurst, a distance of one hundred and twelve miles. He liked this very much as he was his own master, had a comfortable hut to live in and a hut-keeper to attend upon him. He lived there quite alone for two years.' My impressionable daughter smiled as if the man's every experience was a wonder to be admired.

'But at his next place of employment, as Body Constable for Lieutenant Evernden, he saw how contented he and his wife were and lived in their house with them, wanting for nothing. Mrs Evernden was more like a sister to him, he said, and was good to everybody. It was then he first began to think seriously about taking a wife. But how, in this Colony where the women are mostly ex-convicts and outnumbered four to one by men, would he find someone suitable?'

'Where indeed?' said I. I was learning a lot about John Knatchbull.

'He said it was Providence that led him to me,' said Harriet, with a smile. 'Like Mrs Evernden, he saw I was a truly good woman, and he wished to protect me from those who would pretend to have honourable motives but who mean to do me harm.'

'And who would these harmful people be, Harriet?' I asked calmly.

She did not answer but turned her head away as if in shame. Then suddenly she burst out, 'The most dangerous of them is you. John says you are an evil woman, a bad character and even if he has to strangle you he will prevent you poisoning my love for him. So please, Mama, stay away from us all. It is not safe to do otherwise.' And with that she ran off, choking back her tears.

Now I was really alarmed. I felt sure my daughter was now afraid of Knatchbull and was being coerced into this marriage. I had never seen her so full of changing moods and so deluded. She was completely under his spell.

I decided to call the very next day on Mrs Hollowell, using as an excuse the delivery of some shirts I had been making for her husband, and see for myself how things were at Harriet's lodgings in Clarence Lane. The shirts were not due to be delivered until the following week but I stayed up almost all night to finish them.

Next morning when I told Jane that I intended to go there and risk meeting Knatchbull as well as my daughter, she insisted that she would come too. 'He will not know me in my disguise,' she said.

I did not like the idea but she was most persuasive. 'I will say not a word until you have said all you wish to, and even then I'll be most tactful. The wretch will betray himself because of my sly methods, see if he doesn't!'

I had no idea what Jane had in mind but decided to trust her. I admit I was relieved at the thought of having her company.

# CHAPTER 60

## It Would Be a Miracle if the Widow Jamieson Lived
## The Rocks, January 7th, 1844

I meant to include extra buttons with the shirts I had made for Mr Charles Hollowell, and knowing that the ones I needed were sold by a Mrs Ellen Jamieson, who kept a shop at the corner of Margaret Place and Kent Street, I walked there with Jane on our way to Hollowell's. As we came closer I saw that the Widow Jamieson's shop had been recently boarded up. I wondered if the poor woman had been unable to pay her rent and so had been closed down. She too had been a customer of mine at one time but had fallen on hard times recently.

'That is a bother,' I said as we climbed the steep hill to Clarence Lane. 'Now I feel the shirts are not fit to be delivered. Never mind, I shall charge less for them because of having no extra buttons.'

'You're too generous, Mary. If you charged what others do you'd be a rich woman by now.'

I smiled and shook my head. 'I prefer my good reputation to riches, Jane. Ah, here we are. Now change your character, quickly.'

She lowered her voice a pitch, spat on the street and increased her swagger. 'And don't forget to call me Jem,' she muttered. She was so comically convincing as a sailor that I almost laughed.

The Hollowell's lodging house in Clarence Lane was quite large, with a handsome facade of yellow stone and a neat picket fence. I banged the brass knocker and waited. No one came and after a few more knocks I pushed the door gently and it opened. We went into the hall and looked about for a servant, but no one appeared. 'Let's go in,' said Jane, and strode boldly down the passage. I had visions of Knatchbull suddenly opening a door, believing the sailor to be an intruder and knocking her down. I followed timidly. There seemed to be nobody about at all.

However, in the small courtyard at the back we found my three darling grandchildren playing. Mary Rose ran to me at once and flung herself into my arms and Will and Andrew came up and clung to my skirts. 'Where is your mother, Mary Rose?' I asked.

'She is gone to see Mr Fitch. He is in gaol.'

'Oh? And why is he in gaol?' I asked, thinking she was making up a story.

'Because he chopped up Mrs Jamieson with an axe!' she declared.

Jane burst out laughing and almost forgot to be Jem. 'Why, I like that story, Mary Rose! If it's even half true we won't see much of him from now on.'

At that moment I heard Mrs Hollowell hurrying

down the path at the side of the house. She did not look surprised to see us. 'So you've heard the tragic news, Mrs Jones?' she asked me gravely.

'I've heard nothing, except what Mary Rose said, that John Fitch has —'

'Attacked the Widow Jamieson with a tomahawk? It is true. Oh, it is too horrible!' she cried. 'That a man living in this house, a man about to be married in a few days, could rob a poor widow with two children to support and attack her so brutally. They say she will not live. She hangs on by a thread. Her brains were all over the floor!'

'Sssh! The children!' I said and covered Mary Rose's ears. I hoped the little boys were too young to understand. 'Are you sure it was John Fitch who did it?'

'Nothing more certain. There are several witnesses. John Shalless, the builder who lives opposite, saw him go into the shop and Elizabeth Brown of Kent Street, who used to mangle and mend for Mrs Jamieson, tells me she was in the shop when he came in to buy a pint of vinegar. Then he went out and lingered suspiciously outside until all the other customers had gone.' Mrs Hollowell gabbled on as if she could not stop, pouring out the whole story. 'It was a clear night with the full moon riding high and Shalless kept on watching. He saw Fitch go into the shop and shut the door behind him, then he heard sounds as if a hammer were cracking coconut shells, so he told me, and called out to his wife: "He's murdering the woman!" He roused a watchman, then ran to the Glen Albion public house and brought McKenzie, the owner, back with him. By then two other neighbours had come to help. They broke in and found poor Mrs Jamieson lying in a pool of blood. When they found Fitch he cried out twice, "Oh! Don't strike me!" but he made no resistance.'

'And where is he now?' asked Jane, using Jem's voice.

'He was taken to a cell in the Station House where they are holding him before he goes to Hyde Park Barracks.'

'And Mrs Jamieson?' I asked.

'A surgeon is attending her. Her skull is fractured in several places.' She gasped for breath and then continued, 'And the worst news of all is that the blood-soaked tomahawk was found hidden in a mattress in an upstairs room. My husband was called to identify it. It belonged to him. Oh, what a sorry mess!'

'And where is my daughter Harriet?'

'At the Station House, pleading to see Fitch. She believes he is innocent.'

'Poor fool,' said Jane.

'And Mrs Jamieson's children? Were they in the house?' I asked.

'Slept through it all, thank the Lord. They are safe with a neighbour now.' She crossed herself.

'Why do you think Fitch would do such a thing, Mrs Hollowell?' I asked, crouching down and gathering my three grandchildren close around my knees.

'I am puzzled. He comes from a most respectable family in England. His conduct while he lived here was always regular. He must have done it for the money, for he was five weeks behind with the rent. Ah, poor Mrs Jamieson!'

At that moment I heard a step on the path and there

was Charles Hollowell, escorting Harriet, who had been weeping.

I ran to her and held her close. 'Oh, Mama. There has been a terrible mistake! John would never have done such a thing! They will not even let me see him!' She burst into tears. The children, upset to see their mother so distressed, clung to her skirts.

'Mary Rose, Will, Andy, this is Jem who's going to tell you all a story and show you tricks he learned at sea. Your Mama is tired and I'm going to put her to bed to make her better,' I told them.

'Jem' gave me a wink, drew out a tin whistle and began to play the Sailor's Hornpipe, better than most real seamen, I suspected.

I took Harriet indoors, where she had agreed to lie down, after I promised I would go to the Station House to try to see John Fitch. But first I went back to ask Charles Hollowell some questions.

He shook his head when I asked whether there was any doubt that it had been Fitch who'd committed the deed. 'His trousers were spotted with blood on both legs and there were bloodstains on his boots, according to the constables. They found a total of over seventeen pounds on him in notes and silver. It was in the pocket he had torn from Mrs Jamieson's skirt. She was in the habit of keeping her shop money in this outside pocket, so Elizabeth Brown told the Constable.'

'And will Mrs Jamieson live, do you think?'

'It would be a miracle.'

# CHAPTER 61

**Jane's Old Enemy is Accused of Murder
and She is not Sorry
The Rocks, January 18th, 1844**

Mrs Jamieson died today. A coroner's inquest was held on the body and the verdict was wilful murder. John Knatchbull is to be tried at the Supreme Court in five days' time and Jane says she will be there to see he gets his just deserts.

I do not think I will go to the Court with her. I am fully engaged in comforting Harriet, who is broken-hearted. She still believes the monster is innocent. Perhaps grief has swayed her reason. Eliza and Jane have been wonderful nursemaids to the three children. But Mary Rose had a nightmare about a man with an axe who was chasing her.

It is cramped living all together in my small cottage, but I am comforted to have my friends as well as my family close to me at this time. Eliza and Jane are sharing the guest room with Mary Rose, while Harriet and the twin boys share with me.

Our good friends Eleanor Turner and Elizabeth Male are often in the cottage as well, drinking tea and brewing stews and puddings for us all to eat. Jane is no cook and I am distracted by Harriet so I am thankful that they have taken over the task. The gossip runs high in the parlour, as one might imagine, but we keep our voices low for fear of offending the poor grief-stricken girl.

Knatchbull has appeared twice before the Court at Hyde Park Barracks for examination and is now in Sydney Gaol. Today he was taken to the inquest at a public house near the scene of the crime — there was much excitement amongst the local people. The word spread quickly on The Rocks that he was to be marched there between two constables, handcuffed, along the whole of Clarence Street. A crowd of hundreds soon gathered, Jane and Eliza amongst them. It was like a fairground, they said, with people booing, yelling and whistling. They followed the grim little procession to the place where the Coroner's inquest was held, in McKenzie's public house, and there waited in an anteroom with many others curious to know the outcome. There were about ten witnesses inside, including Mr Charles Hollowell, but no one could hear what was said. When the final verdict of wilful murder was announced a great cheer went up from the mob. A few minutes later a coach drove up and the prisoner was hustled into it amidst the hissing, booing and cheering of about five hundred men, women and children. I was glad Harriet was not there to hear it.

She has been allowed to see Fitch only once since his arrest and he has somehow convinced her that his version of the events of January 6th is the true one. He told her that on that night he was feeling very pleased with himself because he had recovered all the debts owing to him and was celebrating this and his approaching marriage by supping with a friend. He sat at supper longer than intended and, suddenly seeing how the time had flown by, rose about ten minutes to twelve to walk home to his lodgings. As he passed Mrs Jamieson's shop he heard the cry of a female. He had seen a person he knew to be a bad character go into the house just as he passed it, so rushed to the assistance of the distressed female. He closed the door behind him so that he could lay hold of the intruder and stop him escaping, but the man quickly put out the light and ran out the back door, securing it against Fitch, who was not aware of what had happened to the woman.

While he was standing there in the dark, feeling 'lost in his mind', the door was broken down by persons from outside and he was found, secured and taken to the watchhouse.

Last night poor Harriet was in a sorry state after hearing this tale. 'I was only allowed to see him for a few minutes,' she told us, beginning to sob. 'They have stripped him of everything he values, even the ring I placed on his finger as a pledge of my affections. He says his cell is full of rats, enough to devour him when they come out at night. He says I must spurn Charles Hollowell, for he gave evidence that John took a tomahawk from his shed and that this was the murder weapon. Oh, he is in such a wretched state of mind, Mama! Is there nothing we can do to help him?'

'We must let the Court decide his fate, my darling,' I said gently.

'Can we not appeal to someone in the Court for clemency? Mr John Stephen will help us, surely. He has always helped us before. Yes, I shall go to see him at once!'

I turned to Jane with a gesture of hopelessness that Harriet did not see. 'No, you stay here and rest. I will go to see Mr Stephen, though I doubt that he will be able to do anything. Stay here with Jane. It is dark and you are exhausted.'

Jane said she would be glad to keep Harriet company and whispered to me that she welcomed the chance to try to talk some sense into her. I bade her to be gentle.

# CHAPTER 62

**Perjury, Innocence and a Lost Love Recovered**
**The Rocks, January 18th, 1844**

As I hurried from The Rocks along the quiet road towards Ultimo House I felt a great wave of relief that I had been unable to express inside my little cottage where Harriet is so miserable. I thanked God it was not her the wretch had murdered. By now, if he had not blundered and revealed his true nature, Harriet would have been his wedded wife and a most likely victim, for a man with so much violence in him cannot control it for long. I thanked God for saving her and my grandchildren, and for the dear friends who have supported me through all of this, for Eleanor and Elizabeth and most of all for Jane.

John Stephen was in his study transcribing documents when I called. He welcomed me, in spite of the late hour. When I apologised he said, 'Think nothing of it, Mary. If you called at the time normal people do, I would not let you in!'

'It seems I gave you the wrong advice about Mr Fitch *alias* Knatchbull,' he admitted at once. 'I encouraged you to think the best of him as he'd committed no crime for so long. Please forgive me.'

'I do, John. As it happens I did not take your advice on that occasion for there was something about the man I did not like. I pleaded with Harriet to give him up but she would not.'

He nodded thoughtfully. 'Is she taking it very hard?'

'She is. He has told her he is innocent and she believes him.' I paused and then said, 'She has asked me to see if there is anything you can do to help Mr Fitch.'

'There is nothing, Mary. Fitch has a powerful defence lawyer, Mr Lowe, but the evidence against him is very strong.'

'I know. And I myself do not doubt he is guilty. But Harriet cannot believe that a gentleman like him, any gentleman in fact, could commit such a crime. Nor does she believe that a gentleman would lie.'

'Oh, the poor innocent child …'

'Well, she has you to thank for this belief, John. You would never lie.'

'Would I not?' He looked bemused.

'I don't believe so. To me you have always been a generous advisor, a true friend and the kindest of gentlemen.'

'And I have never lied?'

'No.'

'Then tonight I am going to disillusion you, Mary.' He sighed. 'It is something that has so troubled me for many years that I decided to see only little of you —

but the time has come to tell you the truth.' He seemed to find it hard to continue. 'Once, and only once in my life, I have perjured myself in court.'

I sat frozen. Surely this could not be what I imagined.

'I was a young man, besotted by a young woman. I knew I was a fool but I couldn't help myself. I helped her escape from the law, harboured her in my house for a week and when she wished to return to her husband I did my best to persuade her not to. I believed she was in love with me. When I realised that she had deceived me for her own convenience I helped her back to him. I was heartbroken, as poor Harriet must be now.'

'I understand,' I whispered. But it was a deep shock to me that he had been the liar, not Jane New.

'I loathe myself for my weakness. You are the only one I have ever told about this, Mary, because I trust you absolutely.' He sighed. 'I was impressionable. Jane was very pretty and appeared to be innocent. She was in fact coquettish and manipulative. I was an easy target. I just wanted to help her at first. I believed she had been unfairly treated because she was an ex-convict. And then I fell in love with her. Or was it infatuation? Probably the latter. I make no excuses for myself. I was a fool.'

'And you perjured yourself in court for her?'

'And to save myself from disgrace.'

'But you had many years of anguish trying to prove your innocence.'

'Almost five years. I deserved the anguish. While I was searching for evidence to free myself of guilt, I lost my ambition. Which is why I no longer practise law but have settled for the lowly position of solicitor's clerk, keeping files on prisoners and carrying briefs to barristers.' He blushed. 'And it is why I still live at home with my mother.'

'Well … your mother is delighted to have you. She has told me so. I have wondered for many years, John, how it was that you managed to resist Jane New's charms.'

'Well, now you know that I did not.'

'You would have been the first who did if you had succeeded. Well, now I will tell you a secret, since you have told me one.'

'What is it?' He looked so eager to hear that I laughed.

'Two, in fact. I'll tell you two. The first is that Jane New has returned from New Zealand for a visit and is at present staying with me.'

'What!' This really shocked him.

'She is as wicked as ever but as she is my great friend I will trust you not to betray her.'

'But surely she will have been recognised by now. She is still listed as an escaped convict.'

'She travels in disguise. I will say no more.'

He drew a deep breath. 'And the second secret?'

I blushed. 'I have changed my mind about that. It is foolish and not worth the telling.'

'Oh no, that's unfair! Come now, Mary, you made me a promise.'

'I did not.'

'Can I guess it then?'

I shook my head. 'No, John, I would rather you did not even try.'

'Well, since we are being so frank with each other, may I tell you one more of mine?' he asked gently.

I was suddenly very nervous. My heart beat fast up high near my throat. I nodded.

'After my case had been settled, I came to your cottage one evening to tell you the good news. Do you remember?'

'Yes.'

'You embraced me so spontaneously when I told you the case had been won, and you seemed so very happy for me that I thought — oh, it was a foolish thing to think — that perhaps you might be falling in love with me.'

'Yes?'

'But I was unsure of myself and afraid of being hurt again so I left without trying to discover if you really did have feelings for me. After that you did not visit us at Ultimo House any more so I concluded that I had been wrong and imagined the whole thing. Soon afterwards I left again for England and we did not see each other for many years.' He sighed with relief. 'And now I have confessed everything.'

Taking my courage in my hands I said, 'You were not foolish to think I was falling in love with you, John, for I had been besotted with you for years.' I smiled, for he looked astonished. 'If only I had learned some of those fine tactics from Jane New you might have been tricked into staying with me that night.'

'Tricked? I would have needed no more than a look! But you kept your face turned away from me after that first embrace and I thought you were suddenly ashamed of it. Is it true that you wanted me to stay with you?'

'It is true. Ask Jane. She knows how I felt.' I hung my head to hide my blushing.

'Jane knows? It seems I was the only one kept in ignorance.' He sat in silence for a minute, then suddenly he burst out joyfully, 'What a fool I have been, Mary! What an utter fool!' He came towards me with a look of humility. 'Can you ever forgive me?'

'I did so years ago, John.'

He took my hand in his and said quietly, 'Is it too late for us to try to recover some of that lost passion?'

I shook my head and smiled at him.

'Then, Mary, let us drink a toast to that.' And he led me towards the sideboard where he poured some brandy from a crystal decanter. We clinked our glasses together and smiled into each other's eyes.

It is strange but this time when I embraced him I did not once think that I should be prudent and wait until he suggested marriage.

# IX
## Resolution

# CHAPTER 63

**The Prisoner Pleads Moral Insanity but at Last Confesses the Truth**
**The Rocks, January, 1844**

This has been a month of great excitement in the Courts, newspapers and public streets of Sydney Town.

'Kororareka will seem so dull after this,' Jane proclaimed as she spread out the new garments she had chosen from my two shops to take back to New Zealand.

At first John Knatchbull's defence lawyer, Mr Robert Lowe, had pleaded 'monomania', or morality insanity, on behalf of his client, claiming that he was unable to distinguish right from wrong and so should be acquitted. But the Judge and jury had declared him guilty.

Next there had been rumours of a free pardon, and that a large sum of money was being sent from England for the wretch. Then word came from Darlinghurst Gaol, where Knatchbull was awaiting what seemed like a certain death sentence, that he had become religious and that he was writing his memoirs, which he hoped would sway the public to forgive him! Finally, there was a strong story that the prisoner had deprived the people of seeing him hanged by cutting his throat with a razor smuggled into his cell.

'Oh, poor Harriet,' said Eliza. 'How can she still believe he is innocent?' She pulled off a bonnet she had been trying on and stared at us sadly.

It was true. The last time she visited Knatchbull, Harriet had told us that he seemed calm. 'He was busy writing his life story and allowed me to read some of it. I was so moved that I asked if I might copy out part of it.' Then she read this part aloud to us: *Life of John Knatchbull, written by Himself in Darlinghurst Gaol. I will open to the eyes of the world such persecutions and deprivations that the hardest of hearts would bleed and commiserate with me in my sufferings and perhaps when I am dead and gone will say I am an injured man.* She lifted her eyes from the page. 'Is it not beautifully written?'

We agreed it was, though Jane and I were repulsed by the man's self-pity.

'He is writing down everything, from his childhood until the present day,' Harriet said proudly.

Harriet visited him one more time that same evening. When she returned several hours later she looked pale and shocked. I jumped up from my sewing in alarm. 'What is it, Harriet? My darling, what has happened? You look as if you've seen the very devil!'

She nodded mutely, then said brokenly, 'He has told me the truth.'

'About the murder?' asked Jane and Eliza together.

'About everything.' She fell into a chair like a puppet without strings. 'You were right, Mama. He is a violent man and I have been a fool. And yet — and yet I still care for him. He begged my forgiveness and I gave it. Oh, how wretched I am!'

I held my daughter close, thanking God, and after she had sobbed her heart out and I had persuaded her to take some beef broth I asked, 'Would it help to tell us what he told you, Harriet?'

She nodded and then began the sorry tale. 'John said he was relieved when I agreed to delay the wedding one week. He told me I was most understanding, for I had noticed that he was silent and distracted and asked what hung heavy on his mind. He told me that although the money owing to him had been promised it would be a few days more before it was forthcoming. I at once had said that we should wait until January 8th to be married and hurried off to St Philip's Church to change the arrangements. He had planned to take a larger and better house than my cottage in Kent Street, but I persuaded him that the cottage was adequate and when we were better able to afford a large house we could move then. He said, "Harriet, you are a most practical partner and my whole soul is devoted to you." He told me that he hoped I was not too sad that he had asked me not to visit you, Mama, or to take the children to you either, until after we were wed. He said he had caught me looking pensive sometimes and on Christmas Day he knew I had shed a few tears in private, which I had told him were tears of happiness. He said he believed me when I said I wanted nothing better than to make him a good wife and to help him forget the suffering he had endured as a convict, and indeed for most of his life.

'He confessed to me then that he had been concerned about the lack of money. He said, "I had told you and my landlady that the sale of the coaster *Harriet* was imminent, and so it was, but much good that would benefit me. I am not the owner, as I told you, but was merely employed to work on board. It pains me that I am not more wealthy, as I was brought up to expect it, so sometimes I find it better to lie. I had several bills which I hoped my brother in England would have signed, so that I could have paid the wedding expenses, but as usual he was tardy. But I had hopes of receiving money the next day from friends who owed me enough to cover the cost of our lodgings for the previous five weeks and for your wedding dress that was to be delivered the next evening." '

Harriet continued: 'The next morning John rose early, drank tea and ate porridge with me before the children were awake, then left our lodgings by seven determined to get the money from those friends who had put him off from time to time. It was a fine sunny morning and he told me that his spirits lifted as he saw the harbour sparkling blue. He strode down to the wharf to the *Harriet* — where he had lived on board her for several weeks before finding lodgings. He roused two sailor friends from their bunks and demanded the cash they owed him. One, still drunk from the night before, said he owed him nothing. John hit him on the jaw. The other took a shilling from his grimy purse and said it was all he had until he was paid in a month. John hit him too, though with less ferocity.

'He said he then went on to Darling Point, a long walk on a hot day, with little shade and the cicadas screeching in the gum trees, to his friend Silas Green, who runs a pawnshop and is a dealer in stolen goods of all kinds and a hard-headed businessman. When John asked for the twelve shillings he was owed, Silas threw back his head and laughed. "Twelve shillings, Fitch? For that fake gold watch you begged me to pawn last month? I've already given you three and that is two more than it's worth."

'John told him the watch was worth fifteen shillings at least and was inscribed with his name, if Green would care to look. Did he think the late Sir Edward Knatchbull would give his son a fake gold watch? Silas told him the salt had got to it and its springs had gone. If he wanted it back he'd be pleased to oblige as long as John repaid him the three shillings.

'John said, "Silas, listen to me, friend. I'm to be married in two days time and need cash in a hurry. Can you not give me a few more shillings on that watch?"

' "Not a sixpence, Fitch," the Pawnbroker replied. "Times are tough in my trade." And with that he turned his back and walked off into the gloom of his cavernous shop. As he left, John said he kicked at a copper kettle which made a great din and put a dent in it.

'Where next was he to go? He had been bargaining on getting twelve shillings from the Pawnbroker, enough to cover the rent and pay for my wedding gown at least. It was true the watch had been dropped in the salt water more than once but the springs were as new. He pledged to get even with Silas Green.

'He had a friend who had once asked if he wanted

employment as a cooper, making barrels for the Albion Brewery, and although the position was such a lowly one, he thought he must go to him now and offer to work there after our marriage, asking for an advance on his wages.

'He followed the water's edge around Farm Cove and crossed the Government Domain, lingering on the way to look at the horses in the Government Stables, which he said he often admired when he passed that way. Then on past Government House, a fine sandstone building which always reminded him, he said, of the house he had grown up in at Mersham Le Hatch. Sir George Gipps is a friend of the Knatchbull family, but John had received not one invitation to his Government House. Thence to Elizabeth Street which he followed for some miles along the edge of Hyde Park until he had left the town behind and passed a cattle market which stank most foully on this blazing hot day. He stopped to quench his thirst at a pump used to water the cattle and splashed his face, neck and arms which he then dried with the kerchief around his neck. "Dear God," he thought, "I feel like the prodigal son come home to his father, taking his swill amongst lowly beasts. Would that I were about to be embraced and taken back into the family fold as he was." Then he staggered on another twenty chains to the Albion Brewery.

'And there was his friend James Newton, manager of the coopery attached to the brewery, standing at the gate waving cheerfully. "Why, you looked scorched, Fitch old man. Come in and take some ale," cried he. John told me that he was so grateful to see a friendly face that he almost wept. As they sat side by side on upturned barrels in the cool of the coopery, John broached the subject of the position he had once been offered. He told Newton he was about to be married and his intended wife, fearing for his safety, had asked him to leave his life at sea and find a job on land.

'Newton smiled at this, he said, and congratulated him on finding such a rare wife who would rather keep her husband safe than have him dead and keep his pension. "But my dear Fitch, when I offered you that job it was some months ago and now I have more coopers than I need, experienced craftsmen who are paid more than the brewery can truly afford, for it is a new venture and most people in the Colony still prefer rum to ale. I am sorry, Fitch. I would like to have employed you for old times' sake."

'Newton was an honest man and John said he believed him. He too had been a convict and had earned his ticket of leave. John congratulated him on doing so well for himself and Newton would not let him leave without half a dozen jars of ale to drink at the wedding. These he packed in straw and put in a sack so that John could more easily carry them on his back. Then he set off on the long walk back to The Rocks.

'By now John was weary and his spirits were low. He looked to his left and saw the Burial Grounds, with their separate sections for Catholics and Protestants and a small patch for Jews. Beyond lay the Benevolent Asylum. Would that some kind person would emerge from there and transport him to a happier life, John thought.

'He trudged on until the sun was low in the sky. On

the way he drank one of the jars of ale and pretty soon he drank another. He had eaten nothing since breakfast and his head was soon whirling. "I could not return to you, my sweet Harriet," he told me, "with nothing but a shilling and a few jars of ale to show for my hard day's work. Why, the wedding gown would be delivered by now and you had no money to pay for it! How could I disappoint my innocent bride? I could not!"

'He devised a plan to get the money he needed. But first he must have something to eat to build up his strength for the task ahead. He entered a public house, and was able to trade the remaining four jars of ale for a good dinner of roast pork and potatoes and a few tots of rum. And still he had a shilling left over! His spirits had lifted and although, he said, he was a little unsteady on his feet he made his way cautiously to our lodgings in Clarence Lane and crept down the side path where he entered the shed at the back of the house. Here he concealed something beneath his coat, buttoned it tightly and emerged again into the cool night air. "The lamps were lit inside the house. I knew that you expected me home by now and would be worried," he said, "but there was nothing I could do about it." He hurried down the steep hill to the corner of Margaret Place and Kent Street.

' "As you know," he told me, "there is a small shop on this corner kept by a widow by the name of Jamieson. She lives alone, except for two small children, in lodgings above the shop and it was my intention to go in there and make a small purchase, perhaps a pint of vinegar which I knew she must get from the back of the shop, and while her back was turned, relieve her of the eleven shillings I needed. I knew she kept silver in a drawer beneath the counter, for I have often seen her open it and noticed that there is much more there at the end of each day than at the beginning. She is an unsuspecting soul. I was sure the theft could be swiftly carried out and I would be undetected."

'John then waited in the shadows opposite her shop until he thought that the last customer had left and then made his way across Kent Street. As he entered she called out cheerfully, "Good evening, Mr Fitch. And what can I do for you?"

' "A pint of vinegar if you please, Mrs Jamieson."

' "Very good. I'll have to go back there to pour it from the barrel. Do you mind waiting a minute?"

' "Not at all." John slid behind the little door beside her counter in readiness to leap behind it and get to the drawer. At that moment who should step out from behind the shelves at the other side of the shop than another customer. He recognised her as Elizabeth Brown of Kent Street. "Ooooh, I see you've got a man behind your door, Mrs Jamieson!" she exclaimed in jest.

'Mrs Jamieson turned her head around as she poured the vinegar into a small jar and smiled, although John said she did not seem amused by the remark. She is a dignified woman. After that what choice did he have but to leave the shop with his purchase? He said he cursed Elizabeth Brown.

'He waited again in the shadows opposite for what seemed like hours. Late customers kept popping in and out. He said he wondered why the deuce the wretched woman didn't close her shop at a respectable hour.

'He said it must have been close to midnight when the Widow disappeared into the back of the shop. Having satisfied himself there were no customers inside, John dashed across the street, entered the shop and locked the door behind him. He intended to take the money he needed from the drawer and make his escape before she came back. But when he opened the drawer he saw to his astonishment that it had already been cleared of its silver and there were only a few coppers inside. He cursed the Widow. She was coming back. Quickly he turned out the light so that she should not know him and grabbed her from behind, covering her mouth with his hand. He disguised his voice as best he could and demanded to know where she had put the cash. "Nowhere you will find it, Mr Fitch. Let me go at once!"

'John was stung by this defiance and the fact that she had recognised him. "Give it to me now or I will murder you!" he cried. But she would not. "You shall not rob me and my children of all we have in the world. How could you do this, when you are about to marry a widow yourself?" She struggled out of his grasp as she said this and turned to face him. He felt his resolve melting under her gaze.

' "Damn you, woman!" he yelled and flung her to the floor in a blind fury. He said he beat her head against the floor until she was silent, but then, as he was ripping the outside pocket from her, which held the banknotes and silver she must have just taken out of the drawer, she opened her eyes and said hoarsely, "Damn you to hell, John Fitch, for I have always known you were nothing but a low thief."

'At that he drew the tomahawk from beneath his coat and smashed it into her skull. He smashed and smashed, he does not know for how long. When he looked at the weapon in his hands he saw that it was covered in hair and blood. He rushed to a room upstairs and concealed it under the mattress on the bed. He ran downstairs. She lay there in a pool of blood. He stared at her in the moonlight and thought she did not look like a woman at all but a corpse in a battlefield. He thought to himself, "I must escape from this nightmare. Poor Harriet will be so worried." He was about to leave when he heard the door at the back being broken down and the sound of many men's voices. He crouched down in the shadows to conceal himself and waited.'

When Harriet had finished speaking we all four sat in silence to digest this gruesome tale. It was the truth, of that we had not the slightest doubt.

# CHAPTER 64

**A Repentant Murderer is Hanged in Front of a Silent Crowd**
**The Rocks, February 13th, 1844**

I did not think that I would ever go to see a hanging. Jane announced that she was prepared to go alone to see the deed done but said she would prefer some company, and so I agreed to accompany her.

We rose at six o'clock although the execution was not to take place until nine. I was surprised to see that Jane had discarded her sailor's disguise and was dressed as a woman, all in black. When I questioned her about the prudence of this, she replied that she was unlikely to be recognised dressed in mourning and produced a widow's veil for her head and face. And so, leaving Harriet asleep and giving instructions to Eliza Jane to keep her company, we made our way towards Darlinghurst Gaol.

I had not crossed the Race Course so early in the morning before and was surprised at how many people were up and about. Men, women and children from all parts of the town were swarming, I realised at last, towards Darlinghurst Hill. As we walked, people chatted to us just as if we were all on our way to some picnic or fun fair.

'He's quite happy apparently, made his peace with the world and asked God that all be forgiven,' announced a woman still wearing her apron and munching on an oatmeal cake. 'He even ate a hearty supper last night, so it says in the newspaper.' She chortled.

'He'll be losing it all once he dances on air!' joked a man with a bundle of parsnips on his back.

They had come to gloat and I wished I was not part of it. At home my poor daughter slept soundly for the first time in weeks because I had given her a sleeping draught.

Since John Knatchbull had confessed to her that he had committed the murder, she had been in a daze. Just last evening I had watched her sitting alone on her bed, shaking her head and repeating what he had said to her after he'd confessed. '*The devil instigated me to do the deed and I did it.*' It was as if by repeating that phrase over and over she hoped to make some sense of it.

As we had come early we were in time to take up a position close to the scaffold. It was now twenty minutes before nine and the mounted police had arrived. They took their places some distance from the foot of the scaffold. Then the foot soldiers arrived. By now the crowd had swelled to what must have been thousands. They were strangely well behaved and created no disturbance, apart from murmuring, almost as if they were about to witness some religious ceremony.

As the bell tolled the fatal hour John Knatchbull appeared dressed most formally in a mourning suit, which Harriet told me had been provided by his relative Governor Gipps. He was accompanied by four men, all clergymen. One of these, I believe, was the Reverend Ross, to whom he had first made his confession of murder.

He was deathly pale but he walked firmly and decisively between two of the clergymen to whom he spoke his prayers aloud. Gradually his prayers and pleas for divine mercy increased in volume until they could be heard even outside the gaol. Now that the fearful reality was upon him I felt that his repentance was real. As he ascended the scaffold there was utter silence in the crowd.

The knot of the noose slipped abruptly to the back of his neck and the struggle of his expiring life began. I could not bear to look and turned my head away, but Jane watched to the end.

When I looked again the body hung limp and the features of John Knatchbull seemed to have collapsed and darkened.

'Please, let us go now,' I whispered.

Jane nodded.

It seemed that the crowd was chastened. They moved away in silence.

Next day it was reported in the *Sydney Record* that '*at least ten thousand persons were present, but amongst the vast assemblage no one was found inhuman enough to disturb the last moments of the culprit; there was not even a murmur and this fact deserves to be recorded.*'

# CHAPTER 65

## Jane Shares One Final Secret with Me
## The Rocks, March, 1844

Jane is leaving Sydney this morning for the Bay of Islands.

She and Eliza Jane are loaded up with presents to take back to their friends and Eliza's family. I have given them several fashionable gowns and bonnets.

'We shall be like duchesses in Kororareka,' said Jane. She was wearing one of her new gowns, for she said she now believed the constables in Sydney had better things to do than look for an ex-convict who had escaped so many years ago.

Harriet and I and my three grandchildren were walking with them to the wharf to wave goodbye. Elizabeth Male and Eleanor Turner had promised to meet us there. It would be a noisy, affectionate and sorrowful farewell.

As we walked down the hill in the sunshine, with the little cart loaded with our packages and the children piled on top rumbling behind us, Jane took my arm and said, 'Do you know it is twenty-five years since we met each other as girls at Elmtree House?'

'I was in awe of you,' I laughed. 'You were so wicked and knew so much more about everything than I did.'

Since I have told Jane my secret I feel so much more relaxed. Yes, I would say I am happy. Jane turned to me with a wicked smile. 'To think, Mary, that you are the one walking out with Mr John Stephen, a gentleman, and I, who always vowed I would get one first, have just seen the only one I even came close to catching dangle from a scaffold.'

'Jane, don't speak so of the poor wretch! He's not been buried three weeks.'

'Ah, but I've already paid my respects. I was there at his burial. Did you read what the newspaper said? "*The coffin was followed to the grave by two gentlemen and two ladies in deep mourning; also a third female, in a black veil, who did not, however, appear to be connected to the other mourners.*" Think if they'd found out who I was, what a delicious scandal it could have been!' She began to parody the newspaper. 'The third female was none other than John Knatchbull's wife, better known as the notorious escaped convict, Jane New.' And she burst out laughing.

'Sssh, Jane. Someone might hear,' I said, looking around us.

Jane dismissed my caution and then said seriously, 'It is strange Mary, is it not, that we are close friends and yet we are so different? You stay in one place yet change a great deal in your mind and soul. I move from place to place yet stay the same. You mature, like a good wine, growing wise and becoming strong. But for all my roaming and adventures my character remains fixed and I have no wisdom.' She paused before adding, 'And not much strength either.' Now it was my turn to laugh. 'You flatter me and do yourself a great injustice, Jane.'

'No, I speak the truth.' She turned then and looked back at Harriet and Eliza Jane, who walked at a distance between us, also arm-in-arm.

'I am glad our daughters get along so well together,' she said.

'My daughter and your God-daughter? Yes, so am I.'

Then she looked hard at me and said, 'I've often seen you looking at Eliza Jane and wondering. Have you not guessed my secret, Mary?'

At this I blushed and stuttered, 'There is an amazing likeness between you two but, how could it be possible? She is —?'

'Half-Maori. Yes. Does it shock you?'

'What! She is your *daughter*? But how could that be?'

'Remember I told you that when I first landed at Hokianga I lived as a castaway for a time on the beach there, knowing no one?'

'Yes, you said the Maori women were kind and taught you how to cook fish and potatoes in the sand.'

'They did. But there was also a man I met at that time. One night there was a storm. Trees were blown down and the waves rose so high on the beach that my crude hut was washed away. I was terrified. Nene and some other young warriors came from the village to help the castaways. All I knew of Nene was that he was a Chief and much respected by his people. He cut boughs so quickly in spite of the storm and made me a shelter higher up the beach. I was sobbing, for I believed the storm would finish us that night. Thunder cracked and rolled as if we were on a battleground and lightning flashed across the beach like daylight.

'Nene offered to stay with me in the hut until the storm had passed. He sat at one end of the hut with me huddled in a ball at the other but when he heard me whimpering with fear and shivering so much with the cold that my teeth chattered he came near. He was wearing a fine glossy mat decorated with fringes and fastened at the neck. This he took off and wrapped around me like a blanket. I was grateful. I saw that his chest was bare and around his neck he wore a small native god carved in green stone. "Tiki will protect us," he said, and was about to move away when I put out my hand to touch the charm. In doing so I also touched his skin and the result was like being struck by lightning. We fell upon each other in a passionate embrace as if we had been waiting an age to do so. How my wet clothes were removed I hardly remember but the urgency to feel his body against mine was such that I must have torn them off myself. When he entered me I cried out with a wild joy that was almost relief. We lay together all through the storm, caressing each other, tumbling and playing. I traced the pattern of his facial tattoos gently with my finger tips and he moaned with pleasure. He stroked my breasts and thighs and buried his face in my hair. Taking some of the ornaments from his hair — feathers, sharks' teeth and a piece of bone — he decorated mine. Then we made love again and again until it was light.'

I felt my eyes go wide with astonishment. 'So he is Eliza Jane's father?'

She nodded. 'After that night I moved with him to his village and lived there for some months without seeing another European. It is strange, but I felt at peace there. I worked in the gardens with the other women. The Chief and the other men in the tribe accepted me because I was Nene's chosen one. He wanted to make me his wife.' Jane smiled at my look of incredulity. 'Nene was a savage but a gentle savage, Mary. I loved him but I didn't have the courage to stay with him.'

'Did he love you?'

'Yes, very much. I hurt him deeply by running away. I think he still grieves for me, although he has another wife and children now.' I looked back at Harriet and Eliza Jane. 'Does she know?'

'She does now. I have told her while we were here, away from the woman she has always believed to be her mother. She is old enough to know it now. Lydia and her husband Captain Wright took me in when I first came to Kororareka and discovered I was pregnant. I was quite ill.'

'So Nene does not know about Eliza Jane?'

'No. I told no one but the couple who adopted her.'

'But how could you bear to give her up?'

'I was afraid to be a young woman making her own way in a new land with a half-caste child. When I told Lydia, a Maori, whose baby she was, she said there could be trouble if Nene found out. He might want to claim the baby, or even to get rid of it, because it was rare for a chief to father a child that was not of pure

Maori blood. She and Captain Wright offered to keep me confined in their house and adopt the baby at birth, saying that it was their own. I agreed. But they have always encouraged me to see as much of Eliza as I wished, and as you see, we get along well together.'

'Better than most mothers and daughters. In fact I envied you when you first arrived!'

'There is no need for envy now. When I broke the news to her a week ago there were tears and angry accusations, I can tell you!'

'So why did you to decide to tell her Jane?'

'It was partly to do with Knatchbull's death. A lot of anger passed away from me when I saw how repentant he was. I don't know … I have always rather hated men and I think it was because of him.'

'Even James New?'

She nodded.

'But you married him!'

'For convenience. I never really loved him, though he loved me.'

'And I know you did not love John Stephen,' I said with a smile.

'No. I certainly did not love him.'

'But you did love Nene?'

She sighed. 'Yes, he is the only man in my life I have loved and I left him.'

'Shall you tell him he has a daughter?'

'Eliza Jane says that she will if I don't. She is determined. She says she would be proud to call him her father. I think he would be proud of her too. I once made him a promise to tell him everything when the right time came. He knew I was hiding something.'

'Will he be angry with you when you tell him? Will he harm you, Jane?'

'I don't think so,' she laughed. 'He might even ask me to be his wife again. They are allowed to have several wives, you know.'

'Oh dear! Surely you wouldn't agree to that?'

'No, no, dear Mary. And yet I am still fond of him. I will tell him soon about Eliza Jane because he's a great fighter and has constant battles against another Chief named Heke. I should hate him to be killed before he meets his daughter.'

'How frightening he must be!' I said.

'Not to me. He is quite a diplomat with Europeans. Most courteous and charming. You would like him, Mary.'

'But Jane, what about Lydia and Captain Wright? Won't they grieve for their lost daughter?'

'I told them that on this trip away from the Bay of Islands I intended to tell her the truth. They agreed that the time was right. They have other children. Eliza will decide which of us she prefers to live with. Perhaps she will live with neither.'

'You always manage to shock me, Jane.' I smiled my approval. 'But I am pleased she is yours. She is so like you in her looks and her manner. She seems to have your courage and sense of adventure too.'

'Thank you for saying that, Mary. If she decides to leave me at least I will remember that.' She turned away; suddenly she seemed sad and frightened.

'Why should she want to leave you?'

'She is still angry with me for abandoning her and lying about her parents,' she said unhappily. 'She has reason to feel anger. I was a coward and now she is punishing me.' Then she pulled herself together and put on a cheerful face for my sake. 'But Harriet will certainly never leave you.'

'Well not for a little while, anyway. Do you know what she said to me yesterday — "Mama, Mr John Stephen is exactly the kind of father I have always wished for. I have thought that since I was a little girl." '

We laughed softly together. 'Don't tell her about his perjury then, at least not until after you are safely wed.'

'Sssh Jane. For goodness' sake. I told you that in complete and utter confidence!'

'Of course you did. Your secrets are always safe with me.'

'Quick. Get on that boat! I am terrified you'll be recognised and dragged off to prison. I've been frightened for you every minute since you arrived,' I told her.

'Ah my dear friend, you make such a fuss. But I would not have you any other way.'

'Nor I you. Even though you did leave me to take the blame for your stolen forged banknotes!'

'You should thank me for it!' she cried, as she gathered together her bundles and hugged the children one by one.

'Why, in God's name?'

'Because if I had not we would never have been transported to a better world and been friends forever!'

'Mama, wait, here are Elizabeth and Eleanor running to say goodbye!' cried Eliza Jane.

'What did you call me?' Jane stared at her.

'Mama.'

Jane looked at me and I saw that her eyes shone with

tears. 'It's the first time in my life that I've ever been called that,' she said gruffly, dragging a sleeve across her eyes. 'It's a shock to me, that's all.'

I passed her my handkerchief. 'I don't think your daughter will leave you, Jane,' I said softly.

We clung together for a long moment.

Then she turned brightly to say goodbye to the others.

# AUTHOR'S AFTERWORD

*Women on the Rocks* is a work of fiction, although it is based on several real characters and some actual events.

I first became interested in writing an historical novel set in the early 1800s on The Rocks when I moved there to live in late 1997. Although there are now tall apartment buildings towering against the skyline, The Rocks was the earliest settlement in Sydney and today it retains much of its sense of history. Walking along the narrow back streets, climbing worn sandstone steps to seldom used pathways from which the harbour could be glimpsed through giant Moreton Bay fig trees, it was not hard to imagine the people who had lived here over one hundred and sixty years ago.

I came across a major archaeological site in Cumberland Street and a tiny museum in Susannah Place furnished as a corner shop of 1844, still with its original privy and open laundry out the back. I found a map drawn and engraved in 1836. It showed the city street where I then lived with only a cluster of cottages and a windmill. Nearby was St Philip's Church, the quarries, and the Military Hospital. A dotted line showed the proposed Government House and public wharf. The rest consisted of a few cottages and pubs tumbling down narrow tracks between the rocks to the harbour and bush. As I continued to explore the steep back streets of The Rocks, I began to hear the voices of my characters.

I have tried to keep the dates of historical events accurate — such as the hanging of the murderer John Knatchbull, the arrival in Sydney Cove of the convict Mary Jones and the escape from the Female Factory of the convict Jane New. But in a few cases I have taken a writer's licence with dates and places. Where large gaps appear in the records I have felt free to invent.

*The real characters:*

*Mary Jones* was fourteen when she was charged with forging banknotes. She was tried at the Old Bailey, sentenced to fourteen years transportation and arrived at Sydney Cove aboard the *Medway* in September, 1820. (*PRO Trial Records. Microfilm 2737.*)

At the age of almost sixteen she was assigned as a servant to *Andrew Frazier*, a Scot aged fifty-six, one of the most successful and respected dealers and publicans on The Rocks. A baker, landowner, importer and exporter, he was an emancipated convict. He was often a guest at Government House. Frazier had a good house in Cambridge Street, a bakehouse, stock enclosure, gardens, wells, storehouses and warehouses and ten servants. He subscribed to benevolent institutions both in the Colony and at his native Montrose, Scotland.

Mary served Frazier for four years and was promoted to the position of Housekeeper. During that time she became his lover. They appear to have lived contentedly as man and wife for some years. In 1821 Andrew Frazier wrote a memorial to the Governor recommending Mary Jones for her 'steady, honest and upright behaviour' and requesting a ticket of leave for her so that she might start a small business of her own. (*SRO*.)

But in September 1824 he met *Ellen Hatton*, a convict aged twenty, transported for seven years for larceny from a person. He petitioned the Governor to be wed. Mary Jones was packed off unceremoniously to the Female Factory to await further employment. She was most unhappy about this and wrote a letter to Frazier pleading with him 'not to forsake the old one for the new one. My time will be up in September and I will be coming out to my liberty. If I ham guilty of aney fault is loving the to well.' Apparently she received no reply.

Andrew Frazier and Ellen (or Eleanor, as she now called herself) Hatton were married on 18 October, 1824. The marriage was not successful. Eleanor liked to drink, dance, spend money on 'vanities' and leave home without permission. In 1825 the couple went before a magistrate to try to settle their differences. But they continued to quarrel, particularly when Eleanor opened 'a disorderly house' near her respectable husband's business. In September 1826 Andrew Frazier petitioned the Governor that his wife, whom he had sent to the Female Factory for 'her shameful conduct', not be allowed to leave. (*SRO Colonial Secretary's Correspondence, Petition of AF.*) Eleanor Frazier petitioned the Governor that she had been 'confined in the Fac-

tory eight months for being at large in consequence of
another woman living with the petitioner's husband'.
The Superintendent of Police was instructed to 'ascer-
tain whether this man has a mistress and is living in
open infidelity as has been stated — He shall then have
his answer.' (*SRO.*)

Mary Jones would still have been at the Female Fac-
tory at this time and it is likely that she met Eleanor
Frazier and they compared notes about Andrew
Frazier.

When he died in 1827, Frazier seems to have
repented of his harsh treatment of Mary and left her a
substantial amount of money. He left nothing to Eleanor.

Mary married **William Baxter**, a Botanist, at
Parramatta on 15 January, 1827. The marriage does
not appear to have lasted long.

Five months later two women were arrested on The
Rocks by Constable Miller for 'outrageously riotous
and disorderly conduct'. They were Mary Baxter and
Eleanor Frazier. Mary, having recently discovered that
her husband William Baxter had a lover, had gone to
Eleanor's house to 'pour out her griefs'. The two friends
shared a meal and 'a cheerful glass' (or several) before
'supporting one another well enough' back to Mary's
lodgings at midnight and causing a complete 'uproar'
outside the house. Fortunately the complainant was
unable to give testimony because he was too drunk, so
the charges against the women were dropped. (*Australian*, 20 June, 1827, cited in *The Rocks, Life in Early
Sydney* by Grace Karskens)

Eleanor Hatton/Frazier married **Mr Turner**, a clerk

who worked at the Female Factory, at St John's, Parramatta on 3 September, 1829.

*Jane Henrie* (*alias* Maria Wilkinson) was described as 'uneducated, Presbyterian, aged 17, a native of Leeds, dressmaker, 5 ft 3 ins, fresh ruddy complexion, dark brown hair, black eyes.' She was convicted of 'receiving', tried at Chester on 27, April, 1824 and sentenced to transportation for seven years.

She arrived at Hobart Town aboard the *Henry* via St Jago in February, 1825. (*Surgeon's Journals AJCP PRO.*) She was assigned to a settler, Mr Officer, for eighteen months before her marriage to *James New*. She married on 24 July, 1826 at New Norfolk, Van Diemen's Land and was assigned to her husband, who was a free man. On 24 September, 1827 James New petitioned Lieutenant Governor Arthur for his wife to accompany him to Sydney. Permission was granted two days later. Jane and James New arrived in Sydney aboard the *Medway* on November 3, 1827. James purchased a public house, *The Mermaid*, in Cumberland Street on The Rocks and Jane worked there, apparently enjoying her customers and making herself indispensable as a hostess. On 18 December, 1827 Jane New stole goods in the dwelling house of Madame Rous. Bailed and at large she was found guilty of other shoplifting and sentenced by the Bench of Magistrates to serve an additional twelve months. On 12 August, 1828 Jane was brought before the acting Superintendent of Police, John Stephen Junior, for shoplifting. Her original sentence had been extended by one year. She was returned to her husband and discharged by the Bench of Magistrates. (*HRA*.)

In January, 1829 she was tried and convicted to death for stealing a piece of silk worth five pounds from Madame Rous. From Sydney Gaol she petitioned for mercy, which was granted and on 10 February she was ordered to the Female Factory, where she was to be kept in second-class until further notice.

In March, on a writ of *Habeas Corpus*, Jane was brought before the Supreme Court and found not guilty. But she was obliged to remain in the Female Factory until a vessel could be found to return her to Van Diemen's Land. She escaped from the custody of the Gaol Constable *en route* to the Factory but was retaken six days later and returned to the Factory, this time in first-class.

A subscription was opened for her in the *Australian* newspaper to help pay the court costs.

While in the Factory she gave presents to the Matron as a bribe.

On 3 April 1829 she wrote a letter to her husband (*HRA*) and two days later he helped her to escape. He appears to have been devoted to her, risking not only his own safety but losing all his property in order to pay her court costs.

Jane's name and description appeared on a list of absconding prisoners published in the *Sydney Gazette* soon after her escape.

On 1 May, James New requested the return from John Stephen Jnr. of affidavits confirming his wife's freedom. On 10 May, Jane New was believed to have sailed as a passenger under the name of James Middleton on the brig *Mary* from Sydney to Van Diemen's Land. On 14 May a collection was being made in Van Diemen's Land for her. But there was no convincing evidence that she ever arrived.

In July 1829 the Superintendent of Police was informed by a seaman that Jane New had escaped to New Zealand from Sydney in the cutter *Emma Kemp*, disguised as the boy Thomas Jones. Another seaman claimed he had seen her in New Zealand, where she kept a brothel of 'native savages'.

In January, 1830 Joseph Turner of Parramatta gave evidence that Jane New remained at large and that, disguised in men's clothing, she lived with her husband, mother and stepfather, Richard Baker at Hunters River.

Jane New was never found.

*John Stephen Junior* was a magistrate and acting Superintendent of Police at the time he came in contact with Jane New in 1828. His family was well connected to the law, his brother a judge and his father a judge of the Supreme Court.

He met Jane when he appeared on the Bench of Magistrates that added twelve months to her sentence for stealing. After that, however, he appears to have championed her, writing in a petition for mercy for her after she was sentenced to death that she was a 'strangely persecuted Female' and describing her trial and conviction as 'an infamous perjury'. He made himself responsible for collecting the signatures of fourteen magistrates and other influential gentlemen to support her plea. When this plea was successful and after Jane was transferred from Sydney Gaol to the Female Factory, he obtained a writ of *Habeas Corpus* to have her released from all convictions and transported to Van Diemen's Land as soon as a vessel could be found. When Jane, not wishing to return to the Female Factory even for a few weeks, escaped from the Gaol Constable and hid for six days before being recaptured, John Stephen fell under heavy suspicion of having aided and abetted her. He was also supposed to have issued Jane New with a certificate stating she was free, when in fact she would not become free until 27 April, 1831.

Stephen was then a Commissioner for apportioning the Territory, a Magistrate and Registrar of the Supreme Court. Governor Darling recommended that he be dismissed from these positions, writing in a letter to Sir George Murray (29 June 1829) that out of charity he would suppose this 'to be the effect of infatuation, and not a wilful determination to misrepresent the facts'. Governor Darling continued: 'Information was received that she [Jane New] was residing about 27 miles from Sydney [at Minto] and a Party of Constables was despatched to apprehend her. It being Midnight when they arrived and Jane New being an adept, she again managed to get off. The Constables then examined the Apartment, which she occupied, found the Bed, which she had just quitted, quite warm and discovered a Certificate to the following effect in a small Box, "Vizt." "I hereby certify that the Bearer hereof Mrs Dickson is free. John Stephen, jnr, JP".' (*HRA*.)

John Stephen denied that he had harboured Jane New in his apartment at Minto. He claimed that Mrs Dickson was his housekeeper and that although she resembled Jane New in appearance, she was a quite different person.

Stephen was determined to get justice and travelled to London, where he petitioned the House of Commons and tried from 1829–34 to get satisfaction. His letters to Sir George Murray and eventually to Under Secretary Hay became increasingly desperate. During this time he felt too ashamed to meet his family and friends and lived at Gray's Inn and Joys Inn, both humble establishments. Eventually he agreed to return to the Colony and submit to examination of the facts. Part of the transcript of the court case is contained in the text.

*John Knatchbull* was the second son of Sir Edward Knatchbull of Mersham Le Hatch in the county of Kent. While still a boy at school, his pranks were those of a bully and he appeared to have few friends. He joined the Royal Navy as a midshipman and distinguished himself serving under Lord Cochrane in South America. He appears to have been proud and overbearing to his inferiors and servile to those in authority. His family was often called upon to pay his debts and when his older brother Edward objected to this, they quarrelled bitterly. When Knatchbull was apprehended for robbing a Captain Dampier at Vauxhall Gardens of a blank cheque and two sovereigns, he protested indignantly that he was a Post-Captain in the Navy and the brother of Sir Edward Knatchbull. Captain Dampier immediately went to Sir Edward and offered to drop the changes, but the latter had apparently had enough of his debauched brother and encouraged Dampier to press ahead. John Knatchbull was committed for trial as 'John Fitch' in August, 1824 and sentenced to transportation for fourteen years.

There were various rumours surrounding the convict Fitch even before his ship left Portsmouth. One was that a lady the prisoners took to be his wife often came on board to stay with him, another that he beat a sickly prisoner whom he kept as his servant to death.

As soon as he arrived in Sydney he is believed to have applied in person to Governor Sir George Gipps (a distant relative) for a ticket of leave. Sir George helped him to find an employer who gave him charge of a small coastal cutter, but the employer soon became insolvent.

There were many rumours after Knatchbull's death about his horrifying crimes. However, according to his criminal record he was convicted only three times: first in 1824 for stealing the bank cheque and two sovereigns, secondly in 1832 for forging a draft for six pounds ten shillings, for which he was sent to Norfolk Island for seven years, and thirdly, in 1844, for the murder of Ellen Jamieson.

In 1843, now fifty-six, he met a young widow named Harriet Craig who had three young children. She was, he wrote, 'as virtuous a woman as ever stepped, and [that] there was not a blemish on her character'. As it appears in the text, Fitch did offer to pay Harriet's rent at Charles Hollowell's boarding house and paid the six shillings for her wedding gown.

He also asked her to give up her position as a servant a few weeks before the wedding so that his relatives would not discover she was employed in such a lowly position.

He planned to rob Mrs Jamieson and then murdered her in much the same way as I have described in the narrative. Some direct speech is taken from Knatchbull's memoirs written by him in the condemned cells, Woolloomooloo Gaol, in February 1844.

[Cited in *John Knatchbull: From Quarterdeck To Gallows* by Colin Roderick.]

*Elizabeth Sibley* arrived in Sydney as Elizabeth Male, aged twenty-one aboard the *Broxbornebury* in July 1814. She was transported for life. Shortly after her arrival she married William Sibley and lived with him on The Rocks until 1821 when she petitioned Governor Macquarie for a conditional pardon, which was granted.

As an emancipated woman Sibley believed she had a right to own some of the property on The Rocks that she and husband had worked hard for. But he was not inclined to share it. This, together with the fact that Elizabeth had young children who died, made their married life volatile. William frequently sent his wife back to the Female Factory for punishment. He also took out advertisements in the newspapers cautioning the public not to trust her and stating he would not be responsible for her debts, as she had left her home of her own accord. Eventually they separated and Elizabeth lived alone on The Rocks.

\* \*

*Certain minor characters mentioned in the text are based on real people:*

*Jane Toomb*, Andrew Frazier's elderly cook, was a convict who had murdered her husband with a carving knife.

*William Wakeman*, who was dismissed as overseer of the Hospital for drinking the 'spiritous cordial medicines', later became a Rocks constable.

*George Cribb* owned a hotel and butchery on The Rocks.

*Sam Hulbert* was licensee of the Sheer Hulk, a public house on The Rocks.

*Ann Hamilton*, a third-class prisoner at the Female Factory, died in her cell. An inquiry was held into the cause of her death at which it was stated that she had been beating her head against the walls and had to be tied down. Eleanor Frazier was one of those who gave evidence.

*Mary Jones*, aged forty-six, was a convict on board the *Medway* at the same time as fifteen-year-old Mary Jones. The older Mary was transported for life for 'Larceny from a Person'. It was not unusual aboard the convict ships for an older woman, recently parted from her own children, to take care of a younger prisoner.

*Constable Samuel Cleme* did allow Jane New to escape out the back door of a house in Philip Street when he was escorting her back to the Female Factory after her trial. He was later dismissed for drunkenness.

*Matron Ann Gordon* was in charge of the Female Factory when Jane New escaped in March, 1829. The evidence she gave in court regarding the escape is taken almost verbatim from the court transcripts.

*Thomas Franklin*, a seaman aboard the cutter *Emma Kemp*, gave evidence in court that Jane New had landed at Sikianga (probably Hokianga) in the Bay of Islands, New Zealand, around the middle of 1829 and 'remained there still'.

*Johnno Johnston* built a public house, The Duke of Marlborough, on the waterfront at Kororareka on the Bay of Islands around 1833.

*James Busby* was appointed to look after the interests of the British residents of the Bay of Islands in 1833. He was not to be called Governor, but Resident. Maori chiefs from all over the area were invited to meet him. Busby and his wife settled on a remote cliff above the sea at Waitangi.

*Tawati Waka Nene* was the son of the Hokianga Chief Tapua, who had boarded Captain Cook's vessel *Endeavour* from his canoe when Cook first came to New Zealand in 1769. Nene was a leader of the Ngapuhi, who lived at Hokianga in the 1830s and early 1840s. Nene was more pragmatic than chiefs like Heke, who proclaimed 'death to Europeans' and often opposed Heke in battle. Nene realised the inevitable outcome of the European influx and was in favour of trade and Pakeha settlers. He had learned from the Missionaries to read and write English and was one of the chiefs who supported The United Tribes of New Zealand, and who encouraged other chiefs to sign the Treaty of Waitangi. A descendant of his, Frederick Nene Russell, held one of the first four Maori seats in New Zealand Parliament in 1868.

*Te Mahanga*, a Bay of Islands man, was the first Maori known to have visited England. He travelled with John Savage on board the *Ferret*, leaving London in July, 1806 and returning to New Zealand in March, 1807. Savage described him as 'a healthy stout young man of the military class, a most affectionate kind-hearted creature'. Sailors had taught him to shake hands and say 'How do you do, my boy,' which he did to passers by in London who stood and stared at him in fright. Savage took Mahanga across London in a hackney coach and when he was asked how he liked it he replied: '*Pai ana whare, nui nui haere*' — 'Very good house, it walks fast.' (Cited in *Between Worlds: Early Exchanges Between Maori and Europeans 1773–1815* by Anne Salmond.

# ACKNOWLEDGMENTS

I am grateful to those archivists and librarians who helped in my search to find out anything at all about the real characters around whom I created this fiction.

The State Records Office in Globe Street and the Geneaological Society in Kent Street, The Rocks, Sydney were my starting points. From there I moved to the Mitchell Library to read extracts from the *Sydney Gazette* and the *Australian*. In Historical Records of Australia the correspondence between Sir George Murray and Governor Darling was found regarding the dismissal of John Stephen Junior, as well as Stephen's letters pleading his case. Court transcripts and records and letters relating to the Female Factory and from prisoners to loved ones were also found at the Mitchell Library.

In New Zealand I visited the Bay of Islands, exploring the waters, forests and cliffs. I stayed at Russell (formerly Kororeka) where I found valuable information in the Museum, at the cemetery and at the Duke of Marlborough Hotel, which is still open for business. I also learned much from a visit to Waitangi where the

Treaty was signed and where the house James Busby and his family lived on top of the cliff still stands.

I would like to thank my researcher Terri McCormack for her assistance in finding invaluable primary source material in Sydney, and to Angela Bowne for legal advice.

Thanks also to my friend the writer, Geraldine Brooks, for her encouragement and criticism of my early drafts, and to my agent, Fiona Inglis.

I am very grateful to editors Judith Lukin-Amundsen and Barbara Ker Wilson and to my publishers, Madonna Duffy and Laurie Muller.

I found many books helpful, but most especially: *Making Peoples: A History of the New Zealanders, From Polynesian Settlement to the End of the Nineteenth Century* by James Belich (Allen Lane/The Penguin Press, 1996); *Leviathan: The Unauthorised Biography of Sydney* by John Birmingham (Knopf, 1999); *A History of Australia 1: From The Earliest Times to the Age of Macquarie* by C.M.H. Clark (Melbourne University Press, 1962) and *A History of Australia 2: New South Wales and Van Diemen's Land, 1822–1838* (Melbourne University Press, 1968); *Depraved and Disorderly: Female Convicts, Sexuality and Gender in Colonial Australia* by Joy Damousi (Cambridge University Press, 1997); *Convict Women* by Kay Daniels (Allen and Unwin, 1998); *The Real Matilda: Woman and Identity in Australia, 1783 to 1975* by Miriam Dixson (Penguin, 1976); *The Rocks: Life in Early Sydney* by Grace Karskens (Melbourne University Press, 1997) and *Inside the Rocks: The Archaeology of a Neighbourhood* (Hale and Iremonger, 1999); *Parramatta: A Past Revealed* by Terry Kass, Carol Liston and John McClymont (Parramatta City Council, 1996); *Anchored in a Small Cove: A History and Archaeology of The Rocks, Sydney* by Max Kelly (Sydney Cove Authority, 1997); *A Most Notable Anchorage: A Story of Russell and the Bay of Islands* by Marie King (Northland Historical Publications Society, 1992); *My Wife, My Daughter, and Poor Mary Ann: Women and Work in Australia* by Beverley Kingston (Nelson, 1975); *The Bay of Islands* by Jack Lee (Reed Books, 1983); *Australian Women and the Law 1788–1979* edited by Judy Mackinolty and Heather Radi Hale and Iremonger, 1979); *Convict Maids: The Forced Migration of Women to Australia* by Deborah Oxley (Cambridge University Press, 1996); *The Quincunx* by Charles Palliser (Penguin, 1989); *Playing Beattie Bow* by Ruth Park (Penguin, 1980); *The Floating Brothel* by Siân Rees (Hodder, 2001); *The Women of Botany Bay: A Reinterpretation of the Role of Women in the Origins of Australian Society* by Portia Robinson (Penguin, 1988); *John Knatchbull, From Quarterdeck to Gallows: Including the Narrative Written by Himself in Darlinghurst Gaol (23rd January–13th February, 1844)* by Colin Roderick (Angus and Robertson, 1963); *The Rocks, Sydney* by Olaf Ruhen (Rigby, 1966); *Between Worlds: Early Exchanges Between Maori and Europeans, 1773–1815* by Anne Salmond (Viking, 1997); and *Colonial Eve: Sources on Women in Australia, 1788–1914*, edited by Ruth Teale (Oxford University Press, 1978).